BIRD GOTTA LAND

THE EDUCATION OF A YOUNG PSYCHOLOGIST

GERALD S. DROSE

Bird Gotta Land: The Education of a Young Psychologist
Published by Lead Balloon Publishing, Atlanta, GA

ISBN: 978-0-578-84930-0

FICTION / Psychological

Cover art by Felice Sharp
Cover and Interior design by Victoria Wolf, wolfdesignandmarketing.com

LEAD BALLOON
PUBLISHING

To Robert Drose and Bill Zeckhausen

ACKNOWLEDGMENTS

I WISH TO THANK MY WIFE, Dina Zeckhausen, for her faith and great patience throughout the writing of this book. She has been my cheerleader, my taskmaster and my occasional editor.

I am also grateful to Cliff Bostock who was with me throughout the 20-something years of my crazy journey toward completing this project. As my writing supervisor/therapist, he shaped many of the ideas (and edited many of the sentences) in this book. If I wrote a novel about the process of writing this book, no one would believe an actual human would be capable of listening somewhat patiently for years to my neurotic excuses for not finishing.

I am indebted to my psychology professors at the University of South Carolina who shaped me as a psychologist and a man. Thank you to Herman Salzberg, Bob Heckel, Randy Engle, and Bob Deysach.

Finally, I want to thank my mother, Carolyn Drose, who read books to me when I was a lazy child and who loves me to this day.

Tiger got to hunt, bird got to fly;
Man got to sit and wonder "why, why, why?"
Tiger got to sleep, bird got to land;
Man got to tell himself he understand.

~Kurt Vonnegut, Cat's Cradle

PREFACE

I BEGAN WRITING THIS FICTIONAL MEMOIR in 1996 as a young psychologist. It is based on my experiences and relationships in clinical psychology graduate school in the 1980's. While the line between fiction and non-fiction can be blurry, the main truth in this book is that I stumbled through much of my young adulthood and only found solid footing with the help of some of the experiences detailed here.

I always hated it when people claimed that they studied psychology to "find themselves" or fix their mental health issues. I used to think my mental health was so excellent that it did not need fixing. And to the extent that I recognized my own psychological struggle, my preference was to hide it. In writing this book and revisiting my earlier life, I admit that my mental health did, indeed, need improvement. In publishing this story as a much older psychologist, I honor a more mature belief that addressing one's struggles is nothing to hide.

Bird Gotta Land begins in 1989. Since that time, the world of psychotherapy has changed dramatically. While the Scientist-Practitioner model of psychology training was a significant model at that time, it is currently so dominant that faculty have little time to develop skilled psychotherapists through intensive supervision.

Granted, the modern psychotherapist must be a good scientist. I appreciate the academic psychologists who taught me to think critically and to reason through complex information. However, this book is not about those psychologists and their important research. It is about the value of what is being systematically eliminated in psychology departments around the country: the artistry involved in deeply understanding the people who seek our help.

I offer this book as a view behind the curtain of psychotherapy and as a form of psychotherapy supervision. Today, new psychologists coming to me for supervision are quite aware that they are not trained to understand people in depth. They have learned a set of specific symptom-reduction tools, but they get lost in their clients' complicated stories, wondering why clients repeat the same painful dramas rather than "fixing their presenting problems."

At a psychology conference in the 1980's I recall hearing the great psychotherapist Carl Whitaker declare: "Techniques are what you use until the therapist shows up."

I hope you will discover the role that the liberal arts play in shaping the mind of the psychotherapist and thus the process of psychotherapy. While our life stories have elements of truth in them, most personal narratives become entrenched. The transformative art of psychotherapy happens when clients understand that their narratives are limiting and keep them stuck. Psychotherapy helps clients imagine an alternative ending.

In 2021, we live in a digital age where information comes at us from many directions. We can even Google our symptoms and download techniques for relief. Yet there is still something irreplaceable about the slow conversation between two people sitting across from each other in a quiet room. The magic of the therapeutic conversation continues to flourish as people increasingly need to better connect to themselves and others, to feel grounded and present.

Bird Gotta Land depicts Stephen's journey from floating through life up in his head to landing solidly inside of his own experience. It is about a therapist learning to show up.

PART I

Chapter 1

ASLEEP

THE ATLANTIC OCEAN is breaking thirty feet from his screened window, and yet he's oversleeping. The ocean's morning rhythm has grown louder in tiny increments sneaking in toward the small shingled beach house. The heavy air that was completely still an hour ago now bends some sunburned oleanders slightly toward the window.

Stephen turns his body toward the nightstand, peeks out of one eye at the clock and discovers that he has overslept by almost an hour. "Shit," he whispers, before pulling the bedspread up to his shoulders and falling back into a dreamy sleep.

Carol is in the kitchen moving to the soulful music in her head as she prepares one last breakfast for her sleeping lover. He'll be moving out after breakfast and she wants their last moments to be special. Stephen is moving to Atlanta, Georgia, to begin graduate school in clinical psychology, while she'll probably live forever on this barrier island off the coast of Charleston, South Carolina.

Carol squeezes oranges and cuts strawberries, waiting for her young poet to awaken. She slips into the room and out of her robe. She slides her long thin body into the bed and presses against Stephen. She kisses his neck, becoming sexually aroused as she does so easily, as Stephen's eyes open.

The tide reaches the breakwater rocks close to the window with a loud crash.

Stephen turns over and pulls her to his chest. They lay together for a minute. He kisses her cheek and they get up and move to the kitchen for breakfast.

Carol is reading poetry by Mary Oliver when Stephen walks into the living room dressed in running shorts and a singlet, his day bag on his shoulder. She meets him at the screened door and puts her hand on his tanned shoulder. She holds out the book of poetry to him. "You never did read this," she says.

"I started it. I just never got very far with it," Stephen says.

"I want you to have it," she says, handing Stephen the book.

"No, it's your book," Stephen says.

Carol frowns. "You're my young poet," she says. She knew that he'd begun disliking her sweet idealizations of him since it had become clear that he was moving. She'd never expected that they would stay together forever. For one thing she was twelve years older than him.

"You have a poet's heart. You have to learn to appreciate poetry. Mary Oliver is a good place to start."

Stephen nods and puts the book in his bag. Carol stands on her tiptoes to kiss him lightly on the lips. They smile at each other and head out the door.

Right now, Stephen wants to be elsewhere. He's saying good-bye, it's too early in the morning, and he knows no good story about saying good-bye. The bright sun jolts him as he steps onto the deck. He squints at the glowing silver sunlight on the gray morning ocean.

As they move to Stephen's twenty-year-old Karman Ghia convertible, he opens the car door and turns back to Carol.

"You gonna stay in touch with me, sweetheart?" she asks, fingering errant hair on his forehead and pushing it to the side like mothers do to their teenaged sons.

Stephen flinches and glances away from her. He turns back to her and smiles. "Of course, I'll call," he says.

"Oh God, I'm going to miss you," she says, hugging him as tears fill her eyes. "I'll always love you, Stephen, so much."

"I love you, too," he says, stiffly, before looking again toward the waves.

"Oh Stephen, God Stephen, you be careful and call me soon, but only when you want to. Got it?" she says, as she lets go of him and backs away.

"I got it," he says quietly.

Carol's so-called young poet, despite his not showing much appreciation for poetry, drove along the narrow two-lane road that slithered through the marshes separating Folly Beach from the rest of the world. Once off Folly, he hopped into Charleston, South Carolina and onto the interstate for the trip to Atlanta. By Karma Ghia, Atlanta is about five and a half hours away which allowed plenty of time to listen to many repetitions of John Lennon's last album, as well as favorites from INXS. All the while, he mused over his reasons for enrolling in a clinical psychology program. He knew he wanted to help others, but his own life circumstances seemed overwhelming at times. He felt, at twenty-seven years of age, that he'd never find a loving relationship of any duration. There was his ex-wife and Carol, but there was also his relationship with his three-year-old son Nicholas. How often would he be able to see him now that he was moving to Atlanta and had sacrificed joint custody with his ex-wife, Charlotte?

Stephen lights a marijuana joint he'd stashed in his ash tray for the trip. The gentle sinsemilla reminds him of his mantra of attempted reassurances that had begun when he decided to move: My family will help out; he's a resilient kid; this education will allow me to take better care of his future; his mother is good to him; and maybe she'll move with him to Atlanta, so we can resume co-parenting.

The reassurances worked for the first hour of his trip until the image flashed of Nicholas's face as they said goodbye two nights earlier. The little boy had a stiff smile as he tried and failed miserably to hide his sadness. The image shifted to the moment when Stephen had to close the front door to leave his son. Nicholas could have easily turned away to his toys and acted as if his father's leaving was routine. Instead, he looked into his father's eyes as he closed the door. The memory of Nicholas's sad eyes brought a rush of guilt and loneliness.

As he got closer to his new home, Stephen also ruminated about his father's recent prostate cancer diagnosis. It was another relationship in jeopardy – irreversibly so, if he died. Just one more thing that seemed out of his control. Perhaps enrolling in a PhD program in psychology was a road to greater self-awareness and better relationships.

Stephen parks in front of a house on the famously posh Tuxedo Road in Buckhead where he's rented a small apartment in the backyard pool house. He walks across the slate pavers toward the ornate front door of the main house. He pushes the doorbell and hears a cacophony of barking dogs. He takes a few deep breaths to try to relax before the door opens and he's greeted all at once by his two new landlords who are attempting to restrain their two dogs, a small poodle and an English sheep dog. "Oh my God," Dan says. "They act like Dobermans in the projects. Come on in."

Randy chuckles and extends his hand to welcome Stephen.

Stephen walks into the foyer and ducks his head slightly as he steps under the two-hundred- year old twinkling chandelier, even though its lowest point is a foot over his head. He surveys the ornately framed abstract paintings crowded together on the ocher walls. Dan, who hasn't met Stephen until now, catches Randy's eye and raises his eyebrows. "Definitely attractive," his look says. "A tenant has to be attractive," he told Randy earlier.

Dan wrestles the dogs away. Randy motions Stephen toward the living room. "This way," he says. "Did you have a good trip?"

"It was okay," Stephen says. "I don't have an air conditioner in my car so it was pretty hot."

"I'll bet," Randy says. "So, you got everything taken care of before you left?"

"I think so. I hope so," Stephen says, following Randy.

Dan walks into the room, cleaning his hands with a dish towel. "I'll bet you didn't know you were moving into the wild kingdom, did you?"

"I met your dogs when I rented the apartment. They're good," Stephen says.

"Great," Dan says. He slaps his hands together. "Let's see," he says, "first, let me get you a glass of iced-tea, and then we'll give you a tour." Dan gestures toward the kitchen.

Stephen shrugs. "Ah, no thanks, I'm okay. I just finished a drink in my car," he says. "I probably just need to start getting my stuff organized in the apartment. I don't want to interrupt; just go back to what you were doing."

"That won't work," Dan says. "What we were doing before was waiting for you and you were late. You're here now. We'll have to find something else to do with our time." Dan wants to throw Stephen off-kilter. His father liked to say that influencing people was like changing the direction of a spinning top. Once the top is knocked off-center, even slightly, the wobbling top can be knocked over with a slight touch.

Dan smiles at Stephen, waiting for his reply. Just as Randy draws a breath for a quick rescue, Stephen says, "I think I'll have that iced-tea, if you don't mind."

Dan smiles at Randy and leads them to the kitchen. He hands Stephen the iced-tea and begins the tour. After passing through every room in the house, the three men walk outside to the pool and the adjacent pool house. They follow a slate path, first under a lattice arbor draped with grapes, then between rows of enormous boxwoods, at times passing brilliant roses, fountains and benches, before finally arriving at a perfect view of the pool. The gray cement pool is designed to look like a natural pond, long and narrow, with grass growing right up to the edge of the stones.

Dan watches as Stephen's eye catches the marble cherub with water spouting from his penis, keeping the pool filled with warm water. Stephen's face does nothing to betray any thoughts he might have about it.

"God, this place is really, um, amazing," Stephen says, glancing at the house next to the pool.

"Thanks," Randy says. "Do you want us to help you get your place set up?"

"Um…" Stephen starts before Dan interrupts.

"Let's show him the back nine, and then we can get him settled in," Dan says.

"Sure, that's fine," Stephen says.

They continue along a slate pathway away from the pool, ending at a natural, untended area. Dan points to a fence about fifty yards away. "Our property extends all the way to that fence, but Randy hasn't had time to finish landscaping this part."

Stephen looks at the area, overgrown with brush and weeds. Randy tells Stephen, "I want to put a perennial garden over there, something that looks natural, wild, but that's next spring's project."

"Promises, promises," Dan says, turning to Stephen. "Don't listen to him. He'll never clear that area. He's too busy. He promised me he'd put in a natural garden with perennials and wildflowers and pathways to those old oaks back there. I believe his design even included a couple of benches for reading and thinking, though who's got time for that? When did you promise to do that for me, Randy, two years ago?"

Dan stands with his arms crossed waiting for a response.

When Randy takes a breath to speak, Dan quickly adds, "All he does is paint these days."

Randy shakes his head. "I never told you exactly what I was going to do, and I sure didn't promise when I'd do it," he says. He turns to Stephen, "I want to do something with this area this spring, but I haven't decided exactly what, yet."

"It does look like a great place for a garden," Stephen offers. "Not that you don't already have a pretty spectacular yard."

"Wait, are you here to work in the diplomatic core?" Dan jokes.

They end the tour in front of the small house that is Randy's studio and Stephen's new apartment.

Randy unlocks the door to Stephen's apartment before handing him two keys to the door.

After Stephen declines their invitation to join them later for dinner, Dan and Randy return to their house. When they enter the kitchen,

Dan turns to Randy and smiles broadly. "Why Randy, I don't know whether to punch you or kiss you. I've got a mind to do both."

"What?" Randy says, grinning.

"Well the new roomy was quite the surprise," Dan says. "I believe you described him as cute. I know the guys that you describe as cute, you know, the guys that we're always trying to fix our friends up with, who we both admit we wouldn't really date if we were single. The new roomy is quite handsome, now isn't he Randy? And I believe you described him as heterosexual. What did you base that on?"

"You think he's gay?" Randy asks.

"I'm not sure," Dan says, hoisting himself onto the recently finished Italian tile countertop. "It's very weird; my gaydar wasn't telling me much. But how many heterosexual men do you think show up for their first meeting with gay landlords wearing hot pants?"

"Those are running shorts. He told me he's a runner," Randy says.

"Please, I'm not stupid. They were about as short as I've seen," Dan says, rubbing his chin with his thumb and index finger.

The conversation is typical of the couple's bantering. Dan initially protested Randy's suggestion they build a pool house and divide the space into a small apartment and a studio for Randy. But Dan couldn't reasonably object. He complained constantly that Randy's painting failed to contribute more to their household. "This way," Randy told him, "I can save the considerable money I spend on renting a studio. At the same time, the tenant adds income. It's a perfect situation."

Dan, who frequently bragged about his income at Coke, felt entitled to expectations that Randy take care of household chores while he lounged about reading the paper and sipping cocktails during his off-hours. "You'll find something else to complain about. But you won't be able to complain about my studio costs," Randy said at the time, as he kissed Dan lightly on the cheek.

In his apartment, Stephen sits on the edge of his bed, marveling for a few moments about the apparent tension between his new landlords. Then he eyes his possessions in the middle of the floor where he'd dumped them on his trip when he rented the apartment. He empties the small bag of necessities and briefly organizes the bathroom. He begins unpacking some books, placing them on a bookshelf next to his desk. He flips through the textbook for his History and Systems of Psychotherapy class. He sits on his bed, opens the book to a chapter on Gestalt therapy and begins reading.

He reads a few pages before falling back on the bed with his eyes closed. He feels uneasy.

He decides to take a shower, go out to dinner, and come home early to finish straightening up. That way he'll feel fresh, so he can focus on getting everything organized. Tomorrow is the first day of classes, but this is also his first evening in Buckhead.

Chapter 2

THE FIRST DAY

COMFORTABLE, OVERSTUFFED DEN CHAIRS arranged in a semicircle invite intimacy, but Stephen is uncomfortable. It's the first day of classes, a new beginning and he isn't ready, a normal thing for him. He glances around the room, then blinks rapidly as his eyes drift from his syllabus to the worn Persian rug at his feet. He follows the pattern of shapes in the rug to the edge and then back, again. Instead of the living-room arrangement, Stephen had hoped for a classroom setup with desks in rows where you could take one toward the back and hide. No such luck.

Stephen shakes his head and squeezes his eyes shut. He surprised himself, but not that much, last night by betraying his plans and staying out until two in the morning drinking beer, talking to a strange woman he had almost no interest in. He even made out with her in the parking lot, leaning against her car. He probably would have gone home with her just to spend the night somewhere besides his empty room except that he knew he had to get up early.

"Fucking idiot," he'd admonished himself when he flopped onto the naked mattress in his apartment and set his alarm clock to go off in a little less than four hours. He knew he'd be tired and hung over for his first day at his new graduate school. Closing his eyes, he looked on the bright side of things, imagining that the next day would likely be low stress, just an orientation day.

Stephen looks to the side and the guy sitting next to him lights up. "Hi, I'm Scott Melvin," he says. The two shake hands. Scott has silver-blond hair pulled tightly into a ponytail. Slightly sunburned, he wears a bright blue t-shirt, faded jeans, and running shoes.

"So, where do you live?" Scott asks.

Stephen sits up straighter. "In Buckhead. I have an apartment behind a house in Chastain Park."

"Not too bad for a graduate student," Scott says, smiling. "But, honestly, that neighborhood is about nothing but money."

"Well, not in my case," Stephen says, thinking, "What's the deal with this guy?"

Scott leans toward Stephen. "I'm in Inman Park, about ten minutes from here by bicycle. Rode in this morning."

"Oh, really," Stephen says, nodding, as if he has a clue where Inman Park is.

"Do you bike?" Scott asks.

"Yeah… Oh, you mean, like, long-distance?"

"Yeah!" Scott brays.

"Some…not really…much," Stephen mutters. "I run, though."

"Great! Me too," Scott says, turning toward the door as Ed Holland walks quickly toward the head of the semicircle.

Stephen instantly recognizes Ed, the co-director of clinical training, from the description given him by a professor at North Carolina where he got a master's degree in experimental psychology. "An athletic looking guy with thick grey hair; looks like an aging Hollywood actor."

Stephen watches Ed smile, shyly, as he slides gently into one of the chairs in front of the blackboard. "Welcome," he says in his quiet voice. "It's good to see all of you. I'm going to give you an overview of the clinical program before describing the 'Intro to Clinical Psychology' course, the first of four required practicum courses that I teach. All of these courses are designed to introduce you to the major concepts of psychotherapy and help you begin the process of understanding yourself as a clinician."

Stephen, still tired, fights against slouching, sitting up straighter in his chair.

"We have an atmosphere here of acceptance," Ed says. "We selected the eight of you from almost 400 applicants. We expect that you'll make it through to get your Ph.D. So, we want you to relax and know that we're on your team, okay?"

Ed's voice is almost soft. His eyes are soft, too, and his light blue gaze gently floats from student to student. "It's our goal to help you become good clinical psychologists," he says. "We start that in this course.

"Having said that, I don't, however, presume that each of you will become clinicians. In fact, it's my experience that only about half of each class has the mix of personality and emotional and intellectual skills to be good clinicians. The other half of our students usually go into research or teaching."

"Half?" Stephen thinks. He was getting his PhD to become a clinician, not to do more research.

Ed was the biggest name in clinical psychology at Georgia University. In fact, his name was generally known by most graduate students and faculty in clinical psychology throughout the country. Ed had published three or four hundred articles, written several important books and was prominent in the early research and theoretical articles in cognitive-behavioral psychology.

Steven remembers some other lesser-known things he'd picked up about Ed from his professor. Ed's noticeably young girlfriends had been the hit of faculty parties for many years. When streaking was the craze, one of Ed's girlfriends dashed naked through the University president's crowded garden reception for an incoming social science dean. Another girlfriend was known to light marijuana joints at department parties, not a huge deal in the mid-seventies, but she'd often bogart them, smoking them like cigarettes. She also downed tons of tequila shots and if a pool was available, she was the first to strip off her clothes and dive in. Stephen smiles at the thought of that.

Ed covers the final entry on the syllabus and announces, "Let's go around the room and introduce ourselves."

"Why don't we not?" Stephen wants to say.

Ed turns to Scott. "Scott, you want to start us off?" he asks. "And then we can go counterclockwise around the room."

"Oh great," Stephen thinks, realizing that he'll be second. He wonders when he'll learn to prepare for important things with a good night's sleep. He looks at Scott who seems deep in thought. Within seconds, Scott is rattling off his accomplishments.

Scott lets everyone know that he has already practiced psychotherapy in Atlanta for ten years after completing his master's in social work from Northwestern University. He's returned to school following the recent publication of his book, "Crazymaking: The Psychiatric Hospital Environment," which he says is "an indictment of psychiatric hospitals that routinely impose the standards of the dominant culture on their patients using a process of labeling and coerced normalization."

Apparently continuing to quote from his book, Scott continues, "The most troubled and vulnerable members of our culture are subjected to the most bizarre and insensitive systems in our culture as a means of what, help?"

Scott holds his gaze steady for a few seconds, then turns to Stephen and smiles.

Stephen looks down. Finally, he smiles and looks up. "I'm Stephen and I've been brought here to carry Scott's books around campus." He waits for a second and then everyone laughs, Scott loudest of all as he warmly pats Stephen's shoulder.

"I, um, have a master's degree in experimental psychology from the University of North Carolina and have been doing applied research at the Medical University of South Carolina in Charleston for the last two years," Stephen continues. "The truth is I wasn't as motivated as I needed to be to make the grades to get into graduate school in clinical psychology and that's why I ended up getting my masters in experimental psychology. I still have an interest in research, but I really want to be a practicing clinical psychologist, which is why I returned for my Ph.D. I have a son, Nicholas, who is three years old. He lives with my ex-wife in Charleston, South Carolina. I'm not sure what areas of clinical psychology I'm most interested in."

Stephen's voices trails off and he turns to the student counter-clockwise from him and smiles. As she begins her introduction, he takes a full breath.

The introductions continue and thankfully for Stephen and the rest, none are as impressive as Scott's. Maggie is into feminist psychology. Sierra is interested in adolescent psychology and describes her previous work in wilderness programs in Colorado. Joe is a lawyer who hates being a lawyer and is interested in psychoanalytic therapies. Larry has a master's in child psychology and refers to himself as a "kid person," with no irony.

Perhaps the most intriguing student is Charles, a married African American minister with two children. "I've been an AME Zion minister in Detroit for the last five years," he says. "Before that, we lived in Ohio and I had a church there.

"I'm here because I believe in education, both for myself and as a means of elevating my people. I want to continue to serve as a minister, but also as a psychologist, a role that I've been playing in my community for the last five years even though I haven't been qualified or properly trained for it. I'm here to get that training and to learn to work with disenfranchised populations."

The classmate whom Stephen is most anxious to hear, Ally, speaks last. The two have exchanged glances throughout the class. Her hair is silky blond, her skin clear pink-white, and her features are slender and sharp. In one smooth movement, she slides her feet out of her Dr. Scholl's onto the chair and tucks them under her skirt.

"I think I'm the youngest person here, and I don't have many of the impressive experiences you all have," she says. Her voice is strained and high-pitched and Stephen feels anxious for her. His anxiety grows as she takes an uncomfortably long pause.

Finally, she adds, "I'm from New Hampshire where it's not hot like it's here today. This morning I thought I'd choke on the humidity." She pauses again. "I guess I always wanted to be a psychologist. My father is a psychiatrist and I've always enjoyed hearing him discuss psychotherapy and I liked my undergraduate courses in psychology. And, you know, I've always wanted to help people. And I didn't know what else to do when I graduated from college, so here I am."

Ally shrugs and smiles uneasily. Stephen sits back in his chair and watches her look down in her lap at her notepad.

Ed smiles at the students. "Very good. All of you, except Ally, have at least a few years of post-graduate work. In fact, we have a policy of not accepting students without either a master's degree or significant clinical work experience. We accepted Ally because she had the highest combination of grade point average and GRE scores of all our applicants, so we felt that she had the raw material to make an exceptional student. I hope that doesn't embarrass you, Ally," Ed says, looking at Ally's bright red face.

"Good rescue," Stephen thinks.

Ed continues. "I think this year's class is as interesting, at least on paper, as any we've had. To say a little about myself, I helped found the clinical program here. I teach History and Systems of Psychotherapy, applied clinical research, and many of the clinical training courses. I describe my orientation to therapy and supervision as narrative and aesthetic." He pauses.

"So, what do I mean by narrative and aesthetic? For me, psychotherapy is a process of helping the client gradually live a deeper and sometimes improved version of their life by helping them learn to adopt new, much more creative stories of their life. It's this new, creative story that makes up the narrative aesthetic," he continues. "This will become clearer with time."

Stephen is puzzled but suddenly recalls Carol's moniker of him as a young poet. How, he wondered, did that relate to this narrative aesthetic?

"I'm particularly interested," Ed continues, "in working with disenfranchised populations and currently one of my grants is to study the communities in Atlanta that have been destroyed by the federal interstate system. Not surprisingly, all of them are African-American."

He pauses and looks around the room. "Now, my personal passion in life, however, is an obsession with seeing the psychology department team win the intramural softball championship. I know it sounds strange, but it's as worthy and important a goal as any I've ever had."

Ed's eyes appear to darken, and Stephen recognizes that he's being very serious, even though what he's said is quite odd.

Ed continues. "I'm sure that some of you find that surprising, but things change as you get older, priorities change, and right now, at this point in my life, that's a very important goal for me. Actually, it's my dream."

Stephen jokes to himself that as you get older, maybe you regress to a child.

"I'm the pitcher on the team," Ed says, "and also usually bat somewhere in the middle of the order, at least in the last several years since I've learned to hit to all fields, to take what the pitcher gives me, as they say."

Stephen notes some classmates squinting with confusion and feels some validation.

"I haven't had a chance to discuss this with Stephen," Ed says, startling Stephen to the point that he fumbles his papers, only catching them from falling at the last minute. "I was thrilled to read in his application materials that he played college baseball." Ed smiles at Stephen. "And I assume that Charles, since he was a college football player, like myself, might be a multi-sport athlete and available for our team."

Ed looks at Charles, who is smiling. "Yeah, I played a little baseball up through high school and can probably help out," he says.

Ed beams.

Stephen is certain he did not indicate anything in his application about playing college baseball. While he likes the image this creates for the other students, he's a little embarrassed since he was actually cut from his college baseball team midway through his sophomore year. He'd become third string when the incoming freshman shortstop had his second two homerun game in winter practice. After Stephen received word that his services were no longer needed, he surreptitiously read the coach's summary report in his athletic chart.

The coach described him as an "athletically gifted infielder," but followed that with: "Struggles hitting the curve ball and in strategic situations he seems to get too much into his head, puts too much pressure on himself, and chokes."

Stephen read the summary several times, especially that last sentence. He could recite it by heart though he never uttered a word of it out loud. He knew it was true in many aspects of his life but did not know what to do about it. Maybe he'd learn something in his classes that would help. As for Ed's team, he knows that slow-pitch intramural softball is a long way from college baseball. The same guy who loses his scholarship from a college baseball team could certainly be a huge improvement on a psychology department softball team.

Stephen, lost in his remembrance of his college baseball failures, suddenly realizes that Ed's story of himself held no information about his personal life, whether he was married, if he had children, none of that. He wondered if Ed still had his crazy girlfriends.

"Okay," Ed says, standing. "I think that's about all we can accomplish here today."

The students stand and gather their belongings. Scott laughs about Stephen's earlier comment about him while Stephen watches Ally walk toward the door, her movement so much easier than her voice had seemed just a few moments ago.

Chapter 3

ATTEMPTED ATTUNEMENT

IN HIS STUDIO ADJOINING Stephen's apartment, Randy looks at the canvas he'd shoved into the closet a few weeks ago. He was captivated by the images but knew something was missing. It was just a couple of vague sketches of masculine forms with interesting layers of colors.

Randy closes his eyes, trying to capture the fleeting mental image that originally inspired the canvas. As before, the image flashes before him and then disappears, like a dream memory evaporates when he wakes up. He sits quietly waiting for the image to reappear.

He opens his eyes. He looks at the canvas in front of him and remembers the figures from a college trip to Italy back when he was trying to be heterosexual. He was traveling alone. Two men were walking down a narrow street, maybe father and son, he guessed at the time. From a distance, he'd watched the outline of their bodies move, oriented toward each other, gently framed in afternoon sunshine that reflected off ancient stone buildings, washed in the colors of Italian earth. As the two men approached, Randy saw the older man's arm around the younger man, his hand lightly draping his shoulder. Randy was swept away by the man's beautiful dark hand, with its thick veins and wrinkled skin, lovingly squeezing the younger man's t-shirted shoulder. As the two men moved out of sight, Randy felt a cold, desperate loneliness.

Looking at the canvas now, he revisits the memory image and realizes that the two men were lovers, not father and son. His internalized homophobia at the time had disguised that little fact.

He reaches into his pigments and finds the russet clay, hand-dug on that Italian trip from a country garden not far from where he'd shuddered with loneliness. He spills a small amount onto his palette and covers it with oil. He stirs, dabs his brush into the shimmering paint and then onto the image.

He sweeps his brush along the inside of the first figure. Quickly, he dabs the brush back in the red-brown pigment and then streaks it around the inside of the second figure. He closes his eyes again. The figures appear and vanish. All that remains is the hand on the shoulder. He reaches for a finer brush and delicately reproduces the hand in its intricate detail, as it rests on the abstract shoulder of the other figure. Only the hand is almost as clear as a photograph.

A subtle change of lighting in the room causes Randy to turn. He spots the shadow of Stephen's head on the other side of the screened door.

"Hello?" Randy calls out.

"Hi," Stephen calls back, tentatively opening the door.

"Hi, hi, come on in." Randy says.

"So, this is where you paint," Stephen says as he closes the door. "You sure it's okay to come in. I don't want to interrupt."

"Yeah, of course," Randy says. "I'm just finishing up and, besides, it's been six weeks since you moved in and we still have barely talked."

Stephen walks around the room looking at the paintings while sunlight streams through the skylights. He looks at a group of framed still lifes of flowers. Some paintings show blooms grouped together in pots, others single roses in vases. "These are beautiful," he says.

Randy, cleaning his paintbrush over the sink, does not respond.

Stephen continues his stroll, stopping in front of a group of abstract representations of human figures. "I really love these!" he says.

Randy turns and smiles.

Stephen moves in front of the painting on the easel, the one that had been in the closet for a couple of weeks. "God this one is really… it's so much more abstract than the flowers…obviously. It's incredible. I mean the flowers are too, but I guess I'm more drawn to the abstract ones," he says, and points back to the abstract paintings on the wall.

Randy prefers the abstract ones, too. Two minutes ago he might have questioned the authenticity of Stephen's compliment, especially about the painting on the easel. But now, with his internal image so clearly before him, he feels exhilarated.

"I'm working with these new images, the more abstract ones. I sell a good bit of the flowers over there," Randy says, motioning to the framed canvases of flowers.

"I like those, too," Stephen says. "I'm just more drawn to the abstract ones."

"Thank you for being more drawn to them," Randy says.

"Is there a story with the painting you're working on?" Stephen asks, pointing to the easel.

Randy stutters a bit then stops and shakes his head. "God, I really can't describe my work very well," he says. "I have trouble with words. I just paint what I see."

"So, you don't have a story of what's going on in the painting?" Stephen asks. "You just paint from… a memory, or do you just start painting and see what comes out?"

"Yeah, I guess, I, well, both." Randy says. "I hope my audience will have their own stories and put them into the painting. What do you see when you look at it?"

Stephen gazes at the canvas and shifts his weight from one foot to the other. How do you say something semi-intelligent to an artist about his abstract work? And then there is the whole gay thing. Presumably, he's looking at two men, one with his arm snug around the other. What is a heterosexual to say?

"I guess for me the figures look like, you know, like lovers walking together. But I'm not sure."

"Actually, I remembered a few seconds before you came over where I first saw these guys," Randy says motioning to the canvas. "I was in Italy and I saw them walking toward me, two men who were so deeply connected, so not alone at a time when I was utterly and completely alone. I was at the lowest point in my life and they seemed so alive."

"So, there is a story!" Stephen says. "It's like the process of abstraction, getting to the core, helps the story unfold. It's funny but that's kind of like the psychotherapy technique my professor seems to advocate – an aesthetic narrative. Do you think the painting is therapeutic?"

"Absolutely," Randy replies. "It's probably why I prefer the abstract images."

The light in the studio dims as clouds cross the sun. Stephen looks away, back toward the flowers. "If you like the abstract paintings more, why do you paint the flowers?" he asks.

"These are how I make money," Randy answers. "The abstract paintings are my art."

"The abstract paintings don't sell?" Stephen asks, surprised.

"I haven't actually tried to sell them much…or really at all. I guess I'm still working on them. I have so much trouble capturing the images that I'm trying to represent in the paint that I haven't really shown them to anyone."

"You must feel like you're getting closer with these, right?" Stephen asks.

"Yeah, I'm still working on them, but I'm feeling closer."

"I'm glad I came in here. This is some incredible stuff you're creating on the other side of my wall," Stephen says.

"That's so nice of you to say. I appreciate your comments more than you know," Randy says. After a moment of silence, he asks, "By the way, how's school going?"

"Good, fine, you know." Stephen mumbles, looking down at his shoes.

Randy smiles. His two teenaged nephews answer questions with about as much elaboration. "You've had six weeks of classes. Are you getting a feel for things?" he asks, probing for specifics.

"I guess. I'm feeling pretty good about things. Right now, though, I'm a little nervous about doing something called an intake interview with a new client."

"What's that?"

"It's a first session with a client. The clients are mostly students or people from the community who want to see someone at a reduced cost for therapy. The first- year students do the intake interview and then refer them to upper-level students for therapy. I think the idea is that we're supposed to help them talk about their problems in a way that we get enough information to match them with an appropriate therapist in the clinic. We do the intake, get feedback about the interview from our classmates and supervisor, and then meet with the client again. During that session we give them the feedback and refer them. I was lucky enough to be the first one assigned this happy little task. The whole class and my clinical professor will be watching behind a one-way mirror while I help the client tell the story of her life."

"Oh my God," Randy says. "That sounds scary."

"Exactly," Stephen says.

"I couldn't do that. How are you supposed to keep your wits enough to do that?"

"Yeah, that's the problem. I'm not sure of the solution," Stephen says. "I've been doing some reading from the different schools of psychotherapy, hoping for an inspiration. Worst part is that most of the other students have a lot of experience and I have none. I got into the program because I have a good background as a researcher. That isn't going to help me much today."

"It's today?" Randy exclaims.

Stephen looks at his watch. "Actually, in about an hour and a half!"

"Wow. That's…soon. But I'm sure you'll do fine. What I don't understand is how in the world a client can come into a room and talk about their personal stuff with an audience."

"Hmmm. Yeah, I guess I haven't thought about it too much from their perspective," Stephen says. He looks at Randy and smiles gently. "Maybe I'll just ask them to paint a picture."

Chapter 4

THE FIRST SESSION

STEPHEN PULLS INTO A PARKING PLACE behind the psychological services center. He has been thinking about Randy's comment about the client's difficulty being observed by an audience. He'd worried about the effect on himself but had not thought at all about how the observation might affect the human being coming for help. Thinking about the client's predicament helped him relax. The interview was no longer exclusively about his grade or impressing Ed and his classmates.

His relaxed perspective evaporated when his classmates arrived. Yesterday they were all graduate students on a mutual journey. Today, he's the beast pacing back and forth in the steel-barred cage while everyone else is on a summer stroll through the zoo, eating popcorn, sipping Coca-Cola and pointing.

Ed walks in and tells Stephen that the client's already in the waiting room. He says that the client's name is Lydia and that she indicated that she was coming to the clinic for help with depression. Stephen goes to get the client, and the rest of them retire to the observation room.

The closer Stephen gets to the waiting room, the more he tries to adjust his gait and his expression to look a little bit more experienced, like he has done this maybe twenty or thirty times before. He enters the waiting room, sees several college students reading weekly news magazines, and calls out his client's name. A tall, slender woman in a black leotard and blue jeans rises from her chair.

"Oh Shit," Stephen thinks, "she's fucking gorgeous." Lydia smiles and shakes his hand. His throat grows a little tighter.

They walk up the stairs together, chatting nervously like teenagers on a blind date. As they enter the large room, Stephen motions her toward two chairs positioned in front of the one-way mirror. She glances at the mirror, tucking some loose hair behind her ear as Stephen sits across from her.

Stephen reiterates what she already knows from phoning for the appointment and materials the clinic mailed to her: "We'll be observed by faculty and graduate students as part of the training clinic's supervision system. This allows the clinic to provide free psychological services in exchange for the training."

She looks shocked. "Really! Oh, I don't know… There are people watching us from behind this mirror?" she asks, pointing toward it.

Stephen clears his throat and answers softly, "Yes".

"I don't…like that at all," she says. She twists her body away from the mirror and bends her head down to her chest.

"Yeah, I understand, but it does allow for supervision." Stephen feels the trickle of sweat on his brow. "One of the advantages for you is that when I give you feedback in a week you'll have the benefit of many perspectives and the years of experience of my professor."

"Okay," she whispers, without looking up.

Stephen clears his throat: "What brings you to the clinic?"

There is a long silence. Stephen wonders if she's going to get up and leave.

"I've just been down lately," she finally whispers.

"Really?" Stephen says, straining to sound empathetic.

She twists her body further away.

"So, you decided to come in because you've been depressed or, um, down?" Stephen says, his voice strained by anxiety.

She looks over her shoulder at Stephen and mumbles: "Yeah, you could say depressed."

She looks away, leaving Stephen alone in the silence.

In the observation room Ed whispers to the students, "She's not going to say anything important unless he gets her to talk about how she feels being observed."

Stephen searches through his pre-arranged list of questions: How long have you been depressed? Have you been depressed before? What kind of family did you grow up in? Were others in your family depressed? Have you had therapy before?

None of those questions feel right. He remembers Randy's insightful comment about a client having an audience. He leans toward Lydia to see her face. Her cheeks are bright pink, and she looks like she's about to cry. Her distress lifts him out of his anxiety.

"You're pretty upset about being observed, huh?"

"There it is," Ed says, leaning back with a satisfied look on his face.

"Yes, I am," she says, turning slightly toward him. "It's just every-thing…everything in my life has been going bad for me lately." She turns in her seat and glances at the mirror. She lifts her eyes to Stephen's.

"I shouldn't be surprised about this. I mean the woman on the phone told me. But, shit, what am I supposed to say with a bunch of people watching?"

"Yeah, it's hard to talk about important things in your life when you're not comfortable."

"Well, yeah, it's distracting," Lydia says, and jerks a tissue from a nearby Kleenex box.

She dabs the tears from her eyes and exhales loudly.

"I guess I'll just focus on talking to you," she says, shaking her head. "I just feel so lost and angry, here, and at home with my family, and in New York when I'm there…everywhere." She looks at Stephen and smiles dimly.

"But I've got to do something."

Stephen nods.

"I'm a ballet dancer. I've been dancing in New York with the New York Ballet. I'm on the second string, so to speak, the 'corps de ballet,' or at least I used to be."

She looks down.

She speaks even more softly and slowly than before: "I've taken a leave from the company because I, um, have eating issues, have since the day I moved to New York, the summer after I graduated from high school."

For the rest of the session, Stephen spoke very little while Lydia talked freely. She was depressed, yes, but the problem that brought her to the clinic was her eating disorder. She was bingeing and purging every day. This elegant ballet dancer was starving herself all day. Then, when her desire for sustenance overcame her, she got huge portions of junk food from the nearest fast-food joint. Some nights she'd devour an entire bucket of fried chicken; other nights she'd stuff herself with pizza. She described her binges as "what you'd expect a football player to eat."

When she finished bingeing, she'd start feeling desperate to get rid of the horrible food. Feeling bloated, nauseated, and panicky, she'd go to her tiny kitchen, run hot water in the sink, and turn on the garbage disposal, a refinement she'd learned in the last few months. Then she'd stick three fingers down her throat and heave.

Lydia seemed almost at ease telling the intricate details of her solitary obsession but was oddly more reluctant to admit that she smoked all day to keep hunger at bay. "We all do it," she said about the smoking. "It's just part of the whole ballet, 'need to look perfect' thing…I plan on quitting soon, though."

Without any direction from Stephen she shifted to talking about her family. She described her father, a financial officer of a large company, as too busy working to pay any attention to his family. While she complained about her father's absence, she seemed most annoyed with her mother whom she described as "sweet, but despicably passive," especially toward her father. From kindergarten to high school, she went to Westminster, a well-regarded private school, and was an A student throughout. She said her friends and classmates were "completely obsessed with success, even if it meant engaging in self-destructive excesses. 'Success at all costs,' should be the school motto," she said with disdain.

"Sounds like she's living that story out pretty completely," Ed whispered to the group in the observation room.

She explained to Stephen that she came to the clinic for free services because she did not want to ask her father for money for therapy.

"Why wouldn't you ask your father for help?" Stephen asked.

"He ridicules my mother for being 'addicted to her therapist.' He used to bring it up when he drank too many Scotches during one of our rare family dinners out. He doesn't say anything to her now. I don't even know if she still goes. I have to admit; I agree with him that I sure don't see where it's helped her very much."

The other reason for her reluctance to ask her father for help was that he'd paid for her to go to therapy three days a week for a year and a half while she was in New York. And every time she grudgingly admitted that she continued to need help for her depression he became "impatient or disgusted or whatever it is that he feels toward my mother. I sure don't need any of that shit," she said.

"Good, it's good she knows that," Ed whispered in the observation room.

She spent her remaining time talking about her therapy in New York. She said that her therapist did not seem interested in talking about her eating disorder. Instead he got her to discuss her relationships with her father and mother. "To tell you the truth he was this little intellectual guy who didn't seem to know anything about the world I lived in…and I don't think he wanted to know either. I binged and purged the entire time I saw him, and he never seemed to care one way or the other."

"Really?" Stephen asked. "That sounds like it wasn't helpful at all."

"Come on Stephen, how do you know that?" Scott mutters.

Ed smiles at Scott. "He's into the counter-transference experience where he's seeing only her reality."

A few minutes later, and only five minutes after he was supposed to stop the session, Stephen uneasily told her time was up.

As they reschedule for a feedback session, Lydia looks back at the one-way mirror. "I almost forgot that thing has people behind it."

Stephen looks at the mirror. "Me too," he says, and smiles at the dancer.

Chapter 5

ROOMIES

THE LIGHTS ARE ON IN RANDY'S STUDIO. Stephen wants to tell him that the interview went well. He peeks in the studio window and Randy waves him in.

Randy shows Stephen the updated version of the painting of the two men walking. Stephen likes the painting even better now. Randy explains how he'll use wax and shellac to give the images the appearance of a memory. He shows Stephen two paintings on the wall that he has done in the way he described. Stephen agrees that they look like a memory or even "a dream image." Randy tells Stephen that the images he has from memory are the same as the ones he has when he's dreaming.

Stephen puzzles over how Randy can know that. "Interesting," he said. "You know, Freud related memory and dreams, but I'm not sure he'd say the images were the same."

"So how did your session go?" Randy asks.

Stephen starts to give a vague answer but Randy interrupts. "Would you like to have a glass of wine or a beer? Dan'll be home soon and I'm sure he'd be interested in hearing about your session."

"Sure, yeah. Just let me go change and I'll meet you."

A little later, Randy and Stephen sit on the screened porch drinking wine as Dan walks into the house, home at seven o'clock, which is early for him.

"Lucy, I'm home," he shouts in an extremely poor Ricky Ricardo accent as he walks into the kitchen.

Randy smiles shyly at Stephen and hurries to greet Dan.

"We're in here," he says, as he walks toward the kitchen.

"Stephen," Dan says, reaching out his hand, "good to see you." Stephen thinks he hears sincerity in Dan's voice. That would be a first.

The three men move to the large den designed as a smoking room. Stephen sits in an old brown leather chair that is perfect mixture of firm support and plush comfort. Dan and Randy sit on a large, wide, comfortable couch. Randy has one leg on the floor, the other curled next to Dan, whose socked feet rest on an ottoman. Stephen watches Dan put his hand on Randy's leg.

"Stephen did an intake interview that obviously went really well," Randy says.

Dan looks at Stephen in anticipation.

Stephen is hesitant at first, but then begins to tell some of the story.

Dan interrupts. "So, she has, what is that…anorexia, where women think they're fat but are really skinny?"

"No, not really, anorexia is close. But it's technically bulimia, since she overeats and then purges. I guess the difference is that she doesn't really see herself as overweight the way she is; she just needs to be thin for her profession. She tries to restrict her calories, because being a ballet dancer means you need to be really thin. But eventually she feels overwhelmed by hunger and she binges. Afterwards she feels ashamed and panicked about weight gain, so she purges."

"That's awful," Randy says.

"What can you do for her?" Dan asks.

"I think I learn that next semester." Stephen says, then chuckles. "I'll meet with her next week and give her feedback from the class and then she'll see someone else for therapy. I'm just glad she talked to me and it went okay."

"Let's toast then," Dan says, "to a successful first session."

"And to our first glass of wine together," Randy says as they raise their glasses.

Stephen looks at Randy. "Has Dan seen the painting you worked on today?"

"No, I think he saw a much earlier version." Randy says.

"What painting?" Dan asks, as he moves his hand off Randy's leg.

"Just an abstract painting I've been working on for a while. I'll show you tomorrow."

"Sure, you will." Dan says, sitting up straighter and looking at Stephen. "He never shows me his work. I don't know if he's ashamed of it or if he thinks I'm too superficial to appreciate it. I don't know why you hide your art from me and now you show it to Stephen?"

"I don't hide my art from you. You never ask to see it."

"Oh, come on, nothing could be further from the truth," Dan runs his hand through his hair and, at least to Stephen, looks very hurt. "Why do you say stuff like that?" he asks.

"I'll be glad to take you to the studio tomorrow and show you my work, okay?"

"Okay," Dan says softly. "You know I've given several of your rose paintings to my friends and family for presents because I'm so proud of you." Turning back to Stephen, he says, "Randy can make still life sexy."

Randy's looks a little embarrassed, but gently squeezes Dan's shoulder.

Randy interrupts the momentary silence. "Hey, we'd love to hear about Carol. Is she planning a visit any time soon?"

"I don't know. She might…I, I'm not sure." Stephen says, before taking a long sip of his wine.

"She might? What does that mean?" Dan asks, looking at Randy and then back at Stephen. "Did you break up?" he asks.

"Maybe it's none of our business," Randy interjects.

"No, well I guess, I mean, we're not really dating exclusively or maybe we're no longer a couple, I don't know. I guess we decided to play it by ear since, you know, I'm living so far away. I'm not sure what to say really."

"That's obvious," Dan says, his tone a little less harsh than before.

"We talk almost every night, but she seems less talkative than before. I'm not sure, but I think she might have decided to end the relationship. I mean, I'm pretty okay with that, though I'd like to continue to talk on the phone and see where we go. But she's the type of person that once she makes her mind up she moves on. I think she's made up her mind that we're going nowhere."

"Long-distance relationships never work, I hate to tell you, especially when you're, what, three hundred miles away," Dan says. "Randy and I moved in pretty quickly, but every time one of us went out of town, we'd call each other, and Randy basically went mute on the phone. I'd say, 'How are you?' and he'd say, 'Everything is fine,' then silence. I thought he was getting a blow job while we talked."

Stephen laughs along with Dan, while Randy grins and shakes his head.

"I hope you're learning how to take Dan. He almost never tells the truth."

"No, I always tell the truth. It's just so foreign to everyone else that it seems like bullshit."

"Come on. That is so arrogant," Randy says, before turning back to Stephen. "Anyway, ignore him," he says. "The telephone is hard for me. I'm such a visual person. Maybe it's for Carol, too. But if she's pulling away, I'm sorry to hear that."

Stephen hesitates. "Really it's okay. I feel like the relationship is probably over at least as boyfriend/girlfriend for several reasons besides the fact that she's 300 miles away."

"If you two breakup let me know," Dan says. "I meet women all the time. I'll keep my eyes open for you. I'm really quite good at match-making. Right Ran?"

Stephen smiles and looks at Randy. "Do you think I can trust Dan?"

Randy shakes his head no, laughing.

"You are so full of shit," Dan says to Randy. "He just can't admit that I'm good at anything, so he won't tell you, but I've introduced several couples and a few of them are still together."

"Who?" Randy asks in complete disbelief.

Dan quickly produces the names of three couples, two gay and one heterosexual.

"You can't be serious," Randy says. "Every one of those couples that you mentioned is always on the brink of breaking up." He laughs. "And I have no idea why they stay together."

"Honey, I just put them together. I don't control them." Dan says, before taking a sip of his wine.

"We want Stephen to have a good relationship, not some relationship where he fights all the time," Randy says.

"Yes, that would be ideal," Dan says. "But do we know anyone in a relationship like that? I mean, one that is at least a couple of years old? Certainly not us!"

"My parents never argue, for your information. Now can you calm down and let Stephen talk?"

"Okay, that's true, Randy's parents don't argue," Dan says. "They're the nicest people you'll ever meet. His mother sends me presents for Christmas and Hanukkah, and they're Baptists. She also sends me presents for my birthday, what else?" he asks, looking at Randy. "Oh yeah, she sends me a card every Valentine's Day saying stuff like, 'With love on this day of love.' I don't even know if Randy noticed, did you, your father gave me a hug last Christmas when they were leaving. I mean a real hug, where he squeezed me and said, 'Take care of my boy.'"

"I heard him say that," Randy says, softly.

"They are wonderful people." Dan says. "On the other hand, I don't see them having a very, how shall I say this, hot sex life."

"Please!" Randy says, elbowing Dan, feigning anger.

"You might have crossed a line, Dan." Stephen says, laughing.

"Can we change the subject back to Stephen and Carol?" Randy asks.

"Only if you promise, with Stephen as a witness, that you're not mad at me for saying what I just said," Dan says.

"I'm not mad at you. The only couple that I have more trouble imagining having sex than my parents are your parents."

"Oh God, you and me, both," Dan says.

"Why do you say that?" Stephen asks.

"My parents hate each other. I mean, more than they hate everyone else."

Stephen watches as Randy slides closer to Dan and leans his head on his shoulder.

Dan closes his eyes and gently kisses the top of Randy's head. It briefly crosses Stephen's mind that they asked nothing about his own parents. Was he already conducting therapy – listening but not saying much about his own experience?

Chapter 6

THE BLIND STUDENTS
AND THE ELEPHANT

STEPHEN LEANS DEEP INTO the back of his chair as Ed facilitates an easy flow of ideas by one graduate student after another giving their analysis of the dancer and her bulimia. Stephen is comfortable today and at least partially he can thank Charles for it. Before class Charles had complimented him on how well his interview went. He'd even laughed about how difficult the dancer was and relayed that Ed had told them in the observation room that Stephen asked the exact question that turned the interview around from resistance to easy flow. "When you asked her how she was feeling about being observed you got right into her reality, joined with her where she was, and it worked. Ed was impressed."

Charles just seemed different from the other graduate students. Stephen was putting his finger on that difference as he was listening to the discussion. Charles isn't competing with him or anyone. Charles treated him and everyone else as an ally in pursuit of the same goal. No one else seemed to interact that way. Even Scott, whose persona was so positive and perfect, always seemed to try to one-up his classmates. Stephen couldn't imagine Scott telling him that he asked the exact question that Ed wanted asked in a given moment. And while it might have been absurd how desperately they all wanted to hear something like that, to Stephen, Charles's reassurance suggested a quiet, loving heart. He vowed to be more supportive of other students, especially Charles.

Stephen looks around the room. Following the feedback from his classmates he'll again meet with the ballet dancer so he's listening intently.

Charles is making the point that the subculture that the dancer lives in is creating her bulimia. That is a point that Stephen wanted to make. Ever since he took cultural anthropology in undergraduate, he couldn't help but view psychopathology through the cultural lens.

Charles finishes: "She's basically being forced to look a certain way and starving herself to do it."

Maggie puts a finer point on it. The dancer is suffering from the patriarchal world in which women must live up to the rigid rules of perfection and control. After an extensive elaboration, the room falls silent.

Larry goes all in on a psychoanalytic interpretation. He thinks that her prior therapy seems to have been of little benefit, and wonders if it's because the client has transferred her resistance from her father to her therapist. He thinks that the client is restricting as an enactment of the lack of nurturance that her father gave her. On the other hand, her bingeing is a reenactment of the over nurturance given her by her mother whom he imagines is over involved with the client because of the lack of a relationship with her husband. Finally, the purging is an enactment of her personal rejection of the inadequate and uneven nurturance of her family.

Stephen wrote frantically in his notebook as Larry talked.

The kid person describes the bulimic behavior in terms of reinforcers. Her hunger made the food extremely reinforcing and the purging allowed her to maintain her weight and ballet body.

Stephen squints and jots, "duh," in his notes.

Ed clears his throat, before saying. "I want to make some comments. First, I'm impressed with your explanations. They're well thought out and show a high level of education in quite varying schools of thought. As I'm listening, though, I can't help but be reminded of a couple of metaphors. One of them is the one about the blind men and the elephant. You know, each of the blind men grabs a different part of the elephant and describes it completely differently from the others based on the feel of the particular part they have. The second is the metaphor about the drunk who stumbles in the middle of the street and drops his keys. Do you know that one?" he asks, and then proceeds without waiting for a response. "The policeman sees him walk over and look on the ground under the streetlight. The policeman asks, 'Why are you looking for the keys over here when you lost them in the middle of the road?' The drunk grins and answers, 'Because this is where the light is.'"

Everyone laughs.

"And we're all a little like the blind men with the elephant and the drunk under the streetlight. And that's okay, we have to start where we start. But I've been using all these models for a long time and find that they prevent us from seeing and hearing as much as they help. What I heard during the session, and can't quit thinking about, is that this young lady who binges and purges in a terrifically self-harming way indicated that everyone she knew who went to her high school was obsessed with success, even if it meant engaging in self-destructive excesses. She's thought about this deep enough to say that her school should have a motto of 'success at all costs.' And she said that with disgust, and yet she's pretty much living out the story."

"Yeah that part confuses me," Stephen says. "I've been thinking of how much courage she has. How does an eighteen-year-old girl leave high school, move to New York, rent an apartment, and join a world-class ballet troupe? And now she's home and oddly feeling better. Could it be that she really didn't want the success that she thought she was living for?"

As Ed pauses to let the students consider all that has been said, he looks at Ally several times, lingering so that she has the feeling of being prompted.

"Ally," he finally says, "I know that you were involved with some well-known eating disorders researchers as an undergraduate. Do you have anything to add to the discussion?"

Silence. Ally feels the force of gravity pulling her body deep in her overstuffed chair. She was learning something fundamental about Ed. He never lets anyone escape anxiety.

Slowly she slides more upright.

"Just that anorexic/bulimic young women are usually perfectionists who perceive that it's necessary to deprive themselves to be thin and thus perfect. I think that describes the client pretty well, right?" she asks, looking at Stephen.

"Yeah," Stephen says. "Except in her case, it's not just perception, right? I mean, to be a ballet dancer don't you have to be very thin?"

"Yeah, I guess it's a reality at least as much as it's a perception," Ally says.

"Did the researchers make any recommendations about therapy?" Ed asks.

"No, I don't think they're at that point in the research." Ally says.

Ally looks away and then back at Ed. Tentatively she adds, "What I thought was unusual about the interview had nothing to do with eating disorder research. It was that Lydia talked for an hour and never mentioned anything about a relationship with a man."

"She didn't, did she?" Ed says. "Stephen, did you find that surprising?"

Stephen had not even considered it. "No, not really. I mean, I guess not. She had a lot to talk about and I didn't direct her there."

"Well, it was a strength of your session that you didn't direct her anywhere," Ed says. "You just, um, danced with her quite nicely and she didn't move in that direction. That's important, let's consider that."

Ed looks at his watch. "It's time for your feedback session with Lydia, Stephen."

As the students stir, Ed stops them. "Just a final thought, our young dancer is a ballet dancer. I was wondering how she'd dance if she was expressing the energy, the desire that she was expressing at night with her eating. It wouldn't be ballet dancing would be my guess."

Back in the observation room together, Stephen and Lydia have been talking for half an hour when there is a short silence. He's looking at her tight, elegant face. She has continued detailing her depression and struggles with food while he has given her the feedback provided by the group of observers. He has carefully explained that she lives in a subculture, whether it's the ballet subculture or the dominant male culture, that requires an abnormally restrictive diet and that her bingeing is her body's attempt to rectify the situation. Her body is in fact trying to reach some kind of nutritional normalcy, which she then rejects by purging. At first she seemed surprised by his explanation, but then with a slight nod, she seemed resigned to it.

And now they sit in silence.

"What kind of dancing do you think you'd do with the energy that comes out with your eating?" Stephen asks, startling her.

Lydia stares at Stephen. She sits up in her seat. "That's an interesting question," she whispers.

"Do you ever leave rehearsal and do anything other than go for food?"

"No. I'm starving when I leave rehearsal."

"Starving for food?"

"Yes, starving for food. But I think I understand what you're saying. Yes, I'm starving for everything. Everything!" she says, looking into his eyes.

"And you never go get anything besides food?" Stephen asks.

In the observation room, Ed smiles. "He's willing to go after it," he whispers to the room.

"I never know anything to get but food," the dancer says.

"You know you're starving for everything, but you don't know what else besides food will help."

She peers into Stephen's eyes. "I guess," she says.

Lydia and Stephen look at each other for a long moment.

"Let's see what our bold young therapist gets for his courage," Ed says to the students in the observation room.

"Do you know how you'd dance if you danced from your desire, the desire you hold back all day?" Stephen asks.

"Raunchy, wild, sensual," she says, with a husky tone that was quite different than her normal feminine voice.

Stephen looks at her questioningly.

She smiles at him. "Raunchy is not quite right. But it'd be very sexy," she says.

"So, you're aware of something important being inhibited that comes out with food?" Stephen says.

"Not until a few seconds ago…I'm trying to understand how I can use that."

"How do you mean?" Stephen asks.

Ed leans back, nodding his head.

"I've got to figure all of this out and get back to New York as fast as I can. You only get a narrow window to do what I'm trying to do. If I can recover from this and get back, there's still hope."

"So you're more concerned with making it as a dancer than understanding the energy that's being held back?" Stephen asks.

"Are you kidding? A lot more!" she says.

"No, I wasn't kidding," Stephen says.

"There has never been any question that dance is my deepest desire."

"But other desires are haunting you."

The dancer squints at Stephen. "Maybe. My whole life has been about becoming a ballet dancer and that's what I want to be. You don't get that, do you?"

"Don't let her intimidate you," Ed says in the observation room. "Say 'Yeah, I get it, but I thought you hated that motto at Westminster where you give up everything for success.'"

"Do you have a boyfriend?" Stephen asks.

Ed spins around and waits for the response.

For the first time in this session Lydia glances at the one-way mirror. She twists slightly away from Stephen.

"I haven't had a date since I moved to New York, which is a long time."

"Is that hard, not having a relationship?"

"I guess. I mean, everyone wants a relationship, right?"

"I guess so," Stephen says.

"I do have some friends, fellow dancers, guys and girls that I do stuff with occasionally."

"Is it hard to be without a relationship?"

"He's willing to ask, isn't he," Ed says.

"Yeah, it's hard. I've been lonely and freaked with the whole big city, big dance company thing. I hate to admit it, but I've been happier since I've been home, even though I feel like a huge failure. And I've been bingeing and purging less. I still do it, but a lot less."

"What do you make of that?"

"I'm not sure. I sleep late. I don't have to dance all day. I've been going out with my high school sweetheart occasionally."

Stephen starts to say something, but she interrupts. "And I have been less depressed."

"And you're saying you're bingeing and purging less, which is great," Stephen says.

"Yeah, but I want to make it with the ballet," she says.

"Yeah. It seems something has been missing in your life that you…"

She interrupts him, blurting out, "Well if you insist on knowing what has changed since I've been home, I'll tell you…"

Just as quickly as she started, she stops.

"What?" Stephen asks.

"Seeing my high school sweetie is the big change. I mean, we're not getting back together, but we've been having some sexual fun." She smiles broadly at Stephen. "Jesus, how Freudian is that?" she says, laughing out loud and settling back into her seat.

Stephen laughs with her, adding, "So having fun is a part of what you've been missing out on?"

"I guess."

"Why do you think you're so quick to give up the fun for dance?"

"It's everything to me."

"Do you think others do it that way, give up their personal lives?"

"I think some do, some don't."

"You said that the Westminster code is to give up everything for success. Is that what you're doing?"

She glares at Stephen at first. "I don't know what to say about that. I don't like to think that… maybe you're right."

Stephen smiles gently at the dancer. She smiles and nods at him. He glances at the clock and sees that their time is up.

As they rise, Stephen reaches his hand out. Lydia shakes his hand, turns to the one-way mirror, smiles, and curtsies.

Chapter 7

EMPATHY AND CONFRONTATION

STEPHEN LIGHTS A FEW CANDLES and fires up a joint, then puts on some acoustic guitar music, a new-agey album he finds instantly grating. Why did he buy that damn thing? He flips through his CDs, but none is quite right. One of the candles burns out and he quickly re-lights it. As soon as he's stoned, he feels lonely and distracted. He opens his textbook and reads a paragraph. He has no idea what he has read. He rereads it. Then he wonders if he has adult-onset attention deficit disorder. As Ed said, with a load of derision: "ADD, it's not just for kids anymore."

He thinks about calling someone. No one comes to mind.

He thinks about his marriage, his ex-wife, and his son Nicholas.

He decides to go out to a bar. It's a dance club, but it also houses a quieter bar.

Stephen sits at the bar, uneasy, not wanting to look as despicably lonely as he feels. From time to time he glances at the TV though he has no interest in the football game.

He orders his second beer, takes an icy sip. He rotates his neck slowly, trying to release the tension. The volume of work for his classes has intensified. He wonders if the exams will be difficult.

He looks around the bar. A mix of laughing groups of people and long-faced single men. He thinks about a presentation he did earlier in the week on Rogerian therapy. The defining idea of Carl Rogers' therapy was that accepting clients just as they are, their thoughts, their feelings, their perceived reality in general, allows them to explore their world in greater depth and, subsequently, to change. Something just did not feel right about that to Stephen, but he presented it as he was supposed to, defending the ideas as best he could. After a lively discussion, Ed offered that Rogers brought the concept of client/therapist empathy squarely into the therapy room and for that psychotherapy owed him an enormous debt.

"On the other hand," Ed had added, "if all you give clients is empathy, you might as well be the neighbor standing on the other side of the fence."

Ed said that Fritz Perls, a Gestalt theorist to be discussed in an upcoming class, argued that most clients come to therapy for "support for their craziness, not to change." Stephen wrote those words on his beer napkin and wondered if that was why he'd gone to therapy in Charleston.

He's grateful that Judy, his therapist, pushed him to follow through on his desire to go back to school and get his PhD, instead of patiently listening and empathizing with his complaints about the ridiculously narrow and seemingly useless research he was doing at the medical university. Instead, she confronted him: "If you want to work for some-one," she said, "then you have to accept the limits of your influence. You can complain about that or do something to change it. You're just too bright and insightful to sit around a medical university doing second-rate work."

He writes, "empathy and confrontation, not always in that order," on his beer napkin.

A compact, athletic-looking woman with a surprisingly delicate face gestures toward the empty barstool next to him. "Is anyone sitting here?" she asks.

"No" he says, feigning indifference. He's a little intimidated by her confident style, and he was so deep into his thoughts that it's as if he's waking from sleep. He folds the napkin and puts it in his pocket.

She slides onto the stool and orders a glass of Chardonnay. When she crosses her legs, Stephen sneaks a glance at her muscular calf. She turns to Stephen, leaning back and sliding some of her hair behind her ear. She smiles very casually.

He smiles back and then looks at the TV.

"Who's winning?" she asks, glancing at the TV, then back at him.

"I think…I don't know," he admits, smiling sheepishly.

"You're not watching then?" she asks.

"Yes, no, I'm not." He smiles at his clumsiness. "Sorry, I'm a little out of it. I've been alone all day and…"

She interrupts, "You're okay with me, baby doll. I'm not looking for someone who's a smooth operator."

"Lucky for me," he says, and they both laugh.

The woman's dressed rather oddly for the bar. She has on a shim-mering silver t-shirt, a short black skirt, black hose, and black heels, everything a bit tight.

"I'm Stephen," he says.

"Teresa," she says.

"Why have you been alone so much today?" she asks.

"I've had some reading to do, and I'm new in Atlanta," he says.

She asks the typical questions: where he's from, how long he's been in Atlanta, questions like that, then he asks them of her.

They sit silent for a few seconds, hearing the low roar of music and conversations. Out of the blue, she reaches for his hand and holds it, looking in his eyes. He notices that her hands are strong, almost rugged. Her touch feels good but the sudden, incongruous closeness gradually begins to feel uncomfortable.

Stephen looks away and Teresa lets go of his hand. He tries to dispel uneasiness by talking about the sudden cold spell.

She ignores his comment. "Don't be intimidated by me," she says. "I'm just more comfortable with physical touch than most people."

He stares at her, having no idea what to say. "Is she coming on to me?" he wonders.

"I'm a massage therapist," she says. "I'm also a macrobiotic cooking instructor." She smiles.

Stephen blinks a couple of times and tilts his head. He takes a sip of his beer and glances around the bar to see if any new attractive women have come in.

"What do you do?" she asks.

"I'm a PhD student in clinical psychology" he says, trying not to sound self-important.

She looks at him and says dreamily, "I bet you're going to be a great therapist. I feel really comfortable talking to you."

He laughs.

"What's so funny?" Teresa asks.

"Sorry," he says. "I've been feeling a little down about school today, but I do hope that the faculty consults you before the grades go out."

She does not get the joke.

"Are you always so negative?" she asks, looking curious.

"You will agree that we haven't spent much time together for you…"

Teresa interrupts once more, "So I couldn't already have that knowledge of you? Don't you believe in love at first sight? You don't think people can instantly know each other? You don't believe that they can fall in love immediately, maybe it's a smell, a taste, something chemical, or an intense intellectual connection that makes it happen?"

"You know, Teresa, this conversation might go a little bit better if you'd let me finish a sentence." He smiles and takes her hand. "What do you think, can we try that?"

"If you insist," she quips.

Stephen leans toward Teresa, "I really don't believe in love at first sight. I think people can have that chemical thing you're talking about and decide that they want to sleep with each other or even date, but love? I'm not sure what love is, but I think it's something more than chemistry."

"That is a depressing way to think, Stephen," Teresa says.

"I got better stuff than that to be depressed about," he says and smiles.

"Really?" she asks, looking at him carefully.

"Really," he says, laughing uneasily.

"I think that it's depressing not to believe in love at first sight," she says. "But tonight, I'll try it your way and accept that the chemistry is more physical than anything else. You want to go next door and dance?"

Three hours later, half-drunk, and exhausted, they fall into bed at Stephen's apartment. Their bodies are lit by the moonlight filling the apartment. Stephen kisses her neck. His tongue follows the contours of her body, lingering on places where her breathing tells him to. He moves lower across her firm stomach and then down into her hair. He takes his time. They moan. Teresa actually shrieks.

The sun rises just above the horizon, filling Stephen's room with that awful morning-after white-blue glow, only a couple of hours after he and Teresa, exhausted from raucous sex, finally fell into a deep sleep. Teresa's eyes begin to open, but she keeps them closed, replaying scenes from the night before. She drifts into a dreamy meditation.

She pulls her knees up to her chest, holding them there, letting her muscles slowly wake up. Now she opens her eyes to look at the man sleeping next to her. He looks as good now as he did last night. She touches his lips and gently massages his chest. He doesn't move.

She decides to get up and fix coffee and breakfast. She hopes he has some orange juice. She walks naked to his small refrigerator, squats down and opens the door.

There is a half empty carton of milk, two beers and a plastic jug filled with water. She tugs open the tiny freezer door. It's almost sealed shut, with ice spreading like cancer into the refrigerator compartment below.

"Oh my God, baby. You need me more than I thought," she says, glancing back at the bed. She wonders if the couple in the main house is awake. She looks at her watch, seven forty-five, and decides to find out.

She puts on her black skirt and shimmering tee shirt. She walks to Stephen's closet and pulls a denim shirt off a hanger. She buttons the shirt as she follows the slate path through the garden in her bare feet.

"Hello?" she calls out, rapping on the partly open back door.

"Hellooo, I'm in heeere," Dan calls out, lowering his paper to see over it.

She walks into the kitchen and throws her hand toward Dan, "Teresa Coskos, good to meet you," she says.

She shakes his hand vigorously.

"Dan Perlow, so nice to see you, Teresa," Dan says, in a tone that shows his annoyance. She should at least apologize for interrupting him in the morning.

"I'm with Stephen," she says, motioning with her head toward his apartment. "I'd love to fix a nice breakfast for us, but I checked his refrigerator and there isn't one thing in it. What are you gonna do with guys like that?"

"I don't think you need me to tell you what to do with him, honey," Dan thinks, having heard Teresa's shrieks last night owing to her volume and that he sleeps with his French doors that open to the back cracked all year around. "You know, he didn't even tell us he had a date last night, much less a spend-the-night guest or I'm sure my partner Randy would have stocked his refrigerator," Dan says, his face gradually forming into a sugary smile.

"Sounds like you have a very nice partner," Teresa says. "I know you're a little annoyed, but can I have a cup of coffee?"

"Of course. I'd have offered you some, but I assumed you were on your way back to Stephen's."

"He's dead to the world," she says.

"Well you must join me," Dan says, pouring the coffee.

"How long have you and Randy been together?" Teresa asks.

"Ten years last month."

"No kidding, congratulations."

"How long have you and Stephen been together?" Dan asks, adding quickly, "I'm kidding, I'm kidding."

Teresa chuckles. Something about this conversation felt oddly similar to talking with Stephen in the bar. "How long have you known Stephen?" she asks.

"He moved in two and a half months ago," Dan says. "We stay pretty busy so…"

"You and Randy have been together for ten years," Teresa says, interrupting. "That's pretty amazing."

"Yeah, it beats my previous best by about nine years and ten or eleven months."

"How long have you been living together?"

"Ten years. I've known him ten years and one month and he's lived here ten years and one month. He basically moved in the day we met. Some of our friends accuse us of being lesbians."

"You just fell in love instantly? How did you know you were in love enough to move in?"

"I can't answer that except to say that I just knew, right away. It was everything about him. The way he answered me when I hit him up on an escalator at Lenox Square. Yes, for real. He was all shy and confused. Then we went to my favorite French restaurant and he admitted he didn't have a clue what to order. I'd never been with anyone who wouldn't fake it.

"He told me he wanted to be an artist, so I asked him to make a sketch of me. He told me he was into abstract art, so it wouldn't be a portrait. We got some paper from our waiter and what he came up with is hard to describe. In the foreground there was a kind of menacing looking abstract mask-like version of me, not flattering at all. Behind the mask was this portrait-like face, a sweet face that looked exactly like some of the pictures from my bar mitzvah. I knew right then that he was everything I ever wanted. He still is. I'm very lucky. Most people don't get to have that. To tell you the truth, I don't think Randy can say that about me, but maybe only one person in a couple gets to feel that way."

Teresa squints at Dan. "That's…an interesting thought," she says.

"I try to have one of those at least once a day when I'm not at work," Dan says. "So tell me about our boy, Stephen. You two must be doing pretty well. He's lived here for two and a half months and you're the first woman I've had coffee with."

"Really! I figured he'd just broken up with a girlfriend. He had that aura about him. I love him," she says. She looks out the window at the pool house. "I only wonder if he'll even remember me when he wakes up. I'm very interested in him, but he has that all too familiar feel of a guy who needs a woman, but who's kind of lost. I have no idea if he's in a place to appreciate what I have to offer."

"I guess that's always the question," Dan says. "I remember wondering that of Randy."

Teresa nods. "I do feel like something special happened between Stephen and me, but I'll just wait and see." She glances out the window again. "I think I better go check on him, but it was nice talking to you," she says, standing.

"Nice talking to you, Teresa," Dan rises to shake her hand.

Teresa walks back to the apartment, crawls into bed next to Stephen, and whispers, "Good morning, sweetheart." She kisses his lips and lays her head on the pillow right next to his ear. She whispers, "The sun is out." She rubs her hand across his chest. "You said you were a runner. Why don't we put on some of your running clothes? I've got some shoes in the car. Let's go for a run and then I'll fix us some breakfast."

Stephen is in that state of sleep where sounds images mix with his playful dream world. He hears Teresa's words as something like a sweet joke, a play on the absurdity of voluntarily abandoning deep sleep, for the harsh reality of daily imperatives. Teresa squeezes his penis and his eyes fly open.

The last time Stephen checked the clock it was five-thirty a.m. He realizes that she's not going away without some kind of response. He sits up squinting, barely able to see her. He sees the outline of her body, the long brown curly hair framing her round face and falling around her shoulders. He thinks for a second, at the most, about complying. He closes his eyes and rubs them with his fingers, sighing deeply. "I can't get up until, you know, later," he says, "maybe around noon."

He moves his elbow, which has been propping him up, and his head flops back on the pillow. Before he falls back asleep, he mumbles, "You go without me."

Teresa stares at the sleeping man before her. Several times she starts to say something to him, but each time she stops herself. Finally, she stands up and says to her sleeping audience, "All right, baby. No problem." She finds a pen and paper and writes her name and phone number. She fishes through her pocketbook for a scarlet lipstick. She goes to Stephen's sink and looks in the mirror. She works the lipstick around her wide lips. She puts the paper to her lips and kisses it fully, leaving a broad red impression of her lips right below her name. She walks back to the bed and lays the paper on Stephen's chest.

"Dan was right," she thinks. "Maybe only one person in a couple falls in love at first sight. Then again, maybe Stephen was right. It's all about a great fuck but nothing more."

Chapter 8

RUNNING

STEPHEN SITS ON AN OFF-WHITE COUCH in a small room. He glances out a window at a bare dogwood tree. He looks at Dr. Henry Smith, a psychologist recommended by Ed. He offers graduate students a very low fee and is renowned for his talent.

Henry smiles at him while rocking slowly in a wooden rocking chair. If Ed hadn't told Steven that Henry was in his sixties, he'd guess that he was about fifty. He looks at the books on a bookcase behind Henry. "The Primal Scream," and "Zen and the Art of Motorcycle Maintenance" lean against each other. Stephen looks back at Henry, who nods and smiles but remains silent.

Stephen says, "I...um, have been thinking about coming in for a few months. As I said on the phone, I'm in graduate school and it's kind of difficult."

Stephen chats on about his classes, distracted by the intensity with which Henry appears to listen. Finally, about ten minutes into the session, Henry speaks.

"You said that you've been thinking about coming since you moved here so I imagine your primary concerns are with something you've left behind or the transition you're making. So let's talk about that instead of your classes… for now anyway."

The words are very direct, but there is also softer, almost questioning tone, which allows Stephen to consider whether to take his advice. "Yes, it has been a… yeah, I think that's true… a difficult transition. And I'm having a hard time with…I moved, and my three-year-old son Nicholas stayed, and I miss him." Stephen says.

"That must be so hard, not being with him," Henry offers.

"It is…Maybe I should give you my background and then move forward to…this," Stephen says.

Henry nods and reaches for his teacup. It's the first time he's averted his eyes from Stephen's. He pulls the warm cup of tea to his mouth and sips it.

Stephen reaches for his Styrofoam cup, takes a long swallow of his coffee, and begins talking more easily. He tells Henry his background information. His parents divorced when he was in college. He has one sister, two years older, a lawyer in his hometown. He was married to his college girlfriend and divorced after three years because of "mutual incompatibility." They have one child, Nicholas. Because he lives five hours away, he has only seen him two weekends since he moved to Atlanta four months ago.

"I don't know how you bear not being able to see your son," Henry says.

Stephen looks at the book just to Henry's right, "The Primal Scream." "Yeah, it's really harder than I thought it would be. I mean, I'm sure he's doing well, but…"

Henry leans forward, "You miss Nicholas, huh?"

Stephen reaches for his coffee and takes a sip. He returns it to the end table, carefully. He leans over, picking up a throw pillow from the other side of the couch while nodding his head.

Stephen squeezes the pillow to his chest. He feels his full sadness as he glances at Henry's face. He takes a few ragged breaths and then says, "It has been very hard. I think sometimes I don't even know how hard it is for him."

Stephen looks around the room. The walls are mostly bare, except for a few small pictures of Henry with small children, presumably his grandkids.

"I'd like to know more about Nicholas," Henry says.

Stephen says Nicholas is "highly verbal," and "very funny." Henry asks for some examples of Nicholas's humor and laughs heartily at Stephen's stories. Stephen talks about his concerns about Nicholas's adapting to seeing him less.

As Stephen talks, Henry notices that Stephen appears to be distancing himself from his feelings.

Henry interrupts, "I'd like to try something. Do you mind?"

"Sure," Stephen says, maybe a little too loudly.

Henry hears the shift, and says, "I'd like for you to talk to Nicholas right now. It won't be Nicholas, of course, so you won't have to worry about how what you're saying might affect him. I just want to make sure what you feel is more real. Okay?"

Stephen closes his eyes for a second. His face tenses. "What the fuck?" he thinks angrily. "How is talking to someone who isn't here going to feel more real?" He opens his eyes.

Henry examines Stephen's face closely and can see that he's angry. "Talk about what you're feeling right now, this moment," he says.

Stephen looks at the clock, and then back at Henry. "Nothing, really," he mumbles.

"You're sure?" Henry asks.

"No, no. Let's, I mean…" Stephen says, sitting upright on the couch. "I'll try. I just don't know what to say."

"Of course, you don't," Henry says. "Just imagine that Nicholas is sitting in this chair," pointing to a chair several feet away from Stephen. "And imagine he has the capacity to understand your feelings. Just tell him how it feels for you to not be with him day in and out. And how you wish you could be there like your father was for you."

Stephen blinks and swallows uneasily. He realizes that he'd casually told Henry about how close he was to his father growing up and how different that was than his current situation with Nicholas. He glances at the clock on the bookcase, realizing that he has been in the room for fifty-five minutes. Isn't time up?

He clears his throat and points to the clock. "I don't want to start, you know, and then have to stop in the middle."

"I'm watching the time," Henry says. "We'll just run over a little today."

Stephen clears his throat. He's struck with his need to do whatever is asked of him, to be polite, and also wants to better understand his feelings about Nicholas. And yet, even though he already trusts Henry, the idea of talking to an empty chair seems way too Fritz Perls, too weird, too scary.

Slowly, hesitantly, Stephen talks to Nicholas. The more he talks, the clearer he becomes, and the words begin flowing. He starts to tell Nicholas about the divorce from his mother. "How do you explain something like that?" he asks Henry, interrupting his talk to the empty chair.

"Just tell him about it," Henry says, pointing to the empty chair. "Nicholas," Stephen says, "Your mother and I were young when we got married. We didn't know how to find similarities in all our differences.

But your Mother and I love you, and we're so glad that you're our son. I miss you so much, Nicholas."

Stephen starts to cry lightly. "Nicholas," he says, "I always want to be there for you."

"I think that's important," Henry says. "You always want to be there for him. But you can't right now. Right? You want him to know that you'll be there for him as soon as you can."

Stephen nods slowly and slumps into the couch.

"I want to help you work with your desire to be in your son's life even though you two are separated. We think of kids as suffering from separation anxiety when they're forced to be separate from their parents. But parents suffer anxiety, too. I'll bet you find yourself running from the difficult feelings you just experienced," Henry says.

Stephen looks blankly at Henry before offering, "I don't know, maybe."

"Well, we better stop," Henry says.

Stephen stands as Henry reaches for his appointment book and writes Stephen down for an appointment the next week. Henry hands Stephen a card with the date and time. Stephen pulls out his folded check for the agreed upon twenty dollars and holds it out. Henry takes the check, holds out his arms and Stephen falls into them. Henry squeezes Stephen for a few seconds, before stepping back. "See you next week," he says.

Stephen is feeling dazed when he leaves Henry's office. He looks forward to a run and the clarity or at least the distraction he always finds there.

Chapter 9

A PRIMAL SCENE

AN HOUR LATER, Stephen is running down Tuxedo Drive. The conversation with Henry about his relationship with Nicholas has brought up a memory of his own father. He's a teenager, dressed in his high school baseball uniform, long hair jutting from his baseball hat. He's walking carefully in his steel cleats across the concrete floor in the men's locker room that is moist with spring humidity and steaming afternoon group showers. He walks to his father's tiny office in the gym.

His father is the head baseball coach at the high school in the next school district over from Stephen's. His teams have won more division and state championships than any other school in the state.

Stephen goes to a different high school and plays shortstop for that high school's team. Because Stephen's school has fewer students it's in a different division, which, fortunately, prevents the two schools from playing against each other. Before Stephen began high school, there was some consideration of transferring to his father's school so he could play for his father's team. With the teams' past successes, he'd have had a higher profile for college scouts.

But Stephen's father said that he didn't like the idea of him transferring to his school because he'd probably have to play a different position than shortstop, which he'd played since he was eight years old. There was a boy Stephen's age who was a superstar and who would be strong competition for him. Stephen had never seriously considered transferring to his father's school, but he was stung that his father had so clearly let him know he was not as good as the other boy. He remembers nervously leaving the room when his father told him that. Thinking about it on his run, he realizes that his father was in a difficult situation and probably didn't know what to do. Still, it hurt, and he hopes he never has to make such a decision with Nicholas.

Now, Stephen sees himself walking into his father's office. He sees the small window-unit air conditioner in the spacious office and remembers its awful roar. In front of the air conditioner, his father is talking on the telephone with a strange smile on his face.

Stephen stands just inside the door waiting for his father. Suddenly, he knows his father is talking to a girlfriend. Something about the unusual smiles and flirtatious tone of voice. His father was home by five o'clock every day, and played whatever sport was in season with his son and daughter until dark. He listened when his children talked, seemed almost always enthralled with their childhood stories. How could Dad have a girlfriend?

"Look I really have to go right now," his father says, swiveling his chair away from Stephen. "It's a bad time." He hangs up, "How was school?" he asks, turning back to his office, glancing around to make sure he had everything.

"Who is she?" Stephen wants to respond but says nothing.

"You ready?" his father asks, motioning to the door.

Stephen does not speak to his father during the ride home while his father chats awkwardly about nothing.

On his run, Stephen turns back onto Tuxedo Drive, only a half a mile away from his house. He tries to understand why he did not say anything to his father.

Stephen walks up the driveway, trying to cool off, his run was longer and faster than usual. He walks toward Randy's studio feeling the gentle, late-day sunshine on his face. He opens the door and sees Randy painting a canvas with yellows and browns. Randy smiles at Stephen and continues painting.

Randy wipes his hair from his forehead with his shirtsleeve. Stephen slides onto a stool and nods to Randy to continue painting. Randy's hand dances around the canvas like a falling leaf in the wind. Stephen becomes absorbed in the movement and the violin music playing on the stereo. He notices how peaceful Randy seems.

"Does painting calm you?" Stephen asks. "I mean it's kind of like meditation, isn't it?"

"It's calming. It's hard to explain, but I just let whatever wants to be seen emerge. It feels very therapeutic. But sometimes, particularly when I'm painting another pot of flowers for a client, it can be very frustrating."

After a few minutes, Stephen, afloat in the effects of afternoon sunshine, difficult memories, and endorphins, excuses himself to take a shower. Randy watches Stephen's shoulders sag as he walks out the door. "See you," he calls to Stephen.

Randy lets the image of a Stephen linger. "Sad," he whispers to himself, turning back to his work, where a sad-looking figure begins to emerge.

Chapter 10

ROOMIES 2

RANDY HEARS STEPHEN AND NICHOLAS, who is visiting, laughing outside the house. He reaches for the wine that Dan just poured for him. "I invited Stephen to join us," he says.

"Excellent," Dan says, rummaging through the Wall Street Journal.

Randy picks up his sketchpad and runs his pencil back and forth across the page, replicating the calming motion of the wine as it was poured. He puts it down after a few minutes. He stares into space.

"What's going on?" Dan asks. "Are you about to ruin my night?"

"It's nothing…I was just thinking about Stephen and Nicholas… how happy they are with one another. Have you enjoyed having him here this week?"

"Absolutely," Dan says. "He's fun, but I think I know where you're going."

"Well, really. Don't you ever wonder what it would be like if we had our own child?" Randy asks.

Dan folds the paper and slaps it lightly on the table. "I know you'd love to have a kid, but as I told you from the start, I don't want to. I had two lousy parents and I'm sure I'd be a lousy one, too."

"Your parents also have a terrible marriage, but you've managed to have a pretty good relationship with me," Randy says. "You're nothing…nothing like your parents. They argue and criticize each other all the time, we don't do that. So maybe you would be a good dad."

"Ran, I don't want you to try and talk me into wanting a child because we're not going to have one."

"I know, Dan. I'm just talking, dreaming, I guess." He picks his pad back up. "I like how Stephen is with him. He's so loving. Did you see how he threw the ball with him for like an hour today? They talked the whole time, even when Nicholas was playing with his cars by the pool and Stephen was reading, they always seemed so connected."

"Yeah," Dan says. "I think he said more to Nicholas during dinner than my father said to me before my eighteenth birthday."

"That is so sad," Randy says.

"Not really," Dan says looking at Randy. "In my house the last thing you wanted was my father's attention."

"Dan, I'm sorry," Randy says, leaning over and rubbing Dan's shoulder.

"He was an asshole, but you know, as he likes to remind us, he never beat us, at least not without a good reason."

Stephen walks through the back door.

"We're in the den," Dan calls to him.

"The little guy's asleep?" Randy asks as Stephen walks into the room.

"Yeah, I told him I'd be up here. If he wakes up he'll turn on the porch light. He was tired. I just hope he sleeps in tomorrow. He woke me at seven this morning."

"Oh, you suffer so much," Dan says, pouring Stephen a glass of wine. He proposes a toast: "To a wonderful father and his great kid."

The three men click their glasses together.

Stephen sits down in the leather chair closest to the fireplace.

"Randy tells me you completely broke off the relationship with deep-tissue gal. What was her name, Teresa, right?" Dan asks, plopping his socked feet onto the ottoman and slumping deeper into the couch. "You want to tell Dr. Dan what went wrong?"

"That was at least a month ago and we only went out for a couple of weeks."

"Why didn't you keep dating her?" Dan asks.

Stephen shakes his head, "I don't know. It just didn't work for me."

"Never mind," Dan says. "If you don't know us well enough to share your innermost secrets, I can accept that."

"I've already told Randy some of it. You'll just give me shit about it."

"What in the world are you talking about?" Dan says, looking surprised.

"Come on," Stephen says. "You know everything is an opportunity for you to give someone shit."

"I promise I'll be serious. Hey, I liked Teresa a lot," Dan says. "When I first met her, I thought she was a bit much, but after I got to know her, I thought she had a cool style. I liked how she dressed. How would you describe how she dressed?" Dan asks, turning to Randy.

"Funky. Sexy," Randy offers.

"She laughed like a man. I don't like that in a woman," Dan says.

"I can't believe you, Dan. I didn't think that…" Randy says before Stephen interrupts.

"I know what Dan means. To tell you the truth, she fucked like a man," he says.

"Meaning?" Dan asks.

"I don't know, exactly," Stephen says, realizing that his hosts might have more experience with that than he. "I guess all I mean is that she'd, you know, go at it pretty hard and then when she came, she'd scream, fall over all spent and dead, regardless of where I was in the process."

Dan nods his head. "That does sound like a few men I've known," he admits.

They all laugh. Dan adds, "I have to admit, Teresa certainly was a screamer. I didn't know women did that. The first night you two were together you had your door open." He smiles and takes a sip of his wine. "I always sleep with our French doors to the balcony slightly open. From, what, seventy-five yards away, she woke me up. She was howling like some kind of beast in the forest."

Randy buries his head in his hands, then looks at Stephen for forgiveness.

Suddenly, they all burst out laughing.

"We need to change the subject, or I'll end up calling her tonight," Stephen says.

They laugh again.

"Well you must have liked her. You dated her for, what, two weeks or so?" Dan says. He reaches for the bottle of wine and tops off everyone's glass.

"I think it was that long. I just... I mean... I liked her, I guess," Stephen says. "I certainly found her sexy. I just don't want a long-term relationship right now."

"Did she want that?" Randy asks.

"I don't know. I just knew something wasn't right, and to tell you the truth she really got on my nerves. I mean, even the way she talked bothered me. I guess I just got tired of her."

"Do you think you'll ever settle down again with one woman?" Dan asks.

"Well, you know, I want to have another long-term relationship... marriage, but..." Stephen says.

"Aren't they teaching you anything at that University?" Dan asks.

"I take Successful Relationships next semester."

"Good. You sure don't want to skip any of those classes," Dan jokes. "I'll tell you right now, to have an enduring relationship, you have to be able to put up with your partner's shit. And everybody's got shit."

"Eloquent," Stephen says.

"What's the longest relationship you ever had?" Dan asks Stephen.

"I guess three years of really trying," Stephen replies. "I was married for three years...and we dated about a year-and-a-half before that. I dated my first girlfriend for about three years. But in both cases, the last year was getting up the courage to leave."

"So really, you've never done what I'm talking about," Dan says. "It takes at least two years for someone to really show you all of who they are. And when they do, you leave."

"That's not really fair. Maybe they weren't the right person," Randy says.

"He was with them for three years. There must have been something right about them."

"Dan," Stephen asks, "how long did you date someone before you found Randy?"

"That doesn't count. I was pretending to be heterosexual, to myself and to women. So it doesn't matter..."

"So none of what you're saying applies to you, right?" Stephen says.

"No actually, I've been with Randy for a little more than ten years, and it hasn't been any picnic, but I've hung in there."

"What are you talking about?" Randy asks, turning to look at Dan.

Dan smiles. "See," he says, tilting his head toward Randy, "You think it's a picnic to be in a relationship with someone whose convinced he's perfect?"

"I don't think I'm perfect. I know that we've both had to deal with the other's shit. I just want to know what you're referring to right now."

"I'm not stupid enough to answer that question," Dan says.

"You did bring it up, Dan." Stephen chides.

"I was trying to be helpful to you, not ruin my evening," Dan says.

"What are you talking about?" Randy insists.

"Just that you get pissed off when I imply that you're not perfect."

"I'm getting pissed at you right now."

"I rest my case." Dan says, leaning forward, slapping his knees and standing. "I think I'll pour another bottle of wine on this fire. Okay?"

Dan walks to the bar and pulls a bottle from the wine rack above it. "I have no desire to start an argument with you, Hon," Dan says, working the cork out of the bottle.

"You guys seem to have a great relationship to me," Stephen says as Dan pours wine into his glass.

"I find myself wanting to go along with you on that one," Dan says, pouring more wine into Randy's glass.

"Dan," Randy says, "you should be a little less brutal and a little more honest. I read that somewhere."

"Kurt Vonnegut said something almost exactly like that. Maybe it was him," Stephen says.

"Lucy's been doing some heavy reading behind my back?" Dan asks.

After a silent moment, Stephen asks Randy, "Is it any of my business why he sometimes calls you Lucy?"

"He doesn't strike you as a Lucy?" Dan asks.

Stephen looks at Dan and then back at Randy. "Since Randy is smiling," he says to Dan, "I assume it's some kind of inside joke."

"God, you are perceptive," Dan says. "Therapeutic intuition?"

"What does it mean?" Stephen asks again.

"Like Lucy, as in 'I Love Lucy.' You know, how shall I say…a tad spacey, but very sexy."

"I never thought of Lucy as sexy," Stephen says.

"Me either, but then I'm gay, what do I know? I'm just saying the spacey part is about Lucy. The sexy part is about Randy."

"And I guess that makes you Ricky Ricardo. I can see that," Stephen says, nodding.

"Well thank you. I found him very sexy. Didn't you, Randy?"

"'I Love Lucy' was before my time," Randy says.

"Oh please. You're the same age as Stephen and he remembers."

"I saw them in reruns," Stephen says.

"Oh, that's great. You two want to make me feel old. Thanks a lot."

"I love older men," Randy says, sliding his hand across Dan's shoulder to the nape of his neck and then slowly through the back of his hair.

Stephen watches Randy's movement. Somehow when Randy moves his hands they always seem to float, as if they do not suffer gravity.

"That feels good, Ran," Dan whispers.

Randy continues his gentle massaging of Dan's head. "Can we change the subject?" Randy asks.

"As long as you continue rubbing my head, we can do anything you want," Dan says.

"When do you find out how your grades came out?" Randy asks Stephen.

"I found out earlier today. I made two A's and a B+."

"That's great! Congratulations," Randy says.

"I'm feeling pretty good about things," Stephen admits.

"You should. You're off to a great start," Dan says.

"Yeah. I'm a little worried about next semester, starting therapy supervision, and I'm also starting a job working in a prison. But for now, the grades were better than I expected, so I'm happy.

"Prison?" Dan asks, raising his eyebrows.

"Yeah, I'll be working in a mental health unit in a Maximum-Security prison. Supposedly, I'll be working with inmates, helping them adjust to prison."

"I'm sure there's a lot of work there," Dan says.

"Yeah, I guess," Stephen says.

The three talk through another glass of wine before Dan, his head supported by a throw pillow embroidered by his Russian grandmother, falls asleep.

"I can't believe he can fall asleep in the middle of a conversation," Stephen whispers

"He's so sleep-deprived," Randy says, as he reaches across Dan and turns the lamp off. "If he stops thinking for five seconds, he falls asleep. He gets up every weekday at five and usually doesn't go to sleep before eleven. He works harder than anyone I've ever seen… We can talk. We won't disturb him."

Stephen and Randy talk in quieter tones. Stephen tells Randy his Christmas plans. He and Nicholas are going to Charleston in a couple of days to see Stephen's mother and his sister and her family. Nicholas will return to his mother's house in the early afternoon on Christmas day.

"You have him Christmas morning? That will be so much fun," Randy says.

"Yeah, we'll be at my sister's house. She has two daughters, one's a year older than Nicholas, the other's a year younger. Nicholas is really close to them. My mother will be spending the night there too, so it should be a fun Christmas."

"Will you see your father?"

"No, he'll be in Clearwater where he lives. I'll probably call him. I mean, I'm sure I'll call him."

"Do you see him much?"

"No, and he never calls my sister or me. He's so passive. He waits for us to call. And he rarely comes to Charleston to see us."

Randy looks at Stephen. "When we talked about him a few weeks ago, you said he had cancer and I never asked. Is it a life-threatening form of cancer?"

Randy watches Stephen thinks about his answer. "I don't think it's serious… like in, 'You have only a few years to live'. But it's prostate cancer that's moved out of his prostate, so they can't operate to remove it. But he seems optimistic about the chemotherapy helping."

"That sounds pretty scary," Randy says.

"Yeah, I guess it means it's serious," Stephen admits. "But my father assures me that he's been told by his doctors that they'll be able to contain the cancer or arrest it or something."

"Oh, that's…good. I guess I'm kind of an alarmist these days. I used to think everyone lived forever until my first friend died of AIDS. And I've seen a lot of reality since then."

"Have you had lots of friends die of AIDS?"

"Yeah. My best friend died last year." Randy says, his eyes suddenly moist.

"Really? Was he here in Atlanta?"

"Yeah, he lived off of Ponce, near Little Five Points."

"Were you involved with his, you know, dying?" Stephen asks.

"Yeah, I saw him almost every day. It was a very horrible death," Randy says.

Stephen watches Randy, whose eyes are focused on the wine he tosses gently in his glass.

Stephen looks at the fireplace as the nearly spent embers hiss.

Randy glances at Stephen and then at the fire. He sits up a little in his seat. "I bet it's going to be hard for you to leave Nicholas when you come back. You two will have had a couple of weeks together."

"It will be hard. I do fine once I'm here with so much to do for school. But leaving him is never easy."

"You're a good dad," Randy says, firmly. "He gets a lot of you when he's with you, but I know you both miss each other when you're apart."

"I know I miss him…and he misses me. But he's got a really good mother. I hope he… I think he's doing fine."

"He seems to be doing great."

"He's a good little guy who, by the way, will be getting me up early in the morning. Much earlier than I like to get up, so I better get some sleep."

Randy looks at the clock. "Oh God, it's late," he says.

As the two of them stand they're suddenly facing each other awkwardly. "In case I don't see you in the morning before you leave, Merry Christmas," Randy says, opening his arms to hug Stephen. Stephen is surprised and uneasy, yet he moves into Randy's embrace.

"Merry Christmas," Stephen says, as he hugs Randy. "You two have a great holiday," Stephen says, walking toward the doorway.

"We will," Randy says.

At the door, Stephen slips his sweater over his head. He looks down the hall and watches Randy support Dan as they walk toward the stairs.

Chapter 11

ASLEEP AND AWAKE

HENRY ROTATES HIS NECK SLOWLY, taps his tea ball on the side of his mug, puts it in a cup on the floor next to his chair, and squints out the window at a car pulling into the parking lot. Another graduate student is discussing the need for safety in the group. Henry had been excited about this group, imagining he'd learn what the next generation of psychotherapists was into. He also welcomed being able to work with Stephen in a group setting. He assumed the group of young psychologists would be adventurous, working on psychological issues beyond his typical client. Instead, the second group session has begun where the first one left off, with tedious discussions of the structure of the group, confidentiality, whether attendance would be mandatory, and all kinds of other details Henry knew could be settled in a few short comments.

Now, Scott wants reassurance that everyone will always be support-ive of differences and respectful. "Assuring nothing useful gets said," Henry jokes to himself. The group drones on about support and respect while Henry begins fighting sleep.

When one of the students finally stops for a breath, Henry tactfully notes that talking about the structure of the group might prevent them from more meaningful conversations.

Maggie agrees, but goes on about setting appropriate boundaries. Henry feels his eyelids closing.

Sierra, who has been listening intently, sits forward and grabs her knees, sending a cascade of hair from her unclasped braid. She looks up and says, in her Colorado Rockies' accent, a hint of a jazz musician's marijuana slur mixed with eyes-wide-open enthusiasm, that she feels, "a deeper level of trust" as a result of the discussions.

Henry blinks. A moment later he's asleep. He wakes up quickly and opens his eyes. Nobody noticed. "Get on with it!" he wants to scream, but everything in his humanistic training tells him to let them continue their very tedious discussion and something important will evolve.

Since getting his PhD in 1955, Henry's been on the cutting edge of freedom of expression in the psychotherapy community, including nude retreats, mixed-sex focus groups in hot tubs, primal scream weekends that left everyone hoarse, couples' groups where participants were encouraged to exchange sexual fantasies, and just about anything else that broke the constricting rules of the culture.

Henry shares stories from time to time about his own life to help clients learn from his experiences. In his half-awake, day-dreaming space, he considers telling the group how his wife Jean, also a psycho-therapist, helped him get rid of the last vestige of his need for safety. Jean got into "cunt positive" therapy that consisted of an extended weekend retreat where women sat naked, examining each other's vulvas.

Henry's first reaction when Jean raised the idea of attending one of these retreats was, "Have you lost your fucking mind? Why don't you spend the weekend with me naked, talking about your sexuality?"

Jean went anyway.

When Henry picked her up at the airport after her first weekend retreat he immediately noticed the change in his wife. She was like a little girl, talking non-stop, laughing as freely and fully as she did on their first dates, then suddenly weeping uncontrollably.

In a calm moment, she told Henry that one of the women in the group compared Jean's vulva to descriptions in the "Hobbit" of earth covered with exotic mosses with tunnels twisting deeper and deeper to a place of infinite possibilities. Henry was speechless.

Jean and Henry made love before falling asleep in each other's arms on her first night home. At about three that same morning, Jean woke with her vagina drenched and aching. She wrapped her legs around Henry and they fucked like teenagers until daybreak. Henry's experience with Jean and the pro-vagina group taught him that everything changes when you abandon your fears, especially fear of your wife's sexuality.

Henry smiles, imagining how the students would react to such a story this early in their work with him. He takes another sip of tea and tries to focus on the discussion. He dozes off again, then jerks himself awake after nearly falling out of his chair. Everyone pretends not to notice.

Henry takes a deep breath and interrupts a student. "I'm not sure this group can be any more clearly defined or any safer and actually still be useful. If relationships are too safe, nothing of importance happens in them."

That finally shuts them up. He glances at the clock. "We have another hour today and I want to move on. Does anyone have a specific issue to discuss?"

Stephen glances around the room and into Henry's eyes. He looks away quickly, hoping Henry will ignore him.

Too late.

"Stephen, do you have something you'd like to bring up?"

Stephen smiles a tight nervous smile, clears his throat, and looks up at Ally, who smiles gently at him.

"I haven't…I've never heard that…the idea that relationships can be too safe. But it makes sense to me," he says. As soon as he says that, he thinks about his conversation with Dan and Randy, how that might be part of what Dan was getting at when he said you have to stick around and plow through the problems instead of pretending they aren't there. Maybe, he thinks, it's possible that you're the least safe when you feel the safest.

"A certain level of safety is good," Henry says, "but beyond that it becomes constricting. A minute ago, I fell asleep and almost catapulted out of my chair. When my eyes opened, I saw all of you looking at me and not one of you commented on it. That is safe, but it's also dishonest, right? That's what I mean by 'too safe.' I want us to talk about what is going on with us in the room, and outside of here, whether it feels safe or not, okay?"

Heads nod and one by one the students relax more in their chairs.

Stephen sits slightly forward in his seat and considers bringing up a conversation that he had with his sister, Michelle, first thing this morning. She called at eight and awakened Stephen from an exhilarating dream.

"Stephen, I have to talk to you about Dad," his sister said, sounding fearful and confused. "He's clinically depressed. He's even been thinking about killing himself."

Stephen sat up, alarmed.

"I've never heard him talk like this," she said. "He said he didn't have any reason to go on. He promised me he wouldn't do anything impulsive, but I think it would be good for you to call him."

Stephen reflects on how she seems so good at everything but dealing with emotional problems. He remembers the day the two of them were sitting on her deck in Charleston, looking out at the marsh along the Ashley River. After a few glasses of wine, Stephen asked Michelle how things were going with her husband Roger.

"Mom told me you and Roger separated for a few months because he had an affair, but I never really knew what happened or how you two got back together," he said.

He looked at his sister and waited.

"I don't really like to talk about it, as you might have guessed," she answered before chuckling a little and taking a long sip of wine. "There's not that much to tell. Roger was having trouble at work, I had my hands full with the girls, and our sex life went down the tubes. He found someone a little younger, with a better body and a willingness to pretend that he was…what is it that you guys want to feel… wonderful… special?"

They did not get much further than that. Nor did they get far in their conversation about their father this morning.

"What do you think we should do for Dad?" Stephen asked.

"I don't know. That's why I called."

Stephen returns his focus to the group. Ally is crying as she talks about her relationship with her boyfriend Ben in New York. She misses him, "but it's more than that. I don't have faith in the relationship anymore. I used to assume we'd be together forever. Now, I don't think so."

Stephen listens closely. He feels surrounded by people – from Dan and Randy to his sister and her husband to himself and his ex-wife – whose lives are a continual struggle because of relationships.

"Ben doesn't talk to me," Ally says. "When we're together we do fine. But what I've realized being here, talking only on the phone, is that we can't really talk about important things. We talk about movies, travel plans… we never really talk about my life."

"That's important to find out," Henry says. "Maybe you could have only learned that being apart."

Ally nods. She looks down and her eyes fill with tears.

"I can see how important this is to you, Ally," Henry says before motioning to the clock. "I'm sorry that we need to stop here. I hope you'll bring this issue up next time we meet. Are you okay to stop here?" Henry asks with a gentle smile.

Ally nods and forces a smile.

As everyone gets up to leave, Stephen notices Scott go quickly to Ally and give her a long hug.

Charles walks toward him, and they talk about the orientation for their job at a prison. They make plans to ride together to their first day of work as they walk into the parking lot. Stephen is about to get into his car when he glances back to see Ally walking by.

"See you in class," she says, smiling.

"Yeah, see you tomorrow."

Stephen drives home, consumed with Ally's smile. As he parks his car in the garage, he thinks about his father.

"Why can't he take care of himself?" Stephen wonders, slamming his car door.

Randy, in his studio, hears the car door. He walks to the screened door and flips it open.

"Hi," Randy says. "Gorgeous day, huh?"

Stephen looks at the sky, noticing it for the first time all day. "Yeah, it's…beautiful," he says, hesitantly.

"You alright?" Randy asks.

Stephen smiles weakly.

"What's wrong?" Randy asks.

"I guess I'm a little worried right now," Stephen admits. "This morning, I got some weird news about my father from my sister."

"Is he alright?" Randy asks.

"I don't know. He told her he was really depressed."

"Have you talked to him?"

"No, I'm going to call him tonight."

"Come in," Randy says.

"Sure," Stephen says and follows him in.

"You have any idea what's going on with him?" Randy asks, moving some paint-stained newspapers from a stool so Stephen can sit.

"Not really. He invites my sister and me to Florida to visit and, I don't know, we just never want to go. He told my sister last night how much that bothers him, but, honestly, we don't like to visit him."

"Why not?" Randy asks.

"We don't like being around his wife. She's annoying as hell."

"What's so bad about her?" Randy asks, mashing his thumb into a thick dab of brown paint on the canvas.

"Basically, she controls everything my father does. When I've visited, we can't do anything without her tagging along. She has to be right at his side to keep an eye on things."

Randy wipes the paint from his fingers and sits down on a stool near Stephen. "It sounds like you're angry at your father for letting this woman get in the way of his relationship with you."

Stephen leans away from Randy. "Yeah, I guess Michelle and I are mad at my father for a lot of things. We're mad at him for divorcing our mother, moving hundreds of miles away, then marrying a woman who's very hard to like."

"You think your dad's depressed because you and your sister don't visit him?" Randy asks.

"It's probably part of it. He also has prostate cancer. He plays golf all day and lives in a small house with almost no yard. He was the kind of guy who was constantly doing things, working with his hands, gardening, building stuff. I don't think playing golf all day satisfies him, and now that's his whole life."

"Why don't you invite him here?"

Stephen looks at Randy and slowly nods his head. "That might be nice. I hadn't thought of that."

Later, talking to his father on the phone, Stephen mentions that Michelle was worried that he was "depressed."

"Depressed? I wouldn't call it that. I was just a little down," his father says.

"You sound down now, too," Stephen says.

"Yeah, well I'm having some minor problems getting used to living in Florida."

"Like what?"

"I don't know, Stephen. It's just different being retired and so far away from everyone."

"Then why did you move?" Stephen wants to ask. Instead he says, "Michelle said you told her that you didn't see any reason to go on."

"Oh, come on, Stephen," he says. "Your sister exaggerates. I'm just a little down with missing my children…and things here could be better."

"What do you mean, 'things could be better?' You mean in your relationship with Donna?"

"Yes, but now isn't a good time to discuss that."

"Is she there by you?"

"No, but she's in the house so…you know."

"I guess I know," Stephen says.

"Let's talk about you for a while. How's school going?"

"I'm fine…school's okay. I miss Nicholas, but I like Atlanta. I've got a real nice place here. In fact, I'd like you to come visit me and see it."

"That sounds good," his father says, in a flat tone. "Maybe this summer we could come up that way."

"The summer is several months away," Stephen says. "You say you miss your children, so why don't you come visit me? What do you have going on that you can't get on a plane and come here for a weekend soon?"

There is a long silence. "I think Donna would be upset if I came without her and…"

Stephen's interrupts loudly, "You know what that sounds like to me? It sounds like she's interfering with your relationship with your children."

There is a longer silence.

Stephen tries to restrain himself, but impulsively adds, "That's what the problem is, you know. Michelle and I'd love to spend time with you, but Donna interferes with that. And that's one of the reasons that you're down, because you're not involved in our lives."

After a moment, Stephen's father sighs. "I don't know what to say to all of that," he says.

"Don't say anything. Change it. I'm just asking you to come visit me and have a good time like retired people do with their children. I'll even play golf with you and you know I don't have any burning desire to play golf."

"Well, we'll see Stephen."

"I'll even let you win. That always lifts your spirits."

"What the hell do you mean 'let me win?' I'm playing in the low eighties these days."

"Don't give me that," Stephen says.

"You know I wouldn't lie about that."

"Well maybe you'd exaggerate, like your daughter sometimes does. I tell you what; I'll call the airlines and make reservations, so it'll be easy on you. How about three weekends from now?"

"I don't know, Stephen."

"Look, just tell Donna that you haven't seen me in in a long time and that you're going for a short weekend. Brace yourself to hear a bunch of inappropriate BS, and just ignore it."

"I don't know, Stephen."

"I'm going to hang up the phone and call the airlines, so you might as well get ready to catch hell."

After another attempt to get out of it, Frank agrees.

After Stephen hangs up, he calls his sister. She's washing dishes as she talks. Occasionally she stops to help one of her daughters with a homework problem, multi-tasking exactly as their mother used to do. She's shocked that Stephen has invited their father and equally surprised that he's agreed to go. She volunteers to call the airlines and pay for the ticket.

Michelle passes the phone to her oldest daughter, Lauren, who insists on talking to her uncle. When she's finished, Lauren hands the phone to her little sister, Gabrielle. Each girl tells Stephen that she loves and misses him.

Stephen sits on his bed and dials his ex-wife's number. After the tenth ring, he places the phone in its cradle and walks toward the door. The kitchen lights in the main house are out. He feels an aching loneliness. Earlier that day, standing in line in the grocery store, he chatted with a little boy about Nicholas's age, asking him questions about his life until his mother looked at him with protective suspicion. He thinks about going out to eat, but he isn't hungry. He decides to go anyway, for the movement of people, the sound of human voices, the hope of a chance encounter with a woman, and the possibility of thinking less about his own life….and all the relationships that seem broken.

Chapter 12

THE PRISON

IN THE PRISON PARKING LOT, Stephen and Charles get out of Stephen's Karman Ghia. They have enjoyed their thirty-mile trip together, exchanging perceptions of faculty and fellow graduate students. They feel close to each other. Today is the first day of a part-time job where they'll work together two and a half days a week.

Stephen and Charles pause for a moment, seeing the prison for the first time. They squint against the sun reflecting off the concertina wire. Wavy horizontal lines of moist heat rise off the silver/white wire, creating a dream-like image that blurs the colorless buildings and guard towers beyond the fence.

To prepare for their work in the prison, Stephen and Charles had attended a one-week mandatory prison orientation program. They were there with new staff, from administrative employees to correctional officers, in a nice university-style building a long way from where they are right now.

Both men are nervous. They wonder how, with their limited experience as psychology graduate students, they'll be able to provide any kind of useful psychotherapy to inmates in a psychiatric unit in the bowels of the prison system. Both prefer to look self-assured regardless of the situation, and in fact they haven't discussed any of their fears with each other.

They each face their fear now as they walk down the grimy cinder-block tunnel that leads to the entrance to the prison. Stephen and Charles grow silent. The only sound in the tunnel is the echo of the two men's footsteps.

At the end of the tunnel they pass through two heavy metal doors to the only entrance and exit to the prison. Stephen looks around at the industrial-weight steel, the bulletproof glass, and hyper-vigilant officers in khaki shirts and pants. Stephen and Charles approach the officer sitting on a stool in front of the entrance. Stephen looks at the handgun snapped into the guard's holster. The wood-grained finish makes it look a little like a toy gun. He knows from the orientation that no officers inside prison can carry a gun. Charles talks to the officer, who gives him directions to the mental health unit.

One of the officers speaks into a microphone: "Your names and the unit where you'll be stationed."

"Stationed?" Stephen asks, and quickly adds, "Mental health unit," in as firm a voice as he can manage.

The officer flips though pages on a clipboard. After a minute, the officer with the gun nods and the officer in the control room flips a switch. A loud jolt of electricity moves the gate in front of Stephen and Charles slowly to one side. The two men pass through the door, then another electric gate, and into the general population of the prison, or "yard." As Stephen and Charles learned at orientation, the yard is the medium-security part of the medium/maximum security prison.

From seven in the morning until early evening, inmates in the yard move about freely, going to school, work, the dining hall, the gym, the library, almost like on a university campus. The exception to this is during "count," which occurs in the early afternoon. During count, every inmate returns to his cell and is locked up while officers all over the prison actually count inmates in their area to make sure no one has escaped or is otherwise "out of place."

In the yard, Stephen and Charles are enveloped by a cacophony of loud talking, laughing, and competing music from portable radios tuned to different stations. Inmates are lined up, maybe four or five wide, in a space about the length of a football field arguing, laughing, and playing little pranks on each other. Except for the massive bodies, it looks like elementary school recess. Today is Monday, fried-chicken day, so the inmates always line up early for the most popular lunch of the week.

The prisoners stop their animated movement when the new guys get about thirty feet from them. They look at Stephen and Charles with a mixture of curiosity and contempt.

"Man, there are some angry boys back there," Charles says, after they have cleared the inmates in line and continue walking toward their destination.

"They didn't seem too friendly, did they?"

"This is some heavy shit we got ourselves involved in. You know that, right?" Charles says.

"This is a weird place, Charles. I don't know who looks scarier, the inmates or the guards."

"Correctional officers, man. Not guards. Remember from orientation. They prefer that, and I think we need them to like us."

They both think that is pretty funny.

They approach the maximum-security area where they'll be working, two identical, three-story gray buildings connected to each other by glass and steel walkways with a small building in the middle. One of the buildings is the "lockup facility;" the other is the mental health unit. A thirty-foot chain-link fence surrounds the entire area, with a row of concertina wire along the top. A prison within a prison.

"I think we have really fucked up. We're going to work with guys they protect those other crazy-looking guys from," Charles says, half kidding.

"Hey, don't forget they're paying us a couple dollars over minimum wage for this shit, so let's try to be positive," Stephen says.

The gate opens, and they walk down a long sidewalk that takes them past the front of the lockup building. Inmates in the cells begin yelling out their steel-screened windows.

"Hey… nice piece of white ass. Come to my cell so I can fuck your hot ass!"

"I think someone would like a visit from you," Charles says, grinning.

Almost immediately another voice calls out. "Hey, hey you, yeah you, you big black dick, come over here and let me stick my big white cock in your mouth."

Then it seemed all the locked-up inmates unleashed their vitriol. Voices as independent and disconnected from each other as the various instruments of an orchestra, tuning up, began spewing sex and hostility.

Orientation had covered that the inmates in lockup were frequently angry and verbally abusive of staff. Various reasons were given for this: First, they felt anonymous, essentially hidden in their own rooms, unlike inmates in the yard who were easily distinguished from other inmates and could be charged with verbal abuse and sent to lockup. Second, the guys on lockup tended to be the meanest, and likely to have difficulty managing the connection between behavior and consequences. So, once they were sentenced to lockup, they essentially threw in the towel on trying to control their behavior. "What are you going to do, lock me up?" was their attitude. Never mind that they were taking a chance on adding more time to their current sentence on lockup. Also, the officers in the lockup facility were always alert to the possibility of thrown feces or inmate physical attacks against them or another inmate. On alert for more disruptive behavior, they were not that interested in playing schoolmarm and policing unkind comments.

As the screams grow louder and louder, Charles and Stephen look straight ahead, feigning deafness like frightened American schoolgirls just off the tour bus, walking by a group of eager young men on some hot Mediterranean street.

"Okay, Stephen tell me what you think is going on with these guys that's got them yelling all that sexual shit at us," Charles asks, looking straight ahead.

"I understand the hostility, making it sexual, that I don't get." Stephen answers.

"If you figure it out let me know," Charles says, as they walk in the door of the high security building. Just inside the door, Dr. Daugherty, whom they haven't seen since their job interview at a much safer place about a month ago, greets them. "You made it. None of those convicts scared you, did they?" he asks.

Stephen and Charles force smiles.

"Well," he says, "we've been expecting you two and want to give you the cook's tour of the place. I want to introduce you to some staff and a few patients. Are you ready?" He waggles his eyebrows at them like Groucho Marx.

"Sure," Charles answers.

The tour is more heavy steel and electronic gates. Dr. Daugherty talks about the organization of the unit as he shows Charles and Stephen through each of the sections, divided according to the degree of freedom the inmates have, determined by their responsiveness to treatment and overall degree of danger to themselves or others.

As they walk out of the Level Two area, where clients are free to move about the unit, and even play games such as ping pong and cards, Dr. Daugherty asks if either Stephen or Charles has ever worked in a state hospital. Neither has. "What you would notice is that here, different from most state hospitals, our patients are more alive. We don't overmedicate. Our treatment team reviews every patient weekly and makes any necessary change, either in treatment approach, living situation, medicine, whatever, immediately. Within a month at most, we want even the most dangerous or suicidal patients moving from the most restrictive level, One-R, to the least restrictive, Level Three, which includes yard privileges."

A white inmate, maybe forty years old, urgently calls Dr. Daugherty to his cell. Charles and Stephen follow.

"Well, Wallace, I heard you were back with us," Dr. Daugherty says.

"Doc, you got to get me off this Level. I'm not going to hurt myself. I need my yard privileges."

"I don't know about your level," Dr. Daugherty says, as he pulls a pack of cigarettes from his shirt pocket and hands the inmate two. The inmate's hand shakes wildly as he places one of them in his mouth, and Dr. Daugherty sticks a lit match through the opening. "I heard you cut your arm up pretty bad."

"No, it's not that bad. I lost control for a little while, but I'm okay now. I love myself too much to hurt myself," he says and then grins.

Stephen moves closer, so he can see the inmate's arm. He winces, seeing the blood stained-gauze and Ace bandage. The inmate notices Stephen looking and raises his arm to him almost proudly.

"The treatment team is meeting today, and you'll get a therapist assigned to you," Dr. Daugherty says with almost no hint of concern. "You know the drill as well as I do. After that, if your therapist thinks you're ready for yard privileges, you'll get them." Dr. Daugherty begins walking away.

"That's bullshit, man. I just got mad because my family didn't show at visitation and cut myself…a little. Now you're going to punish me. What kind of fucking shit is that?"

Dr. Daugherty stops and turns back to the inmate. "Wallace," he says, "next time you get mad, don't cut yourself, and you'll stay in the yard like you want."

He walks away, ignoring the inmate's cursing and pleading. Stephen and Charles follow him back toward the middle of the cellblock as other inmates, seemingly desperate, call them to their rooms. It seems as if everyone is chanting two main themes: "Get me off this level," and "You got a cigarette?"

Dr. Daugherty ignores them and continues talking as Stephen looks through the cell doors trying to make out the images behind them. Behind one of the doors, he sees a dark black man, with mutton chop sideburns, a long Afro, and a haunting stare, take a drag off his cigarette. The inmate's eyes dart from Dr. Daugherty to Stephen to Charles like a hyperactive surveillance camera. Through the long narrow window, Stephen can see the inmate's shirtless body, sculpted with long muscles and no visible body fat. His blue jeans rest on his hips, while his boxer shorts are pulled above the jeans, just below his belly button.

The inmate thrusts his fingers through his Afro, pushing it back so that it stands up about three inches in the front. He takes another drag off his cigarette, breathing in the smoke as deeply as if he were smoking a joint. He exhales a thick cloud of smoke that floats through the door opening and steadily toward Dr. Daugherty, Stephen, and Charles.

Stephen has been looking at the inmate's ripped abs, envying them really, before he looks up directly into the man's dark eyes. Suddenly, like a machine jolted by an electrical current, the inmate begins screaming, so loud and with such a staccato rhythm, that the unit grows silent for him.

"White mother-fuckin' running dogs is what you white mother fuckin' psychiatrists are. Don't look at me unless you're here to call me sir, and your profession, your mother fucking degrees, keep you from using sir even to a man. I ain't no man's woman and I ain't never been no slave, but I've been locked up for ten years for a crime that was not a crime. And if you don't know my lawyer then why am I wasting time talking to you…Why, motherfuckers?"

For a few seconds he glares at Stephen before his eyes jump to Charles.

"I will not be sold into slavery even for a black man and I wouldn't kill none of you, even though you'll try to kill me with your so-called treatment. And yet, I'm on this side of the bars. Can you explain that to me with all your rooms full of psychiatrists and all your pigskin degrees? Someday, motherfuckers, one of you is going to say the wrong thing and then there will be a good goddamn reason to keep me locked in this place where the walls don't lie like you psychiatrist motherfuckers."

His head rocks up and down, nodding, as he grins at his audience.

"Did you hear what I said to you?" he continues, his eyes riveted on Charles. "The walls don't lie, at least not as much as a black man who's more comfortable with those not his kind. I want to know when I'm getting out of this place or at least have a chance to talk to my lawyer. And there ain't nary one of you gonna help me with that."

For an instant Stephen thinks he sees a look of vulnerability in the inmate's eyes. But then they darken, and he screams, "I'm waiting for an answer, motherfuckers!"

into the yard for at least an hour each day. Darnell refuses medication, psychotherapy, and just about everything else we offer him except cigarettes, right Darnell?"

Dr. Daugherty continues without looking to Darnell for an answer. Darnell takes a drag off his cigarette and continues to stare out his window.

"We don't force medication on inmates unless they're actively suicidal. If we feel they're too dangerous to be around others, we simply keep them on Level 1 R, locked up where they can't get to anyone. On this level, they're only allowed to leave their rooms for showers and their mandatory daily one hour of exercise."

"Is it all right if I ask Darnell a question?" Stephen asks, looking at Darnell.

"Sure," Dr. Daugherty answers.

Stephen waits a few more seconds for Darnell to reply, too, but he does not answer.

"What's the hardest thing about being a client on the mental health unit?" Stephen asks.

Darnell glances quickly at Stephen before looking out his screened window. He takes a long drag off his cigarette and exhales through his nostrils. He turns around slowly and meets Stephen's eyes.

"Answering questions filled with lies and bullshit," he says, with a horribly sarcastic grin.

"Yeah…I guess this is a place of, you know, a lot of questions," Stephen says. "I guess I was hearing that there's a lot of restrictions here and you don't get out of your room much. That must be hard."

Darnell stares at Stephen.

"Can I ask another question?" Stephen asks.

Stephen waits and this time, Darnell just barely nods his head.

"It's kind of weird question, but… I was wondering how you stay in such great shape. I mean, being locked up and all."

Darnell smiles. "I do 'bout ten sets of fifty-sixty pushups a day," he says. "And about ten minutes of sit-ups, 'bout four or five times a day… Sometimes I do more."

"Wow," Stephen says. "It shows. Did you play sports before getting locked up?"

Darnell looks out the window.

When it's clear that Darnell isn't going to answer, Stephen continues. "Anyway, it's nice of you to let us see your room. You do keep it looking nice and neat."

Darnell turns and stares at Stephen before looking out the window again.

Dr. Daugherty smiles, "Darnell, I don't believe you have a therapist assigned to you these days," he says. "And I was thinking maybe Stephen and you could work together. You could fill him in on the ways of the mental health unit, and maybe y'all could do some exercises together."

Darnell chuckles at the absurdity of that, but never looks back at the others.

"That sound good to you, Stephen?" Dr. Daugherty asks.

Stephen looks at Darnell, Charles, and Dr. Daugherty. What else can he say? "Yeah, I mean, sure, if Darnell's okay with that… I'd like to work with him."

Darnell turns toward the room. "I don't need no psychiatrist," he says, with less of his usual venom.

"Yeah, of course, you don't," Dr. Daugherty says, winking at Charles and Stephen. "Stephen will just check on you a couple of times a week."

Darnell looks out the window.

"Good, good. Well, why don't I take Charles with me to meet another of our patients and you two can get to know each other a little better. Okay?" Dr. Daugherty asks, looking at Stephen.

Again, Stephen slowly glances around the room, then nods and says, "Sure, yeah, that, um, sounds good."

Dr. Daugherty calls the head officer, who unlocks the door and lets him and Charles out of the cell. The officer looks at Stephen as he locks the door. "He's all right," he whispers, nodding toward Darnell.

Standing with his back against the locked cell door, Stephen spends several painful minutes stiffly asking questions that feel like they rolled off the pages of some bad psychotherapy textbook, and being pretty much ignored by Darnell, before he remembers that Darnell responded to his earlier questions about exercising. The remainder of the time Stephen asks questions that are more immediately relevant to Darnell's life and they at least are able to lightly chat.

After Dr. Daugherty and Charles return, Stephen turns to Darnell, on the way out the door, and holds out his hand to shake. Darnell looks at Stephen with something resembling disdain, but just before Stephen withdraws his hand, Darnell reaches his out.

"Thanks for letting me see your room," Stephen says as they shake hands.

Darnell removes his hand from Stephen's and moves away from him clumsily.

Stephen and Charles pass through the last of the electronic gates, both happy and relieved to get out of the prison. They walk down the long tunnel, which is almost empty because they're leaving a couple of hours before the full-time employees.

They review their experience, agreeing that the most terrifying moment was walking in the room with Darnell in full psychotic bloom.

"You think Dr. Daugherty picked his room so he could watch us freak out?" Stephen asks.

"He was testing us, or maybe just showing us how we have to adopt a self-assured attitude," Charles says. "You know I felt bad leaving you in there alone, brother, but…"

"Yeah, you looked upset," Stephen drawls sarcastically.

"What did you and Darnell talk about after I left?" Charles asks.

"Not too much. I asked some general questions, which he ignored. I asked if he'd teach me to roll cigarettes like he does," Stephen says.

Charles looks at Stephen. "No, you didn't," he says, grinning.

"Yeah, I did. You could say I was building rapport. I've never seen anybody roll one like that."

"Man, you are crazy," Charles says, shaking his head. "He can roll a cigarette; I'll give you that. But what are you going to do if he tells Dr. Daugherty that you want him to teach you to roll cigarettes? I'd guess Dr. Daugherty would assume you don't want to start rolling up legal tobacco for smoking."

"Charles, for a big motherfucking psychiatrist you worry about way too much shit. You know that?"

"Yeah, well, I do approach new situations with some degree of over cautiousness, that's true. What did Darnell say?" Charles asks.

"He laughed, looked at me kind of funny, and said, 'I can teach you.' I think it was one of the only things he said after you left other than that he wasn't going to be subjected to a 19 dot b though d."

"I bet he felt good with you asking about the cigarettes," Charles says, seeming to warm to the idea. "I'll bet that's why he was willing to shake your hand. You're willing to bring almost anything up, you know that?"

"What do you mean?" Stephen asks.

"Well that, and the stuff about his being in such great shape. I mean, there were four men in a crowded cell, inmates were just yelling about wanting to fuck us, and here you go complimenting the guy on his body." Charles laughs and shakes his head. "That's some weird stuff where I'm from. Men just don't talk about each other's bodies, especially when they're standing on top of each other."

Stephen looks at Charles as they open the doors of his car. "I didn't even think about it, you know, like that," he says. "You think it bothered him?"

Charles looks back at the glowing steel surrounding the prison, then turns back to Stephen. "Honestly, it didn't seem to."

"So, I guess it bothered you?" Stephen asks.

"Now you're going to challenge me, huh? I won't say it bothered me. Just, where I'm from it isn't done. Talking about another man's body could be a white man's thing, huh?"

Stephen laughs. "No, I don't think so. I usually don't bring that stuff up either. I was just trying to connect with him, and I'm always looking for tips on improving my rapidly deteriorating abdominal situation…A white man's thing? Come on with that bullshit."

"Well, you know, I'm just living and learning," Charles says with a grin, as they get in Stephen's car. "Do you think Darnell is actually crazy or was all that stuff an appropriate reaction to the context of his life?"

"Hmm, I can see how both of those could be true," Stephen says, before shrugging his shoulders.

Chapter 13

SLOWER

STEPHEN SITS AT A TINY TABLE on the deck at Einstein's, waiting for Ally. She'd invited him to dinner to repay him for helping her with their statistics class. "I'll buy dinner," she said.

Einstein's is packed with animated, attractive urban dwellers. Stephen takes a sip of beer and glances at a woman sitting at a table a few feet from him. She looks like a fantasy woman, maybe from some banana republic, her olive legs crossed with her khaki skirt open to mid-thigh. Her hair is black, and her eyes are exotic, a concoction of blues, greens, browns, and even yellows that are the phenotypic representation of the breeding of opposite ends of the genetic continuum. She's forty, maybe forty-five, and Stephen finds himself unable to look away.

Stephen looks at the woman's husband who seems unenthusiastic about being with her. Stephen watches the couple chat, casually, distractedly, with each other. His thoughts turn to a conversation with Dan and Randy an hour earlier. Dan quizzed him to determine whether this was actually a date or just a dinner between friends. Eventually Dan decided it was a date. He adamantly insisted that Stephen pick up the check, despite Ally's offer. He even insisted Stephen wear a yellow linen shirt he recently bought Randy. As usual, Dan and Randy bantered throughout the hour. They always seem on the brink of an argument, and yet they remain so enthusiastic about being with each other even after ten years. "Can heterosexuals do that?" he wonders, glancing back at the woman and her seemingly bored husband. He spots Ally, stands, and waves.

Ally walks quickly to the table, noticing his lemon-yellow shirt. She has never seen him in anything except blacks, whites, and navy blues. So maybe he dressed up for me, she thinks. "Hi," she says, as she pulls her chair back. The woman with the olive legs appears to notice her as she tilts her head in the couple's direction and begins watching them.

Ally and Stephen work hard at first, talking about their classes and professors, both agreeing wholeheartedly with the other's observations. Within a few minutes, though, they're more relaxed, both leaning forward in their seats, smiling and talking easily. The waitress brings Ally her beer. She takes a sip as a cool breeze blows through the trees moving some strands of Ally's hair off her shoulders. Stephen looks up and notices menacing clouds dancing around the moon.

"Looks like it might storm," he says.

Ally looks at the sky and smiles. "It does," she says, before leaning forward and resting her chin on her fist.

For the second time the waitress asks if they're ready to order. They tell her they need a few more minutes and find that a lot more amusing than she does.

The fantasy woman at the other table leans over and asks, "Is this a first date?"

"Yes," Stephen says without thinking. "How did you know?"

"You've got that glow. You make a beautiful couple," she says, and turns back to her husband, who smiles and nods.

"I hope that's okay, for me to call it a date?" Stephen asks.

"I'm very happy to hear you call it that," Ally says.

They're quiet for a few moments before Stephen leans forward. "I've wanted to go out with you all year," he says.

Ally looks at him carefully. "Really?" she manages. "I figured you were way too busy to notice me. I assumed you were going out with several women."

"Why did you assume that?" Stephen asks, as the waitress returns.

"You guys ready to order?" she asks.

They hastily look at the menu and decide to split a couple of appetizers.

After the waitress leaves, Stephen says, "You were about to tell me why you assumed I was going out with several women, right?"

"I'm not even sure," she says. "You act different about women than most guys I know."

"Really..."

"I guess it's your reputation in the department. I mean, the women say that you're a heartbreaker type. And you've discussed several different women in our group therapy sessions. And I guess you and Ed seem so bonded. He has kind of a reputation as a womanizer, and he acts like you're his soul mate or something."

Stephen looks at Ally, and then at the woman with the olive legs. He takes a sip of his beer. He likes that Ally has noticed that Ed treats him special. He actually feels pretty good about the heartbreaker comment.

"I guess I've talked about a couple of women in the group, you know, in trying to understand myself and my relationships better," he says. "But none of those relationships have been real. I mean, they haven't been important to me. But yeah, I guess the truth is, if we were looking for sure things we wouldn't be out with each other. You spend your time in the group talking about your relationship with Ben. I don't have any idea how free you are to be with me tonight."

Ally's face turns pink. "I'm, um, free. I just don't know how to end that relationship," she says, leaning against the wrought-iron seat back.

"Really…that sounds a little different than what you say in the group. But if you have trouble ending relationships then we have that in common."

"Why is it hard for you to end relationships?" Ally asks.

"I'll tell you if you tell me," Stephen says in a seductive tone.

"You're bad, aren't you Stephen?" Ally teases back.

"Sometimes," Stephen says, reaching out to hold her hand.

Ally puts her hand in his and blushes. "Are you going to tell me why it's so hard for you to end relationships?" she asks.

"I have trouble saying difficult things in relationships. I hate to hurt people," he says.

"I'll try to remember that," she says, smiling.

"Okay, I told you. Now, you tell me." Stephen says.

"I guess it's the same reason as you said. I don't like disappointing or hurting people."

"You can't give the same answer as me. That's not fair," he says, letting go of her hand.

"Well, if it's the same reason…" she demands.

"Well yeah, but there are hundreds of reasons or explanations for, you know, our cowardice. You can't just give the one I gave."

Ally blushes again. "Well I'll have to think about it," she says.

They sit in silence for a few seconds, then Stephen asks, "Should we just change the subject?"

"No, I'm thinking about it," Ally says. She looks around the restaurant. Before her response has fully formed, she says, "I guess the best answer is that I don't like giving up on people or relationships. I have trouble letting go of hope," she says.

Stephen takes a sip of his beer. "That…that's a good reason to… have a problem ending relationships," he says. Stephen has noticed how, in class, Ally never backs away from a challenge even when she appears flustered. He looks at her, the shadows of the clouds and the light of the moon dance over her face. She looks so free and uninhibited.

The waitress arrives with the appetizers and lights the candle that was blown out by the wind.

While they eat, Ally and Stephen talk again about department politics, before getting back to Ed.

"You seem to have a kind of judgmental thing going with Ed," Stephen says.

Ally takes a sip of her beer.

"I can see how what I've said might sound judgmental," Ally says. "But maybe it's a gender difference thing. I mean, how appealing is it to a twenty-three-year-old woman to hear that a man as old as your father dates women close to your age?"

Stephen looks at his date's face. "I guess I've wondered about that myself," he says. "With all he's accomplished, you would think he'd want to date women a little more his equal."

Both sit back and relax, having come to an agreement about Ed's controversial appetite for younger women. As they're finishing eating, the wind and clouds swirl around them.

Stephen looks up as the moon disappears behind swirling clouds.

"The sky is really looking threatening. We better leave," he says. "Do you want to go dancing?"

"Sure, that would be great," Ally replies.

As the waitress brings the check Stephen grabs it and says, "I want to pay for tonight, okay?"

"What? I asked you out and I'm paying you back for helping me with statistics," Ally says.

"Yeah, I know, but you arranged this, so you should get a free night out, right?"

"Are you sure?" she asks.

"Definitely," Stephen says.

"Okay, but only if we go out tomorrow night and I pay," Ally says.

Stephen looks at Ally, who has once again caught him of guard. He loves how provocative she is.

"Wow, um, sure. That's a great idea," he says.

Stephen and Ally ride past warehouses and boarded-up businesses as they look for a nightclub in downtown Atlanta that Randy said was the hot new gay/straight dance club. They left the area lit with attractive streetlamps and now head down dark streets past abandoned buildings with jagged edges of broken glass and graffiti- covered plywood in the windows and doors.

A traffic light turns red and Stephen stops the car. Stephen leans forward and looks out Ally's window. On the corner there are shadows of men. Stephen takes a drag off a joint he and Ally began smoking a couple of minutes earlier and passes it. Suddenly, a large, smiling face with golden-capped teeth appears in the windshield. He sloppily sprays the glass and wipes it with a dirty rag before thrusting his empty hand toward Stephen's face, demanding payment for the chore, and moving menacingly toward his window. At first Stephen hesitates, not wanting to roll his window down and reveal that he's smoking marijuana. But then he decides the man is definitely not a drug enforcement agent. Intimidated, he rolls the window down a couple of inches and passes a one-dollar bill to the man.

"No tip?" the man demands with a frightening look.

"That's the only money I have," Stephen says, rolling the window up.

The light turns green and he eases away.

Ally takes a deep drag and passes the joint back to him.

"That was kind of scary," Stephen says, taking a long hit off the joint. He holds the smoke and then slowly exhales. When he catches his breath, he adds, "It felt like we were in some alternative reality."

"I think we were," Ally says.

"There it is," Stephen says as he spots the club. He turns the car into the parking lot of a machine shop next door to the club. They walk inside holding hands. It's before midnight, so the club isn't crowded, but the dance floor is packed. Stephen and Ally dance under pulsing lights to music that drives the last of their carefulness away. After dancing to exhaustion, Stephen leads Ally from the dance floor toward the bar. They slide between patrons that they hardly notice, working their way to the bar for a drink. They stand together sipping their drinks, talking into each other's ears so that they can hear over the music. They laugh at something, then Stephen leans toward Ally and kisses her deeply. They smile and kiss again.

"I liked that," Stephen says.

Ally leans back to look at him and then pulls him to her. They kiss again.

"Will you spend the night with me?" Stephen whispers and kisses her again.

Ally laughs, "Definitely," she says.

Ally and Stephen get out of his car just as the rain that has threatened all night begins to fall. They move quickly through the door into Stephen's apartment and without thought fall into each other's arms and onto the bed. They kiss and move slowly with each other, touching, smelling, tasting each other as lightning brightens the room over and over allowing their eyes to meet. Stephen breathes in the experience of this sensual woman and whispers, "You smell wonderful."

The first sign of morning light touches the eastern sky outside Stephen's window as Stephen and Ally hold each other close. A cool breeze moves through the window, touches the pink bottoms of Ally's feet and drifts along her body, gently moving the blonde hair on her forehead, curled slightly from sweat, hers or Stephen's?

Ally hears two birds sing to each other. She senses a faint heartbeat, whose heart? She slips into a deep sleep.

Stephen feels her body let go of wakefulness. He runs his hand along her smooth skin as he holds her head to his chest. He too hears the birds outside. He's completely still as he drifts off.

Chapter 14

SUPERVISION: POETRY AND PSYCHOTHERAPY

ALLY NUDGES STEPHEN. "It's nine o'clock," she whispers.

Stephen has his weekly clinical supervision session with Ed at 10:30 on Monday morning. He pulls her closer and smells her hair. He wants to stay in bed with Ally all day. She leans up and kisses him gently, then slips back into sleep.

Stephen slides out of bed.

An hour later, even after a drive through traffic to school, Stephen carries the weekend's love with him. As he walks towards Ed's office, he does not have a hint of anxiety, no self-reflection either, just the euphoria of springtime love.

Stephen checks his watch just before entering Ed's office. Ed sits in the far corner, facing away from the door, reading a book. Stephen lingers in the doorway as Ed moves his head subtly to a primitive percussion beat blasting from his cassette player.

"Welcome to Ed's lair," Stephen thinks, as he admires the odd mixture of statuettes, sculptures and paintings from exotic cultures. Everything is cluttered between books and Eastern rugs and tapestries. Except for the books, browns, blacks, and burnt orange dominate the color scheme. It's a room with very little feminine influence, yet it always has a sedating effect on Stephen.

Stephen smiles at the oddity of this man and his room. Here is a sixty-year-old man, with elegant silver hair and mildly tanned skin, wearing shorts and a t-shirt from a 10K road race. As the most politically powerful professor in the department, he sits in a high-backed rattan chair that's part king's throne, part Gilligan's Island prop. As Stephen walks in, Ed turns, looks over his reading glasses and smiles at him. He lays his book in his lap and reaches for the cassette player's volume button, turning it down just a little.

"Come in, come in," Ed says. "Ringo, say 'hello,' our shortstop is here," he says to his 12-year-old dog. Ringo is a mixed breed dog so oddly shaped and proportioned that almost everyone laughs out loud when they see her for the first time.

Ed motions Stephen to sit down in one of his overstuffed chairs as Ringo slowly gets to her feet and walks over to him. "Good to see you," Ed says, his soft blue eyes resting on Stephen's face.

"Good to see you, too. I'm a little early...I was already here, so I just thought I'd check to see if you were ready."

"Let's do it. I'm just reading for pleasure, a book of poetry by Raymond Carver. You know him?"

"No, I don't think so," Stephen says.

"You read much poetry?" Stephen asks.

"Yeah, I try to read poetry at least a few minutes a day. I just got into poetry in the last five or six years. Before that, to me, it all seemed obfuscation for the sake of intellectual titillation. Now I think they're telling important truths. I'm thinking about doing an elective seminar on poetry and literature for our students, as part of the clinical training. Maybe getting a professor from the English department to participate. Try getting that past the experimental guys who've taken over this department. But I think it's important for our training. At least, it's important for a clinical psychologist to have a poetic heart. We have to have the desire, or maybe a better word is the compulsion, to tell the truth even when the truth is scary. We need to ask questions but know there are no definitive answers, just important moments.

"Poets tell the truth right in the moment and don't concern themselves with whether or not that truth is popular. A poet searches for the truth in an experience and finds ways to make the experience more knowable."

"Then why do so many of them seem to hide their meaning or make it vague?" Stephen asks.

"I used to wonder that myself, but now I appreciate that they express things in ways that can appeal to all our different levels of understanding," Ed says, looking reflectively around the room. "By using metaphor, for instance, poets push us deeper into the experience they're describing. Sure, it's more difficult to get, but that's a small price to pay for a deeper layer of truth."

"Why do you think it's so hard to tell the truth?" Stephen asks.

"I'd like to ask you that question," Ed says.

Stephen looks down at Ringo who lies sleeping and reflects for a moment in silence. "Ok, I'll take a shot. If the truth exists at a particular moment, it's the most personal expression of that moment. We don't tend to like things so personal."

"True, true. Why, though, do we avoid the things that are personal?"

Stephen looks at Ed and wonders if he's stoned, since he's so completely into the associations of the moment and unconcerned with an agenda for their time. He has never had a professor act like that. "Maybe it's that the truth about our existence is pretty pathetic, really, and that's why we avoid it," Stephen says.

"How do you mean?" Ed asks.

"Well let's see. We live in a finite world with a beginning, a middle, and an end. The end means that our world will exist without us sooner than we're comfortable with. Who wants to stare at that very often?"

Ed chuckles, "Yes, nobody wants to die. Do you understand why I say that a psychotherapist needs to be poetic?"

"I think you're saying we have to tell the truth, even the difficult truth, and that truth has to be communicated in special ways," Stephen says.

"Exactly! We also have to go all the way into the experience, even those that scare the hell out of us. Metaphors, the virtual basis of poetry, provide a way to go slowly to the depths without directly confronting everything at once. If we eventually go all the way into the experience with the clients, they'll learn more of their own truth. When a non-poetic therapist is faced with a difficult truth he'll back off and start talking coping mechanisms and medications. The truth doesn't always set us free, but we need to face reality to fully appreciate ourselves and our lives."

"That's really interesting," Stephen says "My landlord is a painter and I sometimes watch him at work. His favorite paintings are the ones that emerge slowly and spontaneously from someplace inside himself. As he moves the brush, the images seem to talk back to him and then he adds a detail. You're talking about a similar experience, right?"

Ed looks at Stephen, smiling. "Exactly! You know it was the Kurt

Vonnegut poem you started one of your essays with on your admission application that led me to rate you so high and ask to be your advisor. Do you remember the poem?"

"Yeah, of course. It's one of the only poems I know by heart."

"Go ahead," Ed says, gesturing for Stephen to recite it.

Stephen steals himself with a breath:

"Tiger got to hunt,

bird got to fly,

man got to sit and wonder 'why, why, why?'

Tiger got to eat,

bird got to land,

and man got to tell himself he understand."

Ed smiles broadly. "When I saw that on your application I said to myself, who else but a guy with a poet's courage would include that on his application. I figured you must be a little bit crazy and thought we'd get along."

They both laugh.

"To tell you the truth, Ed, I feel a lot better hearing that," Stephen says. "I've been thinking you chose me because one of my letters of recommendation said I'd been the shortstop on the department softball team at my last graduate school. I kind of like that it was my including that little poem."

"Well, I have to admit, that recommendation carried some significant weight, too."

Again, they laugh together.

The first day Stephen met Ed he felt comfortable talking with him, but today is different. He feels close to him now, father-and-son kind of close. Not like his own father, but more like he'd fantasized his relationship with his father to be, where they could joke about intellectual things.

"I tell you, the only thing keeping our softball team from winning over the last several years is a consistent weakness at shortstop. Hell, I could play shortstop almost as well as our last couple of shortstops, and I'm washed. I'm looking forward to softball practice in a couple of weeks. Are you ready?" Ed asks.

"I'm looking forward to it," Stephen says.

Ed looks at Stephen and smiles. The two men turn away from each other for a moment and let their eyes wander through the books on the shelves. Ed breaks the silence.

"There was something, I'm not even sure what, about all of your essays, not just the one that included the poem, but all of them that told me you had a poet's heart." He pauses. "What's got you smiling?" he asks.

Stephen feels a little awkward. "I was just thinking about the woman I dated before I moved here," he says. "She used to call me her 'young poet.' It always kind of embarrassed me." Stephen feels his face grow warm.

"You must have liked it too, right?" Ed asks.

"Yeah, I guess I did." Stephen admits.

"You know, our women know us at a deeper level than we know ourselves," Ed says.

Stephen smiles, wondering, "Isn't he the guy who dates women thirty years younger? How could these young women know him at a level deeper than he knows himself?"

"Are you still dating this woman?" Ed asks.

"No," Stephen says. "We quit dating when I moved here."

"I could never make a long-distance relationship work either. I'm not too good at making the ones closer to home work, either."

They smile at each other and fall into silence.

"She was also significantly older than me, which made it sort of a temporary relationship even though we dated for two years," Stephen ventures after a moment.

"How much older was she?" Ed asks.

"Well, about ten years older," Stephen answers, reducing the difference in their age by four years.

"I guess that's something men from your generation do," Ed says, shaking his head and smiling. "I've got a little story for you. I agreed, as part of a fundraiser for a local theatre company, to be one of the mini celebrities they auctioned off for a dinner date this weekend. They were obviously desperate and must have broadened the criteria for mini celebrity. Anyhow, I'm told a woman who was maybe forty, forty-five or fifty bought the date. I know it's pathetically shallow, but I'd kind of envisioned a significantly younger woman. But it's not like I can not go."

"Ed, are you're serious? She's forty something and you're thinking she's too old?"

"I know...I know," Ed says, sighing. "It's just I find more fun with young pleasure seekers. I don't know, women in their forties... and worse, I hear she's a social worker or psychiatric nurse or something... They're always so damn serious."

Stephen laughs and Ed reluctantly joins him.

"That's ironic," Stephen says. "The woman I mentioned earlier was in her early forties. I guess I found her so attractive, freeing really, because she was older and more independent than most of the women I'd dated."

Ed nods his head. "I've never thought of how a woman's independence would be freeing, but I can start with that assumption, go on this date and let her be responsible for making it fun or interesting. And if she's dull, I can drink an extra glass of Scotch."

"There you go," Stephen says, and they smile.

"Okay," Ed says, sitting up straighter. "Now, getting down to business, you told me last time that you wanted to play a tape of a session you did at the prison, right?"

"Yeah, it's a guy I've been seeing three times a week for the seven or eight weeks I've been working there," Stephen says, handing him the tape.

Ed slides it into the recorder on his desk.

"Anything I need to listen for?" Ed asks.

Stephen thinks for a few seconds. "I guess I'd say listen for how I can be helpful. I think you'll notice immediately that he's...difficult."

Ed nods and presses "play" on the recorder.

They hear Stephen's voice. "How you doing, Darnell?"

Stephen motions to Ed to stop the recorder.

"Sorry. I meant to tell you that he's mad at me, fuming as we begin here because I've been negotiating with him for three weeks to let me record the sessions and he's finally given in, but he's not happy about it."

Ed nods and presses "play" again.

There is a long pause where the only sound on the tape is the background noise of cell doors opening and shutting and yelling inmates. Finally, Darnell speaks in a loud clear voice, "You ask me how I'm doin', white man. Don't you know how I'm doing? Ain't you some kind of psychiatrist-gonna-read-my-mind? Go ahead mofo, read my afro-centric world view!"

Ed takes a sip of his ice water.

"Okay, let's see," he hears Stephen say. "Hmmm...you're thinking, 'This white boy don't know his ass from a hole in the ground and sure isn't going to be able to help me.'"

Darnell bursts into laughter. In the room, Ed laughs with him.

"Am I right?" Stephen asks.

"You ain't too far off...I can say that," Darnell says.

"Well, alright then," Stephen says.

Ed pauses the tape. "I like that. I'm glad you didn't insist that you couldn't read his mind and that you wouldn't be so…very disrespectful as to attempt such a thing."

As he presses "play" again, he smiles at Stephen. "See, I don't have to teach you how to be poetic," he says. "You've already got it."

Ed listens to Darnell and Stephen for fifteen or twenty minutes before he turns the tape off. "How have you been feeling with me looking over your shoulder like this?" he asks.

"I'm okay," Stephen says. "I was worried about the beginning, but since you liked that so much…"

"I loved it. We ask our clients to answer all these questions about their lives and if they're not spontaneous and creative we call them resistant. Then when they turn the tables on us, and ask something of us, we ourselves become resistant. You didn't become resistant. You became playful. You got involved. That's all I ask of a beginning therapist is to get involved with the client. You know, I was thinking as I was listening that it's ironic that Darnell is literally in prison. As I listen to my clients, I wonder how the story they're telling about their life keeps them in their metaphorical prison. When you sit with Darnell, ask yourself how his story keeps him stuck in his literal and metaphorical prison."

Stephen glances at the tiny clock next to Ed's chair. His first class with Ally after their weekend together is in fifteen minutes. As he and Ed walk toward the door, he reflects on his discussion with Ally about not letting anyone in their class know they were dating until they made it past the first month. They agreed that including the other students, and especially faculty, could potentially complicate their relationship. A month seemed an appropriate waiting period and even then, they could reevaluate their situation at the end of a month and decide how to proceed.

Ed interrupts his thoughts. "Let me change one thing I said earlier," he says, stopping in the doorway. "It's not really that our women know us at a deeper level than we know ourselves. That's not right. It's that through our relationship with the beloved, for me that's always a woman, we get to know ourselves at a deeper level. That is, if we're paying attention. That's better, right?"

"Yeah, that sounds good," Stephen answers before having the time to think it through.

Stephen almost sprints toward class, his heart beating with new love. When he walks into the class, Ally, who is famously on time for everything, hasn't arrived.

Chapter 15

AUTHENTICITY

ALLY WAS HEADING OUT THE DOOR for class when her phone rang. She answered it and became instantly tense. It was her boyfriend Ben. Her face flushed, and her hands shook. She was hoping it was Stephen, proposing they get together after class.

Ben was calling with great news. He'd gotten a big part in an off-Broadway play. He jabbered on about his part in the play, not even listening for a response from her. He even read a few of his favorite lines to her, never asking if it was a good time to talk or how her weekend had been. She was grateful for the latter oversight. As he talked, her guilt and his apparent excitement kept her from interrupting him. Finally, during a brief pause, she told him that she needed to leave immediately or be late for class.

"Is everything all right?" Ben asked, in a tone that started Ally's guilty heart pounding.

"Of course, what do you mean?" she asked.

He said that he called Saturday night, continued calling almost all night, and she never answered.

"Oh, I just, I got kind of drunk and slept over at a classmate's apartment, so I wouldn't have to drive home. Why didn't you leave a message on my machine?"

He said he wanted to surprise her with his good news and hear her reaction firsthand.

"Oh," she responded.

"Why didn't you call last night?" Ben asked. "We always talk on Sunday nights."

Startled, she blurted out, "Ben, I'm going to be late for class. Can we talk tonight?"

"Okay, sure," he said sadly.

Ally put down the phone. The glow from the weekend was gone. Reality was back, asking for explanations. Ben seemed to care about the relationship just when Ally needed his usual indifference.

Then she hurried toward school.

Ally takes the steps to the classroom two at a time and opens the door tentatively. Ed stops talking and smiles broadly. "Ms. Hansen, you appear to be running late today. Glad to know you're fallible like the rest of us."

Ally smiles and slides into her chair. She looks up and glances tensely at Stephen. Is she having second thoughts about the weekend or just nervous about being late? He shifts around in his chair. He looks back at Ally who looks as if she's listening closely to Ed's opening comments about authenticity in the client/therapist relationship.

"The therapist responds with his or her real experience of the client," Ed says. "It's a difficult concept to teach since it's more about how to be with a client rather than how to do something with the client."

Stephen continues to wonder about Ally and barely hears the discussion. He tunes in long enough to hear Ed say something about how authenticity of the therapist is considered critical by the Gestalt, Humanistic and most analytical schools of therapy. "And while it's difficult to define authenticity," he says, "several studies demonstrate that the client's perception that the therapist is honest and has integrity is critical to a positive and healthy therapist/client relationship."

Ally's anxiety gets another jolt when she hears Ed talk about the importance of honesty. "There's way too much lying going on in this culture," he says. "Lying to make you feel better and others feel better. It's no wonder everyone feels so bad."

Ally imagines herself telling Ben she's started dating someone. "No big deal, it's just lonely here and I want someone to spend some time with," she might say. She imagines Ben's disappointed face, but then she thinks, "Well, what did you expect? If we were engaged, or if you let me talk about my life more, maybe we wouldn't be having these problems." Then she worries about him dating someone. Obviously, if she can relieve her loneliness, he has the right to do the same. What if he falls in love with some beautiful actress? If she tells him she's dating someone, would he ask if they slept together? That thought causes her to feel sick. She wants to run out of the room. She almost jumps when she hears Stephen speaking.

"It seems to me that there must be some limits to honesty or authenticity," Stephen says. "For instance, if the therapist is feeling sexually attracted to a client, I don't think it would be appropriate to share with them or if he finds something they say boring or disgusting..."

Ed interrupts. "What do you think you would you do, Stephen, if you were with a client feeling sexually attracted?" he asks.

"I guess...I guess...I probably would certainly not express it," Stephen says. "That would confuse and maybe even traumatize the client. I guess I'd make a note of it and discuss it in supervision. I'd try to understand how what the client was discussing led to sexual feelings."

"That's a good answer Stephen. Or I should say, it's the right answer for a jury of your peers or a licensing board. But what would you say about the reaction itself, the sexual attraction? Doesn't it just reflect your nature?"

Ed hesitates and looks around the room. "I agree that to act on it would be inappropriate and could cost you your livelihood. But sexual attraction is natural, right? We just want to have it in the proper context." Ed smiles at his audience.

Maggie speaks up and says sexual behavior between therapist and client is sexual abuse and results in a characteristic pattern of post-traumatic stress in the client. She's passionate, clear, and predictable, especially when the subject turns to issues of abuse.

Ed quickly points out that they were not talking about sexual behavior; they were talking about sexual attraction. "Of course, sexual behavior between a therapist and a client results in all kinds of destructiveness for the client. But let's make a strong distinction between attraction and acting on that. One is normal, and absolutely will happen at some point in your career. Hopefully you'll be discussing your reactions with a supervisor. To act on the impulse is narcissistic and destructive. But let's get back on track. We were talking about the importance of honesty with your client."

Ally looks at Stephen, who looks so calm and confident. The professors seem to treat him almost like one of them. She feels a little jealous as she watches him make some other statement about the importance of honesty, but she cannot hear him. She's lost in remembering how kind and gentle he was the whole weekend, never tiring of being with her, listening, talking, laughing, touching.

She thinks about Ben, and then looks over at Stephen, listening to Ed. His body seems oriented away from her, and he isn't looking at her as he usually did before their weekend together. Was he finished with her? Had they stayed too long with each other over the weekend?

She feels lonely and embarrassed. She starts thinking about Ben again. Had she blown it with him for a fantasy weekend? Would she be able to convince him that she was just at a friend's house? He always eventually believed her regardless of the circumstances.

And then her thoughts turn back to Stephen. Was this the way he did things, to have a woman fall completely for him and then disappear? He was so connected over the weekend.

"Ally," Ed says, jarring her from her wondering. "I saw that you have a second session scheduled for tomorrow at three with the client I supervised you on…the angry young man. That's going to be a session that we all observe. So we'll all see one another for observation then," he says before standing.

The room erupts in a welter of sounds and movement. Ally sees Stephen turn away from her and begin talking to Charles. He has his back to her as she slowly gathers her books. He turns slightly, glancing in Ally's direction.

"You want to go get some coffee?" she manages.

"Yeah, that would be great," he says.

"What do you mean?" Charles asks. "We've got to leave in a few minutes for the prison. You were going to ride with me, right?"

"Oh yeah," Stephen says to Charles, and turns to Ally. "Can we talk later? I can call you tonight. Will that work?" Stephen says, as Charles looks on. Ally agrees and decides to visit Atlanta's most alternative neighborhood, Little Five Points, only a short train ride away.

After walking from the train, she heads toward the Aurora coffee shop to get a sandwich, a cup of coffee, and hopefully a respite from her two pressing worries – tomorrow's session with her client and tonight's conversation with Ben. She passes a shop, "Tattoo Voodoo," and looks in the window. She sees several girls only a few years younger than her getting various body parts pierced and tattooed.

She pulls herself away and continues walking but slows as she sees a man standing about twenty yards ahead of her in the middle of the sidewalk. He's wearing a filthy stained winter coat with the collar turned up on his neck even though it's warm and sunny. His long gray hair is matted, and his prickly gray whiskers appear to be about three- or four-day's growth. She wonders why he continues to shave, even if irregularly, despite his obviously having quit just about everything else. She worries that he'll harass her for money. She walks past him as fast as she can.

Safely in the coffee shop, Ally looks out the window, relieved that the man did not follow her. Just one more thing to unnerve her, she thinks. She orders a smoked turkey sandwich with avocado and honey mustard on wheat with a cup of coffee. She walks to the window and looks for the homeless man.

She looks back at the barista who took her order. "There's a man out there who's kind of scary. Do you think he'd bother me if I sat at a table outside?"

"Are you're talking about Harry?" he asks, "Older white man, with long gray hair, heavy coat, paranoid eyes?"

"Exactly."

"Harry won't bother you. He's completely harmless. He's definitely more afraid of you than you are of him."

"I wouldn't be too sure of that," Ally says.

"No, really. He's here every morning when we open and every night when we close.

He used to be a chemistry professor at GU and word is he fried his brain on psychedelics. I've tried to talk to him before, but if you talk to him beyond really superficial stuff he gets scared and walks away. Like they always say, 'Don't judge a book by its grimy cover.'"

As Ally moves outside, it occurs to her that, as a psychologist, it will be her job to resist such reflexive judgments. As usual and despite her academic achievements, a wave of inadequacy passes through her. She thinks about her client tomorrow, an angry young man with suicidal fantasies. He was so dark and confusing, talking about nihilistic writers one minute and the superiority of vinyl records the next, and everything he talked about was in this heavy monotone. And now she was supposed to have a second session with him in front of all her fellow students, her faculty advisor, and her new lover. She knows now, thanks to the apparently homeless professor, that she must confront her fear.

She knows at heart, too, that the same thing that interests her about psychology leads her to love the Little Five Points neighborhood with all its quirkiness and eccentricity – from its thrift stores and head shops to its costumed pedestrians. The painted buildings' exteriors, she describes to herself, as starving artists on LSD. In a way, she thinks, all the images form a kind of poetry Ed talked about. The more you look, the deeper you sink into an understanding of this alternative culture's purpose, just as happens with individuals.

That prompted her to immediately think of Ben. When he visited the area with her, he felt uncomfortable with the area. It had a chaotic feel that seemed to turn him off. She could imagine Stephen partying here all night.

She pulls a notebook from her book bag to make notes for her session tomorrow. Instead she finds herself writing everything she knows she needs to tell Ben that night. She knows they must end their relationship. She'd tried to bring it up last August on her parent's dock, but Ben always changed the subject, and she couldn't press it further. During their almost nightly phone conversations and monthly visits for long weekends since then, they never mentioned their future or even their present. Both of them talked about their new lives in cities far away from each other.

Ally realizes that she and Ben have continued their relationship only because being alone was unacceptable to them. She shudders. Except for her relationship with Stephen that is a few days old, she's completely alone. She buries her face in her hands and sobs.

That night, she makes the call. It turns out to be anti-climactic. Of course, he knew it was coming. She tells him the truth, or most of it, and he understands and does not ask for any details. "He always understands," she thinks, as she puts down the phone, feeling lighter than she has in weeks.

The next day, she conducts the second session with her client, the angry young man. He's like a different person. "I sense that your mood has improved," she says to him.

"Everything is incredible when you're in love, right?" he asks. He tells her he started dating another English major the night after his first session with Ally. They had spent the last several nights sharing their passion for vampire novels, the Sex Pistols and lots more. "She's a vampiress, you know," he says, wryly.

Ally smiles with him and must admit he has a point about things getting better when you're in love.

"My problem, though, isn't falling in love. That's easy for me," the young man says. "The hard part is not fucking it up once I'm in it."

As if on a dime, the angry young man turns to his pessimism about past failures in relationships. Ally spends the rest of the session trying to help her client believe that this new relationship might be different.

The feedback session, except for one comment by Ed, is unambiguously complimentary. Ed's comment is more of a question. He asks

Ally if she thinks there is any reason to believe the client might have been accurately describing his futility in relationships and if she might have been premature in trying to convince him that this time would be different.

"I think," she says, "that if he has a more optimistic view of things he might get a better outcome." She liked her comment even if Ed did not seem convinced.

"But that doesn't matter. What matters is that it's over and I didn't faint or vomit," Ally says to Stephen as they walk away from the clinic. "Let's go somewhere and get trashed."

At around midnight, Stephen and Ally are sitting at the bar in the Highland Tap in a haze of cigarette smoke and a mental fog of marijuana and alcohol, still ravished by their new love. Ally looks at Stephen dreamily.

"I really loved having you there with me today when I was getting feedback," she says. She kisses him lightly on the lips. "Even if I had to worry about being humiliated, I knew that you were there with me."

"You didn't need my support, you did great," Stephen says, wrapping her hair behind her ear. "I thought it went great. I think I've told you that five times now."

"I know," Ally says. "I just like hearing it. Let's talk about something else, okay?"

Stephen swivels her chair in his direction and closes her knees inside his.

"Let's go home and take our clothes off." Stephen says.

"Can we spend the night at my place? It's less than a mile so we can walk," Ally says. "I sure don't think we should drive."

Stephen and Ally walk down Virginia Avenue toward Ally's apartment. They hold each other closely, stop and kiss occasionally, and talk about having sex on one of the lawns.

Chapter 16

SLEEPING, WAKING AND IMAGINATION

STEPHEN IS SITTING BEHIND *the flight controls of a small propeller airplane, the kind of plane that you might find yourself in when flying out of a small town, maybe a small ski town, whose closest major airport is about 150 miles away. You brace yourself as you're motoring down the runway, and it seems like forever before you finally feel the front tires ease off the tarmac. At last, you think, but it seems like thirty, maybe forty seconds before the back wheels lift off. In the interim, you have considered the comparison costs of alternative travel options. At liftoff, you turned around and discovered that everyone else in the plane was staring, stiff-faced.*

Now, Stephen sits in the first captain's seat, straining to see out of the tiny windshield obstructed by pouring rain and slow-moving windshield wipers. "Thank God it's not snowing," he says to his copilot, looking on the bright side of things. He breathes deeply, trying to relax, "First get your emotions under control, then think about what you have to do," his father used to tell him before important times at bat in close baseball games.

He releases his breath slowly, then glances at the copilot. He is surprised to see Charles sitting there. When did he learn to fly? Charles is calmly reading a newspaper, his feet propped against the dashboard. "How can you be so calm in such an awful storm?" Stephen asks Charles.

"I'm always scared; why should this be any different?" Charles replies.

The plane climbs and rocks from side to side in rough air. Suddenly Charles lunges toward the windshield and yells, "Lift this thing up, man, you're going to hit those trees!" Both pilots impulsively rise up in their seats, superstitiously trying to lighten the plane that barely nicks the top of the tallest tree. "You motherfucker, you almost fucked us up!" Charles shouts, then lets loose with more invectives, uncharacteristic for him.

Stephen is speechless, not because of Charles's tongue-lashing, but because he has spotted snow-covered mountains not that far ahead and now the windshield wipers fight to move thick white snow that has begun falling. He hears Charles say something but it is so noisy that he can't make out the details. He knows that it is some kind of apology, and now Charles wants Stephen to high-five to acknowledge the apology. He obliges half-heartedly, concentrating on the mountains in front of him.

He lifts the steering mechanism to climb above the mountains, redirecting the plane almost straight up. He sighs with relief, having missed the mountains, and looks over at Charles for congratulations. But Charles's distracted, looking back in the direction of the passengers. Charles leans close to Stephen, elbows him, and says, "Man, check out that babe in the first seat on the left." Stephen lets the plane even out a bit, looks down at the pyramidal mountain range, and then looks back over his shoulder. He spots his mother in a dress with a slit exposing her *tanned legs. She is barelegged in black pumps and looks like she's lost a few pounds. He can see how Charles would call her a babe. She's drinking a frozen drink out of a very tall, very tacky glass, the kind of glass you might see some drunken reveler carrying at The French Quarter in New Orleans or Underground Atlanta. Stephen squints to read the writing on the glass, "Live soul music at Daddy's Rib Shack."*

Stephen is embarrassed and a little angry that his mother is acting like such a fool. Who drinks out of those glasses anymore, and Jesus, to carry one on the plane? And then it gets worse. Now she seems to be returning Charles's admiration, smiling a smile you never want to see from your mother. And Stephen is furious with Charles; surely, if the situation were reversed, he would not be acting all interested in Charles's mother.

Stephen sees some movement from the back of the plane. It is Ed, running toward the cockpit in a pilot's uniform. Stephen immediately knows he is an off-duty pilot, obviously angry and scared. As he gets closer, he tells Stephen the plane is flying upside down and they need to, "take corrective action ASAP." Ed repeats those words, looking out the windshield with Charles and Stephen.

The three men stare at nothing, nothing, but faded yellow empty space, the reflection of the headlight off the thick clouds. The space turns pink every few seconds as the red lights from the wings blink on and off. They are completely locked into clouds and cannot see a thing. The sound of the struggling engine is all they hear. Charles leans over, slides his hand underneath his seat and pulls out a manual. Stephen notices that Charles looks washed out, kind of a gray-white. Ed, too, is this same gray-white that looks to Stephen as flesh with an absence of the under-glow of human life. He looks at his own reflection in the mirror and is horrified that he has this same coloring, like he and the others are from the same repulsive race.

Charles opens the manual and begins chanting or praying or something. Stephen looks closer and sees the words "Holy Bible" in gold letters on the worn-out book. "What the fuck is wrong with Charles?" he thinks.

"Just as I thought," Ed says. "Look at your gauges, Stephen. They all show that we're probably flying upside down."

Stephen looks at Charles. Both men are horrified.

"All we can do is wait..." Ed says, "and when we get out of the clouds we'll have one chance to get this thing right. Do you want me to do it?" he asks Stephen.

Stephen wants more than anything to please Ed. Resolutely he shakes his head no. He'll handle it.

Charles gives him a casual thumbs up.

The three men stare into the yellow white space as snow accumulates on the windshield. Stephen looks back at his mother, looking out the window with her legs crossed, showing lots of skin. He understands Charles's interest in her. She looks very sensual. If he's going to die tonight, he's glad he's finally realized his mother is sexy.

Suddenly, the plane emerges from the clouds into the dark night. Ed lunges toward the windshield and screams, "Now!" Stephen moves with incredible skill, flipping the plane completely over. He looks out the window in the direction that should be down and sees twinkling stars. Down is up! They had been oriented correctly before Stephen's adroit flipping of the plane. Stephen jerks his head toward Ed who has fallen over and is bleeding from his forehead. "What happened?" he asks his coach.

"I said, 'we were probably...probably upside-down,' not definitely upside-down. I just wanted you to check. Oh no..." Ed says, straining to get up off the floor.

"Oh God, I let him and everyone down as usual," Stephen thinks as he watches the tiny plane head directly downward toward mountains. He desperately tries to maneuver the controls, but nothing is working.

Charles sits calmly, reading his Bible. As the tiny plane spins toward earth, Stephen screams, over and over, "Mother fucker, mother fucker!" Suddenly, he remembers that his mother is nearby. He wants one last look at her before he crashes.

And suddenly he's awake, sitting upright in his bed, saying, "Mother fucker," out loud. His heart is pounding so hard he can hear it. He looks around his room, filled with a pale blue light; the sun sits on the horizon. He thinks he should make himself a cup of coffee and write down the dream for his supervision session with Ed. A few seconds later, he rolls over and goes back to sleep.

His alarm clock wakes him up a few hours later. He forces his feet onto the floor. He has an hour before Ally arrives. He wonders about his earlier dream, the one he promised himself he'd remember as he slipped back to sleep. He remembers being behind the controls of an airplane, an image of the faded yellow clouds, a lot of yelling and loud motor noises, and then a falling plane. A crazy dream. He tries remembering other details as he takes a shower. Washing his hair, he has an image of a bloody head on the floor of the plane. God, what a gruesome dream.

He wonders what has made him have such a bizarre dream. He remembers that Ally is coming over shortly with two doses of Ecstasy. Maybe that is what he's afraid of. It might be a sign of sanity to worry about a drug manufactured by a chemistry graduate student he has never met, and worse still, who was Ally's high school boyfriend. Or maybe it was his feeling of jealousy that Ally scored the drug when she visited the ex-boyfriend at his parents' lake house, conveniently just a few miles from her parents' place at the lake where she spent the past weekend. The first time she mentioned having seen the ex-boyfriend was when he asked her where she got two hits of Ecstasy. Stephen sought details of the reunion while trying to seem cool. Ally assured him that she and the chemist were "just friends," but, hey, he could imagine that she'd told Ben something similar about him when they first started dating.

Stephen's real fear, he understood, was about the effects of taking an unknown chemical. Call him crazy. That same fear was there when he took LSD in college, all three or four times. It was there when he ate some psilocybin mushrooms, though to a lesser extent since they were organic. He'd not lost cognitive skills, at least not noticeably, because of all that experimentation, or from all the years of sporadic marijuana use. Okay, the fucking dream seems clear now, he tells himself, walking into the main house. He's house-sitting for Dan and Randy who left town early that morning for a trip to Paris.

He puts a Leonard Cohen CD on the stereo, perfect music to begin a weekend of sex-and-drug experimentation. He hears Leonard Cohen's deep whisper: "Everybody knows that you love me baby, everybody knows that you really do. Everybody knows that you've been faithful, give or take a night or two. Everybody knows that you've been discreet, but there were so many people you just had to meet, without your clothes, and everybody knows."

He wonders who Ally did Ecstasy with the last time, and how many times, and why he should trust that the Ecstasy will not scramble his brain.

He walks into the master bedroom to make sure Dan and Randy left it neat and clean. The drapes in front of the French doors to their balcony are wide open. He opens the doors and steps out onto the balcony. He's greeted by a cool breeze, the twinkle of sunshine between swaying green leaved branches, and a scarlet cardinal. The bird crouches and then springs forward and flies a short distance to a bird feeder hanging from a branch. He eats quickly and goes back to the same limb. Stephen watches the cardinal look from side to side several times. And then a female cardinal lands on the feeder. She eats and then springs away.

Stephen leans on the rail of the balcony, feeling relaxed for the first time this morning. He thinks maybe it would be fun for the two of them to watch the birds while they're "tripping," at least during sexual breaks. He chuckles at his lasciviousness.

A moment later he hears Ally's car pulling up the driveway. He pulls the heavy arched oak door open for Ally who is enthusiastic as always. They embrace and kiss deeply, their bodies filled with desire and anticipation. Stephen takes her bag and they walk in the house.

"Dan gave us permission to use the master bedroom," Stephen says.

"I can't believe how excited I am," Ally says. "We have the whole weekend together, with no interruptions, in this really cool space," Ally says, as she walks with Stephen's arm around her toward the master bedroom.

"I'm excited, too," Stephen says.

"Wow, what a bed!" Ally exclaims as she walks into the master bedroom.

The couple sits on Dan and Randy's king-sized bed, covered with a heavy gold comforter. The bed has no headboard, but the wall behind the bed is padded with the same comforter-type material and there are stacks and stacks of pillows below. They immediately wrap themselves around each other. During a break for air, Ally leans back from Stephen. "I want to clear something up," she says. "I could tell you were upset about the stuff of, you know, me getting the X from my ex." She smiles self-consciously. "And with me seeing him on my trip without telling you, like it was a secret. Let me say that, really, for me, he's just an old friend at this point. I have no interest in him or anyone else but you. You're all I think about, always. You know that, right?"

The last thing Stephen wants is to look jealous, or worse, like someone who would lose his cool over something as small as not telling him that she saw an ex-boyfriend she had no feelings for. But still. "I can't understand why you didn't tell me that you saw him. I mean, you had to deliberately not tell me, right?"

Ally turns pink. "I guess I just didn't want you to... worry or anything since he means nothing to me. I mean, other than a friend."

Stephen looks at the pinks and whites of the skin around Ally's eyes. "I'd rather know things. I'd rather know you. I don't want you to hold back," he says, then looks away briefly.

"I want to know you, too," she whispers. "I don't want you to hold anything back with me, either."

The drama of the frightened lover only needs an ending. They kiss passionately, opening their eyes to each other the way they did on that first night...during the lightning.

About thirty minutes later, Ally lies across the bed looking out the French doors, her chin propped on her hands as Stephen returns with two glasses of orange juice. She's naked except for pink socks pulled up to the middle of her calves.

"Did you, em, bring the stuff?" Stephen asks, setting the glasses on the nightstand nearest the balcony.

"I did. It's in my bag. You ready?" she asks.

"I'm ready as I'm going to be," Stephen says. "I've got a joint, too. Maybe we should sit on the balcony. I don't want the smoke in the room."

"It's such a beautiful day," Ally says, getting up.

"Don't put on any clothes though," Stephen says.

"Okay, but you need to take this off, too." Ally pulls on his t-shirt. "We have to be equally naked."

Stephen nods and pulls off his t-shirt.

They sit on the padded chaise lounge chairs. Ally hands Stephen his hit of Ecstasy. She holds her juice glass up. "Cheers," she says, dropping the tiny piece of paper on her tongue. She smiles and takes a sip of juice.

Stephen inspects his, as if he could discern any flaw, before cautiously putting it in his mouth. He chases it with the juice. "I hope we don't lose too many brain cells," he says.

"We've got some to spare," Ally reassures, looking away at the trees and gardens below them.

"Speak for yourself," Stephen says.

After a passionate kiss, Stephen reaches for some matches and lights the joint. "This ought to help mellow us out," he says, taking a long drag and passing it to Ally. They sit quietly, gazing out at Dan and Randy's beautiful yard.

A little later. "It's been thirty minutes and I don't feel a thing. I hope this stuff works."

Ally nods her head while gazing at a swaying branch.

Stephen kisses Ally, pulls her on top of him and closes his eyes. Her warmth feels good. When he finally opens his eyes, which he does because he feels momentarily lost, he becomes absorbed in the rich texture of burning sunshine, glimmering gold hair, and moist bodies. After about fifteen minutes of this, the couple decides that they absolutely have to skinny dip in the pool. As they walk to the pool, they stop and kiss every three or four steps. As they reach the pool, they stop at the cherub that squirts water into the pool and have sex with Ally braced against the chubby little angel. A short time later, the two lovers are in the Jacuzzi, laughing about how completely insane they are for having a three-way with a cherub.

Ally shows Stephen the colors of the leaves reflected in the pool water, Monet at Giverny, and then talks about how she wants to always live as they're living right now, consumed in the moment. Stephen agrees, and they make a drug-soaked promise to always live in their experience.

Stephen's consciousness slips back into the reflected colors and a meditative silence falls between the couple. He thinks about his euphoria and decides that it's because he's completely free from any inhibition and isn't distracted by his own thoughts. He's living completely in his senses and that is what creates the euphoria.

About two hours later, Ally's head rests on Stephen's chest. They're back in the master bedroom, exhausted. She slides up toward his mouth and opens hers to him. Stephen lets his teeth gently touch Ally's teeth. He imagines by touching his teeth to Ally's, he can feel what it's like to live in her mouth. He closes his eyes, and with one sense temporarily shut down, his ideas flow. He describes to himself that the flow of his ideas is like mountain water rolling down ancient rock on the way to an infinite sea. As he presses his tongue against Ally's, he wonders if she can feel what he feels, that their tongues are merged, meshed, no longer separate, but something completely different, maybe like those lonely atoms that were so peaceful before they became fused with each other and became capable of rendering the planet into a billion fragmenting fragments whose rotation around the sun initially began in chaos, before forming this beautifully predictable pattern that could be recreated by a small child with the desire to let his hand move as it wants to, around and around in a circle, in an O, in a perfect globe that was once our planet.

Stephen gasps and opens his eyes. He sees that Ally is asleep. He listens to her deep breathing for a moment. He closes his eyes. He breathes in her smell, peeks at her cream and pink skin, pulls her closer, pulls the sheet up to cover her body to keep her warm, before hearing birdsong call to him. He looks toward the open French doors and tries to understand why he has felt so desperate for all these years. He does not feel any of that desperation right now, as he's stopped in the middle of his pleasure. He closes his eyes and thinks of himself as having sprinted, head down, into a primitive rainforest and then suddenly stopped or was stopped to be free and peaceful and observe beauty. There, in a majestic tree, perches a family of cardinals with contrasting colors everywhere around them.

He knows he's living in the moment and dreams of holding onto it or understanding it so he can get to this moment in the future. It's the moment he has always longed for. He has been desperate, so desperate that he's always running, and yet his search has been to be completely still… and simply experiencing the moment. The birds that are always there. He becomes aware of the slow and deep beating of his heart. He follows a bead of sweat from his hairline to the edge of his eye and experiences only that movement. He feels the burning, salty sweat invade his eye. He feels love for the woman in the bed next to him.

Then he flashes on an image of his mother drinking from a frozen daiquiri glass. He sits up in bed. The entire morning's dream returns, from the rain soaked limping liftoff to the death spiral toward the white-capped mountains. He slowly settles back in the bed and closes his eyes. He sees Ed lying on the floor of the airplane in a puddle of blood. No, the man in the image wasn't Ed. It was his father who was the other pilot, the coach who asked him to slow down and pay attention.

Ally slowly turns onto her side and tries in vain to open her eyes. Stephen hears the birdsong. He cannot remember what he was thinking about before the image of his father. He hopes his feelings for Ally are true feelings of love, of being moved to poetry. Can this be a true connection of souls…with Ecstasy? It feels therapeutic, like a merging of the beauty in the world with the beauty of love's too often blocked clarity.

He remembers that he and Ally had committed to each other an hour or so earlier. They had decided that even though they had only been dating for a couple of months they would tell the other students in their next group therapy appointment that they were a couple. And they imagined a future together: "We know where each other's bodies are in space so we're in a kitchen cooking for our kids and we're moving with each other like fish do in aquariums," Stephen offered. "We know and accept each other completely and love each other not in spite of but because of our differences," Ally added.

He closes his eyes and pulls the sheet over his own shoulders while moving closer to Ally. He joins Ally in sleep at the moment a cardinal lands on the iron railing of the balcony. The crimson cardinal, the one from the morning, investigates the room. He bounces up and flips around and spots the female cardinal on the branch where he knew she'd be.

PART II

Chapter 17

SUPERVISION: LOSS AND CONNECTION

IT'S NINE O'CLOCK IN THE MORNING and already eighty-four degrees when Stephen gets in his car and heads to a supervision session with Ed. It's going to be a long hot day, almost as sultry as those days in movies set in the South, the ones filled with betrayal, murder, corruption, bigotry and the like, where the actors speak in Hollywood Southern accents while strutting around with no shirts on and sweating like they're in a sauna.

Stephen arrives and walks to Ed's office. Delores, the 55-year-old secretary in charge of admissions and everything else of importance in the clinical program since the late sixties, greets him. "Where you been hiding your handsome self all summer, Stephen?" she asks.

Stephen smiles at Delores and explains that he has been away from the department because he has been working at the prison and taking it easy.

"Ed's in there," she says, pointing to his door. "I'm sure he'll be glad to see you. After me, he's your biggest fan," Delores says, her eyes twinkling. "Dr. Ed's high as a kite these days, you know."

"What do you mean?"

"I'm not going to be the one to spill the beans, but I'll say this much, he's got a new girlfriend...one with as much...dignity as he has," she says.

"Really..." Stephen says, and before he can ask for specifics, Delores interrupts him.

"You must miss Ally with her being home for the summer. Ally's one of my girls, you know," Delores says with pride.

Stephen stutters but manages to acknowledge that he has missed her just before Ed steps into the reception area.

"We're a few weeks away from the beginning of your second year," Ed says to Stephen, as he makes his customary tea before starting supervision. "How you doing?"

"Good...great. I'm looking forward to starting the semester. I've got NeuroPsych with Coleman, Advanced Statistics with Williams and Supervision with you. I think I've got my hands full," Stephen says.

"I know you're not worried about me. The other two might be worth starting to prepare for."

Stephen nods his head. Ed brings up his favorite subject – the intramural softball tournament. "That was a disappointing loss to the political science folks," he says, as if it were a day or two earlier instead of a month ago.

"Yeah, but we did great in the tournament," Stephen says. "We came within one game of the final four. That's not bad."

"You played great the whole tournament and some of us did our part," Ed says, shaking his head slowly. "But we should have made it past the political science department."

Stephen watches Ed stare out the window and massage his dog's neck. "Who ended up winning?" Stephen finally asks.

"The PE department, or as they like to be called the Big Jocks, of course, the third year in a row... bastards," Ed says, grimacing. "Their closest game was in the finals against the law school. I think they won twenty-four to seven, or something like that...it never was close."

"Next year we beat them, right?" Ed says, his eyes boring into Stephen's.

"The PE department? I don't know about that, Ed," Stephen says, looking away. "I thought we played our best game of the season against them during the regular season, over our heads really, and they beat us by, what, ten runs?"

"Well, maybe I'm dreaming," Ed says, sighing heavily. "I just wish you didn't sound so sure of yourself."

"Well, I don't mean to be negative," Stephen says. "It's just that I've played on a lot of teams. Some won championships, and some didn't, but you usually could tell if, you know, you were close to another team's level. They have a lot more students to pull from, like most of the other departments. And most of their students are ex-college athletes."

"True, but with you at shortstop and Charles's bat in our lineup, I believe we can compete with anyone. You make two or three plays a game that no one has ever made for us...but I'm surprised by your pessimism, to be honest."

"I can see that," Stephen says, smiling broadly. He still cannot believe Ed is completely serious. "I think I'm just being realistic."

Ed smiles back at Stephen. "Realistic is what everyone, optimistic or pessimistic, thinks they're being. You sound pretty pessimistic to me, but you'd probably say that I'm being too optimistic."

"If you're thinking that we can actually beat the PE department, yeah I'd call that a tad optimistic," Stephen says. He laughs, surprised that Ed does not join him.

"You're an athlete. Haven't you found that it's crucial to believe you're going to win the game? Isn't that necessary for optimal performance?" Ed asks.

Stephen blinks. He cannot believe he has been challenging Ed who is regarded as a principal researcher on the effects of beliefs on optimal performance. In fact, Ed's dissertation was the seminal work in the area of understanding how beliefs influence behavior, published at a time when beliefs were not even discussed in academic psychology. His follow-up studies led to the emerging field of applied cognitive psychology.

Stephen knows the research well. "Yeah, I do know that when I've believed in myself and my team, I've played, we've played, better," he says. "I also know your research shows that athletes rated by their coaches as exceptional performers were 'persistent optimists.' They saw theirs and their team's success as a result of their skill and predictive of future success. On the other hand, they attributed their failures and their team's failures to bad luck and didn't think they were predictive of the future."

"How about average athletes?" Ed asks.

Stephen smiles. "Athletes rated as average performers, on the other hand, were about equally as likely to attribute their success and failures to luck or skill. They tended to predict future success only when they had succeeded in the immediate past. When they had recently failed, they predicted failure on the next task, at least relative to the exceptional performers."

"That's an excellent summary of my early work," Ed says.

"Didn't you also study optimal performance in other areas? Like pilots and executives…and the results held up well across different areas?" Stephen asks.

"That's very good, Stephen." Ed says, his expression oddly blank. He sighs and looks at his pudgy dog. "I'd have to pass you on your comprehensive exam on that question. That pretty much summarizes the conclusions of ten years of my research."

Ed exhales and folds his hands on his chest and is quiet for a moment. "I'll be honest. Ten years is a long time in a man's life, and I don't fully believe in that research anymore," Ed says, glancing up at Stephen. "A slight correction, I know that optimists perform better on certain tasks of skill. I just don't think that means as much as I used to think it did."

Stephen hears Ringo chewing intensely on her leg. He feels confused by Ed's words.

"When I started doing that work," Ed says, "I thought I was studying something bigger than optimism versus pessimism. I thought when I talked about being optimistic, I was tapping into something as permanent and as powerful as intellect. I thought I was beginning to understand a concept related to movement in its entirety, as fundamental as the ability to dance or paint or even express sexuality. I thought I was taking a first step in uncovering something important about the mind creating the life or the story of it. I thought that optimistic belief was actually a subset of a larger cognitive style: actually if I'm honest, a product of an emerging self. And optimal performance was something that tapped into the genius behind the shortstop's first step toward the ball even before it leaves the bat or the dancer's movement as she twists around in the air and lands precisely on the ball of her foot or the artist's hand as it moves along a canvas. I actually thought I was beginning the process of exploring all of that."

Ed takes a breath before continuing. "But I was wrong. I think my dissertation chair thought I was psychotic when I wrote a lot of that in my proposal. He shortened twenty pages of that and allowed me to include one speculative paragraph. After all these years, I know he was right. My dissertation should be taken for face value: Optimists perform better than pessimists on certain tasks of skill, especially non-artistic ones."

Ed takes a long sip of tea. He puts his cup down and looks at Stephen. He smiles gently. "Optimism and optimal performance," he says, his eyes twinkling, "are really only relevant if you're trying to win a huge ball game, which one day I hope to do. In that case, I want my shortstop to believe we can win.

"But if you believe that we can't beat the PE department I can't change that. That kind of thinking, that I can talk you out of your beliefs, is the foolishness of the reformed behaviorists around here." He motions with his head toward his door. "You know, the ones who used to claim that our thoughts were irrelevant. 'Epiphenomena,' they called them, like we were products of our 'reinforcement history,' just like rats that had learned to press a bar for food or choose the correct path in a maze. The strict behaviorist didn't have any room for seeing the human being as active in interpreting, understanding, and even determining our lives. Now, of course, they want to call themselves cognitive-behaviorist, but they regard thoughts and feelings as something you can just change, and suddenly everything is better."

Ed is on a roll and Stephen is feeling even more overwhelmed than earlier. He does not quite understand everything Ed is saying but is intrigued.

"My colleague Merv is a splendid example of that," Ed continues. "Ten years ago, at case conferences, he could be counted on to take up fifteen minutes of everyone's time making this big show about how what the client thought was irrelevant. If someone was depressed, he'd want them to contract to have a few positive experiences. If they had anxiety, he'd want them to learn deep muscle relaxation. He didn't care what they were depressed about. I'm not saying that teaching relaxation to an anxious client isn't helpful or..."

Stephen interrupts. "Yeah, I hear your point. Going to the gym is great, learning to relax will help, but what about the real stuff in their lives that needs to change?"

"Exactly," Ed exclaims. "That profoundly depressed patient might have been sexually abused or been to Viet Nam and felt abandoned when he returned or might not know how to give and receive love or all sorts of things that are important to address directly. And Merv thought all of that was irrelevant."

Ed looks at Stephen grimly. "I guess the bottom line is: Can we and should we try to turn our clients toward rationality and away from emotions regardless of the circumstances?"

Stephen smiles and nods.

Ringo rises slowly and slides her head under Stephen's hand. Stephen begins scratching her head.

Ed watches Stephen touch his old friend, before Ringo's legs slowly give way to the pull of gravity and she plops her belly on the floor.

Stephen takes a sip of his tea and clears his throat. "What about the research that shows cognitive behavioral approaches reduce depression, anxiety and lots of other problems?" he asks.

"That's a good question," Ed says, leaning forward slightly. "For years we've been able to show that anxiety, depression, and even personality disorders all get better at least to some extent, depending upon one variable—the degree to which the client experiences a bond with his therapist. Period. Notice I didn't say anything about the orientation of the therapist or the type of therapy they were doing. It's the relationship that's important. Cognitive behaviorists attribute their help to the type of therapy. Of course, others did that in the past.

"For me the story about therapy research isn't that one school is superior. It's that the help begins with the bond between the therapist and the client." Ed looks away for a moment. "I've gone off a bit, haven't I?" he says.

He takes a deep breath and continues. "But getting back to optimism and performance, let me tell you my story. When I was a freshman in high school, I weighed 110 pounds, but I knew I was going to make the varsity football team. Before the year was over, I started at defensive back. I was the only freshman on the team. I weighed 140 pounds when I graduated high school, but I'd been all-conference two years in a row and got a full scholarship to Penn State. I was defensive back there my sophomore through senior years."

"You must have had a lot of talent to be that size and start for a major college," Stephen says.

"I had tremendous desire and belief in possibility; my talent was just a bit above average. The whole time I was in college I knew I was going to play professional football. I knew it the way that I'd known I was going to make the high school team. I thought that if you wanted something bad enough and were willing to work for it every moment of your life, you would get it. And I kept getting it. My obsession with outcome and success was because all I cared about was success. That was everything for me..."

Ed's eyes wander for a moment, as if lost in his memories. "Between my sophomore and junior year of college, I had my left knee operated on. And then the next year, I had the other knee opened up, not the way they do it now, but laid open, where they cut through the working parts to get to the parts that weren't working."

"I've seen your scars when you wear shorts in softball," Stephen says.

"I didn't quit planning to play professional football until none of the pro scouts stopped by my locker and my letters for tryouts were turned down. I had to revise my personal theory of free will to say that you could have anything that you wanted as long as you didn't blow your knees out trying to get it."

"I guess that's an important revision," Stephen says. "If you made that revision then, and your research was based on your own beliefs about your life, why didn't that influence your hypothesis? I mean, you hypothesized that optimism led to optimal performance and your experience with your injuries was that it didn't always work out like that, right?"

"True," Ed says. "That's a very insightful question. The only explanation I have for my resilience in the face of failure is that I was so naïve in my optimism that even when the writing was on the wall, I ignored the evidence."

Stephen sits forward, reaching for his tea. "Did you ever do studies with painters or dancers, more artistic performance?" he asks.

"Some of my graduate students investigated that area. They found it hard to actually quantify artistic performance. The big problem was finding anyone who wasn't pessimistic in the visual arts. It's my experience that the most pessimistic guys on the planet do some of the best art. They might be optimistic about their ability to paint, but general optimism about the world, no, not really."

Stephen thinks about Randy, who seems optimistic. "No one was able to show a relationship between optimism and performance with artistic talent," Stephen says.

"Yeah, because there is no relationship. There are, or course, exceptions, but the most important composers of music, historically, have been among the most depressed and horribly pessimistic people ever on the earth. Writers and artists are for the most part not an optimistic and happy lot."

"And yet you often talk about a poetic sensibility," Stephen says.

"True enough," Ed says laughing. "I'm talking about the therapist's openness to thinking out-of-the-box, bringing creativity to the conversation, hearing the client's story – exactly the opposite of the prescriptive approaches of people like Merv."

"When did you change the focus of your research?" Stephen asks.

"Around '67 or '68. When I came here I was married," Ed says, looking into Stephen's eyes to try to determine if he knew that about him.

Stephen knew that Ed had an adult daughter, but he did not know the circumstances of her life. All the stories about Ed seemed to be about his dating much younger women. He assumed Ed was divorced.

"Let's just say that what I learned next in my life taught me that optimal performance was, for me at least, a trivial concept. What I learned next was that our beliefs, our lives, could be determined by things we have no control over, not the least of which are our losses."

Stephen nods, still feeling a little shocked by Ed's reversals in his thinking.

"The thing that changed my life, that I'm hesitant to get into, because honestly I just don't talk about it, is my wife's death." He looks at his teacup, lifts it slowly to his lips and takes a sip. "Stephen, I'm about to tell you a tragic story about a young woman and death. I don't know if that's something a young man wants to hear," he says, slowly raising his eyes to Stephen's.

Stephen looks at Ed. "I'm okay hearing it if you're okay telling it," he says.

Ed sighs and looks out the window.

"I'd been here about four years when my wife, Cynthia, got pregnant. She was eight months pregnant when she collapsed one day. She called a neighbor who rushed over, but she was already in some kind of shock from blood loss when Sue arrived. Sue called an ambulance and they took her to the hospital... and the doctors saved the baby, but Cynthia died."

"Oh…God that's…" Stephen mumbles.

"The doctors gave us a long explanation. They called it a form of pre-eclampsia. She lost a lot of blood before she got to the hospital and then during birth…she just bled to death."

Ed looks at Stephen, with a brief, sad smile, moves his head from side to side, and sighs deeply.

After a long silence, Ed speaks again. "For me, life was no longer about positive belief and unlimited destiny. It no longer had anything to do with any of that. It was about living and dying and a certain unwelcome randomness to it all."

Ed steels himself with a deep breath before continuing.

"Our daughter, Kelly, lived. Cynthia's parents basically raised her. In a way, maybe she took their daughter's place." Ed shakes his head. "They did a great job of providing Kelly a loving, stable environment. I suppose that's what all kids need. I visited on the academic breaks and when she got older, she came here for the summers. She's thirty, and… we do okay together. She's a social worker, kind of a communist type, you know what I mean, simple lifestyle, doesn't trust material wealth, which she gets from me. I hate to say it, but I don't think she trusts men. That's a surprise, huh? She's probably forgiven me intellectually, but emotionally I think she feels I abandoned her."

Ed looks at Stephen. Stephen clears his throat. "For someone who believed that you create your own reality," Stephen says, "or at least that you could will anything into existence, that must have…" Stephen's voice trails off.

"Yeah. I felt like something…everything had broken," Ed says, shrugging his shoulders. "That's when I discovered that the world included a certain randomness or an error component that I hadn't ever imagined."

Ed looks at the clock. "Okay that's as far as we can go into that. I hate to say it but we're almost over our time and I haven't even listened to your tape. Are you okay going over?"

"Yeah, definitely, I've got plenty of time," Stephen says.

Ed places the tape in the recorder, presses "play" and sits back.

The two men sit quietly for a long time and listen to Darnell rant, as always, about his unfair incarceration, about how psychological treatment is an attempt to enslave his mind, and about the absurdity of Stephen's questions. In between, Darnell talked about situations from his day-to-day experiences: the awful meals, the noise on the unit at night that kept him awake, and the lack of visits from family, which he attributed to the distance they'd have to travel. Ed noticed several instances of a marked contrast in the quality of Darnell's voice as he shifted from ranting about his incarceration to talking about specifics of his life in prison. He stops the tape. "This is the third time you've played a session for me with this guy, right?" he asks.

"Yeah."

"There is a certain... familiarity to them," he says, with a grin. "How often do you see him?"

"Twice a week. I've seen him probably fifty times since I started at the prison."

"That's very unusual... for a guy like him to tolerate that much closeness," Ed says, running his fingers through his gray hair. "My experience is that guys like this chase therapists off before anything positive can happen. My guess is it's your gentleness and respect for him that keeps up the communication."

Ed glances at the recorder then looks back at Stephen. "Do you notice," he says, thinking out loud, "that when he talks to you about things in the prison, day-to-day things, like the food, the noise, that sort of thing, he seems much calmer and sounds saner than when he's into all that stuff about being locked up against his will?"

Stephen nods slowly. He'd not noticed, but it made sense to him to hear Ed say it.

"We'll get back to that," Ed says. "Okay, let's just say some things out loud. He's classically psychotic: delusional, chaotic thinking, has loose associations, probably hallucinates at times. I suppose the treatment team calls him schizophrenic, right?"

"Yeah, paranoid schizophrenic," Stephen says.

"Sure. But let's assume he tells a story that gives his life some sort of meaning. What do you think brings meaning to this guy's life?"

"Ah, I don't know, I guess…getting out…being free…getting back home, that's all he ever talks about," Stephen says.

"I listened very carefully," Ed says, leaning back in his chair, "and I didn't hear him say anything about getting out of the mental health unit or the prison or even anything about life outside of prison."

"Really?" Stephen asks incredulously. "He talks about being wrongfully held in the prison and in the mental health unit almost nonstop. Occasionally, he talks about his hometown. He's from a small farm community, says there's about 400 residents, half of whom are supposedly related to him in some way."

"So," Ed says, "he talks about being held against his will. I'll give you that. But, I didn't hear anything about wanting to be free. The distinction isn't trivial, one implies helplessness, the other implies desire. Now, you said he was from a town full of relatives and he killed someone in the town."

"Yeah, his cousin," Stephen says.

"That's important. But let's go back to the question of what brings meaning to his life. What seems to be the central theme in his life?"

"That he's wrongfully incarcerated and wrongfully held in the mental health unit…" Stephen says.

"Exactly. That's what brings meaning to his life. His life, right now, is living in the mental health unit of the prison, and that life has meaning. The thing that he organizes his primary narrative around is that his imprisonment is wrongful and against his will, right?" Ed does not wait for an answer. "What does he have to do to get out of the mental health unit? Do they just hold people there for the whole time they're in prison if they're psychotic?"

Stephen looks around the room for a moment before he says, "No, usually they just come in when they're actively psychotic and we work with them with therapy and medication until they're stabilized, and then they go back to the regular prison."

"You said he's been in the mental health unit, in fact, in the same room, for ten years. Why, when you stabilize and move others out, has he stayed?"

"I don't really know. I guess because he's so hostile and threatening," Stephen says.

"You said you don't really see him as dangerous though. Are the others that you treat not hostile and threatening?" Ed asks.

"Yeah, some are actually more hostile and a lot of them have assaulted other inmates like he has, and some have even assaulted staff. And we fix them up and send them right back out. As far as I know, Darnell hasn't hurt anyone for ten years…or even broken any of the major rules."

"So maybe Darnell is comfortable right where he is," Ed says. "And maybe the staff is comfortable in some way with him there. He wouldn't be the first person stuck in his symptoms because he's comfortable and appeals to the profession that serves him."

Stephen thinks for a moment. "It's true that everyone likes Darnell in this odd sort of way."

"And look, he has his own private room, and his life has a very specific meaning in that room," Ed says. "He's martyred. He couldn't

162

stand it if he thought that he was living in that room because he felt safe and was being cared for by all of you do-gooder psychology types. He'd want to leave if he thought that. Is he in prison for life?"

"No, actually he comes up for parole every year. He's been in way longer than most inmates in for manslaughter."

Ed nods his head slowly. "Why doesn't he get paroled?" he asks.

Stephen chuckles, "He goes berserk every time he goes to the parole board. He goes in cursing, screaming, giving them the same lecture, he gives everyone on the unit. You've heard it. It's not the type of humble, 'I'll-never-do-it-again-I swear-please-believe-me-speech' the Parole Board likes to hear."

"So, his symptoms prevent him from leaving prison, too," Ed says.

"The staff on the unit who have known him for years think that the parole hearing is too much pressure for him," Stephen says. "He becomes more psychotic when he has to face a roomful of people who hold that much power over him," Stephen offers.

"This is an example of when the poet and the scientist disagree," Ed says, sitting forward in his chair. "The poet has to look at the story of the narrator's life and understand him in terms of the context of his own story. The words, the behavior, may seem crazy, may in fact be crazy according to most definitions, but what is being communicated still comes from this meaning-generating apparatus that he carries around with him, whether he's psychotic or not."

"I think the poet would say that he's got nowhere to go, no home to return to so he keeps himself locked up," Ed says before he looks directly into Stephen's eyes.

Stephen looks away. There is silence in the room as Stephen assimilates the information.

Ed slaps his knees gently and rises.

"That's really helpful, Ed," Stephen says, standing.

Ed walks Stephen to the door. "So, what was our session about today?" Ed asks in the doorway.

Stephen glances at the tile floor shining under the fluorescent lights. "You mean with Darnell?" he asks.

"No, yours and mine, our session. What was the thread that ran through it?"

Stephen looks at Ed's weary eyes and listens to the answer come from somewhere deep inside himself. "Loss," he answers.

"Yeah, Darnell's hometown, my wife..."

"Your belief in optimism and optimal performance," Stephen says, causing Ed to wince.

"Interesting, huh, how just about every word of the session was about loss, and yet I feel peaceful. You?"

"I feel...peaceful is a good description," Stephen says.

"Good being with you, Stephen."

"Good being with you, Ed."

Chapter 18

INTEGRITY AND
COMPROMISE

STEPHEN SITS IN RANDY'S STUDIO swiveling on a barstool. He's about to drive to the airport to pick up his father, but he's captivated by the drama unfolding.

Randy's eyes track Kat, an important interior designer who is selecting paintings for the lobby of a boutique hotel, as she walks back and forth in front of several of Randy's abstract paintings, holding her chin with her right hand and her wine with her left. She stops in front of one of the paintings, stares into space, and moves to the next one. And now she lingers in front of that painting. Finally, she turns to Randy, takes a sip of her Chardonnay, holds her glass in the air, and announces triumphantly, "I want every one of them!" She looks at Randy with a huge grin.

Randy smiles a little bit before turning slowly toward Stephen, looking for some balance for his conflicting thoughts. Stephen beams at him, assuming that Randy must be thrilled speechless.

"Okay, here it is guys!" Kat says, then pauses to take a long swallow of her wine. "I'll give you six hundred each for the paintings." She takes another swallow of her wine, spilling some on her upper lip. She licks at it with her tongue. "And I'll need two more commissioned pieces. I'll pay you seven hundred for each."

Kat looks from Randy to Stephen and back. "Don't you love me?" she says, baring her teeth.

Stephen sees disappointment in Randy's eyes which is very confusing because Randy sold one of the paintings from this series to an artist a couple of days earlier for a hundred and fifty dollars.

"Gosh, I don't know, Kat," Randy says. "I'm not sure I'm comfortable letting them all go at once."

Kat seems amused. "Darling," she says, walking toward Randy. She puts her hand on his cheek and gets up in his face. "In case no one told you, what you do is you sell your paintings for your price, and then what I do is take them and hang them for the world to see." She looks at Randy like a long-suffering mother. Randy leans away from her. The Chardonnay on her breath stinks.

Kat smiles at him, then resumes her slow pacing in front of the paintings. "Okay," she says in her way too enthusiastic voice. "Let me tell you what I'm envisioning for the two commissioned pieces." She carefully studies the paintings, then closes her eyes and speaks almost like she's channeling. "They'll be hanging prominently above the registration desk, taking up about three by six feet each." She turns in the direction of her audience, but keeps her eyes closed. "Okay, okay, I got it."

She opens her eyes and grins at Randy who looks blankly at her. "Let me tell you, the lobby will have these beautiful pale pink walls. Taupe, that's it, taupe is perfect with pink. You know, splash taupe everywhere, taupe in the background, taupe in the figures, taupe every damn where you want it." She looks at Randy and Stephen and laughs and laughs.

Stephen can see that Randy is barely containing strong emotions. Kat walks over to the sink and pours herself some more wine, wine Randy bought after the artist who referred her to him said she couldn't think without a very cold bottle of Chardonnay at her complete disposal. She swirls her glass around, spilling a little bit of wine on the floor as she continues. "Randy, if you want my opinion, your work would be a lot more, I don't know, contemporary," she says, before taking a long swallow of wine, "if you had more pinks, purples, and taupe."

Stephen looks at Randy to make sure he's breathing.

"Those are the colors everyone is hanging these days, Hon. Can I tell you something?" she asks, not waiting for a reply. "I like the ones with two figures." She points with her drinking hand to each of the paintings with two figures, as if Randy and Stephen couldn't pick them out for themselves. "They look much sexier than the ones with, you know, all these figures running around. When you have a lot of figures I get lost and I wonder what's going on with all those people." She walks closer to one of his paintings with several figures and studies it at close range. The figures appear to move along a dark, shadowy alleyway. "I can see the merit in this one," she says in a tone that suggests that she really does not. "But you start putting a lot of figures in these and it begins looking cluttered and the colors in this one are, actually, a bit dark." She grimaces. "You do have to be careful with dark colors. The painting can become... depressing. I mean, I know that's artistic, but you can't get around the fact that depressing reduces the marketability of a piece. It just does."

Stephen is stunned. Could anyone be less sensitive than this woman? He thinks how Kat represents everything Ed argues against. This woman, although in a creative profession, has no depth. She clings to an admittedly compelling capitalist narrative but with no thought of what she's asking of an artist of real depth like Randy. She wants to erase all mystery and darkness in exchange for cash. But the cash, Stephen thinks. It's a lot of cash. Cash can buy freedom, can't it?

Finally, Randy jumps off his stool and walks quickly toward his easel. He picks up his brush and palette and begins dabbing his brush in red paint.

"You know what," Kat says, somehow ignoring everything but her own thoughts. "I have paint chips for the colors for the walls, and swatches for the couches that'll be in the lobby and I just happen to have them in my car." Kat smiles and appears to await applause for her forethought. "Why don't I go right now and get them and that'll give you something to work with?" She struts to the door, swinging her hips wildly from side to side. The sound of her heels clattering on the paint-splattered cement floor jangles Randy's nerves.

Randy looks at Stephen and then looks down. There is an odd silence between them.

"She's.... hard to take. Insensitive," Stephen says, as he walks toward the window, situating himself to keep an eye on her so he and Randy can talk without her surprising them. "But she's talking about several thousand dollars. That part's hard to resist, right?" Stephen asks.

"You heard her. Everything's wrong. Everything she says makes me want to kill her. She wants me to paint from swatches. I refuse to paint abstract images from swatches."

Randy fires his paintbrush toward the sink. It hits the window above the sink and splashes in the sink water below. Dark red paint bleeds across the window.

"Good shot. Is that Kat's blood?" Stephen jokes and falls quiet a moment. "This could be a big day for your career. You're going to do this deal, right?"

"I'm willing to sell her a few paintings, but I'm still working on this series. I'm not going to just let her take all of them. I know what I'm not going to do. I'm not going do any abstract work to match her fucking couches."

"How is that different from painting a still life a particular color or on a particular background?" Stephen asks.

"Actually, I'm not doing that anymore," Randy says. "But these paintings are important to me. They come from somewhere deep inside of me and I'm not going to sacrifice them for money."

"What do you think about this?" Stephen asks, glancing at the walkway to make sure Kat was not on her way back. "When she comes back, why not just take her check and the swatches and say, 'Thank you very much,' and then paint whatever the fuck you want for the commissioned work? If she doesn't like the paintings, you can give that part of the money back."

"I think its bullshit," Randy says. "You heard all that stuff about having too many figures not being sensual. She doesn't know what the fuck she's talking about! And taupe? No, I can't deal with this. That bitch! " Randy turns his back on Stephen.

Stephen has known Randy for over a year and never heard him use the words "fuck" or "bitch" and now he's spitting them all over the place. Kat's head appears in the window, bobbing along toward the studio door.

"Here she comes," Stephen says, walking quickly toward Randy. "Really, Randy, I don't think you want to be too… uncompromising about this."

"I've got them!" Kat says, as she walks into the studio waving the swatches and the check above her head.

"Hey a check! I guess you'll be buying the popcorn at the movies tonight, Randy," Stephen says, smiling.

Randy stares into Stephen's eyes, startling him.

Randy stands up straight. He takes a deep breath before speaking. "Kat, I'm flattered that you like my work. I really am. I'm just not ready to give up all of my work right now. I'm still working on this series. I could sell you a couple of them, but that's really all I can do. I'm sorry if I've misled you."

At first Kat needed a lot of clarification that Randy was not negotiating the price, but when she understood, she immediately decided on two of the paintings and wrote a check for twelve hundred dollars. When Stephen and Randy carried the paintings to her car she said she'd hang them over the registration desk. She also said she'd be back to try to buy some of them later.

Stephen and Randy walk back to the studio in silence. As they walk through the door, Stephen clears his throat. "I kind of don't understand what just happened. You've told me how money is such an important problem in your relationship with Dan, and…so I thought that selling all of the paintings would be a, you know, step toward changing that."

Randy takes a quick breath. "Yeah, money is an issue in my relationship. Dan's been seduced by money in every way possible in his life. He even makes fun of the product he's been working day and night for fifteen years to sell. I have no plans to be corrupted by money. How about you, Stephen?"

"Okay, I get it. This is none of my business. I'm sorry for intruding."

Randy plops wearily on his stool by the sink. He shakes his head. "No, I respect your opinion. I'm just…emotional. I want to know what you see. Tell me what you saw happening in here."

Stephen wipes a line of sweat from his upper lip. "Well, how can you become Dan's financial equal if you don't make certain sacrifices? Another thing, you say Dan has been corrupted by money, but I don't know if I see it that way. He jokes about Coke, but he seems to love his work. And his compromises support your artistic purity, right?"

Randy gazes at the scarlet streaks on the canvas on the easel. "I appreciate your comments, Stephen. I need to think about all of that, and I will. I know I could show more appreciation to Dan for our financial situation. I think I used to do that. I'm not sure why I've gotten so hostile with him about money."

"I've got to get to the airport to pick up my dad," Stephen says, patting Randy on the shoulder. Randy pulls him into a hug. Stephen wonders if Randy has accepted his interpretation of his situation with Dan and money. He also is struck that he'd essentially been blind to the importance of artistic integrity to Randy.

Chapter 19

EVERYTHING IS WRONG

AFTER A QUICK DRIVE TO THE AIRPORT, Stephen darts in and out of the columns of people moving in opposite directions. He wants to get to his father's gate before he gets off the plane since it's always nice to see a familiar face the moment you emerge from that rectangular tube. He lunges onto the train that will take him to his father's concourse just as the automatic doors close.

He slides through the crowd of Friday afternoon well-dressed businessmen, grabbing a support pole, his hand just below a slender, feminine hand as the train lunges forward. He follows the hand, like following a path to a waterfall, from an attractive ring (no diamond), to an elegant watch, up her deep green Armani summer weight wool jacket to her smiling face.

"Hi," she says, her face radiant.

"Hi," he mumbles.

He mumbles because he's intimidated, first by her expensive style and beauty, and then by thoughts about his relationship with Ally. At this point they haven't openly said they're dating each other exclusively, but it's certainly been implied. And through the first month and a half of summer he has talked to her every night, at least once, and not even thought about being with another woman. And he'd be outraged to the point of dissolving the relationship if she decided to pursue a man on a train for the purpose of…what? Indeed, when she told him recently that she'd seen her ex-boyfriend while visiting her parents, he'd been swept by jealousy, even though she repeatedly told him, finally with success, that there was nothing but friendship between them. Certainly, he and this incarnation of Aphrodite were not going to meet and find a closet and fuck like animals before dashing away from each other, her toward her flight, and him to his father's gate just in time to greet him.

He reluctantly looks away from the woman and then as he gets off the train he looks back. She's staring at him quizzically. He smiles and heads toward his father's gate, congratulating himself for his self-control.

The last time Stephen saw his father was a year ago during the last phase of his chemotherapy. His father was shockingly frail then. Probably ten years ago, a local sports reporter described his father as being "a rock of a man with forearms like Popeye, but with a completely gentle soul." That reporter was one of the many ex-high school athletes who continually came back into Frank's life, maybe to introduce a fiancé or to tell him that he graduated from college or was a coach of another high school team. Frank had been a surrogate father for many of the boys growing up in Charleston in the 1960s and 1970s whose fathers were too busy or too drunk to be good fathers.

The surrogate fathering stopped, however, outside of the context of sports. Those young men who would bring their fiancés to introduce them would find Frank courteous but searching for something beyond "Hello" to say to them. He usually resorted to describing their baseball careers. He never seemed to know exactly what the young men wanted from him.

It's also the first time that Stephen has seen his father since he began sounding depressed on the phone. Frank had moved the trip back twice before finally being persuaded to come. Stephen's planned the weekend for Frank to include a trip to his therapist, a day of golf on Saturday, and a Braves baseball game that night. Tonight and Sunday were unplanned.

Stephen worries for a moment that his father will not know how to act around Dan and Randy. Surely, he has never been around a gay couple before. He cannot remember his father ever saying anything, positive or negative, about gay people. He thinks about how comfortable his own relationship is with Dan and Randy. Even hugging Randy earlier felt comfortable. There was nothing sexual or artificial about it. It was a natural way for them to honestly connect.

Stephen wonders why he and his father never hug. He remembers they quit hugging when he was about eleven or twelve, when he no longer wanted to hug either of his parents. He also recalls, several years later, his father saying it was not "natural" for men to hug each other. Well, that explained it! He thinks that maybe he should just reach out and give his father a big hug to put an end to all of that nonsense, which seemed all the more crazy with his father now suffering from cancer and depression. Some of his father's depression had to be related to the distance the two of them felt from each other.

Stephen sees his father walking through the doorway, with downcast eyes, a slight frown, moving deliberately. His skin is pale.

"Dad," Stephen calls out, strained. The two move toward each other and stand in the middle of Atlanta's Hartsfield International Airport shaking each other's hand, smiling, saying things like, "Good to see you," "It's been a long time," and "How you doing?"

As they walk to baggage claim they talk about the flight, the crowded airport, and the traffic on the drive to the airport. Driving home, Stephen begins telling his father about their plans for the weekend hesitating before telling him he has scheduled an appointment for both of them with his therapist on Saturday morning.

After a few seconds, Frank asks, "Why are we going to see him?"

"Well, he's wanted to meet you to get an idea of my family, and he agreed to come in on Saturday as a favor since you don't live here."

"That's nice of him," Frank says.

For a while there is silence as Stephen negotiates the traffic.

Frank is replaying a conversation that he had with his wife before he left. She wanted to come with him. When he told her Stephen had requested some "alone time" with him, she insisted that he not go. They argued for the entire week leading up to the trip, but for the first time in their marriage Frank refused to give in. Earlier in the morning as he sat on the porch of his small ranch house looking across the street while the rising sun turned the black edges of the horizon of the Gulf of Mexico a dark grey, she stood in the doorway and told him that if he went to Atlanta without her, she'd leave him. He slowly shifted his focus from the waves, and he said to her quietly, "If our relationship is that fragile, then you should leave." She said a lot of vicious things before the taxi finally arrived and drove him to the airport.

And now he worried, would she really leave?

Stephen looks over at his father. "I'm worried about you," he says.

"Why is that?" his father asks, continuing to look straight ahead, the morning's awful images alternating with Atlanta traffic.

"I don't know. You seem depressed."

Frank has a momentary image of his wife, her face distorted with rage, standing in the doorway as he got in the taxi. "Well, I've got a lot on my mind these days. Mainly, I'm worried about the cancer coming back. I don't think I can do chemo again."

Stephen feels a surge of panic. "Do you have any symptoms? Have you been to the oncologist?"

"No real symptoms and, yes, I've seen the doctor. He tells me I'm doing well. Then we talk about golf."

"So, what are you worried about if you don't have symptoms?"

"I dunno. It's hard to explain. After you've had the surgery and radiation and chemo, if your blood work's not perfect, you worry," Frank says.

"Your blood work's not perfect?" Stephen's asks, his gaze alternating between the road and his father's face.

"Well, certain readings go up from month to month and he tells me that unless I want to try some new chemo there's nothing he can do."

"Does that mean he's recommending some chemotherapy and you're saying you don't want it?"

"It's not that simple," Frank says.

"Well, then explain it me."

"It's just that if I did have symptoms, I'd probably consider it. It's just my blood work suggests there may be some growth of the cancer, but nothing new shows up on the CAT scan. So it's hard to say, 'sure, go ahead and give me some more of those drugs that almost killed me.'"

"Why do you say they almost killed you?" Stephen asks.

"Because I almost died before. I had pneumonia and was in the hospital three or four times during the first round. Once I had a fever of 103 for almost a week."

"I guess I forgot it was that bad."

"I don't think I told you all the details. I didn't feel right worrying everyone when I was so far away."

"I hope you'll worry us in the future. Michelle and I want to know what's going on; that's why we insisted on you coming here."

"Yeah, I noticed that."

"Good."

"Besides, I've just gotten my golf game back in the eighties. Another round of chemo and I'd have to use the women's tee to hit the green on a par three," Frank says, turning toward Stephen for the first time and attempting a smile.

"I hope you're not really putting your golf game into the formula about making health decisions. That'd be pretty stupid."

"I'm just kidding. I worry about dying of the cure. That's why I don't want more chemo."

Stephen falls silent a moment. "I didn't mean what I said about you being stupid," he says.

"I know you didn't," Frank replies. He gazes emptily at the road, as he thinks about his relationship with his two children, Stephen and Michelle. Lately they have seemed so concerned and yet for the last several years, ever since the divorce they have rarely called. He has seen them for brief, obligatory visits on occasional holidays. He glances at Stephen, who looks back at him. How did leaving their mother cost him so much with them?

Stephen turns into his driveway and his father sits up, noticing the tree-lined drive. "This is where you live?" he says.

"Yeah, I told you it was nice," Stephen says, smiling.

"And your landlords are homosexual?"

"Yeah, you'll meet them tomorrow. They won't try to kiss you or anything," Stephen says, laughing.

"I'm not worried about that," his father says, making a fist and attempting a playful smile.

A couple of hours later, Stephen and his father are at a table for two in a restaurant Dan insisted they visit. It's one of those steak houses where the titans of business supposedly take time to get to know the human side of their colleagues over thick sides of beef and distilled beverages, while they continue to hide from each other like frightened chipmunks.

Stephen swings open the front cover of the wine list and after checking the prices, decides that they might be better off ordering mixed drinks. The room smells good, really, with its mellow mixture of burning beef and cigar and cigarette smoke. A yellow candle flickers between them.

After they order their steaks, Stephen leans toward his father and asks hesitantly, "So can we talk a little about your depression?"

Frank glances from side to side, worrying about being overheard. "Sure," he whispers.

"You said earlier you had a lot on your mind. What are you so worried about, I mean, besides the cancer?"

When his father looks confused, Stephen adds, "Would you say that you're depressed?"

"I guess I'd say so," Frank says. "I'm not sure what depression is, really, but what I've been going through…" He shakes his head slowly. "I've never felt anything like it in my life."

"What do you mean?"

"You're not going to psychoanalyze me, are you?"

"I'll try not to," Stephen says with some impatience.

"You're not legitimate yet, right?" Frank says, forcing a smile.

"Come on, really," Stephen says. "I'm concerned about you."

"I know. I can't describe what I've been going through or at least I can't do it justice." Frank looks around the room. He closes his eyes briefly and picks up his water. "I get up in the morning," he says, quietly. "And it takes everything I have to walk out to the porch." He looks into his son's gentle eyes. "Sometimes I wake up at three in the morning. Other nights I don't go to sleep 'till three and wake up at six or seven. I never feel like I'm really awake, and sometimes I don't feel like I ever sleep." He looks back at his water glass. "It's just...I don't know what's wrong with me."

Stephen pauses and then asks, reluctantly, "Is it, are you and Donna having problems?"

Frank leans back in his seat. "Yeah, we are, but I didn't come here to talk about her."

"Why would we not talk about your relationship with your wife if it's upsetting you?"

"Well, she doesn't really like it when I talk to you or Michelle about her. She thinks you might try to pull us apart."

Stephen flushes and fights the urge to say what he wants to say: "Fuck her!" He shakes his head and stammers. "She's... I can't believe... I don't know how you..." He keeps shaking his head as the waiter brings their drinks to the table.

Stephen watches the waiter walk away. Slowly he turns back to face his father. "Fuck her!" he says, almost rising out of his seat. "I know you don't want to hear that, but what kind of woman tells a man how to act with his adult children?"

Frank looks at Stephen, grimly. "I don't know what to say to that," he says.

A different waiter puts their salads in front of them, grinds some pepper over them, and moves away almost without seeming within earshot.

"So, what are the problems that she wants you to keep from me?" Stephen asks.

Frank looks around the restaurant. He takes a sip of his drink and looks back at Stephen. "Do you really want to talk about this?"

Stephen looks into his father's eyes, then at his Dewar's and water. He raises the glass and takes a sip. "Of course," he says.

Frank takes a deep breath before speaking. "Donna and I really don't have a relationship anymore," he says. "Not like your mother and me. We didn't have an intimate relationship, but we were still good friends. With Donna, it's…I stay out on the porch when she's home to avoid her. We go days without speaking, and those are the good days. In the morning I dread her waking up, and around five in the afternoon I start feeling the same dread about her getting home from work. I'm not sure why I feel all of that because these days she doesn't really give me much trouble. She usually goes into the kitchen or her bedroom and if we pass each other we don't even look at each other. Maybe the dread is just the whole scene, the whole scene of us not looking at each other or speaking… Maybe it's just dreading the final evidence that leaves no doubt about the conclusion that the relationship is dead. That's hard to take. I don't think you can know what that's like."

Stephen looks carefully at his father's weary face. Everything about this chapter of his father's life is wrong, he thinks. He was at the top of his profession as a biology teacher and coach. He seemed happy throughout Stephen's growing up. But now he's divorced from his wife of thirty years, a close friend at least, and married to a woman he dreads the sight of. Stephen feels his eyes well up with tears. He swallows hard. "You can't straighten any of that out? I mean, what are you two not talking about?"

Frank leans forward. "What we're not talking about is the fact that she has done everything in her power to alienate me from my kids," he says. "We've talked about it; believe me. You know I hate arguing, right? She thrives on it."

Frank sighs and leans back in his chair.

"You just confirmed for me what I thought was going on, and I admit I've been really angry at both of you about it. I mean, you're responsible for maintaining a relationship with Michelle and me and your grandchildren who love you, regardless of what Donna does. I've felt like you've gone along with her on some things that you shouldn't have, just to get along."

"I know you've felt that way," Frank says.

"I guess I've mentioned that a time or two," Stephen says, then smiles at his father.

"You have been pretty clear about that, yeah," Frank says, taking a long swallow of his drink. "She seemed so nice when we were dating," he says, looking at Stephen. "It doesn't seem like she cares about me at all now."

Stephen looks closely at the deep lines of his father's weary face, a face that he has always found so gentle. Candlelight dances in the moisture of his father's eyes.

"I'm glad you came here. I'm sure Donna wasn't thrilled," Stephen says.

"We argued, but I'm glad I'm here, too."

"I'm glad you stood up to her and came here. Thank you."

The rest of the evening was easy, with quiet conversation that ended with Stephen turning the light off at around one in the morning. They would have stayed up later, but they had their nine o'clock appointment with Henry.

Chapter 20

A PERENNIAL GARDEN

FRANK IS SITTING BY THE POOL when Stephen jumps out of his day bed to turn off the blaring alarm clock. He looks over at his bed where his father slept, and it's nicely made up for maybe the second time since he originally made it when he set up his apartment. It looks nice that way, he thinks, before he walks outside and calls out to his father, "We need to leave in fifteen minutes." His father is dressed and ready to go.

The two of them rush to Henry's office, getting there right at nine o'clock, a few minutes before Henry arrives. Henry opens his office and Stephen and his father sit next to each other on the couch. Henry sits in his rocking chair and smiles at the two men. "I sure am glad to meet you Frank. I've heard so much about you," he says.

"Gee, I don't know how to take it that you've heard a lot about me," Frank says. "I gather people come to therapy to complain about their parents. I don't imagine you've heard much positive about me."

"Actually," Henry says, "some do come and complain and some, like Stephen, paint a pretty balanced picture of their childhood, which is what I strive for with clients. Stephen has said a lot of great things about you. Let me see if I can recall some of them."

Henry looks away to think. "Stephen describes you as being very affectionate when he was growing up," he says, looking at Frank. "And very involved with your kids, both with sports and with schoolwork."

Henry looks at Stephen to jog his memory. "Let's see," he says, "you said he was a great sports coach, brought beauty into your life by gardening, and generally was a very gentle father." Henry turns back to Frank and smiles. "I'll bet you like that list, right?"

Frank smiles and turns to Stephen, "You said all of that, huh?"

"Of course. I hope you know I appreciate you," Stephen says.

Frank looks at Henry, and then turns back to his son. "We had a pretty good time when you were growing up, didn't we?"

"I sure did," Stephen says. "I feel very lucky to have a father who was as involved with me as you were. I wish I could be with Nicholas as much as you were with me."

"I wish you could, too," Frank says. "His mother is taking good care of him, isn't she?"

"Yeah, she's doing fine, but I wish I could be there with him more," Stephen says.

"Be with him as much as you can," Frank says. "It goes fast."

Stephen smiles and nods.

There is a silence. Stephen looks at Henry. He thinks about his father's depression. He realizes he invited his father to this session in hopes that Henry could somehow perform a miracle and cure his father's depression, in one session no less.

"I thought about this session," Henry says, "and didn't know whether you two had an agenda or not." Henry looks at Stephen.

"Not really," Stephen says. "I wanted you to meet my dad, beyond that, I didn't really... have an agenda."

Henry looks at Frank, implying the same question.

"I just came because I was asked," Frank says.

Henry nods and smiles. "Well I have an agenda," he says, before sitting more upright up in his chair. "I thought it might be good to discuss something that Stephen said to me once, that you two had never reestablished your closeness since you and his mother divorced. I thought we might talk about what gets in the way of that closeness. Would that be alright?"

"Sure, that's fine, yeah..." Frank says, tentatively.

"That's fine. I, you know..." Stephen says with the same caution in his voice.

Henry looks at the two men. "I'm asking each of you the same question: 'What do we need to talk about to help you reestablish the closeness you once had?'"

"Well, the divorce was a confusing time and since then it's been... difficult," Frank says.

"Yeah, the divorce was a turning point," Stephen says, turning to his father. "We talked last night about one of the biggest problems in our relationship," he says.

Frank nods.

"Dad's wife, Donna," Stephen says to Henry, "interferes with our relationship and with Dad's relationship with my sister every chance she gets."

Frank protests, but not too effectively, so the discussion turns to his wife's interference. While father and son disagreed about the nuances of her interference, they were clear that she caused problems between them. They recounted the story of Frank's departure to visit Stephen.

Henry initially found himself thinking the obvious: Frank was married to a shrew. But something nagged at him as he listened to them detail the story of a good man and his shrew. Henry knows how easy it is to blame a third party for whatever ails a relationship between two people.

"I can hear where Donna has caused problems," he says, "but I'm also aware that you two were remarkably close at one time and now you're not. I can't imagine Donna could be so powerful to do all of that. I can imagine her making it difficult, sure, but what have each of you done to cause this?"

Henry knows he's doing exactly what he needs to, disputing a comfortable explanation for the problem. He takes a deep relaxing breath and waits for some resistance.

"I'm not saying she's the only problem," Stephen says, "but she has never done anything to make me feel welcome at my father's house when I visit."

Henry nods subtly.

"She doesn't dislike my kids. I think she just feels uncomfortable around them," Frank says. "I'd say she misinterprets a lot of what they do as…rejecting. And that always causes problems."

"Can you say more?" Henry says.

"If they call and don't have much to say to her on the phone, she gets mad and says they're rude, for instance. They're not being rude; they just don't have that deep of a relationship with her. When they come to visit, she puts effort into the visit and if they don't acknowledge it, she gets angry. I mean, I don't think they should have to make a big deal out of it, but she always seems to."

"She doesn't think they acknowledge what she does to make them feel welcomed?" Henry asks.

Frank looks at his son, and slowly nods.

"Please tell me what she has done," Stephen says with no hint of curiosity.

Henry smiles gently at Frank.

"She always bakes things, does a lot of cooking, and she makes the house look good. She does a lot of stuff before you come," Frank says to Stephen.

"She makes a lot of very unhealthy pastries that my sister and I don't eat," Stephen says to Henry, with a look of disgust that appears to Henry to be a snobbish sneer.

"She doesn't share your culinary refinement?" Henry asks Stephen.

"No, I'm just saying if she wants to join with me and my sister she could try baking things that we want or feel are healthy to eat," Stephen says.

Henry looks at Frank. "Your son has a discriminating palate, huh?"

"I guess," Frank says.

"I'm just saying…" Stephen says, before Henry interrupts.

"It sounds like she puts effort into your visit. It's just that her effort isn't what you're used to or expect. That's not such a terrible thing."

"I can tell you," Stephen says to Henry, "that I always thank her for everything." He turns to his father, "Right?" he asks.

"He does," Frank says to Henry. "She has a hard time believing or trusting what my children say, so she discounts things."

"And you're in the middle," Henry says.

Frank nods.

"Why haven't you talked to Stephen about any of this?" Henry asks. "He's a reasonable guy, don't you think?"

"I… yeah, of course he is. I just don't know what to say," Frank says.

"It sounds like you two have a lot to talk about," Henry says. "Let me introduce something for each of you to consider. Whatever problem has occurred between your wife and your kids was probably inevitable.

In a way, it's a problem that keeps you all from focusing and talking about a bigger problem, a problem I think you're ready to talk about." He pauses and looks at Frank. "You divorced their mother and that changed the family completely." Henry glances from face to face as he leans back in his chair. He reaches for his water again and after a sip, he adds, "The divorce changed everything, and I imagine that's what you need to talk about."

Stephen and his father are compliant sorts, in general, so they take deep breaths and ready themselves for the discussion of the divorce.

"That's probably true…the divorce caused problems…that we need to talk about," Frank says. "I think Stephen and his sister resent me for the divorce and well they should. Their mother never did anything but do the best she could for them. They don't understand me and why I did what I did. And, really, I can't blame them."

Stephen sits quietly, his head turned downward, while Henry and Frank await his response. Finally, he looks at his father. "It's not the divorce now. You just don't call me or Michelle. You had to be begged to come for this visit. You just don't seem that interested in us or our kids."

"So, you each agree the problem began with the divorce," Henry says, "but for you, Frank, you feel that the divorce is still causing problems because you feel like your children don't understand you and why you made the choice to divorce their mother. And, Stephen, you emphasize that you're over having problems with the divorce. The issue now, for you, is you want your father to be more present in your life with you and Nicholas and your sister and her children."

Both men nod.

"Frank, I guess I can see how if you thought your kids didn't understand you, you might become less involved with them," Henry says.

Frank sits up straighter in his seat and disagrees. "I guess I see them as avoiding me as much as me avoiding them because they're mad at me, which I understand."

Henry is about to speak.

"Let me handle this," Stephen says, before smiling at his father. "Okay, let's do this. Would you agree that I call you more than you call me?"

His father slowly nods.

"If I call you three out of every four times we talk, I'm sure that Michelle calls you nine out of every ten times, right?"

His father slowly nods.

"So, who's avoiding who?" Stephen says.

"Whom," Frank says to Stephen, smiling at his attempt to regain his parental position. "I'd say that you call more often, but you always called home. Your mother and I didn't call you that often, right?"

"Ah, no. I think you two called me as much as I called home. I'd say mom calls me about as often as I call her."

Frank nods his head but offers no reply.

"Frank, do you have something to add?" Henry asks.

"I'm not sure what to say. I know he and Michelle were angry at me and I think that has been a big part of the problem."

"I think Stephen said he was angry at the time of the divorce and I assumed that you felt some guilt about the divorce," Henry says.

"Of course, I did," Frank says.

"Did you ever discuss that with Stephen?" Henry asks.

"I don't think so…did we?" Frank asks Stephen.

"Not really," Stephen says.

"Maybe you should discuss the divorce here," Henry says.

"I'm not sure how to explain the divorce," Frank starts. "I thought we had a great family, but for me something was missing in my life. Stephen's mother and I became, I don't how to say it, like brother and sister. I guess I wanted more. And the children never forgave me, and I guess I understand that."

"You feel guilty," Henry asks, "like your kids are still upset with you?"

"How could they not be?" Frank asks. "I left their mother."

Henry nods.

"Yeah," Stephen says, looking at his father. "We were upset with you, but I don't think that's my problem now…and I don't think it's the problem Michelle has either. We just want you to be involved with us."

Stephen and his father look at each other before they both look away.

"You believe your son?" Henry asks Frank.

"I do," Frank says, firmly. "I've never had any reason to doubt his honesty."

Henry nods as he considers the two men before him. He turns to Stephen. "My sense is that as your father feels less blamed by you and your sister, he can get back to knowing how much each of you love him and miss him and that'll help. Can you see that?"

"Yeah, I can understand that. I want to help with that," Stephen says.

"Frank, thinking your kids judged you might have caused you to avoid reaching out to them. And your wife, it sounds like she doesn't make it easy for you."

Frank squints at Henry, nodding.

"You came here today and that's an important start," Henry continues. As he's saying that he's distracted by a startling thought. The three of them had not yet discussed Frank's cancer. He knew from his sessions with Stephen that the cancer was serious.

Stephen watches his father continuing to nod. It occurs to him that his father looks lost. He hears Henry say, "All of this is especially important to figure out because of the cancer, right? "You worry about your dad's health, right?" Henry asks Stephen.

Stephen nods and mumbles, "Of course."

"It's really important for you two to be able to talk about important things. That's hard for fathers and sons to do."

Frank nods slowly.

"How is your health, Frank?" Henry asks.

"I'm, um, doing okay, fine," Frank says, but Henry is no more reassured than Stephen was on the trip from the airport.

"What does that mean?" he asks.

"I'm doing what I can do to make sure that I get the best treatment available… I haven't had a confirmed reoccurrence of the cancer since chemotherapy, which is positive."

Henry hears the carefulness or avoidance in his language. "I know you need support when you have a life-threatening illness. Can you turn to Stephen for support, maybe even talk about your fears, things that come up that are confusing about treatment and such?" he asks.

Frank looks at his son and then at Henry. "I guess I'd like to know from him if he'd like me to do that," he says.

"Of course, I would. Didn't I say that last night?" Stephen asks.

Frank nods, "You did."

Henry's eyes alternate between Stephen and Frank. He smiles, "It's time for us to stop," he says. "I want to say something that I want you two to leave with. I see a lot of love between you two. I hope both of you get more comfortable letting all that love out. I know the whole world has told you to hide it, but I see it and it's really nice. To hell with the rest of the world, right?" Henry smiles and his eyes light up as if he's inviting them into a conspiracy.

Henry motions toward Stephen, "I heard this guy say he wanted to be an important part of your support system, Frank, to help you deal with this phase of your life. Will you let him?"

"I will," Frank says.

"Good," Stephen says. "I really do want that."

"That's the most important thing we could have accomplished here today," Henry says. He pushes himself up from the chair and looks at Frank, "I think it's so terrific that you came in today, Frank," he says. "I know it means a lot to Stephen and I'm just glad to meet the father of this wonderful young man."

Frank reaches out and shakes Henry's hand. "I really appreciate you giving your Saturday morning to us."

"Absolutely, no problem," Henry says, patting Frank on the back.

"I'm glad Stephen's seeing you," Frank says. "I can tell he's in good hands."

Henry beams at Frank. "Thank you," he says. "I'm a parent, too and I just want to say you can be proud of the job you did raising him. Men don't turn out like this without having a great father."

Frank feels like he could weep at those kind words. He takes a deep breath. "Well, I guess his mother and I didn't do too badly," Frank says.

"I'd have to agree with you there," Henry says.

Henry turns to Stephen and spreads his arms. As they hug, Stephen wonders if the session has helped with his father's depression.

Randy, up early on Sunday morning, looks out the window as he pours his coffee. He sees Frank sitting in a chair next to the pool, looking toward the sunrise in the heavy morning air, a frozen image of uneasy solitude.

Randy walks on the slate path carrying two cups of coffee. "Good morning," he calls out.

"Oh, hello," Frank says, pulling himself up from his morning haze.

"I'm Randy, nice to meet you. I guess you're not a late sleeper like your son?" Randy says.

"I'm Frank, nice to meet you," Franks says. "No, I'm not sure where he got that. He's been like that since he was teenager."

"You want some coffee?" Randy asks, extending the cup.

"Sure, thank you."

"How's your visit been so far?"

"It's been nice. We're having a good time."

"You mind if I join you?" Randy asks, motioning toward a chair.

"That's fine."

Randy sits down and looks at the sunrise. "Beautiful morning, huh?"

"Yes, it is. This is great spot to watch the sun rise. The trees, the flowers, it's really nice back here. Stephen tells me you designed all this," Frank says.

"The old oak trees made it easy. I did plant the ornamental trees and the gardens."

"It's beautiful."

"Thanks. I still have some work to do over in the west corner," Randy says, pointing to an area of thick ivy and weeds. "I promised Dan a perennial garden there, but I haven't found my inspiration yet."

"It looks like you have a nice area for it, probably a good mix of full sun and partial shade."

"Yes, it is," Randy says, before taking a sip of his coffee. He has a thought and immediately shares it: "You know it would be fun for us to make a plan for that area over there. Stephen says you taught biology, but you were an expert botanist and quite the gardener, right?"

Frank smiles shyly and nods. He's surprised his son has told Randy about him.

Randy continues, "And I think it'd be fun for him to know his father helped design a garden where he lives. I'd love it if we could work together on that."

"I'd be happy to, but you don't need my help," Frank says. "You've already done wonders with the rest of the grounds."

"Yeah, but I've avoided designing and planting that area for two years. I'm just not inspired. I think we could get some momentum working as a team."

Frank looks at Randy. "Um, sure that's fine if you want," he says.

"Let me get some paper and pastels and let's design it, okay?" Randy asks.

"Sure," Frank says, watching Randy walk quickly to his studio.

Coming back, Randy says, "Frank, let's move these chairs closer to the west corner. Let's walk the area first, and then sit down and draw out our ideas."

As the two men walk through the ivy toward the end of the property, Randy asks a continuous stream of questions about water and sunlight needs, about heat tolerance, and about how much space to allow for plants to grow as they matured. Talking about soil and fertilizer, Randy notices that Frank's voice, initially halting and quiet, has become more melodic and confident.

Randy pulls on the rusty metal fence that is overgrown with ivy. "What a mess," he says.

"We could get some stakes and prop it up," Frank offers. "It would look great to cut the ivy back and plant some rose bushes to grow through the fence and over it. Give it a rustic look."

Randy agrees. "Let's see," Randy says. "We're talking about a few intimate spaces around each oak and leaving the rest, the part that gets full sun, more natural, flowing, maybe even overgrown looking with a couple of paths winding through."

"Let's sit down and I'll draw it out," Randy says. "If we can see it, it'll help us make some decisions about the specific perennials."

Frank sits in his chair sipping coffee seeing the whole garden in his mind. He describes what it will look like in the rain and on sunny days and how to mix in ivy and evergreens so that even in the winter, when the garden has died down and rests, it still retains an elegant form.

Randy sketches every detail of the summer garden. As he changes sheets, to sketch the garden's look in the winter he hands Frank the sketch of the summer garden. "What do you think?" he asks.

"Wow, I'm impressed," Frank says.

"You should be, it's your design and it's incredible."

"Well, I don't know about that," Frank says, looking at Randy and recognizing his kindness. "Are you an impressionistic artist?" he asks.

"No, I call myself an abstract figural artist, but I did some training with these," Randy says, holding up the pastels. "How would you like to go to the nursery with me to help me pick out some of the plants?" he asks.

"You're going to plant things in the middle of the summer?" Frank asks. "You'll have to water them every day."

"We got plenty of water. Getting them in the ground is the hard part."

"Sure, I'll go with you. I've got nothing to do until Stephen wakes up."

A few hours later, Stephen opens his door and squints toward the house. He glances toward the pool and wonders where his father is. He assumes his father must have decided to join Randy and Dan in the house.

He opens the door to the kitchen and sees Dan at the table. "Morning, sleeping beauty," Dan says. "Didn't your mother teach you to brush your hair before going into public?"

Stephen runs his fingers through his hair and pats it down. "This isn't public. Have you seen my father?" he asks.

"Yeah, he's in the outback helping Randy plant a garden," Dan says, glancing toward the window.

Stephen looks and sees his father leaning on a shovel, talking to Randy.

"Damn, they've dug up the whole area," Stephen says.

"Yeah, they've been digging holes and planting stuff for the last couple of hours. I think they've been to Pikes nursery twice already."

"What time is it?" Stephen asks.

"Eleven O'clock."

"God...I didn't want to oversleep. I told my father to wake me when he got up."

"I think he got up early. He and Randy were walking around out there when I got in here at seven or so."

"You're kidding me. I hope Randy didn't mind."

"It looks like they're having a great time to me," Dan says.

"Maybe we ought to go help them," Stephen says, pouring himself a cup of coffee.

"I hate to interfere with their bonding...and I hate to sweat. Maybe we ought to sit here and think about it for an hour or two," Dan says.

About thirty minutes later Dan and Stephen walk out to the garden with a pitcher of iced tea.

"Frank, look who's come to help us," Randy says.

Frank looks up and smiles at his son. He uses a clean spot on his tee shirt to wipe his sweaty eyes, and calls back to Randy, "I don't believe for one minute we can get Stephen to help us out here."

Stephen hates it when his father treats him like the lazy teenager he once was. But it was, he had to admit, pretty damn hot for digging holes and sticking plants in the ground.

"I'd be glad to help," he protests, "you know, some."

"Good. We could use some help," Frank says.

"I made the tea, so I should get the afternoon off, don't you think?"

Dan jokes. "Come on, both of you need a break," he says, motioning them to a table where he has set up the drinks.

"Frank, let's show them what you've designed for our garden," Randy says, sitting down.

Stephen and Dan look at the drawings as Frank and Randy point out some of the finer points.

"I love it," Dan says, beaming. "What a wonderful plan."

"It looks good to me," Stephen says.

Later, after lunch, all four men work in the garden until almost dark. They shower, then join each other for dinner.

As Stephen helps Dan put away the dishes after dinner, Dan says, "Your dad seems to have had a good visit."

"Yeah, I think so," Stephens says. "I've been really worried about him. He's been pretty depressed. But now he seems more like his old self."

"That's great," Dan says. "He sure seems like a great guy. You're lucky to have a father who'd come all the way here just to hang out with you. I'd never see my father if this wasn't the halfway point between Cleveland and his winter place in Florida."

"Really?" Stephen asks.

"Plus, with your dad, you can just tell he loves you. I talked to him this afternoon when you and Randy were doing something, and he told me how proud he was of you. I'm sure my father has never said that to anyone."

"Even as successful as you've been at Coke?"

"My father wouldn't say he was proud of me if I won a Nobel Prize."

"Because you're gay?"

Dan laughs. "No, I'm competition to my father. He spent most of my childhood trying to crush me the way he does any competition."

Stephen looks at Dan, not knowing what to say.

"Anyway, being proud of me or showing that would make it easy for me to dethrone him," Dan says.

The next day Stephen is running down Northside Drive. He feels the rush of euphoria that accompanies his run much earlier than usual. He'd felt closer to his father on the way to the airport than he had in years. The estrangement was gone and so it seemed was his father's depressed feelings. He flashes on an image of his father working in the yard with Randy. He's grateful to Randy for being so good to his father, getting him involved in a project that seemed to help lift his depression after their session with Henry. Gardening is no magic therapy, but focused, meaningful activity sure helped. Randy gave Frank what he needed without knowing it. Or maybe he did know. Maybe Randy's creative work, his painting, really is his therapy, as he has said jokingly in the past. If so, that would have meant yielding to Kat would have meant selling his soul or at least felt that way.

Stephen walks into his apartment, exhausted from his run.

A moment later, the phone rings. His sister, Michelle, has just hung up from their father. After telling her briefly about his trip to Atlanta, he told her he and Donna wanted to visit her in Charleston in a few weeks. Michelle didn't know whether to be happy or upset about how easily her father included the stepmother she loathed until her father added, "I miss you and my grandkids, and I only have so much time to be with y'all so…"

As he listens to his sister talk, he walks out of his apartment toward his father's garden. He sits in the chair that his father sat in near the pool.

Chapter 21

RESISTANCE

STEPHEN SITS ON DARNELL'S STEEL BED and puts the fresh-rolled cigarette into his mouth. He leans forward, letting Darnell light it. He fills his lungs with the harsh smoke. He fights his body's urge to expel it.

Darnell grins, "It's good, huh?"

"It's…it's, you know, I'm used to a little weaker taste, but it's okay."

"Now don't you start smoking again. That wouldn't be cool."

"This will keep me from getting near one for a while."

A northerly breeze blows through the steel holes in the outside window causing the cloud of smoke to dance toward the cell door. Stephen inches back on the bed, takes another drag, and rests his head against the cinder block wall. "I'll probably be high as hell after this," he says.

"You wish, Psycho-Man. I don't have the money to buy that shit in here," Darnell says, watching Stephen for his reaction.

Stephen smiles.

"I bet you smoked a lot of reefer on the street," Darnell says, grinning wildly.

Stephen grins back at him. "I'm pretty conservative these days. I used to get a little wild." He didn't tell Darnell that he and Ally had done Ecstasy a few weeks earlier. He couldn't imagine doing that in Darnell's cell. What was most expansive about their "trip" was the experience of beauty – in one another's bodies and the world around them. He could imagine his mind contracting in the starkness of this space.

"You seem pretty cool, Psycho-Man. Anyway, smoking a little reefer never hurt nobody..." Darnell says.

Darnell leans toward the window and becomes absorbed in the scene outside, a tractor mowing the tall grass. His breathing is slower. His jaw, seemingly always in motion grinding away at his teeth, is still. The skin on his face, always so taut, seems looser.

"What are you looking at?" Stephen asks.

Darnell continues to stare out the window. "It's peaceful out there today. That breeze feels nice, too," he says.

"You ever think about being out there?" Stephen asks.

"Sometimes," Darnell mumbles.

"Really?" Stephen asks.

"Yeah, really," Darnell says, glaring at Stephen. "You want the truth? I think about that every day...about getting me a girlfriend, a nice place to live." He starts laughing.

"I didn't know that. You never mentioned it," Stephen says. "Where do you think you'd want to live?"

Darnell looks out the window, breathes deeply of the warm air. "That I don't know. I think about going to my hometown, but there ain't nothing for me there," he says, shaking his head slowly from side to side.

"What do you mean?" Stephen asks.

"Nobody wants me back there. I killed a man there, remember?"

"That was a long time ago," Stephen says.

Darnell's eyes cut toward Stephen and flash black like they do when he's mad. "Time doesn't change what got me in here. I don't know where I'll be going when I get in the street, but home, that's out."

"That must be tough, feeling like you can't go home," Stephen says.

"It just is…why we talkin' about this anyway?" Darnell says, turning to face Stephen squarely.

Stephen feels a flash of fear. "I don't know," he blurts out. He watches for a reaction from Darnell. "I guess we were talking about life outside of here."

Darnell continues to look Stephen over. "I didn't bring up anything about getting out of here. I won't be going anywhere 'till I max out, which is in another five or six years."

"You know you come up for parole in two months?" Stephen says, watching Darnell's reaction. "What would you do if they said you could go free?"

Darnell glares at Stephen; his eyes open wide. His voice trembles at first, then gets stronger. "Why you talking about this? There ain't one of those white men or those Uncle-Tom-slash-Oreo crackers on that parole board gonna let me out of this so-called psychiatric prison. I've been locked up here, denied my free will and testimony and you come in here lying to me about freedom. You don't know what freedom is."

Darnell takes a quick drag off his cigarette and refuses to look away from Stephen as he exhales all the smoke through his nose.

"I guess I'm just saying… do you ever dream of it? I don't know whether it's possible. I'm just talking about dreaming."

"You dream. I don't dream. They ain't no dreams in here," Darnell says, as he turns and looks back out the window.

"Well, do you think about it?" Stephen asks, his voice stronger and more demanding than usual.

Darnell turns and takes a step toward Stephen. He breathes in through his nose, swelling his bare chest. Stephen sees the anger in Darnell's eyes, but presses on. "If you don't know where you're going, you won't get paroled. I talked to Dr. Daugherty and he told me that you'd have a decent chance of getting paroled this year if you had a plan about what to do when you left here. I'd love to work on that with you."

"This ain't no CIA interrogation of no prisoner, mister, or should I say Doctor of Psychology? And I don't need your phony love or Dr. Daugherty's either."

Suddenly, Darnell's head lifts and he appears oddly prideful. "There ain't one question that you got that I got to answer until my lawyer appears before his majesty the lord." Darnell's eyes begin to flash and dance from side to side. Now he's yelling. "I think you better take your decent chances and get the fuck out of my cell."

Still on the bed, Stephen slides imperceptibly, he hopes, along the wall, closer to the door. "I don't mean it as an interrogation," he says.

Darnell steps closer to Stephen. Suddenly, it seems to Stephen that Darnell might be trying to block his escape route. Darnell lowers his face to Stephen's.

"You've been comin' in here a long time. You know I've let you do that. I," he points at his chest, "let you. No more!" Darnell turns his head away slightly and now he almost whispers, "I don't want you in here no more. You got that?"

"Darnell, I'm just…"

"No, I'm just…no, I'm just nothing," he screams. "I ain't gonna be on no part of some damn interrogation where they say I ain't got no rights because of a so-called mental and or intellectual deficiency that's got nothin' to do with the fact that I served my country in a war that was not a war and then you come in here and do your running dogshit for the establishment psychiatry routine? Get out motherfucker! You hear me motherfucker? I never killed nobody that was somebody and here it is me, yeah me, who served his country and I've been locked up for 10 years for a crime that was not a crime."

Darnell takes a step slightly away from Stephen and then turns back to him. "You lyin' mother fucker!!" he screams so loud that Stephen hears the words bounce back to him from the other side of the cellblock.

"Darnell," Stephen says, his back pressing against the wall, "I was trying to be helpful. I guess I wasn't." The two men's eyes meet.

Darnell moves menacingly toward Stephen and screams, "Get out, you mother fucking, cock-sucking, white commie mother fucker…"

The sound of the key turning in the lock pulls Stephen and Darnell out of their trance.

The door opens slowly, and an old officer moves through it. Stephen looks through the Plexiglas window and sees three other officers lined up outside, looking as paranoid as he feels.

"Hello, gentlemen," the old officer says, calmly. "Darnell wants you to leave, Stephen. Let's let him be by himself and cool off, alright?"

"I don't want to ever see this motherfucker again," Darnell says to the officer, before turning to Stephen. "You got that?" he says, his long finger pointing a few inches from Stephen's face.

Stephen moves his head back, away from Darnell's finger.

As Darnell slowly backs away, Stephen slides in between the officer and the steel door to the safety of the cellblock. Stephen hears the cell door slam shut before Darnell returns to his rant. The last words Stephen hears as he walks through the gate out of the cell block are a variation of a familiar quote: "I've been locked up for 10 years, in violation of my free will and testimony, by this god forsaken land of ours for a crime that was not a crime."

The echo of those words play in Stephen's consciousness as he pulls into the garage next to Randy's new "man truck," as Dan calls it. Seeing the truck, he smiles. When Randy came home with his full-sized Ford pickup truck Dan and Stephen had unmercifully teased him about it. While Randy insisted it helped him with Home Depot runs and other errands, there was a certain glaring truth to the fact that the particular truck Randy bought, perhaps the biggest and most macho on the lot, somehow didn't fit in with the part of Randy that the whole world saw.

Stephen's respite is short-lived as his thoughts return to that tiny prison cell. He wonders if Darnell would have assaulted him had the officers not been so quick to his cell. He wonders why he wasn't really terrified in the moment, too. He was alert, sure, and there was some fear and he was making escape plans, but he didn't feel panicked. At least not as much as he feels afraid now, with his leg trembling against the clutch as he reflects on Darnell's darting black eyes, his rigid controlled movement, his own obvious concern about his ability to control his rage.

He remembers hearing Darnell described as having no control over his impulses in a treatment team meeting from staff members. If Darnell had no control over his impulses Stephen wouldn't have been parking his car an hour after that awful experience. He goes to his room and tries to find a distraction. He wishes he had some reefer. Finally, he decides to drive to the University and see if Ed is there and can talk.

Ed swivels around in his desk chair with the phone at his ear. He motions Stephen to come in, that he'll be available in a minute. After a few seconds, Ed says, "Stephen just came in, so I'd better go." After another few seconds, he says, "You coming over tonight?"

"Good, great, I'll cook...

"I love you, too," he says, hanging up.

"Young love is beautiful, no?" Ed says to Stephen, grinning.

"It sure is," Stephen says. "You've crossed the infatuation barrier with love intact, right?" he asks.

"I don't know. I never really know when my relationships cross that barrier. I just wait for the women to grow up and leave me."

"This relationship is different though, right?"

Ed knows this relationship is different, but still he thinks for a few seconds." I guess so," he says. "For some reason, I have trouble admitting that."

"It shatters your reputation," Stephen says.

"Oh, what reputation is that?"

"You know, that you have one failed relationship after another. This one is much more of an equal than most of your dates over the last several years, right?"

"Yeah, she's definitely that. I guess it's true that my reputation has suffered and maybe I've resisted that. I'm crazy for her and it's different, I agree. Are you just in the neighborhood or is there something you need?"

"Well...yeah, as a matter of fact, I just left the prison at noon and have something really difficult to talk about concerning Darnell. I wanted to see if I could schedule some supervision time with you. I've got kind of an emergency."

"I've got some time right now if you do," Ed says.

As Stephen makes himself comfortable in his chair he thinks about Ed. He's sort of like a perfect parent, never too busy, always so openly pleased to see you, always ready to listen.

"What's happening with our old buddy Darnell?" Ed asks.

"I'm not sure how to get into this. It's confusing to me. I just had a session with him and basically I pushed him too hard. I kind of broke rapport by pressing him on some of the points we discussed about him way back."

Stephen feels as if he's babbling. "I think he just fired me as his therapist, which was the nicest thing he wanted to do to me. I felt physically threatened. Guards came in to rescue me."

"What do you think happened?" Ed asks.

"He comes up for parole in two months. I think I tried to force him into talking about his conflict about leaving prison before he was ready to talk about it. It probably caused him to decompensate. I'm sure he's, you know, pretty psychotic right now."

"Are you saying you should have been less honest with him?"

"Well I don't know about that, but you yourself said that I should take my time and follow him to the point where he begins to talk about the way out of the prison and then show him how he keeps himself locked up."

"I think you should wait until the content of what he's discussing allows you to contradict the beliefs that keep him locked up. You've been patient. You're feeling like his rage means that you've screwed up. Is that right?"

"Um, yeah," Stephen says.

"What do you do in other contexts when people get mad at you?"

"I'm not sure what you mean."

"Do you ever think that someone being mad at you is a sign that you're in fact being honest and that what you're saying is actually very important to say?"

Stephen isn't following Ed and feels mildly distracted and anxious.

"What's going on with you right now?" Ed asks.

"I don't know I feel… a little confused…nervous."

"Now we're getting somewhere," Ed says, laughing. "Confused, anxious, that's the state of a person who is in the pre-learning stage, right?"

Stephen looks blankly at Ed.

"If you were someone who got angry when you were confused, you'd probably want to hit me right now or do something outrageous where the guards would come bail us both out. What I think you're experiencing right now is Darnell's resistance. Anger's sometimes a reaction to an important truth that makes someone uncomfortable. You were confronting him with an important truth and he got mad."

"Yeah, I can see that."

"If you'd told him something like, 'because of the way the system is rigged, it must be awful for you that there is no way out of here,' he'd have happily agreed and where would he be? Still behind bars."

"Exactly where he is now," Stephen says.

"But now there's hope." Ed tells him. "You've taken a position that requires him to face the part of his story that keeps him where he is and maybe, in enough time, to do something to get out. If you simply follow his lead you two will grow old in that cell. Neither of you wants that, I hope."

"I sure don't," Stephen says. "I see what you're saying."

"Don't think someone's anger means you're wrong. That tendency will haunt you forever if you don't learn to distrust it. Anger is one of the signs that you've tapped into the defense structure that keeps your client stuck. That's why someone like Darnell is such a good teacher. More controlled clients won't let you see what's going on inside them. All I'm saying about Darnell is that he's paying a price and you need to keep showing him that he's no different from all of us. If he wants to stay locked up, he can keep on believing there's no way out."

"What if I go back there and he's decompensated and completely psychotic?" Stephen asks, finally revealing his fear completely.

"I guess you do what you do for psychotic patients, get him to take meds, provide support and comfort, and then as soon as he understands you, you start working the new story through. That's all you can do, right?"

"I think that sounds right."

"You've got the kind of relationship with him to help him get through this. And if there's not time for this year's parole, get him ready for next year's. But you're working on the edge and you care about him and he cares about you. That's what you need."

Stephen races down the steps to the quadrangle on his way to the library. He looks up at the same sky he saw before he went to supervision: round white clouds in a medium blue sky, a sky like a child would draw. He feels the same gentle breeze he must have felt earlier, a warm wind filled with memories: an afternoon sitting on the porch waiting for his father to get home from work to play baseball, a late morning on a day he cut school to wander through Middleton Gardens with his girlfriend, stoned on pot and having sex among oak trees as old as America.

He even remembers the day that he and his ex-wife stopped on their front porch, placing their bags from the hospital to the side to gaze, helplessly in love, at their three-day-old child. All of that must have been there before he went into the building, but he missed it before he had a new story of what happened in Darnell's dreary cell.

Chapter 22

RELATIONSHIPS
CHANGE

SNOW FALLS ON THE PANSIES and ornamental cabbages in the window boxes and planters outside of the psychological services center building. Winter semester was supposed to begin today, but a "winter storm," with the prediction of two inches of accumulated snow, led the University to cancel all undergrad classes. It was left to grad-school administrators to make their own determination whether to yield to the panic that a 20-minute snow flurry causes the typical Southerner.

But Southerners do not run the clinical psychology program at Georgia University. It's run by winter people from places like New York, Minnesota, and Pennsylvania. People with suitable winter clothing who accept wintry dangers as part of the human experience. The outgoing message on the answering machine for graduate students left by Matthew Berman, the co-director of the clinical program reflected these winter attitudes. "I braved the snowflakes and made it here in one piece, so I can't imagine it'll be a problem for everyone to get to class or clinical duties on time."

Stephen had hoped classes would be cancelled – not because of snow-phobia but because he'd gotten very little sleep thanks to a midnight-to-four a.m. conversation with his ex-wife, Charlotte. That conversation actually began over the Christmas holidays when she informed him that she was hoping to move to New York to live with a man that she'd been dating long-distance for about a year. She wanted to give the relationship a chance to evolve and she'd been negotiating a transfer with the company where she worked. That left her planning to take Nicholas to a place where she knew almost no one, had no ideas about preschool and kindergarten programs, and to a city that was not all that easy to maneuver for a single mother. She also was wondering if Nicholas could live with Stephen's mother. He already stayed a couple of days a week with her when Charlotte had to travel or work late into the evening.

Stephen did not have a problem with him living with his mother, but that was his second choice. He tried over the holidays to convince Charlotte that he could provide a place for Nicholas in Atlanta, that he had the flexibility with his graduate school schedule, and that it would be in Nicholas's best interest to live with his father. They argued for hours over the holidays, and before Stephen returned to Atlanta, Charlotte agreed to think about the move, and then at three in the morning she finally agreed for Nicholas to move to Atlanta.

Stephen was so excited when he hung up the phone that he pounded his fist in the air. But now, while opening the door to the clinic, he feels overwhelmed with the logistics of the move. He wonders where he and Nicholas will live. There certainly wasn't enough room for them in his efficiency apartment. He wonders about kindergarten classes and how and where he'll enroll Nicholas. He worries about how he'll attend classes, work in the prison, do his research, and take care of Nicholas. All of these were points raised by Charlotte that were easy for him to refute, and he refuted them for two weeks. But now, the complexity of the questions that were so removed from him before was obvious.

He wondered how Dan and Randy would feel about his needing to move without a proper notice. And leaving them would be hard. They had become his best friends in Atlanta. Sitting and talking with Randy while he painted or having dinner with two of them by the pool felt strangely like home. It was going to be depressing moving into a standard apartment after living in the middle of their beautiful world. And he'd miss the garden his father helped plant. He knew that he'd be leaving the apartment sooner or later, but this was much sooner than he expected.

As he climbs the staircase to the group room, he begins thinking about Ally. They'd been talking on the phone every night with her in New Hampshire with her family and she'd been so supportive in helping him address Charlotte's concerns and yet how might she react to the reality of the changes in their life with Nicholas in it? He was longing to see her but also uneasy about the conversation.

The room is empty. Stephen sinks in his chair and begins reading an assigned article he'd not finished. About three paragraphs in, he glances up and sees Ally in the doorway moving toward him with an unrestrained smile. She slides next to him in his chair and kisses him passionately.

"I missed you," Stephen says.

"I missed you, too, baby doll," Ally says.

They kiss again.

"I hope Matthew and Ed don't come in," Stephen whispers, during a long embrace.

Ally kisses him lightly. "Their cars weren't in the lot when I got here," she says.

"In that case," Stephen says, starting to unbutton her shirt.

Ally grabs his hand. "Let's leave our clothes on at least for the next couple of hours," she says.

"Can we be together all day today?" Stephen asks. "I've got supervision with Ed after this and then I'm free. How about you?"

"I'm free after this for the rest of the day. You want to meet at Aurora Coffee and then go from there?"

"I can't wait," Ally says.

Charles clears his throat audibly from the doorway. "Excuse me," he says, grinning. "I assume that you two missed each other over the break."

"Yeah…we did," Stephen says, sliding slightly away from Ally.

"How was your break?" Ally asks.

"Actually, it was very nice," Charles says, before plopping into a chair next to the couple. He reaches his left hand to Ally, squeezing her hand. "We spent two weeks in Mobile with my grandmother. But I don't know if I got enough rest to get back to all of this," he says, before motioning to the room. Charles reaches his hand to shake Stephen's. "What's happenin' brother?" he asks. "Did you get to see that boy of yours over the holidays?"

"We spent most of Christmas together. He came here the day we got out for the holidays. Then we went to Charleston for Christmas. It was really nice."

Ally looks at Stephen. She loves how he looks when he talks about Nicholas.

"I'll bet it was," Charles says. "We still got to get our boys together when he visits."

"That might be easier in the near future," Stephen says.

Ally and Charles casually look at Stephen to hear his explanation for his comment.

"I was about to tell Ally about all of this. It looks like he's really going to be moving here," Stephen says, and then looks at Ally. "Charlotte finally agreed last night."

"Really? That's great," Ally says.

"Man, you must be thrilled," Charles says to Stephen.

"I am," Stephen says.

"Stephen, that is so fantastic," Ally says, with all the right emphasis.

Stephen looks at her. There was not a hint of reluctance on her part, he surmises. He recognizes her unique strength. Whatever she has to do to make things work out, she does it. And she does it without complaining and with as little ambivalence as is possible for a person with some ability to look at both sides of things.

Stephen pulls her close to him while smiling at Charles.

Outside in the parking lot, Matthew, the department co-chair, and Ed drive up in Ed's twenty-year-old Porsche. They're returning from breakfast where they met to discuss the syllabus for the new semester. But the conversation immediately began with Ed telling Matthew that he'd fallen in love with a "wonderful young gal" that he started dating this summer.

Matthew heard that and took a sip of his coffee. He glanced down at the syllabus and restrained himself from saying out loud what he was thinking – that this will be another twenty-something woman whom Ed met while she was drunk and stoned at an academic function. She'll be behind on her rent. Soon she'll move in with Ed and he'll become troubled by her alcoholic behavior. She'll start therapy, like his earlier girlfriends. Ed will pay the bills. Within a few sessions, she'll begin enjoying the AA or NA meetings her therapist insisted she attend. Within another few months she'll begin realizing that Ed has become her ideal father, helping her to take care of herself and at the same time actualize her potential. Then, Ed will actually help her learn to become independent of him. Maybe she'll return to college, or maybe she'll learn to express those blocked artistic gifts. And as she does this, she'll begin the inevitable search for a way to tell her ideal father that it's time for her to leave. He'll scramble around, trying to find a way to fit into her new life. And yet, as an ideal father he cannot block her actualization even when it involves her needing to leave. And then, following the tearful, apologetic, grateful, goodbye, Ed will sit in his office with the music playing too loud, staring at a book of poetry, wondering if he has the energy for a new relationship.

And even though Matthew felt all of this, he was appalled at the tongue wagging that went on in the department about the inappropriateness of Ed's age-discrepant relationships. Yeah, there was a lack of equality in the relationships, but as far as he could tell the imbalance seemed to be in the favor of the young women who seemed to blossom under Ed's tutelage. In fact, Matthew defended Ed from his behind-the-back critics.

And so, it was with passivity and great reluctance that Matthew pushed the syllabus to the side, slowly turned his eyes toward Ed, and said, "So tell me about this new…wonderful young gal."

Ed examined Matthew closely. "You don't sound like you're actually that interested," he said.

Matthew glanced down at the menu and then looked back at Ed. "Well that's true," he admitted. "It's just that I've heard about wonderful women from you before…I don't mean to be cynical."

"But you can't help yourself…"

"No," Matthew said before chuckling, "No, I can't help myself with you, because you're a hopeless romantic."

"For you, hopeless is redundant modifying romantic, right?" Ed challenged, and then smiled at his old friend.

"Not really. I think a little romance is important. A couple of decades of it with twenty or thirty women is...I don't know, Ed."

Ed took a deep breath. "If I start telling you about this wonderful gal are you going to just tune me out?" he asks.

"I want to hear about her," Matthew said, giving up hope of discussing the syllabus, "but please don't tell me you complete each other's sentences."

Ed grinned. "We do, but if you don't want to hear about it, I can leave out that part. Let me think...I guess I should start at the beginning. She bought a date with me at a theatre fundraiser a year ago and we finally went out this summer."

Matthew had to admit that that was a new one.

"I actually didn't want to go out with her because I heard she was in her forties, but then I decided maybe that wasn't that old."

Matthew laughed, but contained himself by shaking his head from side to side.

"We had trouble scheduling the date, but when we finally did go out, we've been together almost every night since," Ed said before taking a sip of his coffee. "The ironic thing," he continued, "is she didn't buy the date because she wanted to go out with me, per se."

Matthew looked at Ed with interest.

"She was at the auction with a friend and read my bio in the program ...basically it talked about my work at The Social Problems Research Institute. She's a clinical nurse. She directs an agency that provides programs in the community for the mentally ill. She'd been trying to get funding for a grant that she wrote to develop a system to coordinate between the different agencies that administer mental health programs for the severely mentally ill and those that provide homeless programs. The whole purpose for the date was to see if I'd help out. I'll have to tell you I had some trouble getting used to the idea that her reason for wanting to go out with me didn't have to do with…" Ed searched for words.

Matthew jumped in. "Your brilliance and good looks," he offered.

Ed looked at him sheepishly. "Of course," he said.

Matthew nodded.

"The grant she wrote is for a program to reduce the fallout from the fucking Reagan administration's wholesale cuts of the funds for the state hospitals."

"I'm sure that's going to be a mess," Matthew said.

"It already is. They've started releasing some of the back-ward patients, some of whom haven't lived outside of the hospital in ten years. Fortunately, I think the Institute has enough benefactor granting corporations that we can help. This young lady I've fallen in love with, and I use that word advisedly, is divorced and has a six-year-old daughter." Ed flashed his smile. "And even though she's somewhere between forty and forty-five, she doesn't look that old."

Matthew exploded in laughter. "I'm happy for you, Ed," he said. "She sounds very different from anyone you've gone out with since Cynthia."

"In fact, I found myself comparing her to Jean last night," Ed said.

The two spent the rest of the breakfast reminiscing broadly, about Jean and the earlier times in the psychology department when Ed and Matthew were making up the curriculum that trained most of the psychologists practicing in Georgia.

Chapter 23

RELATIONSHIPS CHANGE 2

ED GRINS AT THE STUDENTS seated in the partial circle as he and Matthew walk through the doorway. Matthew frowns as he quickly scans the room to see who did not make it to school.

"Well, it looks like almost everybody braved the frozen tundra and made it to class," he says. "Anyone know where Scott is?" he asks.

"I talked to Scott yesterday," Stephen says. "He was too sick to go for a run. I'm guessing he's still sick." Matthew shakes his head disapprovingly. He thinks nobody is ever too sick to attend class.

"The reason we assigned so much reading over the holidays," Matthew says, "is that this is your last class directed at helping you understand what it means to be doing psychotherapy. You'll get a lot more from your supervision over the next two years, and hopefully throughout your life.

"At this point, we explore the factors that make for a successful therapeutic relationship. Over the next several weeks we're going to be reading and discussing the contributions of Freud, Jung, and other psychoanalytic writers, as well as Fritz Perls and the humanists."

Matthew glances around at the students, then turns to Ed to pick up the ball.

"Yeah," Ed says, before looking out the window closest to him. His gaze lingers on the bark and branches of the old oak tree outside the window. The limbs are draped in white flakes while the bark appears a darker brown in their reflection. "The snow seems to be picking up a bit," he says.

"Before I say a few words about the research in psychotherapy, let me say that, as usual, what we believe affects the questions we ask and ultimately the answers that we get. I hope you gathered from the reading that the nature of the therapeutic relationship and the question of what is therapeutic continues to be a series of very complex questions. Our focus now will be on how these questions have been addressed by the theoreticians and scientists working in this area."

Ally yawns and slides down a little in her chair. This is always her body's natural response to Ed's frequent and wonderful digressions. She isn't bored, just relaxed. A few minutes later, Ed is talking about the archetype of the healer. "In western culture this was originally the priest, and in many less intellectualized cultures, so called primitive cultures, it was the shaman who was the spiritual leader and usually the expert on medicinal herbs and roots. In the West, however, when the priests were dethroned by scientists, the physician took over as healer. Psychology is the first profession to challenge this role for the physician. Psychology evolved because of Descartes's insistence that mind and body are separate. Thus, physicians were left to heal the physical body with physical techniques. Psychologists and priests were left to work with the mind. This is why there is so much natural competition between physicians and psychologists. They're competing for their role as healer. I'd also argue that it's why physicians are most comfortable with behavioral psychologists since they're not trying to heal, but simply correct behavior. In this way, behavioral psychologists are not archetypal healers, but more the archetypal schoolmarm. Physicians are comfortable with psychologists in that role."

There is a roar of laughter since it's known that Ed takes shots at behaviorists every chance he gets and means every word of it. Even students with behavioral orientations can't resist the charm of his steadfast fight even if they disagree with much of the content.

"Ed, I believe in our jointly developed notes," Matthew says, holding his paper up as if to offer proof, "it says that you're going to describe some of the questions that the research has begun addressing before I begin an overview of some of the theoretical issues in this area. Is there any chance that we can return to our plan, now that you have taken another chop at the feet of the behaviorist?"

Matthew and Ed smile at each other warmly.

"Sure, I'm all about making your life easier," Ed says. "But I don't like the image of me at the feet of the behaviorist."

Matthew shakes his head like someone who has suffered so much. "Okay," he finally says. "I'm going to spend whatever time Ed hasn't squandered, I mean used, reviewing the syllabus."

Over the next eight hours twelve inches of snow swept into Atlanta and chaos erupted on the roads. Despite all the warnings and cancellations, most people yawned and went to work. No one could have imagined a snow of this magnitude falling on the undefended city. A line of wrecked, stalled, and grid-locked cars formed from downtown Atlanta to every suburb.

Stephen, his coat zipped to his chin, his gloved hands wrapped around his hot coffee cup, watches the snow grow blinding as he sits under an awning just outside the Aurora coffee shop in Midtown. He's taken with the beauty of white snow sticking to the dark bark of winter-bare trees, and the washed-out images of cars crawling along Piedmont and Monroe Avenues while he imagines repeated permutations of conversations with Randy and Dan about Nicholas moving to Atlanta.

Now the moving beauty of Ally, like a fawn in snow with her blond hair, white scarf, and tan coat, enters the snowy field. He puts his coffee cup on the table and hugs her. He has missed her over the Christmas break much more than he'd suspected he would. She gets a coffee, and they sit close, the only people braving the snow outside.

"I know you have to be thrilled about Nicholas moving here," Ally says.

"I am…really," he says. "I'm having a little trouble figuring out how it's all going to work though."

"I've been thinking all morning about an idea," Ally says. "Now, don't go and reject it until you think it over. Okay?"

"I'm…open to your ideas," Stephen says, before kissing her cheek.

Ally steels herself with a breath. "Um, what do you think about you two moving into my place? I have an extra bedroom, where I already have a single bed. The only problem is I don't have much closet space."

Stephen smiles. "I don't know, that's a nice offer," he says, "but…"

"It would solve a lot of your problems," Ally says.

"Yeah, but I don't know how it would be for Nicholas to move in with me into your place. He likes you, of course, but I don't know… I think I need to solve this first and then we can work on that in the future."

Stephen squeezes Ally and kisses her lightly.

"Is that really what it is or is it that you don't know if you're ready to live with me?" Ally asks.

"I'd love to live with you. I love waking up with you, going to sleep with you. It's just the timing isn't right. You know?"

"Yeah, I guess." Ally says.

"That's a really generous offer," Stephen says. "I love you."

"I love you, too," Ally says. "You know, I'm a little scared about this change. I'm really happy for you and for us, but...I just worry that maybe somehow you'll get too busy or...What I'm saying is that I don't want to lose you and I want to be a part of your life with Nicholas if we can figure a way and I know we can."

"I want to work it all out, too. One thing about Nicholas moving here is that we'll all have a lot time together," Stephen says.

"You're amazing, Stephen," she says. "I love hearing you say you love me in the daylight... and with the snow falling."

Stephen kisses her head.

"This is really quite romantic, sitting out here in the wicked cold watching a snowstorm. I'm surprised with you being a southerner that you can tolerate this," Ally says.

"It's so beautiful I've hardly noticed the cold," Stephen says. "So maybe you should let go of your stereotypes."

"Maybe I should," Ally says. "After saying that, I'm embarrassed to say this, but I'm a little worried about the streets freezing over."

"Really?" Stephen asks.

"This is a serious snow we're having," Ally says, "And the traffic is getting heavier. I think this could get ugly."

"You want to go?" Stephen asks.

"I think we need to," Ally says. "But before we go I want to say one more thing about all of this. I know it's hard for you to ask for help, but I can be a big help. I want you to ask if..."

Stephen pulls her closer. "That's probably a good observation. It's hard for me sometimes. I'll try to remember to ask. I've been thinking all morning about talking with Dan and Randy about all of this. I'm going to have to ask them for help, either to get out of my lease or to make some changes to my apartment."

"What kind of changes?" Ally asks.

"I can't live for very long in my efficiency with Nicholas there, too. It's going to be hard for me to ask, but I've been thinking about asking if they could expand my space. There's a large closet on the other side of my room. Randy uses it to put paintings in when he's sort of half-finished or stuck about what to do next. I was thinking if he could use another storage area, they could close off that room on his side and open it up on my side and it'd make a nice little bedroom for Nicholas. But I don't know..."

"You could ask...his studio is huge. I'm sure he'll do whatever he can to help," Ally says.

"I'm not worried so much about Randy. If he can make it work, he will. Dan is another story. I'm pretty sure Dan won't approve. He's nice to Nicholas, but I don't think Dan wants anyone else living there. Sometimes I wonder if he even wants me there."

"I'll bet Dan will be fine with it. That sure would solve the problem."

"We'll see," Stephen says. "Can we go to my place?"

"Of course," Ally says. "Maybe you'll get a chance to ask them about the changes today."

After a slow drive on winding neighborhood roads between Midtown and Buckhead, Stephen and Ally park in Stephen's spot in the three-car garage. They high step through the virgin snow, now four or five inches deep, walking toward Stephen's apartment.

Randy walks out of his studio and slides his jacket over his tee shirt. "Can you believe this?" he asks, motioning toward the new world.

"It's beautiful," Ally says.

"Did you have trouble getting home?" Randy asks.

"Not really. We went back roads the whole way and the roads weren't that bad," Stephen says.

"Dan just called from his car. The interstates are almost completely impassable," Randy says, as he leads Ally and Stephen into his studio.

"Is he going to be able to make it home?" Stephen asks.

"I hope so. Apparently, the interstates are the worst. He just left his office and says he's going to go the back roads, but he heard all the roads from his office were packed."

"Oh no," Stephen says. "He's probably going to be pretty upset when he gets home."

"He didn't sound too bad. He said he was going to make an adventure of it. I'm sure he'll update me from his car phone. Anyway, I went to the store a couple of hours ago and got lots of groceries so if we're snowed in we can last a few days. I just heard on the radio that they expect it to continue snowing like this for at least the next five hours or so."

"I hope you and Dan are okay with me moving in until the snow let's up," Ally says.

"The more the merrier," Randy says.

Stephen looks at Ally. Somehow, he senses that she thinks this is the ideal time to bring up the conversation about Nicholas. That's confirmed when she raises her eyebrows at him and tilts her head in Randy's direction. He looks away and then looks back. Suddenly, he acquiesces. "Randy, something happened last night that I have to talk to you about," he says.

"What?" Randy asks.

"I talked to Charlotte and she is going to be moving to New York, which is a very long story, but Nicholas is going to move to Atlanta and live with me." Just like that it was all out there. No wondering how or when to say it.

"Really," Randy says. "You must be thrilled."

Stephen nods, "I haven't really had time to get too excited. I've been overwhelmed with the details. I've got to figure out what to do with the living arrangements."

"What do you mean?" Randy asks.

"I don't know what to do," Stephen says. "I've been thinking that I could either move into a two-bedroom place, or maybe, if it works for you and Dan, we could figure a way to make my place a little bigger, if that's even possible. If we could do some work on my place to make a little more room, I could borrow some money from one of my parents or my sister for the work and pay some more for rent. But I know that would inconvenience you and Dan, and so I want to ask for that, but I want both of you to feel that you can say no."

"Why would we say no? We love Nicholas. How is he going to be any more trouble for us?" Randy asks. Randy looks around the room. "I guess we could do something by moving a wall and adding some space. The build-out wouldn't cost much because I could do the work. You could even help me. You know what's a natural thing is for us to close the door space to my closet and then open it on your side of the wall. It's a perfect little space for Nicholas," Randy says, walking toward the closet.

"That's...I was thinking that might work," Stephen says.

"I could close this up with some sheet rock and open it up on your side. I could even use the same door," he says, opening the door. "It'd probably take me about as long to clean all this junk out as it would to sheet rock it and put in the door on your side."

"That would be a cozy little room for Nicholas," Ally says.

"Are you sure you could do without your closet?" Stephen asks.

"I can always find a place to hide my offending paintings," Randy says.

"What do you think Dan will say... about all of this?" Stephen asks.

"I think he'll be fine with it," Randy says, though conviction was noticeably absent from his voice. "I'm just so happy for you. I know how much you miss Nicholas when he's not here."

Randy is smiling at Stephen when the phone rings. It's Dan. He has traveled about a mile in a little over thirty minutes. The roads are covered with wrecked vehicles, but he feels reasonably certain he'll make it home alive.

Stephen fills Randy in on some of the details about Nicholas's move and they spend some more time planning the expansion before Stephen and Ally leave Randy alone in the studio. Randy's thoughts immediately turn to the impending change. Having a child in his home would certainly be an adventure. Randy immediately feels sad, the sadness of being childless, the only thing he ever regretted about his life. But now there was a child moving into the house. Even though that was going to make things more complicated it would be good for everyone, even Dan. The very difficult question was how to help Dan see that. How do you encourage Dan to see how important it is for them to help Stephen have what he wanted most, Nicholas moving in with him? You just say it straight out. Let him have his hysterical reaction, and then wait for him to get over it. And then build the space and Nicholas moves in, and Dan sees how wonderful life can be with a new life in it.

Randy looks at the painting on the easel. He feels calm, although he knows it's going to be an emotional evening. Ever since Stephen started calling his painting therapy, he's become even more aware of the power of images to alter his feelings.

The phone rings. "Dan?" he asks.

"Yes, darling, it's me," Dan says. It's his fourth phone call since he left his office. "I just turned onto our street and should be in our driveway in a minute. Please, pour me a scotch and greet me at the door."

"I'll be there," Randy says.

Chapter 24

CONFLICT AND CHANGE

IT'S AN HOUR AND TWO STRONG COCKTAILS since Dan arrived home. He has barely paused for a breath, describing every horrific detail of his trip home from the office. The scotch and shoulder massage begin to take effect and Randy decides it's time to break the news about Nicholas.

"There's something important we need to talk about," he says.

Dan looks around, panicky. "Is it the dogs? Has someone else gotten AIDS?"

"It's nothing like that. It's just…Stephen found out today that Nicholas is going to be moving to Atlanta to live with him."

"Really? Is his ex-wife moving to Atlanta?"

"No, she might a year from now from something he said. I'm not sure of the details, but for at least the next year, Nicholas is going to live with Stephen. I think you understand the situation, right?"

Dan looks at Randy. "I don't know what I'm supposed to understand," he says. "So, just tell me what you're saying. Tell me how this news requires a serious conversation between you and me."

"I know you're going to react poorly to this..." Randy starts, before Dan interrupts.

"Then why don't you spare both of us that?" Dan says, glaring at Randy.

"Okay, okay," Randy says. "I thought maybe we could do some renovations to Stephen's space and make it nice for Nicholas to move in."

Dan looks closely at Randy and then to the side. His eyes focus on multicolored squares on a Russian tapestry hanging on the wall, a family heirloom, given to him by his grandfather on his graduation from Wharton. With almost no intonation, he says, "Somehow I thought you might want to do that." His eyes stay on the tapestry. Randy notices and thinks how Dan is calming himself with an image just like he does with his painting. But it did not last long.

"It makes sense. Stephen is a wonderful tenant and we've got the space," Randy says. He explains the plan to extend the apartment's space to the studio's adjoining closet.

Dan notices the excitement in Randy's voice. He cannot remember the last time that Randy reacted to anything having to do with their life with that much enthusiasm. He feels sad, then angry.

"Why do you do this to me...to us?" he asks, the pressure of restrained anger in his voice. "Why can't we have our wonderful life without you always needing to do this to us?"

"Do what? I'm suggesting that we expand the space that we rent to Stephen. He has already agreed to pay for the materials. I just need to change the closet."

Randy watches Dan's face turn redder as Dan assumes from what Randy has said that Randy and Stephen have made some kind of plans without consulting him. "You've told him that he can do this. You've told him without asking me that he can move his child into our house."

Randy jumps up. "I did not. I told him that I'd have to check with you first... I did. I told him that we always make these kinds of decisions together. He just said if you agreed, he'd pay for the materials."

"Oh, that's fucking wonderful. So, either we do this or I get to be the bad guy. I'm sure you said how perfect it would be if only rigid Dan, the guy who pays for most of what goes on around here, would just be a decent human and go along with things."

Randy sits back down. Calmly, he says, "I can't understand why you wouldn't want to do this for Stephen."

Dan stares at Randy. "I'm not interested in this conversation," he says, before taking a long drink of scotch.

"Of course, you're not, because you know you're wrong," Randy says.

"Fuck you," Dan yells. Dan can see that Randy flinches. He sighs and shakes his head. "I had a very hard day and you're making it worse."

Dan walks to the coffee table and picks up the Wall Street Journal. He begins skimming the headlines.

Randy looks at him. "I can't believe you don't want Nicholas moving in here," he says.

Dan flips the paper over looking at the Marketplace section.

"Let me rephrase that," Randy says. "What are we going to do, just let Stephen and Nicholas move somewhere else? Where is Stephen going to find a place this nice for Nicholas to live? We live in the best school district in the state, we have a great yard..."

"School district? The kid is five. He won't be starting school for two more years. How long do you plan on these people living here?"

"Stephen and Nicholas aren't 'these people.' Stephen is our friend and Nicholas is his son. He's in kindergarten. They go to public school for kindergarten these days. I'd like for us to be supportive of Stephen and Nicholas."

"Oh please. I don't mind supporting you, but I work hard for my money."

Dan walks back to the bar and pours more scotch into his glass.

"You don't support me," Randy says, standing. "Why do you have to say stupid shit like that?"

"Let's see," Dan says. "Because when I met you, you were driving a ten-year-old truck, going down to visit your aunt in Jacksonville to interview for a job as a landscape architect for some redneck company. And now you live here… and get fussy when someone wants you to paint a picture using specific colors. What an ungrateful…" Dan hesitates, knowing he's going too far.

"I'm not Eliza Doolittle. I cannot stand it when you act like you made me a member of the respectable class. That is so fucking insulting."

"All I'm saying is I've given you a damn easy life and you know it." Dan reaches for his glass and swirls the ice around.

"Listen, Dan. I pay a third of your mortgage payment. I don't get any of the tax benefit for that. I think you get that. I've completely renovated this house…one room at a time, and completely changed the entire landscape. I take your fucking laundry to the cleaners. I shop for everything we have. I moved my studio here to save on rent, so I could afford more of the mortgage payment. I built my studio and the efficiency that Stephen rents which together brings in enough money so that essentially, I pay half the mortgage. And I have no legal claim to the enormous value of this house that comes from all of our work. And right now, you big powerful man, I'm leaving… your… house."

Dan blinks. "Go ahead," he says, his voice a little quieter than before. Randy walks out of the room.

"Get the fuck out of here," Dan yells.

"Fuck you!" Randy yells, as he walks down the hall toward the kitchen and the back door. Dan flinches when he hears the backdoor slam.

Echoes of Randy's voice and the slammed door fade, and now there is silence. Dan walks to the couch and sits. He takes a sip of his drink and looks down at the Wall Street Journal but leaves it next to him on the couch. Randy's list of his contributions to the home was startling. Surely, he'd heard it before. So why did it seem impressive this time? And Randy seemed so angry. Dan hoped he'd come back soon. He'd try to be more reasonable if he did come back.

But he'd not change his mind. Even if Randy contributed a lot to their home, it did not mean that Dan had to do everything that he wanted. Maybe Randy just needed to hear from him that he appreciated all that he did. He sure would like to hear some appreciation from Randy, too.

Dan turns around and strains to look out the window at the moment the lights go on in the studio. Great! Randy can get absorbed in his art and all he can do is read the paper or watch TV. And he was home early and would be hungry soon and the restaurants would be closed because of the weather.

Dan hates the silence.

"Fuck him," he says out loud. He slides off the couch and walks to the kitchen. The immaculate kitchen is quiet, too. He walks to the window and looks toward the studio. His eyes wander to Stephen's window. He thinks about what it would be like for Nicholas to live there. He's not sure what it is that he objects to so strongly, but he trusts his intuition that the change wouldn't be good.

Stephen's door opens. A yellow light lengthens onto the walkway. Dan steps back so that he can observe without being seen in
the window. The light disappears. Shadowy images of Stephen and
Ally move toward the studio. The studio door opens, lighting the
walkway again. The two figures disappear inside, and the light
withdraws. The only thing besides silence in the kitchen is the hum
of the refrigerator.

"What are you doing out here with the king at home?" Stephen asks,
as he slides onto a barstool.

"I don't know. He's in a bad mood because of all the stress of getting
home. I decided to get away from him," Randy says, hoping that would
satisfy Stephen enough to change the subject.

"Oh," Stephen says. "Does this have anything to do with, you know,
the thing about Nicholas moving in?"

"Um, not really. It's not really about that," Randy says, showing
gross ineptitude at lying.

"So, he didn't like the idea. I didn't think he would," Stephen says.

"No, don't worry about it. He's just in a bad mood. We'll talk more
about it later. I'm sure it's going to be fine."

"Okay, but I don't want this to be a problem for you or for Dan and
I'm flexible. So don't let this be a problem, okay?" Stephen says.

"So, you and Dan have been arguing, right?" Ally says.

"Well, yeah, a little, but it doesn't really have to do with Nicholas
moving in. We're having our recurring argument about whether or not
I have the same rights as him, and as I said, he's just in a bad mood."

"I'm sorry you're going through that," Ally says.

"Thank you…I'm all right. Really."

Stephen notices Randy seems to relax with Ally's supportive comments.

"What are you doing for dinner?" Ally asks.

"I'm probably going to paint for a little while and get a sandwich. Do you have food in your fridge?" Randy asks, looking at Stephen.

"We're fine," Ally reassures.

"You're a beautiful couple," Randy says.

Ally squeezes Stephen's hand. "He told me he loved me today in the daylight."

Randy grins and looks at Stephen.

Stephen smiles like a shy child. "Okay, have a good therapy, I mean painting, session and don't let me be the cause of problems between you and Dan," Stephen says, as he takes Ally's hand leading her to the door.

"Any problems that Dan and I have, whether or not we're talking about you, have to do with us," Randy says.

Stephen fumbles for the doorknob as he considers Randy's statement.

"I appreciate you saying that," he says.

Dan has returned to the study and arranged himself on the couch so that he can see when Stephen and Ally leave the studio. He watches the reverse sequence of the lights and images, and then stillness. He points the remote at the TV, turning it on. Maybe something decent is happening elsewhere. He flips from one station to the other.

After three rotations through all the possible choices available from his cable, he tries to read the Journal, but his eyes are blurry from the alcohol. Finally, he pulls a quilt to his shoulders, curls in the corner of the couch, and falls asleep.

About two hours later, he wakes to the sound of Randy coming in the back door. He spends a few minutes in the kitchen and then runs upstairs. Dan hears his heart pound. He's angry. How could Randy treat him like this over something so small that has nothing to do with him personally? But he's also terrified. What if Randy decided that he was such an asshole that he couldn't put up with him anymore? He fights the desire to rush to Randy.

Randy sits in a chair in their bedroom, looking out the window while eating a turkey sandwich. He takes a sip of his Diet Coke. He knew in advance that Dan wouldn't want Nicholas moving in. But he also knew that allowing Nicholas to move in and keeping Stephen living there was the right thing to do. It was right for Stephen and Nicholas, for himself, and it was right for Dan.

Randy is so sure that he's right that it does not matter how long it takes Dan to see that. He'll wait. He finishes his sandwich and walks toward the shower. He turns the water on. And he's finished with Dan treating him like a second-class citizen. He can wait him out on that, too. He won't do anything until he gets a full apology, and this time he will require a commitment to the subject of money never being mentioned in a fight again. Never. He takes his clothes off and gets in the shower.

Randy lathers his hair with his eyes closed as Dan walks quietly into the wide area leading into the bathroom. He marvels at the body of the man he loves. Randy rinses the soap from his hair and catches a glimpse of Dan walking quickly away.

Dan sits in the same chair in the bedroom where Randy was earlier. Randy walks into the bedroom holding his bathrobe tightly closed, communicating his desire to hold himself away from Dan. He turns away from him and begins brushing his hair in a mirror.

Dan is disheartened as his eyes follow his lover's movement. Finally, he offers, "This is a ridiculous argument. We both know that...I wish you could understand that all I'm saying is that I want to keep things the way they are. That's always the way it is. I never want to argue with you… I hate this stuff, but you constantly bring this on us. Why can't you just let things stay the same and let us live our happy life?"

Randy sits on the bed and turns toward Dan. "I didn't bring this on us. Life brought this on and I want us to support Stephen on this."

"Can we talk about us?" Dan asks.

"I'm talking about us and I'm talking about me and what I want," Randy says.

"Even if it contradicts what I want and need?" Dan asks.

"I could say the same thing. What you want contradicts my desire to be generous to a good friend," Randy says.

"That's not the issue here," Dan says.

"That's what the issue is for me," Randy says.

Dan can see that Randy is sad. He wants to hold him, but he stays put. "This is so unnecessary," he says, "for us to be fighting over this. I can't believe I finally get home at a decent hour and this is what I have to deal with."

Randy glances at the clock. It's still before eight o'clock. "I want to spend the rest of the evening close to you, too, but this is important," Randy says.

"Come on, Ran," Dan says.

"Before we do anything, I want you to apologize to me for that bullshit about me being some kind of kept man. You've promised not to bring money into our arguments and you do it every time."

"I didn't say anything about you being a kept man," Dan says.

Randy stares at him.

"What?" Dan asks, and giggles nervously. "Okay, if you thought I was talking about money that way, I'm sorry," Dan says.

Randy turns and looks at him. "What a pathetic attempt at an apology," he says.

"What I was talking about had nothing to do with money," Dan says. "It had to do with fairness and how you impose your will on me and change everything to suit you."

Randy wants to throw his hairbrush at him but simply turns away and brushes his hair.

Dan stands up and walks to the French doors and looks out at the back yard. "Why do you always make me deal with this shit?" he asks.

Randy turns and stares at Dan's back. He knows that Dan will keep repeating the same accusations. "Goodnight," Randy says. He leans over and turns his lamp out. He slips out of his robe and under the covers. He turns away from Dan onto his side.

Dan stands completely still. He's shocked that Randy is so resolved about all of this. A dim light from outside allows him to see the long, shapely figure under the blanket. He feels lonely. He'd expected to have sex, but that certainly wasn't going to happen. He plops in bed, jarring Randy a bit. He lies in bed at first with his eyes open, then he forces them closed, only to find them open again. An hour later he looks at the clock. He can't recall insomnia of more than five minutes in the last ten years. Of course, he's trying to go to sleep earlier than normal and he's pissed, but finally he falls asleep.

The next morning, Dan is sitting at the very elegantly worn eight-seat farm table that he and Randy considered quite a bargain when they found it in an antique store in the north Georgia mountains. They "restored" it by adding appropriately placed dents and scratches in addition to shoring up the joints. He's looking at his front yard as he sips his second cup of coffee. God, he loves his acre of beautifully manicured, wonderfully landscaped front yard. Suddenly, he has an image of his lawn covered with large primary colored children's cars and radio flyer wagons and bicycles. He spontaneously yells, "No!" He glances around to make sure no one heard him.

He feels stronger this morning after getting more sleep than he has gotten maybe since high school, even though Randy walked straight past him without speaking on his way to his studio a couple of hours ago. "Fuck him and his self-righteous bullshit," Dan thinks. He flips the TV on to check the weather and road conditions. He noticed when he went to get the undelivered newspaper that the road was deep in snow and did not have a tire track on it.

Today would have been a perfect day to go to work and bury himself in a bunch of detailed financial reports and forget about all of the social work being proposed at his expense in his own home. Instead, now he's locked into his home without his partner who is probably painting guys with gorgeous dicks, sublimating his sexual frustration. Isn't that what Freud said art was about: allowing artists and their patrons to experience their sexual frustrations and perversions in socially acceptable ways? He'd have to ask Stephen whether or not that was still the prevailing view in psychology. Maybe that's why Stephen calls Randy's painting therapy. Dan thinks about some way of getting Randy to see his point. He thinks about different ways to say what he has already said several times. He knows that never works. And he misses Randy.

He'd love to get back in his warm bed with him.

He wanders around the house before finding himself walking down the stairs to the basement. Randy has his studio; the basement was supposed to be Dan's work area. When Dan and Randy first moved into their house ten years ago, before his job at Coke became completely consuming, he did all of the woodworking and most of the electrical wiring for their expansions. As he reaches the bottom step, he remembers how much he loves this area of his house even though he rarely visits it.

He has every woodworking and electrical tool needed for home construction and repair. He walks to the potbelly stove, opening the front door. He fills it with some dry logs from last year. These should have no trouble burning. He lights the fire. Immediately, some of the dampness leaves the room.

He turns on the fluorescent lights above his workbench. He looks at the cluttered countertop, a situation that he never would've allowed a few years ago. When was the last time he was in here, maybe a couple of weeks after they returned from their trip to France, and then just to unload the two-hundred-year-old wine racks they bought?

God, he missed this place, with all its simplicity, things that worked by turning this or fastening that. Nothing at Coke, at least not at the senior vice-president level, worked anything like that. In fact, you never knew how or why something worked, even when you got your dreaded revenue numbers. All you ever knew was whether you made those numbers. Then when you did make them, you doubted their meaningfulness, and began the mad pursuit of the numbers for the next quarter that had to exceed the previous numbers by an arbitrarily derived percentage.

He walks over to the wine racks. The racks were from an ancient winery and were chipped and bent, just the way Randy wanted them. But when they arrived after being shipped across the Atlantic, a few of the support beams were broken. He promised Randy that he'd weld them together and help install them in their new wine cellar, which Randy had built with rustic stone floors, stark white walls, and electric candles for lighting. They even built a separate staircase to the kitchen so that they could invite guests into the wine cellar for tastes. But the cellar was absent the requisite wine racks not to mention the wine. It didn't matter. Randy sure didn't care anything about wine. What he cared about was creating a wonderful wine cellar and, except for the racks, he'd done that.

Dan examines the broken pieces. He walks across the room to his welding equipment and slaps away some cobwebs from his machine.

He picks up the welding gun and carries it while rolling the machine in the direction of the wine racks. He walks back and gets the gas tank and mask. He returns to the wine racks. He squats down and examines the broken parts. He presses the two pieces together. They fit nicely.

Quickly, he walks to the workbench. God must have provided the snow of the century for something other than a wasted day off, he thinks. He searches through drawers of one of his cabinets and pulls out some thick welding wire that is perfect for the job.

He carries two pairs of vice grips and the wire to the wine racks. He squeezes the broken parts together, fastening them with the grips. He turns on his welding gun. Gas seethes out the long thin nozzle. He clicks the lighter spark in front of the gun igniting a steady stream of blue heat. He adjusts the flame down a bit.

His posture, his movement, even his internal image of himself is his grandfather, his father's father, who taught him how to weld. The wrinkled, straight-backed ninety-five-year-old man was still alive. Watching his grandfather with a welding gun was like watching Randy with a paintbrush. Every move was so graceful. Even in his eighties, with his dime store reading glasses, he could lay the flame on a thin wire and drip liquid metal exactly where it needed to be with none of the excesses of younger, less artistic welders.

The old man, as Dan's family called him, hadn't always been a welder. Born in Russia, he headed a prosperous construction company founded by his father. In 1917, the anti-Semitic Communists forced the family to flee to Germany where he started a company of his own. It too prospered until 1932 when the banks prematurely called in loans against Jewish-owned business as part of Hitler's effort to wrest control of industry from his adversaries. Again, he had to abandon his business and his company, this time moving his wife and three children to America, a country where he knew no one and didn't speak a word of the language. That and his weariness kept him from starting another business, so he became a welder, making enough money to create a comfortable middle-class life for his family. But he also had a dark side. Dan's mother told him that the old man had been abusive to his children throughout their youth.

Perhaps so, but he was nothing but supportive to Dan, whose father treated him with icy contempt much of the time, even refusing to pay more than half his tuition at Harvard, despite being one of Cleveland's first millionaires. His grandfather stepped forward and paid the remaining balance every semester. Most importantly, his grandfather explained to him that his father's refusal to pay, like his general contempt, was because he was jealous of Dan's brilliance and all of the opportunity ahead of him. After that, Dan was able to listen to his father's ranting without absorbing any of it as true.

At least as much as Dan learned to loathe his father, he developed a deep love for his grandfather. Sitting here now, he realizes that he shared his grandfather's acumen as a businessman and a welder. His heart swells.

Besides small doses of his mother, Dan cannot think of anyone else in his family he likes being around. There were no stable relationships in his extended family. Even his parents went weeks without speaking to one another when he was a kid, barely acknowledging his own presence. So when Randy stormed out last night, Dan felt that old familiar dinnertime knot in the pit of stomach like maybe he'd be alone forever. In the past, the knot always sent him to Randy talking or yelling or maybe even pleading to try to find some resolution to any conflict. That lonely feeling still felt like it might last forever.

Everything was different for Randy. Everyone stayed married in Randy's family. And arguments, even if perhaps too rare, were followed by forgiveness and deeper commitments. So, Randy could be calm.

And Dan had to remind himself that Randy was angry, he wasn't ending the relationship.

Dan bears down on the wire melting it along a thick line fastening the broken parts. He works along the line over and over until he feels that it's sealed. He reaches back and turns the gas off. The flame disappears. He examines the rack and slowly releases the gripping vice. The steel stays solid. He moves to the next broken joint, presses the two parts together and clamps them with the grips. He turns the gas on, again.

Meanwhile, Randy spreads his third color over a light pink trying to get the mix of colors right for the skin on Ally's face. The hair, fine streaks of gold, yellow, and light tans, and even a touch of silver, was right. Everything about her skin was wrong. He tries to imagine her gazing eastward into morning sunlight, but the colors were wrong. He throws the brush into the sink, hops onto his stool, and looks back at the annoying painting. Could he suck any worse?

He wonders what Dan is doing. He slides off the stool and walks to the door. He opens it and is slapped by the thin, cold air. He leans on the doorframe and looks toward the house. How did he end up in such a difficult relationship? On the other hand, he was in a relationship with a man who was brilliant and capable of extreme kindness. Not to mention that everything in both of their lives worked better because they were together. He sighs deeply. His arms are heavy, even though he has only painted for three hours, and must admit that most of what he has painted has been awful.

Dan returns the welding equipment to its place. He reaches for a rag and wipes the soot from his hands. He looks in the small mirror hanging over the sink as he scrubs his hands with mechanics' soap. He's drenched in sweat even though it's probably fifty-five degrees in the room. His hair is covered with soot, while his face has streaks of black on it from his hands brushing against him when he removed his mask. He kind of looks working class and very butch. He wishes Randy could see him.

He wants to make up with Randy, but he wants to be understood first. He looks out the basement window and can see Randy leaning against his door. God, he loves looking at Randy and he wants to show him the wine racks.

He opens the basement door. "Ran," he calls out.

"What?" Randy responds, a little bit of disinterest in his tone.

"Come here, I want to show you something."

Randy walks to the basement door.

"What happened to you?" he says, startled by Dan's sweaty, dirty clothes.

"I've been welding all morning. Come here," he says, before guiding Randy to the wine racks.

"Oh Dan, they're incredible. I can't believe you fixed both of them so fast." Randy puts pressure on the repaired joints. "They're solid," he says.

"After they cool, you can put as much weight on it as you want. They're as good as new. I need to file some of the excess off," Dan says.

"No, I like it just like this. They look even older. Let's put them in the cellar."

Dan and Randy carry the racks to the wine cellar. Randy opens the door that connects the basement to the wine cellar. They place the racks against the back wall. They go back into the basement and move the tasters' table and chairs into the room. Randy turns on the lights. "Now all we need is some wine," he says.

"Why don't I get a bottle of Champagne from the fridge and we can celebrate by having a glass in here," Dan says.

"I need to work this afternoon," Randy says.

Dan feels hurt that Randy isn't more enthusiastic and won't abandon his work for an afternoon with him. He forces himself to persist. "Can't we just have one…buddy."

"Okay. I can have one," Randy says, before smiling at Dan.

Dan returns with the bottle and two glasses. He releases the cork, bouncing it off the ceiling, before directing the bubbling wine into each glass.

"To our partnership," Dan says, before raising his glass toward Randy's.

"I'll drink to that, even though it hasn't felt like a partnership around here lately," Randy says.

Dan frowns, but clicks his glass to Randy's. "I could say the same thing, but I'm trying to celebrate us right now," he says, before sitting down on one of the uncomfortable iron chairs.

"I want to celebrate us, too," Randy says. "I love you. I just want you to…"

Dan interrupts Randy. "You just want me to agree with you."

Randy sits down. "I want you to treat me like an equal, let me make some of the big decisions," he says.

"Why can't we make the big decisions together?" Dan asks.

"Of course, we can make them together. But you won't talk about the decisions. You want to talk about how you've rescued me from the gutter," Randy says.

"I just get upset because you act like I'm crazy because I don't immediately agree with you," Dan says.

"I'm not saying you're crazy. I just feel like I've got intuition about some things that you won't listen to," Randy says.

"Same here," Dan says.

"Okay, I sure can understand that. But what do we do when something like this comes up, something where there isn't an easy compromise?" Randy asks.

"Well, if there isn't an easy compromise I wish we could say that if we're going to change the status quo we should each have a veto," Dan says.

"You can't be serious?" Randy says.

Dan looks at Randy, confused. "Yes, I'm serious."

"I could choke to death in that kind of environment," Randy says.

Dan stares at Randy.

"What makes you think I don't treat you like an equal?" Dan asks.

"Because you don't," Randy says.

"I treat you like an equal, most of the time, don't I?"

"Yes, until you get mad at me and then you start that Henry Higgins stuff, which makes me want to kill you."

"I think of you as an equal, but I'd like to get something back from that," Dan says.

Randy bursts into an angry laughter. "What do you mean? What if I said that? 'Dan, I think of you as an equal, but sometimes I want to get something back from that.' How does that sound?"

"That's not exactly what I said."

"Yes it is, and it's exactly what it feels like. You want to acknowledge that we're equals until we disagree, and then you start talking about our mortgage and me being a kept man, and all of that doesn't lead us to discussing whatever it is that we're disagreeing about."

Dan is alarmed that Randy seems so quick to get back to his anger. "You're right. Let's try to stay cool. Can we talk about Nicholas moving in here?" Dan asks.

Randy looks at Dan. He takes a sip of his Champagne. "If you think we can talk about it without getting in a huge argument again," he says.

"I'll try, if you'll try to understand me," Dan says.

"I'll try."

"I thought about it. You know what his moving in here means to me? It means that I might lose my peaceful place to relax and connect to you and people that we invite over but can also invite to leave. I don't mean like kick them out, but just…"

"I know what you mean. I like being able to be alone with you, too. Has that changed since Stephen moved in?"

"Yes, actually it has. I'm not complaining, but it has changed some and I worry about any more changes. I've not always had good luck with change," Dan says, a reference that Randy immediately understands is to his family growing up.

"I know," Randy says.

"I want to know that if things are not working for me, that we can change things. But most of all I want you to understand that I'm not being mean or uncaring when I say I want to be cautious about Nicholas moving in. I'm protecting what we have, which is worth everything to me."

Randy notices that Dan's eyes are filled with tears.

"You…what I have with you…means so much to me," Dan continues. "I have to protect that."

"I love hearing you say that," Randy says. He reaches across the table and squeezes Dan's hand. "I love you."

Dan leans closer to Randy. "I love you, too." He says, as he fights his tears. "So here's what I propose…we make this change. We have Nicholas move in, change the apartment, but on a one-year trial basis. We give Stephen a new one-year lease and if any of us, Stephen, you, me, any one of us, doesn't want to renew the lease at the end of the year, there's no questions asked?"

"I love that," Randy says, before squeezing Dan's hand again.

"See, I can be reasonable," Dan says.

"Thank you for putting so much thought into this. You're such a special man," Randy says.

"Thank you. Now, can we go get in bed and have some great sex?" Dan says.

"Let's go!" Randy says, jumping up from his chair.

"You have no idea how hot welding makes me," Dan says.

"Oh yes I do," Randy says, brushing the soot from Dan's face.

Chapter 25

ART AND CHANGE

THREE MONTHS AFTER NICOLAS MOVED to Atlanta, Stephen and Ally return from dinner with Dan and Randy, who asked a blushing, clearly flattered Ally to pose nude for him. She quickly accepted. Now, Stephen tells Ally he needs to do some reading for his dissertation, so he'll be staying up after she goes to bed. Ally can't remember a time when she and Stephen haven't had sex and fallen asleep together.

"Is anything wrong?" Ally asks.

"Um, everything's, you know, fine," Stephen mutters.

Since she'd been fighting sleep on the way home from dinner, Ally brushes her teeth, washes her face and gets into bed.

"Are you sure you have to work on your dissertation tonight?" she asks, smoothing the covers down and exposing her bare shoulders.

"Um, yeah. I'm meeting with Ed tomorrow," Stephen says, not looking up at her, which is something he never does.

"Are you sure? Because you seem different, like something's bothering you."

"I'm fine."

"You seemed quiet at dinner," she says.

"Yeah, I just, you know, I don't know."

"Something is bothering you, isn't it?" she asks.

Stephen's chest bounces with a muted chuckle. He starts and stops a couple of times before getting his words out. "I guess... I wish you weren't so eager to pose for Randy."

"Really?" Ally asks. "Why?"

"I don't know, I think it's...I just don't get why you'd want to do that."

Ally looks at Stephen in sheer bafflement. "It's just not a big deal," she says, "but it's flattering to me. We both love Randy's art and this is a chance for me to be a part of it, in some way. I just think that would be really cool. What girl wouldn't want to pose for an artist as talented as Randy?"

Stephen is quiet because he doesn't have an answer to that question. He searches for some way to say, "Don't do this!" other than by saying it. He searches for words to hide his jealousy and possessiveness and whatever else he's feeling, not wanting to look pathetically weak. Really, what he feels like doing is yelling, "Fuck you and your, 'what girl wouldn't want to pose for an artist,' bullshit!" Since there's no socially acceptable way for him to say any of that, he's speechless.

"What's going on?" Ally asks.

"I don't know, I guess I don't want to be messing with this bullshit when I have to read for my dissertation," Stephen responds.

Barely noticeable red splotches surface below Ally's eyes and eventually on her neck. She wants to say that he sounds like he's dismissing her, like he doesn't really care about her. Finally, she asks: "What do you mean, 'this bullshit?'" unconsciously distorting her face the same way he did on those words.

"I'm really on deadline with this dissertation reading and I don't want to talk about this right now."

After some silence, Ally says, "Okay, I guess we can talk about it later."

"Yeah, that would be good," Stephen says.

Ally looks over at Stephen who appears absorbed in his reading. "Are you going to kiss me goodnight?" she asks.

"Sure," Stephen says. He gets up and walks slowly, heavily toward her. He puts one knee on the bed, leans across and kisses her lightly on the lips.

Ally looks at Stephen. "Goodnight," she says wistfully.

"Goodnight," Stephen says, his eyes not quite meeting hers.

The next evening, Stephen sprints toward the big house through harsh rain, his jacket over his head. Entering the kitchen, he pushes his wet hair out of his face, and calls out, "Hello" to let his landlords know they have company.

A few seconds later Dan walks into the kitchen. "Hey buddy… a little wet, huh?" he asks, smiling.

"Yeah, I just put Nicholas to bed and thought I'd check to see what you guys were doing."

"Come on in. Randy went to Homo Depot to be with all the other queers with big, um, trucks."

Stephen smiles, nervously, feeling the usual discomfort that characterizes his first minute or so with Dan, who opens the refrigerator and hands him a beer.

"I believe I'll pour myself an adult beverage," he says, leading Stephen to the den. He grabs a glass and pours scotch over four or five ice cubes.

"How was your day?" Stephen asks, settling into the couch.

"It was good. It's quarterly numbers time at work, which is my favorite. Everyone else dreads it. But I just get my guys to bring me their numbers and I look them over, and if they're good, I go to the executive committee and brag. And if they're not so good, I go in and tell them how we're going to do better. What are they going to do, fire me? Where are they going to find another guy who works as hard and puts as much energy into things as me? I used to take a double dose of prescription antacid four or five times a day the week of the numbers and I'd still wake up at four a.m. with this ungodly heartburn and horrible swirling…terror. Now, I sleep with a grin on my face. And the difference? I recognize my uniqueness, how hard I work, and how if they want to fire me over some numbers, I'll go somewhere they won't fire me over numbers."

Dan takes a long drink of his dark gold scotch. "But I won't bore you with more details. So how are you doing?" he asks, sliding one leg onto the couch.

"I'm alright," Stephen says.

Dan looks closely at Stephen. "You sure?" he asks. "You didn't seem yourself last night."

"Really, I, well, I don't know," Stephen says, surprised.

Dan laughs. "You're so articulate when you're being evasive."

"I'm fine. What do you mean?" Stephen asks.

"Come on, Stephen, I thought you psychologists were supposed to be able to talk about anything."

"I don't think I'm being evasive," Stephen says.

"Are you telling me that you weren't pissed last night when Ally agreed to replace the bowl of fruit in Randy's next series of paintings?"

"I didn't know Randy meant it as a series," Stephen says, with a concerned frown.

"Maybe he didn't. Really, I have no idea," Dan says. "But weren't you pissed about Ally's agreeing to pose nude?"

"I guess I wasn't pleased about it."

"Do they teach you to talk like that in your graduate program?"

"Okay," Stephen says, and smiles. "Okay, I was upset. Maybe pissed. I still don't get it. I just wish it wouldn't have come up while I'm working on my dissertation because I don't need the distraction."

Dan smiles and takes a sip of his drink. He waits for Stephen to say something and looks distractedly around the room.

"What?" Stephen asks.

"I don't know what to say, really. So, it was just bad timing?"

Stephen stares at the spectacular Ficus tree that stands in the corner of the room, its delicate top branches pressing against the ceiling. He thinks about the two or three Ficus trees he's had over the years that never made it through the relocation stage from store environment to home environment. He takes a long swallow of his beer. "I'm not sure what it is, really. I just don't like the idea of Ally's naked body hanging in someone's house," he says.

"You know what. This Glenlivet is so good I can't watch you drink a beer. I'm pouring you a drink," Dan says. He gets up and begins fixing the drink. "Look at it this way, it's not like Randy is going to paint a portrait of her. Sometimes I can't tell whether the model is a man or a woman, even though I know it's a man because Randy doesn't paint women."

"Until now," Stephen says, before taking the drink from Dan.

"Yeah, but you hear what I'm saying?"

"Sure, except his most recent paintings are pretty realistic," Stephen says.

"But he covers them in layers of, what is that?"

"He uses waxes and shellac to make it look kind of dreamy," Stephen answers.

"Maybe you can tell him to paint Ally more abstractly."

"I can't tell Randy how to paint. He'd be totally insulted. I don't know. I just don't like the idea of this…"

"Randy has this way with people that they don't confront him. Do you know what that is?" Dan asks.

"It's not that I can't confront him. It's just that it's his art. I can't tell him how to do that." Stephen puts his beer down. "Can I have a scotch?" he asks.

"Have you considered just telling Ally that this bothers you and asking her not to do it?" Dan says as he makes Stephen's drink.

"I actually kind of did ask," Stephen says. "I probably wasn't as clear as I could have been. I guess I feel foolish or weird or controlling or something fucked up that I, you know, don't want to be."

"What are you worried about?" Dan asks. "That she won't think you're avant-garde enough? If that's it, that's just stupid. I'll tell you, one of the advantages of being gay, at least if you deal with it by coming out, is that you learn that you do better when you quit trying to twist yourself into something you're not. For me, that's when I learned to really live. There are other advantages to being gay, by the way, but that's for another time. What could possibly be wrong with asking Ally not to pose? What I think is odd is that Ally wouldn't know that you'd find this a little upsetting."

"When I think about it, I think what happened was I said I didn't understand her wanting to pose and she sort of ignored me and said something about how flattered she was by Randy's offer. Then she said something really fucked up like, (as he quotes her, he mimics her movement, turning his palms up, opening his eyes wide, and shaking his head from side to side) 'What girl wouldn't want to pose for an artist as talented as Randy?'"

Dan roars with laughter.

"Yeah, I thought it was funny, too," Stephen says.

"I wonder how Ally wouldn't think that you'd at least have some sort of reaction," Dan says. "Your reaction seems pretty normal. Does she expect that you're not supposed to be possessive and jealous about her naked body? I thought that was something we learned about relationships by the time we were teenagers, that some degree of ownership is inevitable … God, I'm almost empty," Dan says looking into his glass. "Let me freshen yours," he says, getting up.

"Sure," Stephen says as he swallows the remaining Scotch and hands Dan his glass.

Dan hands Stephen the drink and sits down. "So, I have another theory. Do you think that maybe Ally just wants to hear you say no?"

Stephen thinks for a moment. "I have no idea," he says.

"I'm saying that a girl, a boy too, by the way, sometimes wants to be told 'no' as a way of being possessed. It's an old and very sexy game, but maybe straight people are too serious about sex and possession to play with it."

"If that's going on," Stephen says, "I'd have to say it's completely unconscious. Ally's pretty straightforward, and naïve in a way. I've considered some version of what you're saying. What I think is that Ally's used to pushing for what she wants and used to getting it, too. I think I told you. When I first met her parents this fall, we stayed in a bedroom in a hotel suite shared with her parents and grandparents. And some mornings we slept later than everyone and sort of stumbled to the breakfast table."

Dan chuckles and nods his head.

"I'd get dressed, but Ally would come out in her wrinkled silk pajamas and her hair looking all messed up and everyone was sooo accepting. It was a little like 'The Twilight Zone' at times. Her grandmother would ask us how we slept. Was the bed comfortable? I was waiting for her to ask if we needed to borrow some condoms."

Dan and Stephen laugh hard and long.

"There's something pretty neat about that, right?" Dan asks. "I mean, we all wish our family accepted us just as we are."

"I guess. Her grandparents are pretty cool. Being flexible enough to cross two generations and even talk about the bedroom, not just tolerate and ignore it. You know?"

"Sometimes grandparents have an easier time accepting their kids than parents. At least, I've seen that with friends who've come out to their families. The grandparents are cool, and the parents vomit all over the place. Of course, you and Ally weren't coming out, but you were staying together, unmarried, and not bashful about it. Some families would be squeamish, but to have them all so accepting is great. I guess that's why you two found each other."

"What do you mean?" Stephen asks, sitting up straighter.

"I guess I assume your family accepts you. I don't know about your mother, but I've met your father and I had the feeling that whatever you were into he'd think was great. You know what I mean?"

Stephen takes a sip of his scotch and slowly nods his head.

"I like your dad. I had the feeling that however you wanted to live he'd find a way to accept it. Maybe it was because he said how proud of you he was over and over or just how he did whatever you seemed to want to do."

Stephen looks blankly at Dan.

"I just had the feeling that he accepted you ... completely."

Stephen puts his drink on the table next to him, folds his fingers together and looks at them. He thinks that he needs to call his father as soon as possible. It's been almost two weeks since they talked.

"You want another?" Dan asks pointing at Stephen's glass.

"Sure," Stephen says. "I do like that Scotch.

"Isn't it easy to drink? Anyway, maybe that has nothing to do with anything," Dan says. "By the way, Randy's family is just like Ally's. When he came out to them, each of his parents wrote him separate letters telling him how much they loved him and wanted him to be happy. Ally and Randy have a lot in common. Maybe that's how he got you into this mess."

"What do you mean by that?" Stephen asks.

"Nothing, we're talking too much about your life. When do we explore all of my problems?" Dan asks, trying to backtrack.

"Why are you suddenly being evasive?" Stephen asks.

"Don't try that psychotherapy manipulation on me," Dan admonishes.

"Fuck you!"

"Don't you flirt with me just 'cause you got troubles at home," Dan jokes.

"Go ahead, Dan, really. What are you talking about?"

"Okay. Wasn't all of this Randy's idea?" Dan begins.

"Yeah, but for Randy, asking Ally to pose is all about working with the colors and textures and angles of her body," Stephen says.

"Oh my God, he's got you brainwashed! Come on, Stephen. Look at what he's doing. He's used to being indulged. In all honesty, I did tell him it might have bothered you and he was all, like, 'Oh my God, I had no idea.' It's all about his need to push the erotic, and to have very little awareness of anyone else's feelings. Of course, he wants to make sure Ally is comfortable with it. I think he asked her five times if she was comfortable..."

"I noticed that," Stephen interjects. "You seem angry at Randy all of a sudden."

"I'm just telling you what I experience... a lot. Don't misunderstand. I love him dearly. But why do you think he asked Ally what she thought and not you?"

"Because it's her body!" Stephen takes a quick sip of scotch.

"Sure, but why do you think he never even looked in your direction?"

"Again, I assumed it was because he looks at nudity differently than I do. I didn't think a whole lot about his motives."

"Why didn't you think the same thing of Ally? Maybe she thinks of nudity differently than you. Maybe she doesn't see it as sexual, necessarily. Maybe she sees it as an art form."

"I guess that's my point. I don't want her to see her body as an art form for everyone to enjoy. I don't like the way that sounds, but that's the truth. I guess I don't understand how you suddenly got into all your resentment about Randy."

Dan chuckles. "I don't understand it either. Look, I try to tolerate Randy's desires that have nothing to do with me and enjoy the ones that do. That's what you'll have to do with Ally and don't ever forget, she's used to acceptance. She's going to always expect you to accept whatever she finds interesting and important."

"Great, that's fucking wonderful … and probably pretty fucking accurate. I never thought about the cost of having overly accepting parents: The kid grows up with no consideration for how his or her desires affect others. I need to remember that with Nicholas."

Dan rearranges himself on the couch. "Some of this stuff we're saying I haven't really thought about before. I was just thinking about the opposite extreme, which would be my parents. Anytime I wanted anything that challenged their values or perspective on things, I got my ass kicked. Sometimes literally. So, when I want something, I always consider every possible way it might affect everyone involved. I'm not saying that's good, but I guess that's why I never understood Randy when he claimed he had no idea something was going to upset me. I never used to believe him because if it was me, I'd have thought of every possible way he might react."

Stephen stares at Dan and says, "Talking to you really helps. I feel like I understand things at a deeper level."

"Why thank you." Dan says as he swirls the golden liquid around in his glass. "I should've been a shrink." He thinks for a moment. "No, I couldn't sit there day in and out listening to people's insecurities." He takes a sip of his drink while he continues to ponder the idea. "But if they paid as much as Coke pays me… and without the travel…"

"I don't think of being a psychologist as something you weigh out, like you're doing. For most of us, it's a calling. You, on the other hand, are called to use your insight into the human condition to make tons of money for a corporation and yourself."

"But not necessarily in that order," Dan says.

"But you're a pretty good listener and you do have insight," Stephen says.

"Make sure you tell Randy that."

"Why do you always do that?" Stephen asks.

"What do you mean?'

"Any time I pay you a compliment if Randy's around, you ask him if he's heard it. If he's not with us, you ask me to say it to him. It's like you're saying Randy doesn't find you special."

"I do that?" Dan asks. "I guess that sounds…insecure?"

"I assume you know Randy thinks you're special, so it never sounds quite right. You're the one who needs to hear the compliments, not him."

"I'll drink to that," Dan says, getting up. "You need a refresher?"

"Sure," Stephen says, handing him his glass. Stephen looks closely at Dan as he pours the drinks.

Returning with the filled glasses, Dan says, "I'm going to give what you just said some thought."

"I guess we've got something in common around our insecurities," Stephen states.

"And our gals have something in common, too, around their dismal lack of regard for our feelings," Dan responds.

Stephen holds his glass out. Dan clicks it.

"Let me ask you," Dan says, "what are you going to say about Ally's desire to pose for Randy? As I figure it, you can say 'No,' and that can range from, 'Please don't,' to something bold and barbaric along the lines of 'If you do, we're finished.' On the other hand, you can begin the next phase of love where you learn to tolerate the exhaustingly intolerable in your partner and say 'yes.' But then you have to figure out how to do that without resenting her."

"I'm going to, you know, tell her to forget what I said last night and enjoy becoming part of Randy's work," Stephen says.

Dan smiles, "As long as you don't blame it on me if you turn out to regret it," he says.

The men are playfully and drunkenly arguing over that when Randy walks into the room.

"Behold!" Dan says, pointing at Randy. "The Avant Garde has arrived."

Stephen and Dan fall together laughing.

Randy stops and looks cautiously at the scene in front of him.

"Don't worry, Ran. We've just had some very good Scotch while sharing the misery cast upon us by modern art," Dan says, before raising his glass toward Randy. "Cheers."

Chapter 26

APHRODITE WHISPERING

ALLY STEADIES HERSELF with a deep breath before opening the screened door to Randy's studio. "Randy," she calls out, as she swings the door open and steps into the studio. As she moves from the brilliant sunlight to the more muted light of the studio, her eyes struggle to adapt. She sees Randy, washed in white sunlight from the skylight above him. He reaches for a paint-splattered towel and rubs it between his hands. As he walks toward her and out of the direct light, his smile appears, and his skin turns olive. Ally watches as he glances at his t-shirt to make sure it doesn't have paint on it, and then spends another moment wiping paint from his fingers. He reaches for her, pulling her into a strong hug.

Randy carries a large, blank canvas back to the easel. He lifts it onto the easel. Ally notices his long, defined bicep through a tear in the right sleeve of his T-shirt. She likes arms like Randy's. She also likes the feeling of being so close to a sensual man who has no apparent sexual interest in her.

Randy turns to Ally. "Do you still feel okay about doing this?" he asks.

"I'm a little nervous, but I'm okay," she says.

"Do you need anything or have any questions or..."

"No..." Ally says and smiles politely.

Randy smiles back. "Okay, let's begin," he says. "I'm going to put this stool next to you, so you can sit when you get exhausted, but I just want you to stand right here." Randy slides a bar stool about ten feet from his easel. "You can get undressed in the bathroom if you want. There are hangers for your clothes and a robe behind the door, if you want to wear that for a bit...you know while you adjust to the temperature in here."

"I don't need to hang these clothes up," Ally says, motioning to her jeans with tears in both knees and tee shirt. With that, she pulls her shirt over her head revealing her slender midriff and a somewhat loose-fitting bra resting on her breasts. Randy stirs the paints on his palette as he looks at her skin while she undoes her jeans and lets them drop to the floor. She steps out of them and is standing in long purple socks and loose underpants. Randy turns away from her to the blank canvas and plays with the afterimage, watching Ally's colors move about, the innocent navel just above her underpants and the tender nipples pressing against her bra. His breathing is shallow, which he recognizes as a gentle arousal.

He turns back to her as she's stepping out of her underpants. She bends down, picks them up, and tosses them into a corner with her jeans and tee shirt. She's naked except for the purple socks that are pulled up to the middle of her calves. "Can I leave these on?" she asks, momentarily breaking the spell. "Just for a few minutes, my feet are a little cold. Maybe I'm getting cold feet about this." She smiles nervously.

Randy remembers what his mentor taught him about models. "If it's a model's first time, paint what they present to you. Chances are, they'll present something unique about their own sensuality." This contrasts with the professional model, who may have posed a hundred times and has long ago lost her own narrative about her sensuality. Randy recalls telling this to Stephen, who said, "That sounds like therapy. A stranger like the psychologist can bring out a patient's narrative quicker than an intimate friend."

Randy squints, watching the colors blur: light golden hair hanging below her shoulders, round pale breasts, a mound of curling hair that is darker than the hair on her head, smooth legs, and the purple socks that give the expression of humility, or something being held back, yet to be revealed.

"I like leaving the socks on," he says, in a voice that sounds to Ally like he's far away.

"Okay," she says, with a slight smile. A breeze blows through the west window of the studio. Ally brushes her hair back off her face. She notices Randy looking at her and smiles bashfully.

Randy pushes his brush into the colors on his palette as he gazes at Ally's face. He focuses on the pigments, blending shades of yellow, ocher, cadmium red, and white. He looks up into her sapphire eyes, the color of Colorado mountain lake water. He turns to the stark canvas and plays with the image he sees before him. He looks at the angle of her body. Her head appears to float above her neck, effortlessly, like her spirit pulls her up in defiance of gravity. Nothing in her posture reflects any diminishment of energy. Randy is possessed with the sun covering her hair, a shawl of white sensitivity, he says to himself. He works his brush in and out of the colors he has mixed on his palette, and onto the canvas. Suddenly, on the canvas, the mix of colors of Ally's hair are perfect.

In the next few minutes, Randy draws in the outline and the specifics of Ally's face and moves his hand toward the part of the canvas where her body will be. He continues in a flurry of movement before a clear outline of her body emerges. Now there is reality on the canvas and everything changes, like he's tracing over someone else's work or filling in the empty spaces left behind.

As Randy works, Ally finds herself feeling lonely. A cool breeze blows through the studio and she feels her nipples harden. At first, she's embarrassed because she looks too … sexual, though she recognizes that Randy is far away from her. She wonders how much longer Randy will paint and if he'll ever speak to her. Then he does.

"How are you doing?" Randy asks. He blushes when she's slow to respond. "I'm sorry. I've just gotten carried away in my work. I completely forgot to check in with you. I space out sometimes…"

"I'm okay. I'm a little tired and very curious about how things are going for you. You look like you're working very hard."

"I'm great. I've been completely lost in the paint. I'll let you look at it in a minute when we take a break. I know you need one. I've just been on a roll. When I'm on a roll I sometimes forget to eat lunch and paint until I'm too weak to go on."

Ally likes to please, but she didn't have an inkling of how bored and stiff she'd feel posing for Randy's art. Maybe fifteen minutes later, Randy announces it's time for a break. He flips his brushes into the sink. "Why don't we go sit by the pool?" he suggests.

Ally puts on a robe and walks with Randy to the pool.

"That water looks too good. I'm going in," Ally says, stepping out of her robe and diving into the pool. After a couple of underwater laps, she gets out of the pool, and Randy, who has retrieved a towel from his studio, flips it to her along with her robe. She towels off and wraps herself in the robe, before spinning the towel in her hair.

She plops down in a chair next to Randy.

"You're so comfortable with your body," Randy says to her.

"Well, you've looked at my naked self for a few hours. There's no need to hide now."

"How is this going for you?" Randy asks, motioning toward his studio.

Ally looks at Randy appreciatively. "I'm doing fine. I hope I'm doing okay for you," she says.

"You're doing great. I appreciate your patience," Randy says.

"Not a problem. It's a little hard to stay in the same position for so long, but I know it's necessary."

"How's your body holding up?"

"I felt a little stiff. The water felt good though. I needed to get my blood flowing again."

"The good news is I'm close to finishing. I just need you for maybe an hour more at the most. I need to have you here while I experiment with how I want to finish the painting. Then we're done."

"Don't rush on my account."

Randy smiles at Ally. "All I really have left is to imagine what you'll look like when I'm finished, from an overall perspective. The question left to answer is, what will be the background that allows the figure to tell a particular story. Right now, I have the figure pretty much the way I want her. I need a story and I'll keep you as an inspiration for a while longer if you're okay with that.

"I can't wait to see it."

"As soon as she, you, um, the piece speaks to me, I'll show you."

"Great," Ally says.

"Did Stephen talk to you about me posing for you?" Ally asks, as she and Randy lean back in their lounge chairs and absorb the warm sunshine.

Randy turns his gaze toward Ally while considering how much he should reveal from his conversation with Dan. "Dan told me Stephen was a little upset. I haven't talked to Stephen. I hope everything is okay with you two."

"I think everything is okay, but I don't really know. We talked about it this morning in between classes. He said he wanted me to go ahead and do it. He was, I'd say, quietly angry the night we first talked about it. Today he seemed okay. He confuses the shit out of me sometimes."

"Relationships are confusing," Randy says. "Dan told me Stephen was upset. They talked about it some."

"I think he feels threatened by it ... which makes no sense to me," Ally says. "It really feels controlling and I've had enough controlling men in my life."

"You and me, both," Randy says, grinning.

"Is Dan controlling?"

"Not so much these days, but it's always part of our struggle."

"I just don't understand why he wouldn't want me to pose for you," she says. "He loves your work. He talks about how much he loves to watch you paint and how much he's learned by talking to you about colors and composition and your approach to creativity and art. I mean, I asked him to tell me what the problem was and he couldn't really explain it to me."

Ally pulls her robe tight around her neck.

Randy has watched her face transform as she talked. The point of her chin is tucked inside her robe, her skin is tight and gone are the sprinkles of colors, replaced by a glowing, pink. A young, sullen girl, Randy thinks.

"He pretty much said I was an exhibitionist last night. It felt like he reacting to me like I wanted to work in a strip club or something."

"Really?" Randy says, almost yelling.

"Well, he didn't really say that. But it felt like he thought I was being cheap or something. It was really insulting."

"That doesn't sound like Stephen," Randy says.

"I was shocked. It was like he turned on me, or like he was someone else. He had this angry look on his face or maybe it was a look of disgust. I wanted to run away from him."

"God, I'm sorry you went through that, Ally."

Ally's eyes become teary. "It was really confusing. I love him and then he acts like … I don't know what to do. I woke up at three in the morning that night and couldn't get back to sleep. I was so upset I couldn't even nap back at my place before class. And then last night I tried to get him to talk about it on the phone, but we really didn't get anywhere. I slept some last night because I was in my own apartment, but I still woke up at five this morning wondering what to do. And then he told me this morning that he wanted me to go ahead and pose. I started to cancel, but I want to do this, and you wanted me to do it, so I said, 'fuck it. I'm doing it."

"I feel like you have to approach relationships like that…be yourself and let the other person adapt to you." Randy says. "Of course, you have to adapt to them, too."

"I have a lot easier time adapting to them than I do being myself."

"Me too," Randy says, and then looks away and chuckles. "Dan has no trouble being himself and a lot of trouble adapting to me."

"You have this shit with Dan?"

"Oh yeah. It's the main, um, shit that we have."

"How does it work with you and Dan?"

"Gosh, I don't know, Ally. The thing for me … is that I love Dan.

And he's a very powerful man, and so I have to stand up to him or I become his version of me. And I really don't want that."

"What do you mean by 'his version of you'?" Ally asks.

"Who he'd like me to be. Like if I'm reading this right, Stephen probably wants you to be, something like, more conservative sexually or at least with nudity. But then he probably wants you to be hot sexually, and how would you do that by being conservative? It's a similar bind that Dan has with me. He'd hate me if I sat around the house and did nothing. But when I focus on my career and it's inconvenient for him, we fight."

"I can't believe he wants you to give up your career."

Randy looks at Ally. "I'm not really saying he wants me to give up my career. He doesn't want that. He just doesn't want my career to inconvenience him at all."

"Yeah, like Stephen, who wants me to be sexual, but doesn't want it to have any negative effect on him."

"Yeah. What a couple of assholes we've gotten ourselves involved with," Randy says.

Randy and Ally laugh together.

"A sense of humor," Randy says, "is essential for dealing with the nuances of the American male, if I do say so myself."

They laugh again, and Randy watches Ally let go of her robe. "Dan told me something after talking to Stephen," he says, "that really helped me understand Stephen's perspective. He said Stephen wants to hold a part of you separate from everyone else, to hold the sensual part of you for himself."

Ally looks away from Randy, first toward the sun, and then toward the sun's glare on the pool water before speaking. "I've been feeling crazy lately … and I've been feeling like there's no way Stephen and I are going to get through whatever it is we're going through."

"I used to wonder about that with Dan, too, in the middle of an argument," Randy says. "I look back and wonder how we stayed together. I don't think like that anymore. I know we'll be together forever."

"How can you know that?"

Randy smiles. "We've made it through so many crazy times," he says. "I can't imagine what would break us up. Plus, I don't want to spend my life with anyone else, and I'm sure Dan feels the same way."

"That's so…great," Ally says, frowning over not being able to express more of what she feels. "How did you get from living with all this anxiety to knowing that you would never break up?"

"That's been a long road. When I met Dan, he was so sure of where he was and where he was heading, and I was so, well, not sure of any of that. I fell in love with him instantly, as a man and, if I'm honest, as a guide for my own journey. I moved in the day I met him. I guess you've heard that story."

"I love that story."

"We love it, too. People think only lesbians move in on the first date. When I moved in, Dan wanted to take care of everything. He wouldn't even let me pay rent. I started working on my own as a freelance landscape architect, so I didn't have much of an income. But I built a pretty good business after a year or so, started making pretty good money, but I knew my first love was painting. I told Dan I wanted to paint full time, quit designing gardens for Buckhead Sierras, and he completely freaked out."

"Really?" Ally asks.

"Really! Actually, it surprised me that he reacted that way, too. He said things that I've had to work very hard to forget. Actually, I haven't really forgotten," Randy continues. "I've just decided that the things he said have nothing to do with how he feels about me. It's just what he says when he's hurt and mad."

"What did he say, if you don't mind me asking?"

"Let's see…" Randy thinks for a moment. His memory reverts to Dan's face distorted with rage. He hears Dan's words. He sorts through them searching for something decent to share. Finally, he offers, "The nicest thing that he called me was a gigolo," Randy winces. "That's not that terrible is it?"

Ally thinks and then agrees.

"Okay, I have a better one," Randy says, smiling. "He told me I didn't give good enough blow jobs to live here for free."

Ally and Randy burst into laughter.

"The worst thing he did was when I left during the argument, he threw almost all of my clothes into the front yard."

"You're kidding?"

"Nope. I'm telling you, Dan has been crazy at times. He doesn't really do stuff like that now. You know what I did when he threw my clothes in the yard? I refused to pick them up. I gathered the clothes that were still in the house, moved in with a friend, and told Dan that I'd talk to him when he picked up all my clothes, had them cleaned, and returned every stitch to my closet and chest of drawers. He called me a day later, begged me to come home, and promised me that my clothes were back where they belonged. We sort of made up after that, but really, the argument went on for months."

"So why was he so pissed about you wanting to paint full time? Didn't he know you were an artist when you first got together?"

"Well, what he said was that it was about losing my income. And I wanted a studio, which costs money. That's why I built the studio here, and the apartment."

"Does he complain now?"

"Dan complains, because he just does. But I guess our relationship is better than anyone else's that I know … except for maybe yours with Stephen."

"You feel like we have a good relationship?" Ally asks.

"Yes, I do."

"When you told me what Dan said about Stephen wanting to have a part of me separate from everyone else … doesn't that seem like another way of saying he's being possessive, or am I missing something?"

"I think what Dan meant was that a certain level of possession is just a normal part of love. Letting go of that possessiveness is another important part of love. I guess that's why people argue."

Ally sits up in her chair. "That really makes sense," she says. "I haven't thought much about this from Stephen's perspective," Ally says. "I just hope it's not too late for us."

"How could it be too late?" Randy asks.

"This just seems to have changed the way he talks to me. He's so distant. I asked him at school if he was going to come by here when he got through and he gave some bullshit excuse about needing to go to the library to work on his dissertation. For a guy who's been procrastinating for the last several months, he's sure gotten his act together. I think he's trying to decide whether to break up."

"Stephen is way too smart and too in love for that. He doesn't want to lose you. Not to mention, you've basically become Nicholas's stepmother. Look, it's hard to believe in a relationship when you're in the middle of a crisis," Randy says. "But I promise you, he wants this relationship with you."

Ally looks at Randy, slowly smiles at him, and relaxes back in her chair.

A couple of hours later Randy and Ally are in their positions in the studio. A gentle breeze blows through the studio. Tan, gold, and silver strings of hair swirl over Ally's creamy shoulders, disappearing behind them before springing back into sight. Randy is captivated by the dance. Whispering hair, he thinks. He reaches for a fine brush and dabs into some synthetic gold paint he has squirted next to similar silver paint on his palette. He sprinkles specks of gold away from the head of the image all the way to the edge of the canvas. He gets a new fine brush and dabs it in the silver paint and makes similar specks of silver among the gold.

A few minutes later, Randy tells Ally to take a break. As she stretches her hands to the ceiling Randy leans against the wall and gazes at the colors, the curves, and angles on the canvas. Ally is standing beside her stool stretching her arms up high. Randy's breathing is shallow and high in his chest as feelings of sexual and emotional arousal present themselves to him. He looks back at Ally and then again at his representation of her. He sees an image of the completed painting, at first it's a fleeting image, and then it slowly unfolds as a stable image. It's almost portrait-like in places, with exact lines and colors, with abstract wisps of hair spinning away from her. The image drenched by a midday sun absorbed in her hair, bleaching her shoulders and breasts. He then sees the entire image suspended in a dark black and brown background and covered with layers of wax and shellac so that the sensual woman is buried beneath the surface, a distant dreamscape. An emerging Aphrodite, he hears himself say.

"Aphrodite Whispering," Randy names her, smiling, and then remembers that Aphrodite's beauty caused as much jealousy as love.

Chapter 27

COMING OUT

TWO HOURS AFTER MODELING for Randy, Aphrodite, disguised as Ally, is sitting on the futon looking at her jealous lover, Stephen, who is gazing silently out the window. Ally takes a breath and asks, "What is it about me posing that you don't like?"

Stephen sighs and turns to face her. "For starters," he says, "don't you think there's anything wrong with being naked for the world to see? Don't you think it's ... exhibitionistic to want to do that? Don't you believe that some things are private?"

"No, I don't think it's wrong. I do think some things are private and I wouldn't pose for Playboy. But this is Randy, and this is artistic. And I hate to hear you say I'm exhibitionistic. I want to be proud of my body."

Stephen's face is completely tense. "This isn't about being proud of your body. It's about showing people your body. I want you to be proud, too. Show it to me and be proud of it. Look at it yourself and be proud. It's gorgeous. Love it. Do you have to want to show it to everyone?"

"It's not about showing my body to everyone."

"Oh really," Stephen scoffs. "Don't you think it'll be a little awkward walking around the gallery at Randy's fall show with everyone glancing between you and the naked blonde in the painting?"

Ally's skin turns bright pink. She looks away from Stephen. "I didn't really think about that," she says.

Silence.

"So, what do you want to do, break up?" Ally asks.

"I don't know. I want you to have said to Randy when he brought this thing up, 'Oh that's flattering, but I can't really do that. It's just too ... too something or other."

"Then why did you let me do it if it was going to bother you?"

"Why should I have to tell you not to do it?"

"Because I wouldn't do it if you said it bothered you that much. It wasn't that important to me."

"I think I made it pretty obvious."

"You said it was upsetting, but then you also told me to go ahead. I figured you knew it was something you needed to get over."

"That I needed to get over? Are you kidding?" Stephen nearly shouts.

"How am I supposed to know what's going on with you? You told me to go ahead." She pauses. "Look, it's done. Can we get past this now?"

"I don't know. I don't know how to get past this," Stephen says, falling back on the bed, his forearm draped over his eyes.

"You want me to leave?"

"Go ahead. Yeah, why don't you go?"

"I didn't say I wanted to leave. I was asking." Ally cries softly. "You really just want out of this relationship, right?"

Stephen squints at her.

"That's it, right? You were having a great time being single. You've done the marriage thing and now we're getting serious. I'm serious about you. And you, you're bailing, and this is your excuse."

"That's fucked up," Stephen snaps. "I'm not looking for a reason to bail. I'm looking for a reason to stay. I don't know if you have the same idea about common decency toward your partner as I do."

Ally wipes her tears. "You can be a pompous ass, you know that?"

"I'm not being pompous. I'm telling the truth. Maybe we have different values."

"I get that you disapprove of my nudity," Ally says, "but you were not true to me or yourself when you didn't say how you felt. That's some fucked-up psychology, you know?"

Ally looks sadly at Stephen. "Why is this happening?"

"Because you're real clear that being nude in a context outside of our sex life is okay with you."

"Are you serious? I was nude in front of Randy who is painting an artistic representation of me. It's art, not Playboy magazine."

"I know, but ..."

"Yeah," Ally interrupts, "we've gotten too close and you're scared, and this is just some bullshit way to break up with me."

Stephen grins. "You're such a natural psychologist yourself."

"Fuck you!"

"Fuck you!"

Silence.

Stephen takes a long, full breath. "I'm not looking for a way out. I'm just pissed that you didn't just turn to Randy when he suggested a nude and say, 'A nude might be a little too much. How about some other type of work?'"

"This conversation is insane," Ally says.

"So, leave me alone with my insanity," Stephen says. "Nicholas's bus will be here in an hour and I'd like to go on a run and clear my head."

"That's how you want to leave this: you saying I'm too morally corrupt for you? You're the one that fucked half a dozen women your first semester here."

Stephen smiles. "That's nice," he says, nodding his head. "Use the stuff I revealed in group against me. As I recall you were very accepting of me when I talked about those relationships. You said, a couple of times as I recall, that you thought my night life sounded exciting and that I shouldn't feel guilty about sleeping around since the women were probably using me as much as I was using them. By the way, I never felt guilty. I just felt like it showed bad judgment."

Ally stares at Stephen. "I was being generous before I knew how judgmental you could be."

"Don't forget, Ally, you're the one that spent the weekend with me when your boyfriend was calling from New York."

"Fuck you!"

"Fuck you!"

Ally walks to her car, her fists clenched with resolve. For the first time since she began seeing Stephen, she's convinced that he isn't the right man for her. She opens the car door, glances over her shoulder hoping to see Stephen walking toward her, waving a white flag.

Fuck him, fuck his stupid bullshit, she thinks as she swings her car door wide open. As she falls into the seat, she glances up again.

No Stephen.

She bursts into tears and starts to drive.

Stephen sits on his bed and is jolted when he hears Ally's car door slam. He thinks about going to her, but he cannot get himself to move. Bitch! Fucking bitch!

He wonders if she was right. Maybe he was getting scared about being so committed in the relationship. His life would sure be easier not trying to make another relationship work. And for all that was wonderful about Ally, she didn't seem to get what a pain in the ass all of her freedom could be to others. And Atlanta was filled with lots of gorgeous women. Why had he chosen to limit himself to the one actualized woman who was so in touch with her sexual freedom that she'd want to flaunt her body for the world to see? Perhaps he'd be better off with a gorgeous lawyer who makes a six-figure income.

In his stupor, Stephen hears the familiar squeak of brakes from Nicholas's bus as it stops at the house a few blocks away. He trots down the driveway hoping to be standing at the curb when the bus stops. He longs for the smiling face of his son, always a ray of love and possibility, and an antidote to his dark loneliness.

The door opens, and Nicholas bounds off the bus. He flips his book bag to his father. Stephen waves to the bus driver as he closes the door.

"You have a good day?" he asks his son.

"Yep."

"What did you have for lunch?" Stephen asks as he walks next to Nicholas, who says he doesn't remember. "If you're hungry, I'll make you a peanut butter and jelly sandwich."

"Yes!" Nicholas replies. He goes to his room. Stephen heads to the kitchen. He glances at his answering machine and sees that there is no message. He looks at the clock and knows Ally has had time to get home and call him.

Nicholas reappears in his bathing suit. He grabs the door and is about to run to the pool when he stops. "Where's Ally?" he asks.

"She's at her place. She had some stuff to do."

Nicholas examines his father's face. Stephen feels like his little boy can see through him. Nicholas shrugs and splashes into the pool within seconds. Stephen finishes making the sandwich and puts it on a table outside. "Help yourself," he says.

"Is Ally coming over tonight?" Nicholas asks after a few minutes of floating on his back.

"I'm not sure. She's pretty busy," Stephen answers. "Now, get your butt up here and eat your sandwich."

Nicholas wraps himself in a towel and slides into a chair. He grabs the sandwich and takes a big bite.

"When is Monica coming over?" Nicholas asks, referring to his favorite babysitter.

"She's supposed to be here at seven. I might cancel her since it's not really a good night for Ally to go out."

"I thought you and Ally were going out with Dan and Randy?"

"We are or were. I'm not sure. We might do that another night. You and I might end up going out for Mexican. Would that be all right?"

"Sure," Nicholas replies. After two bites of the sandwich he jumps back in the pool. Then the phone rings.

"Hello," Stephen says into the phone.

"Hi," Ally says.

"Hi," Stephen says.

"Is this what you really want?" she asks.

"I don't know what I want," Stephen says, with some indifference.

"How can you say that?"

"I didn't ask for any of this."

"Neither did I."

"Right."

"Why do you say that?"

"I just, I don't know."

"Is Nicholas there? Where did you tell him I was?"

"I told him you had stuff to do."

276

"Good. I feel bad him being in the middle of this."

"He's not in the middle."

"Yeah, I just mean …"

"I know what you mean. He's okay."

Silence.

"I want this to be over," Ally says.

"Yeah, I wish it was over, too."

"You could make it be over."

"I could?"

"You could tell me that it's over for you and it would be over for me. And then I could come over and we could go to dinner with Dan and Randy as planned, and it would be over."

Silence.

Stephen clears his throat. "It's that easy?"

"It's that easy for me. I love you and want to spend the rest of my life with you and this is a small thing given all that means to me."

Stephen swallows uneasily. "I miss you," he whispers into the phone.

"Oh, I miss you, too," she says. "I'll be there as fast as I can get there. I love you."

"I love you, too."

Stephen and Ally are holding hands in the back seat of Dan's six-day-old Jaguar, while Dan and Randy squint through the rain-covered front windshield as the wipers struggle with a true Atlanta downpour.

"I can't see a thing," Dan says.

"Pull over then," Randy says.

"I'm only going ten miles an hour."

Randy starts to respond, but doesn't want to distract Dan, who is already distracted by his rear-view mirror view of Ally and Stephen kissing.

"This is the perfect place for romance, you two!" Dan says.

Randy laughs and explains. "We're on Cheshire Bridge Road. It's kind of like the city's red-light district. Look around."

Stephen and Ally peer out the side windows. Beads of rain dance down the windows, occasionally capturing neon reds and purples, blues and greens from signs inviting men into strip clubs, sex stores, lingerie "modeling studios" or jack shacks and various Asian "spas." There are other businesses along Cheshire Bridge, mostly antique stores and a sprawling '50s-era motel.

"So, we're eating in a strip club?" Stephen asks.

"Yeah," Dan replies. "And guess who's doing a guest performance. It's Ally! You do approve, don't you, Stephen?"

Ally tries to suppress her laughter but lets it roar when Randy begins to laugh too. "Okay, okay, I'm good now," Stephen says, "Well, mainly good, but not laughing-good."

"Oh, sorry," Dan says unconvincingly. "You know how I am. So, we're eating at an Atlanta institution, The Colonnade. The place is a trip, especially on Friday nights like this. The clientele is a famous mix of so-called 'gays and grays,' the grays being mainly senior citizens of the heterosexual persuasion. You'll see widows with sky-high blue hair walking to a table with an oxygen tank. But the classic Southern food is actually very good."

After adding their name to the waiting list, they find a table in the bar. As soon as the waiter takes their order Dan asks to learn more about Ally's session with Randy. "Forgive my earlier joke, Stephen. I know you're having some difficulty with the whole thing, but I saw the painting and it was beautiful."

"The painting is beautiful," Stephen says. "The crazy thing is I think it's a dream image of Ally that I feel like I had. The flowing hair that turns into golden fragments. I swear it was like I'd seen that. It was Randy's image, of course, but it felt familiar."

"I'm thrilled you like it," Randy says.

"Me too," Ally says.

"I can't even imagine how I reacted so crazy about this now."

"I think it was old fashioned heterosexual panic," Dan cracks.

"No, really, somehow even after spending so much time with Randy I thought of it as a painting of Ally naked, not painting her sensuality," Stephen says. "As soon as I saw it, I got that it was more about her beauty, her energy, her colors and really the fact that she was naked, it wasn't about that."

"I don't think your reaction was that hard to understand. You naturally sexualize Ally's body so it's hard for you to detach enough from that to see it as her body. You want to possess it. There's nothing that complicated about that. It's also important that you learn to let go of that. And look what you each got for it. A beautiful painting and you seem closer than ever."

"Dan you're a wise man, you know that?" Randy says.

"Yes, yes I do know that," Dan says. "And I won't add anything to that since Stephen pointed out to me last night that I sometimes ruin your compliments."

Randy looks at Stephen and then back at Dan. "I think I understand, and I think I'm glad to hear that."

"I'm so glad you love the painting, Ally," Randy says.

Dan nudges Randy and points toward the bar. They both suddenly get up and hurry to the bar to greet an older woman seated there.

Ally touches Stephen's hand. "I'm so glad we made it through this together," she says.

Stephen looks at her innocent blue eyes twinkling in the bar light. "Me too," he says, squeezing her hand.

Ally looks into Stephen's eyes. "I hated upsetting you, but everything can't always be just the way you want it. I have needs, too."

Stephen starts to protest but he thinks about how easy it has been for Ally to change just about everything in their relationship to help him make a home for Nicholas. "I'm lucky to have you, Ally. Even saying what you just said to me is special."

Stephen pulls Ally into a kiss. When he and Ally look up from their kiss, Dan and Randy and the older woman are standing before them. "This is Jenny," Dan says, "my good mother during a period when I needed a good mother desperately."

After some chatter at the table, Dan talks intimately with the woman for another minute or so before they embrace, squeezing each other with their eyes closed.

As Dan and Randy settle back into their seats, he explains that he used to come to the Colonnade a couple of nights a week when he first moved to Atlanta and Jenny did her best to convince him that he was good person even though he was gay. Stephen notices that Dan seems sober, even humble. Dan only transitions back to the Friday night gaiety after the silver-haired lady slides her little body back onto her stool and, looking back at Dan, holds her drink into the air, and smooches a kiss at him. Dan blows a kiss at her, and watches for a moment as she turns away from him toward a skinny twenty-something man sitting next to her.

Dan slides close to Randy and leans his head on his shoulder. A waiter arrives and announces their table is ready.

Chapter 28

CHANGING STORIES

THE DISSERTATION IS TO THE PHD PROGRAM what the booby-trapped golden idol is to the archeologist in "Raiders of the Lost Ark." The perils for graduate students, however, are not deviously designed death traps, but inner voices of subversion. Almost inaudible voices often take over, basically saying, "You're not good enough," causing avoidance and, for many, complete paralysis. For some, the subversions start even before writing, when they're researching ideas for their dissertation.

Stephen began reading articles for his dissertation at the end of his third year of graduate school. Ed had been very active in directing his reading and even offered a general outline of his proposal. But Stephen remained resiliently stuck. Ed had seen other very good students become blocked, take a job in the community, and never return to finish.

After months of watching, Ed gently compared Stephen to his client Darnell, who had remained stuck in prison until he became willing to accept Stephen's help and get a clear goal in mind. Darnell also accepted placement in the group home for psychiatric patients that Stephen and a prison social worker arranged where he now resided. "It only took us a couple years to get Darnell out of prison. Hope it's not that long for you," Ed joked.

Even with that gentle nudge, Stephen continued reading and outlining and reading and outlining and producing nothing. He had, in fact, set some kind of record for the amount of reading and the lack of writing in a nine-month period, or at least that's what Ed said to him. Meanwhile, Ally got her outline done and approved by her committee. She was more than halfway through completing her proposal.

Stephen was sitting on his bed surrounded by pages of notes and scrunched-up outlines when Ally called. She had exciting news. Her parents, Tom and Judy, had invited them on an all-expenses-paid three-day weekend training at a retreat at the beach near Savannah, Georgia with Mark Miller, the psychodrama guru whose workshop Tom had taken Ally to the year before. This year he'd invited Stephen to attend the training while Ally and her mother would entertain Nicholas on the beach.

It was hard to turn that down though Stephen's first thought was that he needed to stay in town and work on his dissertation. But he decided to go. He threw his outlines and overflowing files of Xeroxed articles into the trunk of his car and headed to the beach with Ally and Nicholas. He was reluctant, yes, but also relieved to have an excuse to avoid his dissertation.

Ally, Nicholas and Stephen join Tom and Judy who are already settled on the beach in chairs near their hotel. As soon as they get settled, Tom invites Stephen for a run. Stephen begins lacing up his running shoes while feeling the anxiety that he felt the first time he met Ally's parents. There was something so nice, so enthusiastic about their desire to connect to him that it made him want to resist. And Tom especially seemed to want to be close to him even though they barely knew each other

Before they break a sweat, Tom begins explaining the general psychodrama model. He has thoroughly rehearsed what he wants to say to Stephen, because he's so excited about having him attend the sessions with him. "Let me outline it. Mark either calls on a participant or someone volunteers to work with a psychological drama, a psychodrama, from their life. It can be a real event, like a trauma, or it can be an abstract sort of representation of a recurring family psychodrama, or even a dream. The participant, whom Mark calls the 'protagonist,' chooses group members to play real-life family members. Mark then orchestrates a reenactment of the protagonist's drama. It almost always produces a profound emotional response. Then, Mark constructs another, competing psychodrama. This time, actors are chosen to represent supportive, ideal figures, usually parents, who provide messages the protagonist needed to hear. These are also the messages the protagonist needs in his present life. All of the characters only speak what Mark whispers to them."

Stephen says he thinks he understands but Tom notices his hesitation. He begins describing one of the psychodramas where a young woman who was abusing alcohol and being sexually reckless was the protagonist. "When she was growing up both of her parents were neglectful. Her father was alcoholic and almost totally absent as a parent and her mother was neglectful because she was completely overwhelmed with trying to deal with the father and generally kept her head in the sand. Mark got two participants to play the role of parents. They essentially ignored the young woman or dismissed her concerns. At one point, Mark asked her to explain a painful event in her life, a situation where she got drunk and had sex with a man she didn't even like. Then he had the parents turn their backs and walk away as she was describing the situation. At another point, she described a blackout and Mark got the people playing her parents to reassure her with useless statements like, 'Everybody drinks a little too much occasionally. You shouldn't worry about it.'"

Tom shakes his head and looks at Stephen, who is silent, before continuing. "The young woman completely broke down. She was weeping as she described this one-night-stand where she woke up with a man whose name she couldn't recall in a home she'd never seen. And Mark had her father in the drama say in a reassuring voice, 'I've done that a few times. It's nothing to worry about.'"

Stephen chuckles uneasily.

"Then, the ideal parents were chosen. They gave her feedback like, 'If I had been there, I'd have told you to protect your body. I'd have taught you how to protect your body, how to take care of yourself.' And then he'd have the neglectful parents say something like, 'I don't think you need to worry so much about all of this, honey.'

"Then he'd have the neglectful and ideal parents battle it out with contrasting feedback- the ideal mother and father assuring her she should listen to her instincts and protect herself and even cherish her body while her neglectful parents kept assuring her that her behavior was okay and nothing to be concerned about. It was just this back and forth until suddenly the young woman started screaming at her neglectful parents, 'You're crazy, you're crazy,' and then she burst into tears and cried like a child."

After a few more strides down the beach, Stephen asks, "Was this young woman saying that she wanted help with the drinking and the um…sex…recklessness?"

Tom looks at Stephen and then straight ahead. He runs for maybe twenty yards while considering the question that to him is very odd and a bit irritating.

"Yeah, she was," he finally says. "She was really crashing the morning after the alcohol binges and sexual liaisons. She said that she sometimes stayed in bed all morning and promised herself not to do it again. And then that very night she might repeat at least some part of the self-abuse. So, her pain was telling her to protect herself, but she'd been taught not to listen to that pain."

Stephen wipes the sweat from his eyes. He thinks he may have detected some annoyance in Tom's voice. "Not to sound like her parents," he says, "but I was just thinking that maybe she was drinking some and being promiscuous some, you know…not like she was out of control." He glances toward Tom but turns away when Tom looks at him. He doesn't want to invite a dialogue about this. "I guess I was making sure that she defined the behavior as a problem, and it sounds like she did."

"She did," Tom confirms adamantly.

Tom elaborates on another psychodrama while Stephen attempts to listen to the description of the critical and ideal voices. Stephen's thoughts have been set swirling by the bright sun, the moist air, and the glorious endorphins from the run. His feet pound along the bright sand.

He returns to Tom's voice, hears words and occasionally whole sentences, while struggling to make meaning of them. "At some point," he hears Tom say, "Mark showed each client how they actually choose the negative, critical or neglectful voices, almost as if they preferred to listen to them, while turning away from the supportive ones because it was what they were used to." A little later Stephen hears, "At some point, when they took in the ideal messages, it was like you could see something completely different in their eyes, even their posture was different."

Stephen nods and the two men run for a couple of minutes in silence. For Tom, it's a chance to replenish his oxygen with some deep breaths. Stephen is thinking. Something about all that drama and the immediate change didn't feel right. True, it was pure genius to take the primary family relationship, isolate the principle drama from that relationship and put it in the room with the client. To then take that same drama and turn it on its ear was incredible.

Before thinking further, Stephen asks, "Was the idea that these people were cured in this brief psychodrama? I mean, from all of these complicated problems… alcohol and sexual, um, overindulgence or whatever. Is the idea that they're now free from all of this?"

Tom thinks about that for a minute while struggling to get a full breath. He glances at Stephen, lines of sweat stream down his dark cheeks. He hears skepticism in his voice. "I think," Tom says, "Mark would say that they were not so much cured, as they had a new awareness of the unhealthy versus potentially healthy voices in their head."

"I guess another question I'd have is how can someone take in messages that are completely different from the messages they've heard all of their life and actually be affected by them? Isn't it maybe that the client plays along because of the staging? There's the powerful therapist, the audience, and the scripted dialogue that suggests the client should be affected by all of this? I mean it really is theater of a sort: performance art."

Tom starts to say something but doesn't want Stephen to think he's being defensive. "Those are all good questions, especially whether the effect endures after the client leaves the room and walks outside into the sunlight."

Stephen looks at Tom and appreciates his being able to join with him in questioning work he's excited about, so he goes on without caution. "One thing that comes up for me is that maybe this psychodrama is more of an indulgence of the clients' pathology than a solution. My mentor at GU says that people come to therapy when they're stuck in a story. He says that they're stuck because they're afraid to move forward. So, the young woman who is drinking and having indiscriminate sex is stuck and the process you're describing might just reinforce it. For her to change, she needs to have a way of working with what she's afraid of that the story actually helps her avoid."

Tom is jolted when he hears Stephen dismiss just about everything he described. Okay, it's certainly not a cure, and maybe the new messages are hard to take in, but now the whole psychodrama is a misdirected indulgence, according to Stephen: pretty fucking arrogant, his daughter's boyfriend!

Stephen who has not noticed Tom's demeanor change goes on. "I mean she's drinking and having sex but what is she avoiding?"

After twenty more yards, Tom almost screams, "Intimacy!"

Stephen is almost stopped by the truth in Tom's answer.

Tom hears his feet slap the wet sand, and feels the steam rolling in with the waves a few feet away. He sees his family lounging near the surf a hundred yards ahead. He tells Stephen that he's going for a swim, and deliberately does not invite him along. He takes his running shoes and socks off and stuffs the socks inside the shoes. He flips the shoes into the dry sand, sprints into the surf and dives into a wave and away from the temptation to tell his daughter's boyfriend that he's an arrogant son-of-a-bitch.

After dinner, Tom slips into bed next to his wife, who is reading.

"My legs are really aching," he says.

"I'm sure they are. It sounds like you and Stephen ran a long way," Judy says, somehow managing to sound critical in her tone.

"We went a little too far or a little too fast," Tom says, then asks Judy to rub his legs. Judy puts her book down and moves to the foot of the bed.

"That feels great," Tom says, closing his eyes. After a minute of soothing, he says, "When I was running with Stephen he kind of pissed me off…and impressed me at the same time."

Judy stops rubbing his legs. "I hope he didn't know that you were angry," she says.

"Keep rubbing my legs, please," Tom says.

"Did you…argue?" Judy asks, as she returns to the massage.

"It was fine," Tom says, deliberately giving less information than he knows his wife wants.

After maybe thirty seconds, Judy quits massaging his legs and lies next to him.

Tom's deep sigh fills the room.

"I don't want you two getting off to a bad start," Judy says.

Tom turns his head on the pillow toward his wife. "Why do you worry about that?" he asks.

"Because you both seem, I don't know, so much alike, according to what Ally says anyway. You're passionate about ideas, you're competitive, and you're in the same field. I just want you to focus on things you can agree about."

"I said he impressed me. Why aren't we talking about that?" Tom asks, looking in Judy's eyes.

"What impressed you about him?" Judy asks, closing her eyes.

"I'd rather discuss why you worry so much about my doing

something wrong. You know, I make my living talking to people. I don't know why you act like I'm a bull in a china shop."

Judy raises her eyebrows and smiles at Tom.

"I'm going to sleep," he says, leaning over and clicking the light off. The moonlight outside the window immediately brightens the room.

On the other side of the wall, Stephen and Ally lay in their bed. Stephen is lost in the movement of the moonlight dancing with the tall palm trees across Ally's face. She looks at the silhouette of his head, propped on his hand, and wonders out loud what she did to deserve such a beautiful man.

They kiss. The sheet rests delicately around Ally's waist. Stephen kisses her breasts that are the color of moonlight.

"You're so beautiful," he whispers so as not to wake Nicholas who is asleep on a cot in the corner of the room.

The young lovers go on like that, confessing their love, kissing, moving with each other as time slows for them.

In the lull between kisses and endearments, Ally asks Stephen what he and her father talked about when they were running. Stephen thinks about the question. "He told me about his experiences with psychodrama. It sounded pretty interesting, overall, but part of what he described sounded like something that Ed would say is an indulgence that might reinforce the client's pathology."

"Really?" Ally says, looking away from him. "Did you tell my dad that?"

"Yeah, I think I said something like that. I hope I didn't piss him off, but it sort of just came out."

"I wonder how he took that," she says, as her eyes dart around Stephen's face.

"I started not to say anything," Stephen says.

"No, don't do that. My dad wants to know what you really think. I'm sure he was impressed with your insight. I just know he's always searching for something, and if you found a flaw in his latest thing…I bet he felt a little discouraged."

"He didn't seem discouraged… I didn't think so, anyway."

"Don't worry about it. He's always searching, but he's also open to new ways of looking at things. I'm sure he liked you giving him something to think about," Ally says. "Are you nervous about tomorrow?"

"Yeah, a little bit. I mean, with your father there it's going to be a little weird."

"Do you think you'll do your own work?"

"God no, I can't imagine what I'd talk about, but I'm looking forward to seeing it in action," Stephen says, before leaning in for a kiss.

Mark walks into the room with such grace and confidence that Stephen has no problem identifying him. He sits on a blue exercise mat with his legs crossed. Another man joins him and introduces Mark as the father of "movement psychodrama" and assures the participants that the two-day workshop would be like no other experience they'd ever had. He then asks each participant to share their name and expectations of the workshop.

After a few introductions, it's Stephen's turn. He's uncomfortable as always in these situations but manages to say that he's getting his PhD and was invited by Tom to participate to learn Mark's model of psychotherapy. "I'm, um, excited," he says, avoiding eye contact with Mark.

"You seem tense, Stephen," Mark says. "Is there something going on in your life that you're bringing in here today that is causing the tension?"

"I think it's just, you know, being in a group, and being here with my girlfriend's father."

Everyone laughs except Mark, who smiles while his eyes trace the young man's body and then return to his face. "It seems larger than that," Mark says, before gazing expectantly, prompting Stephen to consider his observation.

"Well, I've been worrying about my dissertation. I've been reading and not writing, if you know what I mean."

"Avoiding?"

"Yeah, I'm actually very good at that. I've been perfecting it with my dissertation. In fact, I've missed a couple of deadlines. I'd say I'm pretty blocked." Stephen resisted that label when Ed used it and now he hears himself offer it up.

Mark nods and smiles. "Okay, Stephen," he says. "So, you're here to do some work on expressing yourself. I'd like to help you with your writer's block. Would you like to be free to do your writing?" Mark asks.

Stephen wants to resist but responds, "That would, we could, yes, that would be okay."

Mark continues gazing at Stephen. "Stephen, I notice that your hands are clenched," he says.

Stephen immediately releases them.

"You want to let go of whatever it was you held in your hands that quickly, huh?"

Referring to his clenched fists, Stephen says, "It's just a habit. I think I sometimes tighten my fists when I'm nervous."

"Really?" Mark asks. "Would you tighten your fists again?"

Stephen nods. He clenches his fists tightly.

"Your jaw is clenched, too," Mark says. "Do you feel that?"

Stephen nods tentatively.

"You agree, but you don't seem too sure. Are you sure you can feel your jaw being clenched?"

Stephen nods firmly.

"I want you to focus your attention on your hands and your jaw and anywhere else that feels clenched. And then let yourself become more of whatever that is."

Tom watches as the young man's entire body becomes rigid, clenched. He wonders what kept Stephen so relaxed during their run.

"Good, now can you listen to the message that comes with the clenched hands…the clenched jaw…the clenched body?"

"I guess I want to protect myself."

"Your shoulders are tight, aren't they Stephen?"

Stephen rotates them. "Yeah, they feel stiff," he says.

"Focus on the stiffness, the clenching. Listen to what your body is saying? Can you sense that message?"

"I guess I'm afraid of looking stupid. I mean I don't know what to say. I'm not usually very good at understanding my body."

Tom laughs to himself. Stephen had plenty to say to him the day before and he sure wasn't stupid.

"I want to work with you right now on these important feelings and the messages they carry. Is that what you want?" Mark asks.

Stephen nods, this time a little slower than before.

"Why don't you just sit with those feelings for a minute," Mark says before turning to the others. "The way I teach, as I'm sure most of you know from the workshop description, is by doing. And what I do is focus in on the physical body of the client and pay attention to that. And Stephen's physical responses are already present in the room, so I want to interrupt the introductions and focus on him. Is that all right with everyone?"

The psychotherapists sitting in a circle are motionless and wide-eyed until he asks for their approval and then they nod in unison like a drill team. Tom jokes to himself that they would have downed cyanide-laced Kool-aid at Mark's suggestion after watching him home in so quickly on Stephen's issues. Not one of them had noticed the clenched fists or jaw until Mark saw it, and then it was impossible for them not to see them. They want to learn to see as well as Mark, and they want to see where all of this is going.

Mark gets to his feet. "Very good," he says to the room. He drags a wooden chair into the middle of the room before turning back to Stephen. "I'd like you to come sit in this chair."

Stephen walks to the chair, looks around the room, and sits.

Mark slides a chair a few feet away from Stephen and sits in it. "Okay, Stephen," he says, "we're here with your tight muscles, your fear of looking stupid, which I'd guess is what your writer's block is all about. And I'm noticing that your fists are clenched, again."

"I guess I'm afraid of what I said earlier: of looking stupid, maybe not knowing what to say."

"Really," Mark says.

"I don't think of myself as stupid, but sometimes I block and don't know what to say and I wouldn't want to waste the time here."

"You don't think of yourself as stupid," Mark says, "and yet you've used that word several times. And you also tell us that you're not very good at understanding your body…and you worry that we'll all discover all of this. Do you have a sense of where this voice that calls you stupid in so many ways comes from? Who has criticized you in that way?"

Stephen sits very still.

"Okay," Mark says, "just describe what you saw or heard or experienced internally there."

"I heard my sister telling me that I was stupid. She had a right to call me that." Stephen looks at Mark. "It was a memory of a time when my sister was helping me study for a calculus test and I hadn't done any of the studying or homework to prepare and she got really mad."

"So, you had a very specific recollection of that?"

"Yeah, but that was something that happened fairly often when she tutored me. She'd get really angry or become disgusted with me because I hadn't prepared. Truth is, I wasn't a very motivated student, so I was usually unprepared when she tried to help me."

"Oh really. Okay," Mark says. He gets out of his chair and walks away from Stephen. "Stephen, we're going to bring your psychodrama into the room more fully by enrolling some others to play members of your family. I want you to pick someone to stand in for your sister, at least for this version of your sister, who I'll call your critical sister."

Stephen raises a finger passively toward a woman who immediately jumps to her feet and walks forward.

Mark reads her nametag and introduces her as Connie. "Connie is going to be Stephen's critical sister and say only things that I tell her to say. I'll whisper to you, Connie, and you'll repeat what I say verbatim to Stephen and with the same intonations I direct you to use. I want you to assume the role of his critical sister, but I only want you to say what I tell you to say. All right?"

Connie nods.

Mark looks back at Stephen. "I want you to listen to what your critical sister has to say about you blocking when you want to express something important."

Mark whispers in Connie's ear. Connie takes a deep breath and says to Stephen, "Why don't you just relax?" her voice carrying a hint of disdain.

Stephen looks at his critical sister and then down at his hands. "I'm fine," he mumbles.

Mark walks toward Stephen. He stops a few feet from him. "Connect to your hands there. What's going on with them?" he asks.

Stephen looks at his hands. They're even more clenched. There is a long silence.

"I'm not sure," Stephen says. "Nothing, really…I think," he says.

Mark whispers to Connie again and Connie repeats his words: "This is pretty easy stuff, Stephen. All you have to do is pay attention to what's going on in your body and tell us."

Stephen feels dazed and mumbles, "This is stupid."

Tom shifts uneasily in his chair. He's saying essentially what he said in a kinder way yesterday.

Mark moves quickly back to Connie, and whispers in her ear. Connie says, "Why don't you pay attention?"

Stephen looks at Connie and then at Mark. "I don't feel anything," he insists.

Connie repeats Mark's whispered words. "How can you sit here in the room with all of us waiting for an answer and come up with, 'I don't feel anything.' Of course, you feel something."

Stephen stares at Connie.

"What do your eyes say to your sister?" Mark asks.

"That she's being her impatient, smarter-than-everyone-in-the-room-self," Stephen says.

Mark whispers to Connie. "I'm just trying to help you do better," she says.

"Yeah, well you're not helping," Stephen says.

Again, Mark whispers to Connie. "You're hard to help," Connie says.

Stephen stares at a cheap chandelier above his critical sister's head.

"Are you trying to do your part?" Connie asks.

"Yes, I am," Stephen says.

"You seem distracted," Connie says.

"No, I'm not."

"Maybe you're just being lazy…you have to admit, you can be pretty lazy."

"I'm not really lazy anymore."

"So, you tell me why you're not responding to the questions well."

"I'm just a little confused with all of this."

"Maybe you're just slow."

Stephen and Connie look at each other.

Mark moves away from Connie, to the back of the room, and watches them stare at each other. "I'd like to hear from your parents on this issue," Mark announces. "Stephen, what would your mother and father say about this. Are you slow?"

Stephen turns away from his critical sister to Mark. "They think I'm less intelligent than her," he says, nodding toward his critical sister.

"Okay, Stephen, I'd like you to choose someone to stand in for your critical mother and critical father."

Stephen points to his selections. "Good," Mark says, before turning to the two. "Come down behind Connie." He instructs the critical father to rest his hand on the sister's shoulder. He takes the mother's hand and rests it on the critical sister's other shoulder.

Mark whispers to the man who looks at Connie and speaks lovingly, "You're so smart," he says, before turning to Stephen, "Stephen, let your sister help you. You have your strengths, but you have a hard time learning and your sister can help."

Mark whispers to the woman who looks at Connie, filled with a mother's love, she says, "You're such a genius." And then she looks at Stephen. "You have other gifts, Stephen, but please let your sister help you with the difficult things," she says.

"What are you feeling now?" Mark asks Stephen.

"Like this is pretty accurate. I mean, that just about sums up the feelings about her intellect and mine in my household."

Mark leans close and whispers to the critical mother, "But we loved you, you were always so sensitive," she says.

Mark moves close to Stephen's critical father. "We never thought that you were stupid, it's just that your sister was so smart. It's just a relative thing," he says.

"I don't really want to hear this," Stephen whispers as he looks at his hands.

"Tell them that," Mark says.

Stephen looks up at his critical family and shakes his head.

"Don't be intimidated, you can do it," his critical father says at Mark's prompting.

Mark walks quickly to Stephen's critical mother. She says, "Speak up, Stephen. We're waiting. We're patient, but we don't have all day."

An agonizing silence, occasionally interrupted by Stephen taking a deep breath, seemingly in preparation to speak, follows, but he says nothing. Mark directs Stephen's critical mother closer to his side. She leans down as directed and looks in Stephen's eyes, "What's wrong with you, son? We just want to know what's wrong with you. Can you express yourself?" she asks, and then moves away from him and rejoins her family away from him.

Stephen's arms fall to his side like broken branches. He glances around the room, avoiding the eyes of his critical parents. Finally, he finds a pattern on the Turkish rug on the floor in front of his chair and follows it with his eyes from one design to another, from one side to the other, and then back again, over and over. After a minute, he looks at his critical mother again and tears begin streaming down his cheeks.

Mark walks to Stephen and puts his hands on his shoulders. As he gently rubs his shoulders he whispers, "I need you to choose someone to stand in for your ideal father."

Slowly, Stephen raises his eyes and motions toward a kindly-looking man, Brad. Mark guides him to Stephen's side. He places Brad's hands on Stephen's shoulders and motions for him to continue to rub them.

Mark asks Stephen to choose a woman for his ideal mother, which he does quickly. Mark moves Stephen's ideal mother next to Stephen and motions for her to begin massaging his heart.

Finally, he asks Stephen to choose another of the participants to stand in for his ideal sister and when he does so, Mark seats her in a chair almost directly between Stephen and his critical sister.

Mark whispers in Brad's ear. "Stephen," he says, as Mark instructed, "if I had been there, it would have been different. I wouldn't have allowed your sister to try to teach you something when she wasn't emotionally ready to be a teacher."

Mark whispers to Brad, who parrots his words as sincerely as he can say them. "It takes a lot of maturity and patience to be a teacher and know how to bring out the best in her student. Your sister wasn't ready to assume that role. I wouldn't have allowed her to teach you before she had the necessary emotional and intellectual readiness."

Mark hands Brad the box of Kleenex. Brad gives it to Stephen who gasps for air as he looks at Brad with sincere appreciation. Brad watches as Stephen tries to dry his face as his tears continue.

Mark whispers to Brad, who says, "I'd have been sure that you were taught by someone who knew how to bring out your intellectual gifts. I'd have done it myself if I could have. Even if I couldn't, I'd have made sure you got what you needed."

Mark whispers to Brad again. He repeats the words emphatically, the way Mark said them to him: "I'd have done whatever was necessary to cultivate your unique and beautiful gifts."

Stephen looks back at Brad while struggling to stifle his crying.

Mark whispers to his ideal mother. "If I had been there," she says, "you'd realize how smart you are and how much you have to say."

Stephen looks at his ideal parents and then looks at Mark. He sniffs and catches his breath and says to Mark, barely audibly, "This is stupid." He catches his breath and speaks clearer. "This is stupid… There was no one there that thought any of this."

Tom, who has been watching the drama, feels tense. "Is it all going to fall apart?" he wonders. Stephen doesn't appear to believe the change that Mark is trying to make. He realizes how invested he has become in whatever it was that they were doing.

"I take it that's true, Stephen. These are ideal parents. See if you can hear them? Try not to resist their wisdom," Mark says.

Mark bends to whisper in Stephen's ideal sister's ear. She looks at Stephen and says, "If I had been there, I would have been your biggest fan."

Stephen seems confused, as he stares blankly.

Mark moves quickly away from the Stephen's ideal family and puts his arms around his critical parents. He whispers in both of their ears.

Stephen's critical mother says, "This is probably too much for Stephen," she says.

"Maybe we should slow down," his critical father says.

Mark moves quickly to his critical sister. "Why don't you answer them?" his critical sister asks. "Are you blocked?"

"Fuck you," Stephen says to his critical sister.

Mark motions to the ideal mother and father to vigorously massage him. He moves his ideal sister out of the chair, onto the floor in front of him. She sits at his feet and looks up at him.

Mark rushes back to his critical father and whispers in his ear. "Foul language is used by the ignorant, Stephen," he says.

"Your sister was just trying to help," his critical mother says.

"She was being an asshole," Stephen says.

"Do you have to talk like that in front of your mother? We're all here to be helpful. We don't know what you need, but we're trying. Maybe if you could tell us…" his critical father says.

Mark rushes to his ideal sister. "If I'd been there, I would have been patient and methodical. I would have tapped into your gifts as a learner," he says.

Stephen looks down at his ideal sister and then says to Mark, "I don't really like it when she says stuff I know my sister wouldn't say."

"You don't want to believe it would have been different if your sister would have been patient?" Mark asks.

"No, I just don't believe she thinks it's her fault." Stephen says.

Mark goes back to his critical sister. "It wasn't my fault. I wasn't the one that didn't prepare."

"You should have prepared more, son," his critical mother says to him, at Mark's prompting.

"You should have known that you didn't learn very quickly and put in extra work," his critical father says after visited by Mark.

"I hated calculus!" Stephen yells, and then more quietly he adds, "and besides, she told me that she could teach me." Stephen points accusingly at his critical sister. "She told me that she could teach me everything I needed to know in a weekend. So, I didn't prepare because she made it sound so easy."

Mark rushes to his ideal sister who repeats him. "If I'd been there, I wouldn't have gotten mad when things got difficult. Of course, it was difficult to learn calculus. Anyone who tells you differently is lying. I wouldn't have made it sound so easy and I wouldn't have gotten mad when you struggled."

"Tell him, 'struggling is part of the process of learning,' and massage his neck," Brad hears Mark whisper to him. He repeats the words to

Stephen while he moves his right hand up to the back of his neck and begins rubbing him deeply.

"If I'd been there, and your sister was trying to help, I would have helped her deal with her own difficulty teaching and controlling her emotions. It would have been different," his ideal mother says, with Mark standing at her side watching Stephen closely.

Mark builds the tension further. He moves quickly to Stephen's critical sister. "I made it sound easy because it was easy, and you just were kind of slow," she says.

"Kind of slow," his critical father says.

"You always were kind of slow, but you had other gifts," his critical mother says.

Mark moves back to the ideal family members. "You weren't slow. If I'd been there, you would have known how smart you are," his ideal mother says.

"You have important things to say," his ideal father says.

"I want to read your dissertation when you finish," his ideal sister says.

Mark walks to Stephen's critical sister and whispers, "You never could focus for long enough. Who knows why."

Tom watches as Mark looks closely at Stephen, whose breathing is very shallow. Mark walks to him and asks him to stand up. He asks Connie, his critical sister, to stand also and moves her to a few feet in front of Stephen. Mark walks to the back of the room and watches the two stare at each other.

"What do you want to say to her?" Mark asks from the back of the room in a booming voice.

Silence.

Mark walks back past Stephen and whispers first to his ideal mother and then to his ideal father.

"She'll be okay, just tell your sister what you feel," his ideal mother says.

"You don't have to take care of your sister anymore. She needs to hear the truth," his ideal father says.

"What do you want to say to her?" Mark asks Stephen.

"I finished my Master's thesis. It's 150 pages and was published in a significant journal. I must have some ability to focus."

"Did your sister ask to read any of it?" Mark asks.

"It wasn't the kind of thing she'd want to read. It was pretty boring, actually. It was an experimental study comparing different learning styles."

"What does your sister do?" Mark asks.

"She's a lawyer," Stephen says.

"What kind of law?" Mark asks.

"She helps companies write contracts when they're buying and selling companies."

"I'm sure that's some pretty titillating reading," Mark says, and then roars with laughter. He turns to the room inviting, with an ironic smile, everyone in the room to join with him. Everyone laughs on cue.

Mark moves quickly to his ideal father who then repeats his words. "Your sister has trouble dealing with your accomplishments."

Marks whispers to his ideal mother. "You don't have to protect her anymore," she says.

Stephen stares at his critical sister sitting in front of him.

"Why won't you let her read it?" Mark asks.

"She wouldn't be interested in it," Stephen says.

"But you haven't asked," Mark says.

"No, I haven't," he says.

"Would it mean something if she read it?" Mark asks.

"Yeah, I guess," Stephen says.

"But you don't ask…"

"I just don't think she'd be interested. Maybe change that. I think she would read it, but be unable to find anything positive about it because it would threaten her."

"Why do you worry so much about her?" Mark asks.

After a long silence, in which Stephen follows the pattern of the rug below him with his eyes, he looks at Mark. "I love her," he says.

Mark walks closer to Stephen. "I can tell that, but you're so mad at her you could hardly be in a position to show her the fullest expression of your love, much less your writing."

Mark turns and walks away from Stephen.

Stephen calls out to Mark. "I'm not really that mad at her."

Mark ignores the comment as he walks to the back of the room. When he's as far away from Stephen as possible, he turns around and looks at him. "I want to say this clearly, Stephen. We've all watched you rage at your sister here." He begins walking back toward Stephen, "That makes it hard for me, for us, to believe that you're not very mad at her."

Mark stops several feet from Stephen and motioning toward his critical sister he says, "Tell her how mad you are because of her unrelenting criticism. Tell her you know now that she was threatened by you. Tell her how you internalized her criticism, which became a subversive voice in your head. Do that or forgive her for misunderstanding complex things when she was a kid."

"She still treats me like I'm not quite as smart as she is," Stephen says.

"And not quite as important, also, right?" Mark says.

Stephen quickly agrees.

"Do you still think she's smarter than you?" Mark asks.

Stephen looks away again.

"And so, your block protects both of you," Mark says. "You from having to compete on a stage with your sister and her from having to feel inadequate relative to you if and when you do it. These are feelings that you're both comfortable with."

Mark prompts the ideal sister to ask, "How did you write your master's thesis?"

Stephen looks at her and then away.

"Your sister wants to know how you accomplished writing your thesis. Don't you want to tell her?" Mark asks.

"She doesn't want to know, really," Stephen says.

"Or you don't want to tell her," Mark says.

Stephen looks at Mark and then at his ideal sister. "My thesis chair and I came up with an outline. Then we estimated how long each section would be and put the proposed completion dates on a calendar. I then met with him once a week. We went over what I'd written and where I was in my outline. We set goals for the next week and I went back and wrote some more."

"What kind of feedback did he give you that helped you keep moving?" his ideal sister asks, after being visited by Mark.

"Mostly he was positive, but he told me when I was losing focus or not developing an idea enough. He was really honest and encouraging."

"He sounds pretty ideal," Mark says.

"He really was," Stephen says.

Mark whispers to his ideal parents and then his ideal sister and one by one they acknowledge how much focus and dedication he was capable of.

Mark moves away from Stephen and begins speaking to him, and to the rest of the room. "You know, all along I've been wondering how our young writer here completed his master's thesis. It's not easy to do a thesis, as many of you know. He did that and yet he has been blocked doing his dissertation. What is different now during his writing than before during his writing of his Master's thesis?" Turning more directly to Stephen, he continues, "It sounds to me like your mentor was an ideal mentor, an ideal father, and provided the kind of nurturance and direction that you needed to block out the voices of criticism, and also to help you tap into your own genius. I imagine that is how you'll do your dissertation, too."

Mark and Stephen smile at each other.

Slowly Mark turns away from Stephen and speaks to the room. "So what have we done? We've put this courageous young man's unconscious process on stage. He wasn't aware of the beliefs that were guiding his procrastination and now, because of a memory image that flashed when we paid attention to his anxiety, I believe he is.

"He's making a choice to procrastinate or not write. It's a choice based on an unconscious belief that he's in some way not enough… even though we can all see that he most certainly is… It doesn't matter whether his parents or sister even believed what we presented. It doesn't matter whether the events even occurred as he remembers them. He believes it this way and that belief is getting in the way of his writing.

"The ideal parents and sister that we created were ones with the characteristics that he needed and still needs. They have given him the message that he was and is good enough. Will those new messages unseat the old ones? I think of that as a lifetime journey and whether we're trying to recover from our childhood injuries or thrive in spite of messages that may have been unintentionally given us, it's a journey we all should embrace.

"Let's take a break."

Chapter 29

CHANGING STORIES 2

STEPHEN AND TOM ARE A MILE INTO the last run of the week-end and once again in different places. Tom is wanting to debrief about the workshop and see if Stephen is still skeptical about the ideas. He has hesitated to be the one to bring it up because Stephen hasn't volunteered about his psychodrama experience.

Just before joining Tom for the run Stephen got a call from his father. Frank had been pressured by his wife to call after a report from his doctor that his cancer was in the bones of his legs and spine. He'd had cancer for four years and it was the first time that Stephen considered that he'd die from it. Didn't people in good shape and with a decent mental attitude survive these things?

Stephen was in his hotel room alone when he got the call. Ally let him sleep in and was on the beach along with the rest of her family happily entertaining Nicholas. After hanging up, Stephen's body had not allowed him to move. He recalled his father describing one of his symptoms of depression as not wanting to leave the difficult comfort of his bed. His father, a simple man, seemed to easily master almost every athletic or physical challenge he ever faced and yet somehow was always overwhelmed by the complexities of emotion and relationships. At least he called about this latest setback, but how is he ever going to handle dying? How does anyone deal with that? Stephen got out of bed if for no other reason than to stop himself from thinking.

There's very little wind on the beach and the southern sun almost aches on Tom's skin. He wants to bring up the discussion of psychodrama when it feels natural. Casually, he asks about his father's health. "How is your dad?" he asks. "Ally told me a while back that he had prostate cancer."

Stephen considers several ways of answering, while his legs grow heavy. The damp air from the surf offers little relief from the heat. He thinks through various ways to tell Tom that his father isn't doing very well. The heat and his emotional wariness cause him to abandon his carefulness. "My father's cancer has apparently spread to his legs and spine," he says, adding, "I don't really know what that means, but that's what he told me on the phone a little while ago."

Tom turns his eyes toward Stephen. He sees the sweat around his mouth. His expression shows his pain. In the brief time that he has known Stephen, he's always seemed to be smiling or smirking or showing some similar expression that seemed vaguely not self-effacing enough for Tom. He lingers on this new expression.

He looks ahead at the almost empty beach. "Oh, I'm sorry, Stephen…to hear that," he says, slowing to a walk. "Let's walk," he says. "My legs are hurting like hell."

"Sure," Stephen says.

"How's your father coping with the news?" Tom asks after he and Stephen are walking together.

"He seemed fine on the phone. It's really hard to tell with him... He sort of holds things back."

"How are you doing?" Tom asks.

"I don't know," Stephen says, as he wonders how he's doing. "I guess in some way I'm still hopeful. His oncologist told him that there's a new chemotherapy that might arrest the spread of the cancer. So, I guess there's hope."

Tom starts to tell him that it seems that there is always a new chemotherapy and hope. But there is also always the inevitable spread of cancer, at least once it's as aggressive as his father's appears to be. He chooses his words carefully. "I know there are some drugs that can slow the spread down, but it sounds like your father's cancer is pretty aggressive."

Stephen feels a moment of anger: Why does everyone have to be so negative? He says, "I guess I want to have some hope. I don't think being positive can be a bad thing...at least for my father."

"I agree," Tom says. "I think being hopeful can make an enormous difference. It can make the difference in months, even years in some cases."

"You believe that keeping a positive state of mind can affect physical symptoms?" Stephen asks, feeling much more desperate about the answer than he wished to be.

"I know it can. But with cancer as advanced as your father's, the effect might be more limited than in some cases," Tom says in a caring tone of voice.

Tom looks closely at Stephen's pained expression. "What's most important," he says, "is for you and your father to realize that your time together is limited. I'm not saying his death is imminent. I don't know that much about cancer and chemotherapy. But of course, for all of us, our time here is limited. We don't like to think about that. But cancer has invaded your father's bone system, I don't know Stephen…"

Stephen watches Tom shake his head from side to side and fade away from finishing his thought, and he knows intuitively that it's because there is no way for him to finish without saying something out loud that Tom wishes to spare him.

Tom and Stephen walk toward the waves and continue their walk in the shallow water letting the waves wash up on their running shoes. Tom begins talking about his own father's death. He talks over the next couple of miles about how his father died slowly, as most do with cancer, so he felt blessed that he had time to say goodbye. He tells him that it was important because he felt that he and his father never had an honest conversation about their relationship until it was clear that his father was dying. He tells him about how his father's illness and imminent death changed the way he viewed his father, the man who had made him endure nightly cross-examinations in his effort to educate his children, an effort that left Tom feeling hostile and rebellious. He tells Stephen that he's still confused about how he could feel a way about his father one minute and then suddenly feel completely different when he realized that he was going to lose him.

"Do you still have the positive feelings about him…the ones that you had as he died?" Stephen asks.

Tom glances down at the wet sand, before returning to Stephen's face. He sighs. "Yes and no," he says. "I definitely have a more mature, less judgmental view of him. But I do still remember how he made life difficult for my brother and me. I just wish he could have shown a little more of his…humanity, compassion, maybe…or just played with us more. But he didn't know how to do that. Your father must have done that with you."

"Yeah, he did," Stephen says. "Why do you assume that?"

"I was just watching you with your son. He's lucky how much you put into him."

Stephen walks for a few seconds, then looks at Tom and nods. "Thanks," he says, softly.

The two men turn around and head back. As they walk along and talk easily each of them spend short periods absorbed in the glittering sunshine on the ocean water, the sandpipers scampering ahead of them, the pelicans gliding inches above the cresting waves, and the cheerful children climbing over the waves, making their way deeper into the water.

Tom has been looking at the shrimp boats frozen on the horizon when he glances ahead and spots Ally, Judy and Nicholas in the distance. "Why don't we sit down and talk a little more before we get back," he says, motioning with his head at the family on the beach.

Tom looks back at the shrimp boats. "I have a suggestion about you and your father," he says. "Make sure that you get some time with your dad as soon as possible. You don't know how much time you've got left."

Stephen nods, digging at the sand with his hand. "That's a good suggestion," he finally says. "I also want to help him get into the right mental frame and, who knows, maybe he can reverse the progression of the cancer."

Tom looks at Stephen, admiring his conviction. But he knows his hope will deceive him.

Tom wants to revisit the discussion of psychodrama. He asks Stephen if he's "in a place" to talk about the workshop.

"Sure," Stephen answers, honestly.

"I've been wondering how the workshop went for you. You had some objections to the model beforehand. Did participating change your thoughts?"

"My God yes. I can't tell you how powerful that experience was for me. Maybe it's wishful thinking, but I've been obsessed with wanting to get back to school and get with my mentor and come up with a plan for my dissertation. But here's what was weird to me. All that stuff he had my parents say and even most of it he had my sister say, they never said. At least not out loud, and yet it felt exactly right."

"I think that's because Mark hears the overall message of the memory and what the body is saying and then puts it in the way that he assumes you're remembering and believing it. So, when you were anxious and told him the memory that was blocking you and that you had assumed your parents thought your sister was smarter, he just had your critical parents say out loud what you might have thought. I don't even think he'd say it was necessary for them to have thought it. Just that you experienced it that way. He doesn't think he's replaying actual events. And the antidote is to have these ideal parents present the opposite healing message."

"So, it's not what actually occurred," Stephen says. "Yeah, I get that because in my case the only thing that actually occurred is my sister got mad at me when she was tutoring me. I did think and do think my parents think my sister is smarter than me. I think she's smarter than me. She certainly was when we were growing up. But all weekend I've been wondering if I'd have been smarter if I'd believed differently."

"In that way, maybe it's similar to your mentor's narrative model. You have an old story you've been comfortable with and are stuck because you haven't wanted to change it. I mean, unconsciously."

"Yes, it's exactly like that."

"Good stuff," Tom says, wrapping his arms around his knees and pulling them closer.

The two men look out at the rolling blue waters that has little dabs of white caps before becoming a sea of grayness at the horizon.

Stephen's head rocks back. He closes his eyes feeling the warm sun on his face and the cool drip of sweat on his neck. He hears a wave pound the sand twenty feet away. He thinks about visiting his father.

Chapter 30

PRESENCE IN LOSS

STEPHEN LOOKS TO THE WEST out the window of the cab. The deep blue water of the Gulf of Mexico is speckled with distant boats: some darting, some meandering, some still. He has been in one of those boats, relaxed, exhilarated, free. Now he's in a cab wondering what condition he'll find his father in when he gets to the hospital.

The cab rolls along the wide four-lane road seemingly forever, reminding him of that familiar dream where you spend the entire, awful night trying to get somewhere important, you're just not sure where, and you never get there. He wonders if that's a universal dream, a result of these experiences or perhaps a preparation for them.

Finally, the cab pulls up to the hospital entrance. Stephen hands the driver his money across the front seat. As he's about to slide out the door, the driver turns toward him. "Hope everything's all right," he says.

Stephen tries to smile. "Thanks," he manages, realizing that the cab driver has picked up on his anxiety.

Stephen hurries inside. He's filled with regret, even amazement at his ability to deny his father's failing health even over the many months after learning about the progression of the cancer into his father's bones. He'd talked to him on the phone but hadn't been with him. Hadn't sat with him. Talked to him. Told him he loved him.

The receptionist directs him to the ICU on the fifth floor. Waiting for the elevator, he breathes in the hospital smell, which is a smell like nowhere else, a smell people describe as antiseptic. That's not what a hospital smells like. It smells of blood, human waste, decaying bodies, and, yes, antiseptic spray. The odor is even stronger in the ICU.

Privacy curtains left open reveal patient after patient, mini-computers, rolling stainless steel medical tables with blood-soaked surgical paraphernalia, nurses leaning over patients. Stephen strains to make sense as the nurse describes his father's condition. "His vital signs and sensorium are within normal limits. But his platelets were extremely low when he got here and so far he's been unresponsive to cognitive assessment."

"What do you mean?" Stephen asks, making no pretense at understanding.

"Oh, I'm sorry. Your mother said you were studying to be a doctor."

"I'm not studying to be that kind of doctor," Stephen says, politely. "And, ah, she's not my mother. She's my father's wife."

Stephen feels uncomfortable having corrected the nurse. He tries to apologize, saying his concern for his father has exhausted his politeness.

"It's completely okay," the nurse says.

"Is he going to be all right?" Stephen asks, standing in front of a curtain where the nurse has stopped him, behind which he assumes his father will be.

"His doctor will discuss his prognosis with you. He'll be here in the morning." The nurse puts her hand on Stephen's shoulder and gently massages it. "He's pretty stable right now, but he did lose a lot of blood, so we have to watch him closely. It's good you're here," she says.

Stephen nods his head and steels himself with a deep breath. "So, his wife, Donna's here with him?"

"She left an hour or so ago. She said she had to check on their dog. She said she'd be back in a few hours. There's someone from the hospice here. Donna signed her in. Her name's Ayala."

The nurse slowly pulls back the curtain.

Stephen's father's head sits lifeless above white sheets. The color, the life, seems gone from his face. His eyelids are slightly parted, revealing dark pupils. His green irises seem to have disappeared. Stephen watches closely, hoping for a blink, but he's distracted by movement and sound coming from a very large silver-haired woman, whispering in his father's ear while fingering and kissing a gilded angel. "You can let go when you're ready," she says. "It's okay."

Stephen walks a step closer, puts his hands on the bed next to his father's feet and leans closer to him. His movement has caused the woman to quit nattering. His father appears frozen, like an image he's seen in a movie, maybe where some children discover a body in the snow and then flee in horror. Stephen looks in his father's vacant eyes. He's seconds away from breaking into tears when he sees something change in his father's eyes. Slowly, the large black holes between his eyelids narrow and become filled by the deep green color of his irises.

"Dad?" Stephen whispers.

"Stephen," his father mumbles, before moving his tongue slowly back and forth over his lips. "Stephen?" he says again, a little clearer this time. His eyes blink wide open.

Stephen moves quickly to his father's side and grabs his hand and begins squeezing it. "Dad, are you okay? I love you. I was so scared that...I'm so glad you're okay."

"Stephen...I don't know," his father says.

"Don't worry about a thing. I'm going to make sure you're okay," Stephen says as he rubs his father's shoulder. Stephen glances at the woman who is watching him closely, before returning to his father. He watches his father's eyes slowly close.

"Dad? Dad?" Stephen says.

"Don't worry, Stephen, it's part of the process of letting go," the woman blurts. "I'm Ayala. I've heard so much about you." She puts down the angel and reaches across Frank's chest to shake Stephen's hand. He moves his free hand to hers. She grabs it and moves it up and down too many times.

"Did you see ... he just passed out or something? Do you think we need to tell the nurse?" Stephen asks.

"No, hon. They have him wired up like a Christmas tree. If one of his lights went out they'd be in here in a second. But you know, that was magic what just happened between you two." Ayala's eyes twinkle with tears. "I've been with him for two hours and Donna was here all morning and neither of us has seen him move an inch. He's just had that blank stare. And he saw you and," she snaps her fingers, "everything changed."

Stephen looks up at Ayala. "Were you here when the doctor was here?" he asks.

"No, Donna was. She said your Dad's oncologist told her that the passing out and bleeding were his body's rejection of the new chemo. He said there was nothing more he could do for him."

Steven looks down and feels unsteady.

"What I think he meant was that there would be no more chemo, which if you ask me, is a good thing because it's always the chemo that kills 'em."

Stephen feels panicky. "Kills them?" he repeats.

"Yeah, I told your dad. Once it's in the bones, and you've been through three or four chemos, from here on in, the chemo's worse than the cancer. But your father wanted to try one more. It's hard for people to give up hope, even when it's clearly time." She looks down at Frank and smiles at him the way women smile at babies. "He's resting comfortably now. You want to get some coffee and talk?"

Stephen stares at the woman whose name he has suddenly forgotten and speaks softly to hide his outrage. "Um, no, no I don't. I want to sit here with my father. You go ahead, please."

As Ayala leaves, Stephen massages his father's hand, warming it. "It's cold in here," he says to his father and himself. Stephen starts to cry.

In too short a time, Ayala returns with two cups of coffee in her hands.

"Oh honey," she gasps upon seeing Stephen's wet face, "are you okay?" She rushes to Stephen's side. "Honey, I know how deeply, deeply you hurt. It's okay. Your Dad is letting go and you have to do the same."

Stephen breathes in deeply and mysteriously finds himself relaxing even though just a few seconds earlier he wondered if he'd ever quit crying.

"Ayala is an interesting name," he says, suspended between wanting to be nice and equally to be sarcastic.

"I took that name after my husband died. His cancer started in his prostate just like your dad's. It was a terrible process. What I realized after he died was that I spent every minute trying to keep him alive and what I should have done was to help him die."

"Really," Stephen says, with a positive tone that hides his extreme desire for her to shut up. He's pretty sure he's never met anyone with poorer instincts for what to say and how and when to say it.

It's almost like he's watching someone demonstrate everything he has been taught not to do as a psychotherapist. She can't stop giving advice about outcomes Stephen cannot consider. Plus, he thinks, she's just this awful presence: big face, big hair, tight spandex shirt wrapped around humongous boobs, and, oh my god, the shirt is even a little low cut.

Still, a part of him is appreciative. She was looking out for his father when he wasn't able to be there. "Maybe I'll have that coffee," he says, motioning to it.

"Honestly, Stephen, he looks great compared to earlier today. I think he may have escaped his critical period."

"What do you mean by critical period?"

"When people are gravely ill, there are critical periods, which I believe is their soul wanting to leave this place, and them not being willing to let go." She shakes her head. "It's so hard to let go."

"I appreciate everything you've done for my father. I really do. But I mean, you're just freaking me out. How do you know what his soul wants? That's just a very odd thing to assume, don't you think?"

"This is a very hard time for you. I can certainly understand that," Ayala says, with almost grating empathy. "I think it would be best if I came back tomorrow after you've had some time with your father." Ayala leaves just as the head nurse comes back into the room. "The doctor just ordered that your father be moved to a private room on this floor," she says, as an orderly moves quickly past her and begins preparing the machines and the bed for the trip.

"Is that because he's improved?"

The nurse looks at Stephen with patient eyes. "The doctor will discuss his…"

"Prognosis, I know. I'm not asking for anything beyond tonight. I just…"

"I told the doctor that you were here from out of town and that we had a private room where we could continue the same level of monitoring and it would be much more comfortable for you. There's a lounge chair that opens up into a bed. That's the only reason we're moving your dad."

"That's so nice of you," Stephen says, and suddenly he's over-whelmed with uncontrollable tears and mucus and lands in the arms of the nurse. She holds him as he sobs. Even though his eyes are closed he can sense that someone has entered the room and opens his eyes to Ayala, who heard the news of the room transfer and returned to offer her help.

"I'll take him," Stephen hears Ayala whisper to the nurse as she moves forward. The nurse seems hesitant, but slides from under Stephen, letting him fall onto Ayala. Ayala whispers for him to, "Let it all out honey, come on, don't hold back." After four or five times of hearing this chant, Stephen struggles to support his own weight, wipes his face, and insists he's fine.

A minute later, Stephen is walking down the hall with Ayala. She has taken his arm and is cradling it to her side, like the father of the bride.

"It's so nice that they're moving Dad to a private room," he says, trying to be polite and communicative.

"Yes…" Ayala says, seeming to hold something back, perhaps insider information that only a seasoned angel of death would know about.

Stephen turns to face her outside his father's new room. "Something in your tone sounds pessimistic," he says.

"Well, I didn't want to say it," Ayala replies, "but it's not necessarily a good sign that your father is being moved to a private room. Many times, it's a doctor's way of allowing the family some privacy around dealing with death and dying issues. By the way, honey, do you know your father does not have a living will?"

"No, I don't. I didn't even know that he needed one," Stephen mutters.

"Yeah, he hasn't brought it up to you because he's basically been in denial about dying."

"I don't understand why you keep saying all of this stuff to me. It's like it's not bad enough my father has almost died, you want to make sure I don't think there's one chance in hell that he might actually live."

Ayala takes a breath. "I just know," she says, "how families fight to keep people alive, and then the people who are dying suffer. It's because of denial. I try to break through that denial."

Stephen takes a step back. "I just got here, and it's my plan to do everything I can to help my father get better. I can tell you I'm not ready for him to die. I'm here to be with him, and I don't think you know as much as you think you do about his life expectancy."

"I know your father is in the fourth stage of cancer, and many times people only live a few months once they reach that point."

Stephen stares at Ayala. He moves closer to her, points toward the elevators, and asks her very nicely at first, "Please leave, and take your talking angel." He feels his anger rising and almost yells "Get out of here."

He follows Ayala to the elevator repeating the word, "Leave," until Ayala disappears.

Stephen returns to his father's room. Just before he enters, the nurse comes out of the room and walks right up to Stephen and stops. Her eyes rest on his watery eyes. She smiles so gently that a tear emerges from his right eye and rolls down his cheek.

"Are you gonna be okay?" she asks. "My name is Julia. I'll be here for the next few hours."

"I'm just upset," Stephen says, his lips quivering. He turns away slightly and wipes his tears.

"Of course, you're upset," she says, pulling a tissue from her pocket. She hands it to him. "You wouldn't be human if you weren't upset."

Stephen wipes his eyes. "I'm sorry. I'm just so worried about my father," he says.

"You don't have to apologize to me, sweetheart. You just relax, spend some time with your father, and call me if you need anything, okay?"

Stephen nods.

Julia moves like she's about to walk away and then stops. "By the way," she says. "Ayala…"

"Yeah, I shouldn't have…"

"No, I'll just say that she's worked with several families I've seen here. You're not the first person who's run her off. She has horrible timing and almost no grace, but her heart is in the right place."

"Yeah, I should apologize to her…"

"I'm not saying you need to do anything. Hospice workers have a different perspective on life and death, but they try to be helpful. In Ayala's case, I don't know that she's ever gotten over the loss of her husband. She tries to help everyone else do things differently than she did with him. From what she told me, she handled his death pretty much the way all family members handle death. She kept her hopes up until there was no more room for hope, and then she faced it. There doesn't seem to be any other way to do it."

Stephen wipes his eyes again. "That helps, thanks. I'm getting the impression that you're telling me my father is very sick. I appreciate your telling me the truth…and your compassion."

Julia nods her head, as she looks around the hall and thinks about what to say. "While your father is quite ill, nobody, not the doctors and certainly not Ayala, can predict how much time he has. We'll have to wait and see how his body recovers from the adverse reaction to his chemo and how the cancer progresses. Your hope can help your father. There will be plenty of time for reality. Let's go check on your dad," she says, leading him through the door.

After taking his blood pressure and heart rate, Julia reassures that Frank is much improved from just a couple of hours ago. "So, he's stable right now. You need to make yourself comfortable, spend time with your dad, and if you need anything just call for me."

Stephen walks to the lounge chair next to his father's bed. "Okay," he says, working his face to a slight smile. "I'm all right," he reassures.

"Good," Julia says, smiling like an old friend. She turns away and cuts off the overhead light as she leaves.

The moment she closes the door Stephen feels lonely. He slides into the chair. He reaches over and pulls his father's hand from under the sheets, sliding his fingers through his father's.

After a few minutes, he lets go of his father's hand, stands up, and walks to the window. He looks down at the crowded parking lot. A car backs out of a space and pulls away. He watches an old man walk slowly toward the hospital entrance carrying a bouquet of flowers.

He returns to his father's bedside and takes his hand again. He wants to call his sister. She needs to know what's going on. But right now, Stephen cannot let go of his father's hand. He closes his eyes and begins feeling peaceful somehow.

He's visited by images of his father. He sees him working in the garden with Randy. He has a much older image of his father standing on a pitcher's mound, throwing a ball to him and other ten-year-old boys.

His eyes moisten.

The next image is of his father in a crisp, white baseball uniform, hitting groundballs to high school athletes. This image is followed by the same man, slightly grayer, grinning, completely in love, as he holds Nicholas a few minutes after he was born. He tells Stephen with tears in his eyes that he wishes he could convey to him how much meaning and pleasure this little boy will bring to his life. Then Stephen clearly sees his father dancing awkwardly at his wedding. Then his father is sitting in Bones, his menu resting against his chest, confessing that he's depressed. And finally, Stephen sees the image from earlier, in the ICU looking…lifeless.

He's crying quietly, but at the same time he's thinking about Ed's obsession with the psyche's images. He's often said they're autonomous, erupting under their own power in the psyche whether waking or sleeping. They're often like metaphors, pointing us toward truths we may not comprehend cognitively. Stephen's life with his father has passed before his own eyes, signaling how important his father's love has been. The experience also announces a major life transition to fatherlessness.

Now, he watches his father's eyelids open, naturally, like they had just closed the moment before.

Slowly, Stephen stands up so that his father can see him. "Hi," he whispers, and wipes his eyes.

His father eyes dart to the sound of his son's voice. "Stephen," he whispers, gazing at his face. "I'm glad you're here."

"I love you, Dad," Stephen says.

"I love you, too," Frank says.

That was the first time either of them had said those words to each other since Stephen's childhood and they came out comfortably.

"You all right?" Frank asks.

Stephen chuckles. "Yeah, I'm … I didn't think you were going to make it," he says, fighting tears. "You scared me."

Frank looks away briefly and sighs. "I scared myself. God, that was the oddest experience of my life."

"What do you mean?"

"I'm not sure what happened to me," Frank says.

Steven squints at his father.

Frank shakes his head from side. He looks over his shoulder at the medical equipment. He looks back at Stephen. "This is too much. I never thought it would come to this."

"Never?" Stephen asks with a slight smile.

"You know what I mean? Yeah, we're all gonna die, but a long time from now. I just felt it, dying, like it was right now, right here, and it was the strangest thing."

"Yeah, this all shocked me, too. Michelle wanted to be here. She's ready to come at a moment's notice."

"She doesn't need to be here. Not now, anyway." Frank tries to sit up but is unable to move more than a few inches. "What just happened is hard to explain," he says, then coughs.

"Just relax. We'll have plenty of time to talk," Stephen says.

"I'm alright. I want to tell you about it. In the other room, I felt like I was losing my life. It wasn't so much like I was dying, really, but it was just like I was a million miles away."

"Like you were leaving your body?"

Frank blinks. "No, not really," he says. "I don't know how to explain it. I was in my body, but I was so deep inside I couldn't get to it…my body. That makes no sense, I know."

"Yeah, maybe none of this makes any sense," Stephen says, nodding toward the medical equipment.

"Yeah, that's true, but…" Frank's eyes open wider.

"What?" Stephen asks.

"I just remembered Ayala, my hospice caseworker. I always knew she was morbid, but…" his voice trails off and he closes his eyes.

"What?" Stephen asks.

Frank shudders. He opens his eyes. "It was like she'd completely gone mad. I mean, she always says crazy stuff. I call her a new-age holy roller. But I was lying there not knowing what was going on and she kept telling me, 'Follow the angels to Jesus, follow the angels to Jesus.' At one point, she put this angel figurine right up in my face while she was saying all this crazy stuff."

"Yeah, I heard some of that," Stephen says.

"I wanted to get her away from me but my body wouldn't move. My tongue couldn't even form words. I couldn't do anything but think."

Frank raises his eyes to his son. "And then I saw you. I felt this change come over me. Everything inside me changed. I suddenly knew I'd be able to speak if I could just concentrate and be patient. I concentrated for, I don't know, how long were you standing there?"

Stephen looks away for a second. "I don't know … maybe three or four minutes?"

Frank stares at his son in disbelief. "It seemed a whole lot longer than three or four minutes. I started feeling so tired I was scared I'd fall asleep before I could say anything. And then I heard myself say your name and everything felt normal. Except it felt like I'd been awake for two days and that's the last thing I remember."

Stephen smiles, "You fell asleep right after you said my name for the second time," he says.

"How long was I asleep?"

"A couple of hours."

"It didn't seem that long. It seemed like I was asleep for less time than I was trying to say your name."

"Time is weird that way, huh?" Stephen says. "By the way, you might have wanted to tell Ayala to get the hell out of here, but I actually told her that."

Frank smiles, gently, at his son's young honest face. "Good," he says, "I'm glad."

"I wasn't very nice to her. I hope that's okay."

Frank looks back at Stephen. "That's fine … what did she do to you?"

"I saw some of that stuff with the angels and the chanting. To me, she seemed to want you to die."

"There's no room around here for any of that," Frank says.

Stephen squeezes his father's hand and fights with tears. "I have so much to tell you and I was afraid I wouldn't be able to."

Frank squeezes Stephen's hand, weakly. "I'm okay now," he says. "Damn chemotherapy almost killed me."

"I'm glad I can meet with your doctors while I'm here. I should probably call Michelle now. She'll want to know how you're doing. Can you talk to her?"

"Yeah, sure, but I don't know if I can take any more of my kids acting like I'm dying."

Stephen is a little taken aback when he realizes that that is exactly how he has been acting. He smiles when he hears his big sister's voice. He assures her that their father is stable before giving her some of the details. He hands the phone to his father, who says, "I love you, too."

At the whiff of death, Stephen thinks, all this "I love you" stuff just flows right out of all of us after being contained for…. years. Why does love come forth during tragedy more than in everyday life?

Stephen listens while his father downplays the seriousness of his illness and makes baseless reassurances that his condition was, "a temporary setback," and something that he'd probably recover from, "in a couple of days."

Before they hang up, Michelle asks to speak to Stephen. "Call me when he goes to sleep," she says, and Stephen can hear that she's still sniffling from crying.

"I will. I love you, big sister," Stephen says.

Silence. Michelle had not heard those words in a very long time from her younger brother.

"I love you, Stephen," she finally says.

Stephen puts the phone in its cradle.

"I'm glad to hear you two talking like that," Frank says.

"We tell each other we love each other every couple of decades," Stephen says.

"You should say it more often."

Those are Frank's last words before he falls into a deep sleep. Stephen watches his father sleep for a few minutes before Donna walks into the room.

She and Stephen hug each other cautiously.

"How is he?" she asks.

"He's okay. He's resting right now. He was up for thirty or forty minutes talking and being himself."

"I'm really very relieved. When I called the nurses' station and they told me he was awake I couldn't believe it. I thought we might have lost him. This latest chemo is because the cancer is continuing to spread. Did he tell you that?"

"I didn't know he was starting new chemotherapy until you called this morning."

"I hate to hear that he's not telling you what's going on. He doesn't want to worry you, but I've asked him to let you know. I've been through this with both my parents. You never know what to expect, but it sure helps to have all the information."

Stephen looks at Donna. Somehow, she was transformed from a shrew who jealously guarded her relationship with his father to this caring woman who was trying her best to keep him informed. All of that seemed to have transpired after his father returned from his visit to Atlanta, himself transformed from a passively detached man to someone willing to stand up for what he wanted. He might have changed how honestly he related to his wife, but he was still the same mystery man when it came to talking about his illness.

"It has been hard, especially being so far away," Stephen says. "It helps to know that he's in loving hands. That makes a big difference to me...and to Michelle."

"I love your dad," she says. "He's my white knight. I'll do anything I can for him. He'd do everything for me if I needed it."

"He gives a lot," Stephen says, his body feeling heavy again with grief.

Donna suggests that Stephen get something to eat. "I'll watch him," she says. "And if you need to take a walk, feel free."

Stephen wanders to the cafeteria, eats some coagulated soup and a stale roll, before returning to his father's room. When he opens the door, he sees his father smiling at Donna who is sitting right where she was when he left, holding his father's hand.

The three of them talk for an hour before Donna says she has to go home and get a decent night's sleep. Stephen immediately senses that her leaving is an act of kindness, of love, allowing him and his father to have time together. Stephen walks her to the door and this time they embrace fully.

"Thank you," Stephen says, and then looking at his father, he continues, "We're going to get him better and get him home and then you and I are going to have to stay in better touch."

"It's a deal," she says.

Stephen walks back to the lounge chair next to his father.

"She takes good care of you...and you need that from a woman. I mean, even before you got sick."

Frank smiles at his son.

"The whole man-woman relationship stuff isn't easy, is it?" Stephen asks.

"I don't know if it's easy for some people, but for me it's always been damned hard," Frank says.

"I guess I inherited my ineptitude for it from you."

"I guess you did," Frank says. "But I thought you and Ally were doing well?"

Stephen looks at his father. "Yeah, we are. I'm just kidding," he says.

"I'm not. I've been good at a lot of things, but relationships haven't been one of them," Frank says.

"I think probably most people could say that," Stephen says.

"I know I always wanted more from my relationship with your mother and never knew how to get it. You get one chance to live a life … and not a whole lot of instruction." Frank looks at Stephen. "Your mother was a great mother to you and Michelle. Really. And she was a good wife. I probably made a big mistake leaving her. It hurt everyone. I was lonely with you and Michelle leaving the house and your mother and I were just friends. I underestimated being good friends. Donna and I are good friends now. We had to work to get there. Well you know about that…But your mother and I had a special friendship and I didn't know how to appreciate that."

"Mom always asks about you when we talk."

Frank looks at Stephen blankly and then turns away. "You're a good son, Stephen," he finally offers. "I've been blessed with great kids."

"I feel blessed, too."

"You've always had a very kind heart," Frank says. "From the time you were a small child, as soon as you learned to talk, you were always very loving, very sensitive to others. Your sister was more …standoffish. In a way, you two were the opposites of the conventional stereotypes. But your decision to become a psychologist was perfect."

"But of course, she was the smart one, right?"

"Why do you say that?"

"It doesn't matter anymore. I feel okay about myself these days. It helps that I'm getting a PhD. You did let me know that I was good with people and emotions when I was a kid. I'm sure that's why I'm in graduate school in clinical psychology and it's really where I belong. I really appreciate you for that. You were, are, a great father."

Frank closes his eyes and sighs. "You were a damn good shortstop, too," he says. "If I could have just taught you to hit the curveball a little better, there's no telling how far you could have gone. You know with the curveball, follow it with your eyes, keep your hands back, and if it's a good one, try to foul it off or serve into right field. You can't try to do too much. Of course, you can't ever try to do too much with a really good pitch. Just hit it where you can."

Stephen grins at his father. "Are we really sitting here in the hospital at midnight, with you hooked to a bunch of medical equipment, telling me how to hit?"

"You were a good hitter, no doubt, but to be a great hitter you have to handle the curve ball."

"I think I've heard that somewhere before," Stephen says, smiling warmly.

Julia walks in.

Stephen rubs his father's neck as she checks his pulse.

"You two going to go to sleep tonight?" she asks.

"We've got a lot to talk about and nowhere else to be," Frank answers.

"I'm going to go to sleep in just a minute," Stephen says to placate her.

After Julia leaves, Frank says, "One of the things I despise about being sick is that strangers feel like they have the right to tell you what to do and when to do it."

"We'd really better get some sleep," Stephen says, yawning.

"Okay, if you say so," Frank says. He pulls his sheet closer to his chin. "I've had a good night talking with you."

"Me too. I'm glad we're here together," Stephen says.

The light from the parking lot coming through the blinds creates lines across the two men's bodies. Stephen pushes his chair backward into a reclining position and closes his eyes. For twenty or thirty minutes, he reviews the events of the day while unconsciously being soothed by his father's gentle breathing. Suddenly, the sound of Frank's breathing disappears. Stephen springs up from his chair and looks at his father. In the dim light Stephen watches his father's chest slowly rise and fall. He slumps back in the lounge chair and is soon asleep.

Chapter 31

MAJESTIC DUNES

THE NEXT MORNING, the oncologist walks into the room briskly, clutching Frank's patient chart, and smiling brightly.

"Hello Frank," he says, loudly, causing Stephen to begin forcing himself into consciousness.

"Hi," Stephen hears his father whisper back, apparently in an attempt to let him sleep.

Stephen forces his eyes open and pulls himself up in the chair. The smiling doctor glances in his direction and offers, "Good morning," to him. Stephen rubs his eyes and looks closer at his father, who looks like he's been awake for a while.

Frank smiles at him. "Dr. Smith, this is my son, Stephen," he says. The doctor nods at Stephen without making eye contact.

"The nurse's note says you two stayed up all night talking," the doctor says in a voice way too powerful for the hour.

Frank looks annoyed. "We have a lot to talk about, but it wasn't all night I assure you," he says.

"Rest is important," the doctor says, "but having good conversation is important, too."

Frank likes this guy. "Stephen's studying to be a clinical psychologist," he says.

"Really?" the oncologist says, looking in Stephen's direction. "Maybe I can get him to help you stay motivated."

"You're worried about his motivation?" Stephen asks.

"I worry about all my patients staying motivated," Dr. Smith says.

Stephen doesn't like the answer. "So, there's nothing in particular about the way he's doing things that you're worried about?" he asks.

Dr. Smith looks at Frank and smiles broadly. "I think our man here is doing everything he can," he says, as he raises Frank's forearm by grabbing his wrist. He checks his heart rate, and then continues the examination by checking his vision and breathing.

"Well Frank," he says, "you've had a crisis with this new protocol, one that gives us definitive data. You've made it through the crisis. Your breathing's fine, your heart and your circulation are fine. You're ready to leave the ICU. Keep it up for a couple of days and you can go home. As for continuing with this chemotherapy, I'd have to say your body spoke up and gave us a definite 'no.'"

Stephen looks closely at his father.

"I agree," Frank says. "Whatever that stuff is you had them put in my veins, I don't want it anymore."

The doctor smiles gently at Frank and then there is an odd silence in the room. Stephen watches the doctor run his hand through his thin blond hair. He glances at the chart and then looks up again, asking, "Any questions?"

Stephen realizes that if they don't quickly come up with questions they'll be left sifting through the clues in the doctor's utterances. "Um... does that mean you'll be discontinuing the chemotherapy?" he asks.

Stephen and the oncologist make eye contact for a brief moment. "Yes," he says. "When we get this kind of reaction from an initial administration, we're very likely to get a similar reaction from any subsequent administration. In fact, if we administered a subsequent dose, your father might not be so fortunate."

Stephen looks at his father who appears to be barely listening.

Stephen takes a deep breath before asking, "So what's next?"

Dr. Smith crosses his legs and slides his chair all the way against the wall.

Stephen is mindful of what Ed has taught him. If you ask a question that you really want an answer to, wait until you get it. Impatience interferes with the transfer of the most critical information in a conversation. He sits quietly, defeating his own instincts.

Suddenly, the doctor stands up. "Well, I'd say that's up to our patient here," he trumpets while smiling and patting Frank's leg. "I'm going to be the second-string doctor for now. His primary care doc will be taking the reins from here. I'll stay in close contact with him and certainly be available for any consultation. But since we won't be doing any chemotherapy for now, I'll have to defer to the primary care physician."

Stephen waits to make sure that the doctor has reached the end of his thought. He glances at his father who appears to be listening dispassionately, maybe even peacefully, like the discussion is about something far less grave.

"So," Stephen hears himself say, "I guess what you're saying is that there isn't an alternative type of chemotherapy or treatment that can be used at this point to treat his cancer."

The doctor takes in some air, sighs, and admits with a subtle nod that that is what he has said.

Stephen nods back at him and looks at his father, who makes a very sad attempt at a smile. Hopelessness distorts time in the room.

Frank is elsewhere, lost in memory, his mind flooded with images of youth. He has gone to a place where he loved to get lost as a kid. He's standing at the foot of enormous sand dunes on Isle of Palms, dunes that rolled on for at least a mile and stood maybe three or four stories high. He remembers challenging friends to see who could climb them the fastest, a competition that required knowledge of the slippery slope of fine sand that could send a climber all the way back to the bottom in a matter of one wrong step. He remembers a summer, maybe when he was about thirteen, when he never lost a race to the top. The participants endured cuts and scrapes from the ubiquitous spindly vines of cactus that wound through the dunes. He liked to give those dunes credit for one of his simple truths about competition that he passed along to the players he coached. Both winners and losers get hurt in competition. The winners don't notice their pain because they're elated. For the losers, the pain of losing exacerbates their physical wounds. The takeaway from this was to hold nothing back on the way to victory, even if the cost was getting hurt.

And those dunes were majestic, fantasy-like in proportion, before a great hurricane roared in and claimed all of them. Frank could see the image of those dunes as clearly as he did when he was thirteen years old. In his hospital bed it's exactly like he'd watched, as torrential rains turned the brilliant yellow-white sands death-gray. It was like he witnessed the surging sea pound at the base of the steadfast dunes, over and over, until there was no more reason for battle. The stiff soaked sands collapsed into the sea, became the sea, majestically.

Frank's eyes are wet when he opens them to the doctor who has just squeezed his forearm. He listens passively. "Now the game is to keep you comfortable," he hears him say, as he squeezes his arm again. "And then to help you get back on your feet so you can do the things you need to do."

Frank speaks softly, "That all sounds good to me," he says. He turns to his son. "Dr. Smith told me before we started this round of chemo that I'd be back on the golf course as soon as it was finished." He turns back to the doctor and says, "I guess I can get back out there as soon as I recover from this latest setback, right?"

Stephen watches the doctor look away and take a breath. "Yeah," he says, slowly nodding, "but let's not get ahead of ourselves here. I want you to focus on getting better first, and then we can talk about golf," he says.

"That's exactly what I plan to do," Frank says.

The doctor turns to Stephen and frowns. "I think we need to be thinking in terms of comfort and finding a place where your father can get the focused support and oversight that he needs. What he needs now is twenty-four- hour nursing care at home, if that's where he's going when he leaves here. Otherwise, we might need to look at alternative placement."

Stephen glances at his father, whom he correctly surmises is lost somewhere on a golf course. He has completely escaped the doctor's grave call for twenty-four-hour surveillance of his health.

"I hear what you're saying," Stephen says, as he looks at his father.

As Dr. Smith stands up Stephen hurries to his side of the bed to shake his hand. As he reaches his hand to the doctor, he notices a thin line of sweat along his freshly shaven mustache. The doctor shakes Stephen's hand and then turns and reaches for Frank's outstretched hand. They shake intensely.

"I appreciate you," Frank says.

"You hang in there," the doctor says.

Frank continues holding his hand, "Thank you, Dr. Smith."

It is the last time Stephen and his father will see Dr. Smith.

"I'm glad you were here to meet Dr. Smith," Frank says. "He's a good guy, don't you think?"

"Yeah, he did seem like a really good guy. How are you doing with the fact that he said there are no more chemotherapy options?"

Frank looks into Stephen's eyes, and begins to speak. Then, he lowers his eyes. "I don't know," he says. "Did you think he said there were no options for the future?"

"Yeah, that's what he said... I think."

"Well, chemo's been my hope for a few years. I guess now I've got to rely on myself."

Stephen smiles while feeling sad. "You know you can count on me to help you as much as I can," he says.

Not long after that, Donna returns and stays with Frank while Stephen drives her car to his father's house. He'd planned on napping for a few hours, but woke up in about forty-five minutes, clear eyed and alert.

He puts on his running clothes and goes out the front door and across the street to the beach, running out to the surf line. He replays the sequence of events of the last twenty-four hours: His father's seemingly lifeless body in the ICU; his father's eyes springing open; images of that crazy death-and- dying woman praying and braying; the side of his father's face as he stared at him wondering if he'd wake up again; the sound of his father's soothing voice in the darkness as they stayed up late talking; the sound of his sister's choked tears on the phone; and, finally, his commitment to his father that he'd help him as much as he could.

His commitment to his sister to call after he met with the doctor jolts him. He glances at his watch. He has run thirty-five minutes away from the house. He turns around and picks up the pace to get home and make the call.

Michelle's secretary seems to have been waiting for his call and quickly connects them.

"Stephen?" his sister says. "How is he?"

A couple of hours after meeting with his father's oncologist, Stephen has no idea how to characterize his father's health. "It's kind of hard to say, really. What I know is that his oncologist says that he'll be discontinuing chemotherapy." He takes a breath. "He also said that dad needs twenty-four-hour nursing care and implied that it might be long-term."

"Really," she gasps. "Does that mean that he's ... disabled?"

"I don't know. Right now he can barely move in his bed. But I don't think anything is damaged. I mean, the doctor said he has recovered from this crisis which was brought on by the chemotherapy."

"So, it's not the cancer, it's the medicine?"

"It's the chemo," Stephen says.

"So maybe if they stop the chemo..."

"Yeah, I think there's still hope that he can recover and be a lot better off." Stephen says the words for Michelle and finds that he feels better.

"Did the doctor say anything about recovery or prognosis?"

"No, not directly."

"How is dad doing?"

"He's pretty sick. He seemed much more himself this morning. We had a nice time talking last night and he's in pretty good spirits. He's weak though. His arms are really shockingly thin," Stephen says, before the image of his father's flesh lying next to his arm bone causes him to wince. "He doesn't look very good. His bones are sort of pressing against his skin."

Michelle breaks the silence that follows that description. "Do you think he's not eating?"

"No, he's not. He told me he hasn't had a meal since a few days before the first round of this latest chemotherapy."

"Why isn't he eating?"

"He says he's lost his appetite. Says he can't make himself eat."

"We have to get him to eat. That's the only way he's going to recover," Michelle insists.

"I know. I was thinking about going to the grocery store on my way back to the hospital. Maybe I can pick up some apples and bananas, maybe some fresh bread. I thought about sneaking a beer into his room."

"Don't do that."

"I was kidding."

"You better have been," Michelle says. "How does he seem, with being so sick? Is he handling it okay?"

Stephen hears his sister's sniffling.

"Actually, he seems to be doing pretty well. He's very open about all of this. We had a really nice talk last night."

"I'm sure he can get stronger if we work with him. I have to believe that he has a few good years left," Michelle says.

Stephen thinks about that. It's hard to imagine after what he'd seen. But it's harder to imagine his father dead.

"Maybe you could talk to him about his nutrition and exercise," Michelle says. "I just read about the effects of broccoli and spinach on the growth of cancerous cells. And I read articles all the time about the health effects of exercise. Did the doctor say anything about his diet?"

"No, he didn't say too much of anything beyond the fact that he was turning Dad over to his internist and would no longer be on the case unless…"

"Unless?"

Stephen thinks for a moment. "Actually, he didn't say how he'd be coming back."

There is a long silence. "Really," Michelle finally says.

"There's a pretty good bit of negativity around here. If you meet his hospice case worker, you'll see what I mean."

"He has a hospice worker," Michelle says.

"I think she volunteered to work with him because his cancer was similar to her husband's. Her husband died, and she's...I don't even know how to describe it. Dad calls her the angel of death, but I'm not too sure of the angel part. I'll tell you all about it over a beer sometime."

"How is Donna handling all of this?"

"Great. She's wonderful. We're extremely fortunate."

After a silence, brother and sister begin coordinating their schedules, making plans to fly in and out of Florida to cover the care of their father for the next couple of weeks. With the scheduling covered, they returned to exploring ideas about helping their father become more aware of and focused on the role of nutrition and exercise in his recovery.

Chapter 32

PRESENCE IN LOSS 2

STEPHEN AND MICHELLE WERE ABLE to vary their trips so that their father was being consistently monitored for about a month after the day he fell watering his plants and wound up in the hospital. A nurse came to the house a couple of times a day to monitor the pain medicines that were progressively being increased. Somehow Stephen and Michelle were able to discount that they were watching their father's skin turn grayer, and his movements, even his thinking, becoming more rigid, until finally Donna requested a conference call with them. She wasted little time. "I asked to talk to both of you because I need to tell you both that your dad isn't going to get any better," she said. "Your dad is dying… and I'm not talking about a year or so from now."

The period of silence on the phone was not as long as it might have been had Michelle and Stephen not wanted to appear supportive of Donna, who was balancing at least two days a week on her own. They both agreed to talk to his doctor about more specifics. It wasn't the complete answer Donna was looking for, but at least they would call the doctor and maybe he'd let them know how dreadfully ill their father was.

Stephen was alone in his apartment during the conversation. Anticipating that the conversation might be difficult, since Donna had scheduled it, Ally had taken Nicholas to Chastain Park and was going to meet Stephen in an hour at a restaurant. When Stephen hung up he walked toward his screened door, leaned against the doorframe and stared at nothing. Slowly he began realizing that Donna had spoken truths that he'd hidden from himself. His father was dying, yes, and he'd probably be dead in a few months.

Later, Ally helped him think through what he should do which started a chain of events that lead to him getting a leave of absence from the clinical program. Next, Stephen and Ally made arrangements for her to move into Stephen's apartment to take care of Nicholas, with Dan and Randy agreeing to help out as needed.

Stephen moved into his father's house. He wasn't there to be with his father to keep him alive. He was there to help him die, just as Ayala had suggested in her tactless advice. During the first couple of weeks, Frank continued to take the IV nutritional fluids when he was in bed, which he'd been doing since his hospitalization. He consistently complained that the fluids upset his stomach and took smaller and smaller amounts and tried various anti-nausea drugs. When he refused the fluids, Stephen felt a great sadness, but he didn't fight back. Stephen kept his sister informed and when his father spent his second day in bed without getting up for any reason, his sister drove to the airport and flew in on the first available flight.

Stephen and Michelle walk barefoot along the edge of the warm surf at sunset. They stop and turn toward the setting sun. The sun appears to ease itself onto the horizon, an orange globe on a gray sea. The clouds low on the horizon light up pink like they're enervated by the sunlight.

Stephen thinks about his father lying in bed. He watches as Michelle wipes a tear from her eye. He clumsily puts his arm around her shoulders. It's the first time he's seen her cry since she was maybe eleven or twelve and she got mad at him for seeing her that time. It's also the first time that they held each other in a real way since they were small children.

"When I'm lying in bed waiting to die," Michelle says, as they begin walking again, "make sure you play classical music for me. And play it loud, okay? I can't imagine what Dad must be experiencing, but somehow it calls for beautiful music."

"I will," Stephen says. He wonders why his sister assumes that he'll outlive her.

They continue their walk.

Stephen looks back out across the waves. "This death stuff is very hard, isn't it?" he says.

"Yeah, it is," Michelle says. A few more steps down the beach she adds, "It seems I'm never prepared for the next inevitable crisis in life."

"It's hard to prepare for losing your dad, especially when you've been estranged."

"You feel estranged from him?" Michelle asks, stopping.

"No, not anymore," Stephen says, looking toward some houses along the beach. "I did. I never understood the divorce. I guess that's not really true. I understood the divorce, but I never accepted it. I still don't, really."

"That kind of surprises me. I always thought you and Dad sort of understood each other; like it was a male thing or something."

"That doesn't surprise me. You always make human problems into male/female things."

"I admit it. I don't really understand men. I mean, in a complete way. Can you say that you understand women?"

Stephen is about to say that he does when Michelle waves him away. "Trust me, you might understand girls, but you don't understand women. I understood boys, but I've almost given up on men. And you might as well recognize your limits with women."

"I'll try to remember that. Did you know that dad brags about you all the time? He talks about what a brilliant lawyer you are to everyone who will listen?"

"He does?" Michelle asks.

Stephen begins walking again. "He knows every detail of your cases. He told me the other day how much money you saved a company five years ago in an acquisition deal. Donna and I were talking about you when he was asleep, and she knew all about the same case and a lot of other stuff about your work."

She smiles. "He's always made me feel special. I'm hard on him, I know. I never understood how he could just walk out on our mother."

"Dad told me the first night in the hospital that he regretted his divorce from Mom," Stephen says. "He said that he underestimated how important the friendship part of his relationship with mom was."

Michelle shakes her head gently and looks as if she's about to cry. Stephen puts his arm around her waist and they continue walking through the wet sand. After a few minutes of silence, Stephen asks, "Does Mom ask you how Dad is doing?"

"Every time I talk to her," Michelle says.

"Me, too."

"Did you know that when Donna asked for help, before you got your leave from school, Mom offered for Dad to move back to Charleston and into her house?" Michelle asks. "She wanted him to be in Charleston where she could help out and it would be more convenient for old friends and family to visit. That shocked me."

"Yeah, she mentioned that to me, too. I wonder if she feels sort of left out, not being a part of all of this?" Stephen asks.

"I think she does, not that she'd ever say so. It's been fifteen years and she loves her independent life. She'd be doing it for us...and for Dad. Actually, I think she was relieved that we worked something else out."

Stephen nods. As they walk on in silence Stephen watches a lone pelican slowly flying a few feet above the breaking surf. "I feel so fortunate to be so involved in Dad's dying," he says, "and I appreciate him being so open talking about his life as he's dying. It's been amazing for me."

Michelle glances at her brother, who has always been a mystery to her. Somehow, he just seemed to go all the way into experiences like this one, experiences that she spent most of her time wishing didn't exist.

Two days after he said goodbye to his daughter and a month after it had become clear to everyone that he was dying, death came to Frank with a morning rain as his son slept soundly in the medical recliner next to his bed. A few seconds after his father's death the rain intensified, pummeling the roof of the tiny ranch house across the street from the Gulf of Mexico.

Stephen stirs and peeks at his father.

No movement. Death is still.

He sits up and looks into his father's eyes that are…open. His eyes had grown narrower and darker with impending death and were now black.

Slowly, like a man who is touching something for the first time, he moves the blanket back and touches his father's rigid hand. Stephen's head shakes from side to side with sadness. He lies back in the chair, his wet eyes closed.

His next step seems well planned, even rote, though oddly he'd never consciously imagined it. He walks into the kitchen where Donna sits reading the morning paper. He nods to her and she walks toward him touching his shoulder lightly. He touches her arm, tries to whisper something, before they fall into each other's arms. After a long hug, she goes to be with Frank.

Stephen walks into the kitchen and sits at the table. Heavily, he leans forward and picks up the phone. His sister answers before the first ring is complete. She has been waiting for his call. He tells her that their father died, peacefully, while it rained. She covers the phone, puts her face in her hand and cries.

Briefly, they comfort each other and then there is nothing left to say.

Stephen walks out onto the covered front porch. He sits in the chair closest to the front door, the one his father always sat in when they talked that last month. He feels the windblown moisture on his face.

To the east the sun is rising, but looking straight ahead, all that Stephen can see are menacing clouds and storm waves that rise and fall onto the ivory sand.

Chapter 33

THE PSYCHOS

IT'S BEEN TWO WEEKS SINCE Stephen's father died. Now, sitting in Henry's office Stephen struggles to explain how he's feeling.

"It's kind of like when I was a teenager, alone watching TV, before cable ... and the 'Tomorrow Show' had just gone off the air. The national anthem plays while they show the Blue Angel planes shooting across a blue sky... and then the screen goes blank. Oh yeah, then there's that test pattern, shrill beeping noises, and I get out of the bed and push the button to turn the TV off, before remote control. And with the TV off I'm hit with the realization that I'm alone and left to my own resources."

"You feel alone, empty?" Henry asks.

"Yeah, empty is right." A sad expression comes over his face as he looks out the window at the pink dogwood blossoms on the tree just outside the open, screened window. The two men sit very still while a soothing spring breeze cools the room. "But you know I really don't … feel like talking about it today," Stephen says.

"I sure want to help you with your emptiness," Henry says.

Stephen perks up. "Look at that bird," he says, gesturing toward the window. A tiny bird has landed on a branch of a dogwood tree.

Henry turns his head and spots the bird. It's a delicate bird with an olive-colored breast and a purple tail. "That's a green breasted mango," he says. "I've never seen one in person. It's a type of hummingbird you don't usually see around here."

The bird leaps into the air and is gone.

"You must know a lot about birds to know the name of a bird you've never seen," Stephen says.

Henry turns back to Stephen. "I grew up on a farm and my father used to love birds. He talked about them a lot. Back then I found it boring, but I learned most of the names of birds and now I've grown to love them myself. These days, I enjoy sitting in my back yard, watching and listening. There seems to be real drama with birds if you pay attention. Sometimes I feel connected with my father when I'm sitting out there."

"Really," Stephen says, looking back at the books. "I didn't know you grew up on a farm."

Henry nods, leans forward closer to Stephen, his proximity imploring Stephen to look at him. "Are we going to talk about that emptiness?" he asks.

Stephen looks away. "God, I don't know if I can. I don't know what else to say, really."

"It's probably not a place you can talk from, at least not yet. Maybe if you let yourself just feel the emptiness something will come up."

Stephen looks at Henry. He's a little disappointed to be left with that. He begins massaging his brow.

"Can you say what you're feeling now?"

"Sad," Stephen whispers. "Just sad."

Suddenly his eyes are filled with tears and he cries from deep inside.

Henry moves silently to the couch. Stephen feels the couch slump under his weight. Henry puts an arm around Stephen's shoulders. Stephen leans into him.

Henry holds Stephen as he cries. Henry sees a different bird on the same branch of the same tree. The deep magenta tail indicates that it's a male mango. He smiles, while his eyes become moist with sadness.

Three months after that session, Stephen stands on a baseball field waiting for a bouncing ball, a barely moving meditation for him. The Psychos had made it to the Georgia University intramural softball league playoffs four years in a row, but this time they had won four straight games and were now playing the PE Department, or as they call themselves, the Big Jocks, for the championship. This was, of course, Ed's dream, or fantasy, as Stephen thought of it.

Stephen played shortstop for the first time when he was seven years old, and he rarely moves as gracefully and comfortably as when he's standing between second and third base. He forces his fingers to the ends of the finger holes of his glove, curls them with his throwing hand, and pounds the pocket a few times. He repeats this process over and over on the field, making sure that the pocket of the glove is as well-formed and as shallow as possible so that he can feel the ball when it lands in his glove and can quickly get it out for the throw. Every microsecond can make the difference between out and safe, winning and losing. He pounds the glove again as a ball thrown by the first basemen bounces on the grass, then the Georgia clay, before landing in his glove. He pulls it out as he slides forward, plants his right foot for an easy return throw to the first baseman.

Stephen turns and looks into the outfield. He breathes in its familiar smell of fresh-cut grass and travels back in time to his childhood. He's probably eight or nine. The only thing that exists for him is a scuffed-up baseball about to make contact with his father's bat. His eyes are fixed on the ball as the bat sends it darting to his right. He moves three quick steps to his right, reaches his gloved hand across his body, and backhands the ball. "Throw it," his father yells, as the little boy buries his right foot and fires a throw that his father catches chest high in his thick, bare hand, the bat still in the other hand. "Good throw, big man," his father says, as he flips the ball again in the air and Stephen fixes his eyes on the ball.

Stephen turns back to the infield, returning to the moment in front of him. He spots Nicholas in the stands, his baseball hat, too big, resting on his ears, hiding eyes that watch his father's movement. Stephen misses his father for the first time that day. He takes a quick breath as another bouncing ball comes his way. He takes a step to his right, catches it backhanded, plants his foot and fires it. The ball makes a loud "fwap," as it lands chest high in the first baseman's outstretched glove.

Stephen looks back at Nicholas. He's watching. He's sitting with Ally, Dan and Randy. Stephen was not happy when Ally invited Dan and Randy to the game. Failure was awful enough without an audience. But of course, that was not how Ally looked at things. They were all there for support, win or lose.

The first baseman, Richard Engle, nods his head in Stephen's direction, communicating "Good throw." Richard, a 44-year-old experimental neuropsychologist, has been playing first base for the Psychos for ten years, since he started as an assistant professor in the department. He calls out Charles's name and flips the ball in the air. The bright white softball lands on the deep green grass, bounces once and into Charles's glove at third base. Charles throws the ball wildly to first. Richard lunges to his left and is just able to knock the ball down.

Stephen looks over at Charles. "You're not going to choke on us, are you?" he chides.

Charles smiles broadly. "I'm gonna be alright! You take care of yourself."

Stephen laughs. "Richard's on your dissertation committee, right? One really bad throw to him could mean some bad shit for you, brother."

Stephen glances at Richard, who throws the ball to him. Again, the ball takes one hop before settling in his glove. Stephen snaps the throw, the ball landing in Richard's glove, belt high.

Stephen looks back at Charles. "I'd just hate to see four years of work go for nothing," he teases.

"You better go on, man. I don't joke about that stuff," Charles deadpans. "You're a little too cocky since your dissertation got approved."

"All right just remember he likes you to throw 'em letter high."

Charles laughs, "I'll do the best I can. You can count on that."

Stephen watches Ed, standing on the pitcher's mound, remove his cap and tip it in the direction of his fiancé and his daughter. It's the first time Stephen has seen Ed's thirty-year-old daughter, Kelly. Ed had described her to Stephen as "a thirty-year-old, Marxist, social-worker type," which conjured an unattractive image to Stephen. As he looks at her slender, athletic build and soft features, he wonders why he assumed that she was unattractive.

Kelly didn't come to town for the softball game. She'd stayed over an extra couple of nights after attending Ed's engagement party, which took place the night after the Psychos won their division, the win that enabled them to be playing in tonight's game for the championship.

On the field under the bright lights, Ed looks at Stephen. "We're going to rewrite our story here today!" he commands.

Stephen nods and smiles before looking over at the opposing dugout where some of the best athletes in the state of Georgia appear somehow sleepy and casual like they're getting ready for a pickup game after a church picnic. Some are swinging bats, some are tossing balls, and most are chatting with their teammates or their girlfriends or wives. Each one of them moves with the grace of an athlete even though some of them, a few of the older professors, are twenty or thirty pounds overweight. Stephen and Charles are the only players on the Psychos who could make the PE department's team. Stephen nods his head from side to side as he asks himself a question that he has no answer for: "How the fuck are we going to beat these guys?"

Stephen looks over at the leadoff hitter, William Terry, who played defensive back for a big ten-conference football team two years ago and is now a graduate student at Georgia University. Stephen has noticed him stretching for the last several minutes. He watches as he sits in the grass with his legs spread wide open, his head bent forward so much so that his forehead rests on his left knee. Slowly he rises up and then leans forward toward his right knee, until his forehead touches it.

"Fuck," Stephen thinks. Except for William's height, he's maybe five feet eight inches, everything about him is oversized. His huge shoulders are squeezed into an extra-large white mesh t-shirt that he's cut off, exposing his muscular midriff. As he walks toward the batter's box, there's a dancer's spring in his steps.

Stephen hears Ed call out to his defensive group, alerting them that the warm-ups are over. It's time to deal with reality.

Now, William stands at home plate, laughing confidently about something one of his teammates has hollered.

Ed watches him carefully. Ed likes it that he seems overconfident. He knows that especially in big games, extreme overconfidence will betray even the best of athletes. Overconfident hitters will try to do too much and try to collect homeruns rather than put together hits to produce runs a little bit at a time. He knows that the first couple of innings offer a possibility to outthink the hitters before they begin taking things more seriously and focusing their athletic talents more appropriately.

Ed looks at his buddy, Matthew, who has been catching him as long as the two of them have been professors in the clinical program. They have gone over each batter and developed a plan of attack. Matthew holds his glove, Ed's target, a few inches outside of the strike zone. Ed takes the ball out of his glove, flips it high into the air and watches as William's body uncoils toward the ball, but stops. The ball drops into Matthew's glove about five inches outside and deep.

"Ball one," the umpire calls out.

Ed's next pitch is again on target but deep, but this time inside by three or four inches, and again Terry resists.

"Ball two."

Stephen glances at Charles who looks back at him with concern. Neither needed to worry about Ed. Ed was where he belonged right now and both pitches were within an inch or two of where he and Matthew wanted them to be.

While Ed is a little surprised William resisted his offerings, he's able to see the concern in William's eyes. He's worried about Ed. Will he be wild and unable to throw him strikes? Sure, it would be great for the team for William to walk, but that's the last thing he wants. He's not worried about the team. He knows they're going to win by a lot of runs. All he wants is to hit the ball as far as he can and then run as fast as he can.

Now Ed loops the barely rotating pitch this time about an inch closer to the plate than the first pitch, but still a few inches outside and deep. "Close enough" was how William read the pitch. Every intentionally built muscle in his body brought the bat toward the ball. But because the pitch was outside, he had to reach further for the ball than he'd intended and could only get a portion of his strength into the swing. The ball sailed off his bat high and fairly deep to center field where Carl Wilson, a first-year graduate student in experimental psychology, retreated a few steps before watching the ball land in his glove.

One out.

The second batter, Stan Jones, had been a strong forward on Georgia's basketball team several years ago. He returned to Georgia for graduate school after five years of playing professional basketball in Europe and five years of being rejected by the NBA at tryouts. At six-feet-seven, he was too small to play power forward in the NBA and too slow to play anywhere else.

Ed pitched him the same way he had the leadoff hitter, teasing him with bad pitches until he too swung at a pitch several inches outside. He lined it hard and deep to right field and into the glove of George Anderson, a child psychology professor who was almost fifty years old, but still had excellent speed and covered right field, as Ed put it, like a blanket.

Now there were two outs in the first inning and Branch Smith, Ed's nemesis, at bat. A couple of years ago at a crowded meeting of the coaches, Branch referred to Ed as "the old gray-haired fart who pitches for the Psychos," and then acted surprised and apologetic when he saw that Ed was in the room.

Ed contained his desire to throw the ball into Branch's ear as he watched him, from Ed's view, preening before adjusting his cup after stepping into the batter's box.

Ed plans to start him off with a pitch a few inches inside. Maybe his rage distracts him, but as he releases the ball he grimaces while the wide white ball turns easily toward the middle of the plate, crossing the plate about at Branch's belt buckle. Branch swings easily and hits a line drive that sails over the centerfielder's head, hitting the base of the fence.

Branch was looking smug, at least to Ed, as he stood on second base, clapping his hands in the direction of his team shouting over and over, "Drive me in. Let's get this first big one." Ed frowns at him, then glances at Stephen, who quickly calls to him. "We just need one out, Ed. Let's get the batter."

Ed nods and turns to face the next batter.

Charles Carruthers is the catcher for the Big Jocks. He's a former all-American tight end at Georgia University. The Psychos had played against the Physical Education department three times in the two years that he'd been in graduate school. In that time, he'd probably batted twelve times and Stephen couldn't remember him making an out in any of those bats. He couldn't forget a homerun he hit that went over the left field fence, over seven or eight rows of cars parked behind the fence, over a row of overgrown red-tipped shrubs and out of sight.

Charles was always polite and respectful of everyone. Even now, with the head of his department standing on second representing the first run of the game, he smiles at Ed, obviously trying to convey his respect for the gray-haired pitcher who would have thrown the ball at his head for a slight chance to beat him.

Ed moves the ball from his glove to his bare hand and looks at Charles. He flips the ball into the air in a slow arc that reaches ten feet before it descends toward the outside corner of the plate and about waist high. Charles has all his weight on his back foot, where it should be, and when he determines the pitch is going to be a strike, he whips the bat in the direction of the ball, reaching just a little further out than he likes to. As he makes contact with the ball, all of his weight shifts dramatically from his back foot onto his front foot. His large hands pull his long metal bat, yanking the ball on a line that literally sizzles toward left field.

At shortstop, Stephen takes one quick step toward leftfield, springs into the night air, his glove hand extending as far above him as possible. The brilliant white softball lands in the top of the webbing of his glove as his body spins away from the infield. As Stephen pulls the ball from his glove, Charles, who is halfway to first base, claps his hands and nods toward Stephen as a show of respect.

Three outs.

Ed waits for Stephen on the pitcher's mound, greeting him with an almost vicious high five before they both trot toward the dugout.

"We need a bunch of singles. No swinging for the fences, guys," Ed calls out to his team when he reaches the dugout.

And that's the way the Psychos played it. After their leadoff man lined out to centerfield, Charles, Ed, and Stephen all hit line-drive singles to the outfield. So when Richard Engle came to bat they had one run in and one out, with Ed on third and Stephen on first. Richard hit a deep fly ball to right that scored Ed from third base. When the next batter grounded out, the Psychos led two to nothing after one inning.

The next couple of innings only fueled Ed's dream. He tormented the next several batters as he had the earlier ones. The Big Jocks were swinging so desperately all they could do was hit high fly balls to outfielders who were camped out by the fences waiting for the balls to fall into their gloves. At bat, the Psychos were patiently waiting for strikes from Branch, who like Ed was trying to get them to swing at bad pitches. When Branch was forced to throw strikes, the hitters were taking easy swings and guiding the ball into the holes in the defense for base hits.

When Stephen trotted out to shortstop for the top of the fourth inning the Psychos were leading five to nothing and the only base runner for the Phys Ed department has been Branch's two-out double in the first. Stephen looks into the dugout and watches the mostly young, beautifully athletic men studying Ed as he tosses his warm-up pitches. Stephen takes a deep breath, realizing that only three more innings of way-above-average softball was all it took for the Psychos to live the dream for which Ed had summoned him from Charleston. He jams his fingers deep into his glove, folds them over with his right hand, bends his body so that he's almost in a squat position. "Let's get this first out," he yells.

Ed turns toward the batter. It's the former defensive back, wide receiver and leadoff hitter, who is no longer casual. His first time at bat he'd hoped to hit one over the trees beyond the fence. Now getting on base is all that concerns him.

Ed can see that he's a changed hitter. Hell, he'd probably love a walk this time just to get something started for his team. And by now everyone in the dugout has compared notes and figured out Ed's strategy of getting them to swing at pitches that were too far out of the strike zone for them to get their full power into their swing. They'll be patient.

Ed has an intuition that William won't be swinging at the first pitch, assuming that Ed will again pitch him one out of the strike zone.

Ed pitches the ball and he and William and everyone else at the game watch as it floats easily across the middle of the plate and lands in Matthew's glove.

"Strike," calls out the umpire.

William pounds at his cleats with his bat. A lesser athlete would have let his frustration continue to the next pitch. Instead, he takes a deep breath, visualizes a smooth swing and contact with the ball, and steps back in. Ed's next pitch is a little outside but William, no longer trying to yank the ball out of the park, is satisfied to serve it on a line drive to centerfield for a base hit. That hit, soft and sagging as it was, changes something on the Big Jock side of the field. Now they're clapping and yelling to the next batter to "Keep it going." They'd apparently been taken into Ed's dream, too, so mesmerized by just three innings of being shut out that they were lifeless. One hit changed that. The next hitter also lined a single to the outfield.

Branch settles into the left-handed batter's box and begins adjusting his batting glove on his right hand. "What kind of person wears a batting glove in softball?" Ed wonders, then thinks of a list of insulting answers. As he's insulting the batter in his head, he senses Stephen's presence on the mound.

"You all right?" Stephen asks.

Ed nods impatiently, wondering if Stephen is implying he isn't pitching well.

"We got 'em right where we want 'em, right?" Stephen says, grinning.

Ed looks sternly at his young friend.

"I want to get in this guy's head," Stephen continues. "What do you think about this? On the first pitch, throw the pitch a foot inside so there's no way he can swing at it. As you pitch the ball, I'm going to take off for second like we're anticipating him pulling the ball to right or up the middle. I'll be leaving a huge hole at shortstop and he'll see that."

Ed squints, then nods.

"The next pitch," Stephen continues, "I'm going to go ahead and set up right up the middle, basically behind second base. But this time as he's about to swing, I'm going to take off for the hole. You throw it toward the outside part of the plate, perfect for him to hit it to the hole, and I'll bet you he'll punch it right to me and we'll turn two."

Ed glances around the field while considering the proposal. He curls his lips and nods vigorously.

Stephen runs back to his position.

This strategy isn't something that can be easily done in baseball because the ball gets to the batter too quickly to allow infielders to alter their position much. Also, in softball the batter has more of an opportunity to steer the ball to specific locations. The key is that the batter has to oblige by taking the hole given him. Stephen is betting on two things. Branch will want to show his team-player orientation and take a hit that is given him rather than trying to hit the ball harder. He's also sure that Branch would love to make the Psychos look foolish by upsetting their apparent strategy.

Ed glances around the infield before stepping on the pitcher's rubber and glaring in at a guy he loves to hate. He takes the ball out of his glove and flips it high and way inside. Branch steps away from the pitch, watching out of the corner of his eye as Stephen sprints toward second base, apparently anticipating that he'll pull the ball to the right side of the field.

Stephen's movement and the wild pitch by Ed unnerve Branch. He steps out of the batter's box and walks around. As he moves back into the batter's box and begins swinging the bat easily, he watches in disbelief as Stephen positions himself just on the first base side of second base. He has left a gaping hole on the left side of the infield.

Branch likes that they're shifting for him. That's what teams do when they respect the power of a batter, give him a hole to hit a single through so that they can keep him from hitting to his power and maybe hitting a homerun. He steps out of the batter's box again, feigns adjusting his batter's glove while he thinks. Stephen is pushing at the clay below his feet, trying to look casual as he peeks at the batter, trying to get a sense for what he's going to do.

Without consciously considering it this way, Stephen has offered Branch a very seductive opportunity to add to the story line of the PE department's domination of the intramural softball league. With athletic grace and overall strength, they had not lost a playoff game in four years. Here's a chance to add that they out-smarted a bunch of smart-assed intellectual shrinks.

Branch steps into the batter's box, takes a slow practice swing, and looks back at Stephen, still standing near second base.

"Come on, come to me," Stephen chants like a mantra, as Ed releases the ball. The ball floats in space and heads toward the outside of the plate perfectly placed for a left-handed hitter to punch to the left side of the infield. As the ball nears home plate, and after Branch has committed to the pitch, Stephen sprints toward his abandoned position. Branch reaches for the pitch and slaps a line drive toward left field. Stephen takes two quick steps, stretches his glove hand across his body, as the ball hits the clay a few inches from his glove. The ball shoots into the webbing of his glove. Stephen whirls back around and slings the ball to the second baseman who has hurried to the base. The second baseman catches Stephen's throw, steps on the base, and fires a perfect throw to first base and the outstretched hand of Richard Engle.

"Out!" the umpire at first base calls out.

Branch, who has crossed the base a millisecond after the loud "Fwap" of Richard's glove, hollers, "No," to the umpire.

Double play.

Ed stands on the mound his right fist stretched high above his head. He walks toward Stephen grinning. "We're going to finish rewriting this story, right?" Ed says.

"Yes, we are," Stephen says, nodding. Stephen holds two fingers in the air, and yells, "Two outs."

Ed throws Charles Carruthers, the next batter, almost the same pitch that got him out on his first bat. This time Charles has adjusted his swing. Instead of trying to pull the outside pitch, he aims his swing toward right field, positioning his weight and strength perfectly. He launches a high drive that turns heads the way those low-flying fighter jets at air shows do when they zip by. The ball clears the right-field fence, rattles between several pine trees and disappears. Tiny branches and pine needles float in the wind as Charles steps on first base on his way to a casual trip around the bases.

The next batter hits the first pitch from Ed over the left-field fence. Suddenly the score was the Psychos five and the Big Jocks three. Stephen glances around the field and notices a dramatic change in his teammate's energy level. The general baseball chatter that goes on without being noticed is now noticeably absent. And now the dugout of the Big Jocks is electric. A game that seemed shockingly in the Psychos favor just two batters ago seems completely altered.

"Let's get the batter…two outs!" Stephen hollers to his teammates.

Ed floats a pitch toward the plate. The pitch is well placed but hit as hard as any pitch thrown in the game. At third base, Charles moves his glove about two inches and the ball sinks deep in it for the third out.

The Psychos sprint to the dugout, almost as if they're running away from something. Ed waits for Charles and Stephen at the entrance to the dugout. "Good defense," he says to both of them. "Start us off," he says to Charles, who is leading off the inning. "A single's as good as a homer here. Let's have a big inning."

Charles throws his glove on the bench and grabs his bat. "You gonna' bring us home if we get on?" he yells back at Stephen as he walks toward home plate.

"Just get on, I'll keep it going," Stephen yells back.

Charles and Ed do exactly what they needed to do. Both lined hits to the outfield. As Stephen flips Ed's bat toward the dugout and steps into the batter's box, all the Psychos call out encouragement.

"Just a single," Charles yells from third base.

"Tell your story," Ed yells from first base.

Stephen blinks and begins moving the dirt around in the batter's box. He looks up at Branch, who stares back at him. Stephen digs at the clay nervously. Stephen knows they need a single. A line drive somewhere in front of the outfielders would be perfect. He thinks about what he wants to do. He decides to swing if the pitch is away from him and drive the ball to right-center. If it's anywhere else, he'll let it pass. He can be patient. A hit to right center would likely score Charles and get Ed to third and, more important, keep the rally building with no outs. An out right now would hurt.

Branch flips the ball high and towards the inside part of the plate, the pitch that Stephen had committed to letting pass. But the pitch is exactly where Stephen loves them and he can't resist. As it reaches the inside corner of the plate he swings with everything in his body. The ball soars into the dark sky and towards the left center field fence with the look of a homerun, or at least a long double. Stephen sprints toward first base. As he approaches the base he looks up and sees Ed, who has raced for second, sprinting back toward first base. He looks up from there and sees the center fielder beginning to slow down. The ball lands in his outstretched glove ten feet from the fence. He fires the ball back to the infield. Charles has tagged up from third and scored, but now there is one out.

Stephen trots toward the dugout. The players in the dugout greet Charles and him with high fives, before yelling encouragement to Richard, the next hitter. Stephen stands next to Charles considering the possibilities of his bat. If only he'd resisted the pitch and been patient. He kicks at some dirt in the dugout.

Stephen watches the rest of the inning haunted by his out. They could have had a big inning going had he not abandoned his plan. And Ed wanted him to tell his story. He did that all right. His frustration eased some when they managed to score two more runs but still he had to wonder what might have been.

A couple of innings later, Stephen, standing at shortstop, starts thinking about Mohammed Ali, the great boxer who sometimes played with his opponent for a few rounds before getting serious. When Ali turned serious, the fight would end with a flurry of punches before he stepped back and watched his defeated foe topple to the canvas. That reflection was prompted by on-field activities. The Big Jocks had spent the last two innings lining balls all over the field. A few of them hit the fence while a few sailed over it. Only great defense had preserved the dream for the Psychos before Branch of all people put the Big Jocks in the lead when he hit the foul pole in right field for a homerun.

Stephen watches as his favorite professor stares at Branch who trots around the bases as slow as a human can run deliberately extending Ed's suffering and his own ecstasy.

Stephen walks to the mound to help Ed regain his composure. As Stephen repeats the obvious scenario, which was that they still had another turn at bat, and they had their good hitters coming up, he notices how deep the lines in the corner of Ed eyes look when he's red-faced and sweaty.

Nodding in the direction of Branch, who almost stopped before stepping on home plate, Stephen says, "Fuck him!"

After another hit, Ed steadies himself on the mound. Stephen was right. If they could just get out of this inning behind by only one run, they should be able to win it in their half of the sixth inning. The challenge was to get two outs without another run scoring.

Ed looks in at the batter. He'd give him something low that he had to reach for. Ed looks at Matthew's glove that calls for the pitch right where he wants to put it. He moves his hand backwards and then forward, letting his hand open up releasing the ball. It floats easily toward the outside part of the plate and is greeted by the force of young strong arms. Had the bat not made contact with the ball it would have landed in Matthew's glove without him moving it an inch. Nevertheless, the ball flies past Ed, heading toward center field, before he can react. Stephen darts to his left, lunges for the ball, spearing it with his glove a step before he drags his foot across second base and fires it to Richard for an inning-ending, potentially game-saving double play.

The Psychos are exhilarated as they run into the dugout, knowing that they had somehow escaped the knockout blow from their heavy-weight opponent. Ed greets each of them as they come off the field, imploring them to "make it happen now." While Matthew would lead off the inning, the combination of his bad knees and lack of power would usually mean he was a pretty sure out. Luckily, he'd be followed by the top of the order.

Stephen and Ed stand next to each other as Matthew bats. Looking straight ahead at the action, Ed says, "This is all I wanted, to play our best and have a chance to beat these guys. The only thing left is the ending. Will we be the guys celebrating, or will they?" He slaps Stephen on the back. "You said your father was a baseball coach, right?"

Stephen stares at Ed and barely nods.

"What would he tell you to do when you get up to bat?"

Stephen turns to watch Matthew's fly ball land in the center fielder's glove for the first out. Finally, he offers, "He'd tell me to slow everything down, make a plan and don't change your plan…and don't get in the batter's box until you clear your head of all thoughts except hitting."

"That's great advice. I'd only add that there is a story being written here today and you and I may have a chance to tell a really good one. You want that chance, Stephen?"

"Yes, I really want that," Stephen says with a forcefulness that causes Ed to smile.

"I can see that," Ed says.

Right after that, Kevin chopped a pitch over the head of the pitcher. At shortstop, Terry races for the middle of the diamond while Kevin sprints toward first. Terry grabs the ball just before it hits the dirt for a second hop and fires it to first base. It looked to Stephen like Kevin's foot was descending toward first base at the moment Terry released the ball and yet the ball somehow still arrived just before Kevin's foot landed on the base.

"Out!" screamed the umpire. Many of the Psychos complained, but he'd made the right call.

Stephen watches as Charles walks to the plate. His talk with Ed has left him wanting that last bat, that last chance to change his and the Psycho's story.

Charles hit the first pitch thrown to him over the shortstop's head for a single, causing Stephen to leap into the air, shaking his fist toward the heavens. Ed is up next, and Stephen will follow. Ed turns to Stephen on the way to home plate. Stephen has never seen Ed's face so hard, so fierce with determination. "Drive me in," he says to Stephen, his mouth barely moving. Stephen starts to say something, but Ed has already turned away and is surveying the situation.

A few seconds later, Ed hits a line drive that follows the white chalk line all the way to the left field fence. The hit was so perfectly placed that it allowed Charles to make it to third and Ed to second before the left fielder could get the ball back to the infield.

Stephen stands at home plate looking out at the Big Jocks who are now huddling in the middle of the field. The first baseman, a young professor who played college baseball suggests that they walk Stephen and pitch to Richard. When Branch disagrees, he insists. "He's hit us every year. Hard."

"So has the guy after him and remember that guy got a hit last bat," Branch counters. "And I had this shortstop fucker eating out of my hand last time."

Branch looks around the field, before looking right at the young professor. "We got this guy last time in the exact same situation. The other guy followed that with a hit. We don't have to wonder about what they'll do in a given situation, we've been there."

Branch waits a few seconds before barking "Right?" Then immediately, "We're going after him. We'll go four deep in the outfield. I'll give him something that he thinks he can hit out of here. He'll fly out, and then we celebrate. Let's do it," he says, before turning his back on the meeting.

As the infielders return to their positions, Stephen takes a practice swing while wondering what is next. He's ambivalent about the prospects. He'd be relieved by a walk; it removes the pressure from him. But it would take away his opportunity...his moment. That's how his father and sister said they approached these situations.

Stephen learns of their decision when he sees Branch waving for his outfielders to play four deep. Stephen glances in the direction of Nicholas but pulls his head back toward the field before he sees his fans.

From somewhere inside Stephen's psyche, the part that keeps him from being all the way in these situations, comes the memory of his last baseball game in his senior year of high school where he made the last out in a similar situation. That game was played on a cold early May evening in a small town at the foothills of the Appalachian Mountains. The moment of Stephen's memory was him at bat with his team behind, one to nothing, with two outs and the bases loaded. The noise was deafening and mostly in support of the hometown team and against Stephen and his high school.

The young star standing on the mound looked to his catcher and nodded his head at him. He wound up and threw a pitch that was as fast as any pitch he'd thrown all game. Stephen's swing and powerful contact caused the pitcher's head to jerk in the direction of left field to find out what the story of his last high school game would be.

Fortunately for the young pitcher, Stephen took his biggest swing and the bat swept through the strike zone with a slightly upward trajectory. And unfortunately for Stephen, who had dreamed of creating an unforgettable story, the upward orientation of the bat, which was maybe only three more degrees than optimal, sent the ball twenty feet higher than was necessary and the useless height was of no small consequences.

The ball sped into the thin night air and the left fielder for the team that would ultimately have the story to tell, forever, raced toward the fence. When he stopped at the fence and stuck his glove in the air there was a moment of absolute silence while everyone watched the ball fall into it. Stephen stood a few yards from first base with his hands on top of his batting helmet staring at the scene of another team celebrating a few feet from him. As he walked around the pitcher's mound where the celebratory pile was forming, he saw his father in the stands clapping his hands and yelling encouragement to him. "You did everything you could. You almost got it," he heard him say among the chaos of sounds.

Stephen hung his head and continued walking. His father knew better. A level swing, a swing not calculated to hit the ball as far as possible, would have sent the ball on a line and not given the left fielder time to get to it. And Stephen would be at the bottom of his own pile of young men.

Stephen is digging his back foot into the batter's box as he glances out at Branch who is ready to pitch when he remembers his father's words, "Slow everything down. Don't do anything until you know exactly what you want to do."

Stephen scrambles out of the batter's box and calls, "Time out!" He glances over at Ed on second. "Slow down," he commands himself. He takes a deep breath. On the second breath, he makes his plan. He isn't going to swing unless he gets a pitch on the outside of the plate and then he's going to swing smooth and straight, no upper cut. "Level swing... outside pitch," he says to himself as he screws his foot into the batter's box.

Branch looks at him, takes the ball out of his glove and then waits. He's giving Stephen a few seconds to think outside of the moment. Stephen waits, wide-eyed.

Branch flips a pitch that falls a couple of inches inside. Stephen isn't even slightly tempted. He raises his hands and lets the ball fall into Carruthers's glove.

"Ball," the umpire calls out.

Stephen and Branch go through the exact movement before the second pitch. And then the pitch falls in the identical spot and again Stephen lets it pass.

"Ball two," the umpire says.

Now Stephen steps out of the box and takes a practice swing, exaggerating the movement of the bat downward as a reminder not to swing up. It occurs to him that Branch is unconcerned about walking him but wants him to swing at a pitch off the plate. He's throwing them close to a strike and inside hoping that Stephen will take a big swing and fly out. Stephen knows that Branch has his weakness figured out. He assumes he'll over-swing on a pitch inside where he likes them. No wonder, he did that last bat and probably in past games, too.

Stephen takes a little more time moving the dirt around in the batter's box. Stephen does not want to walk for the same reasons that the young professor playing first base wanted to walk him. Objectively, he knows that Richard isn't as good a hitter as he is, especially right now with all his thinking clear and his concentration focused. It's weird, he can observe how into the moment he is, and he doesn't feel the slightest pull to leave the moment.

As he takes another practice swing he changes his plan. He can count on Branch throwing another inside pitch, and if for some reason he doesn't throw it there, he can just take it even if it's a strike. When Branch releases the ball, he shifts his feet so that he's six inches further away from the plate.

Branch flips the ball and it falls toward Carruther's glove on the outside part of the plate. Stephen loads his weight on his back leg and moves toward the ball and at the last possible moment stops.

"Strike one," the umpire says.

Stephen steps out of the batter's box and wipes his cheek with his sleeve. Branch out-thought him. He's about to jump back in the box, but as before he slows down. He takes a deep breath. He looks out at Ed. He glances toward the outfield, still deep. He can't guess on the pitch this time. He'll take a level smooth swing and hit the ball on a line wherever it's easiest to hit it.

Stephen sets up in the batter's box, screwing his back-foot in. He looks out at Branch who again hesitates before pitching to let Stephen's mind wander. Stephen's thoughts are where they should be, level swing, he repeats to himself over and over until Branch obliges and releases the ball. Stephen shifts his weight onto his back foot as the ball lilts toward the outside corner of the plate. He strides toward the ball and when it's a few feet from Carruthers's glove he swings and lines the ball toward right center field.

The ball lands on the outfield grass and skids toward the center fielder who, because he was playing deep, fields it on the third hop. As he gathers the ball in, Ed rounds third base and heads for home with the potential winning run. As Stephen reaches first base, he stops and watches the play at the plate.

The next period of the lives of the men on the field is less than two seconds but takes place in several different segments. First, there is the ball disappearing in the outreached glove of the center fielder whose right leg slides forward and plants under his body, and then his body heaves forward followed by his right arm. Out of this fierce movement, emerges the crucial white ball streaking through the dark sky in a race against the second segment. That is Ed's body moving quickly, even with the gait of an older man struggling against difficult knees.

Then there is the segment with Charles Carruthers balancing his weight for maximum reaction to the simultaneous incoming ball and determined professor. And then there is the segment where the blurring ball is stretching toward Charles, an absolutely perfect throw that lands in Charles's glove before he slams it to the ground thus creating an impenetrable barrier. Within that segment is the human body full of grace and defying friction as Ed slides headfirst passing three feet to the right of home plate. And then at the very moment that his body is about to shoot past home plate, Ed reaches his left arm back for the plate. As his fingertips scrape across the back of home plate before Charles can reach him with his tag, the final segment begins.

This segment is split into reciprocal images. The Big Jocks hurry off the field and only glance back toward home plate where through the haze of clay dust they can see the other side of the image, a heap of Psychos in an unbridled catharsis, rolling and laughing, fifteen feet behind home plate where Ed's sliding body eventually stopped.

No one imagined that ending, not even Ed, he later admitted. Dan had brought a cooler with several bottles of too expensive champagne, the first of which he opened ceremoniously as the Psychos and their families began their celebration. (Dan also acknowledged later that given what Stephen had told him he'd planned it more as a salve for healing wounds than for celebrating.)

After most of the Psychos and their families had gone, Ed opens the last bottle of Champagne. He pours everyone's plastic cups full and puts one arm around his daughter and the other around his fiancé. He looks up at Stephen, who smiles at him.

"Does it feel as good as you hoped it would?" Stephen asks.

"It feels better. I'm sweaty, covered with dirt, and completely relaxed. The last time I felt this good was when I took Mia to see the area where I grew up. We put the top down on my old Porsche and drove through the Shenandoah Valley. It was early spring when the sun was melting the last of the snow, and we drove past wooden farmhouses, manure-soaked fields, and what was it we felt, Mia?"

"Young," Mia says.

"Young," Ed says, nodding. "Young and filled with hope." Ed sighs. He holds his cup in the air. "To our hero," he says, motioning to Stephen.

Stephen clicks his cup to everyone's and they all take a sip.

"This must bring back memories of past baseball games for you," Matthew says to Stephen.

"Not really," Stephen says. "I don't think I've ever played in a game where I was sure my team was going to lose, and we won. And the truth is, I never got a winning hit in the last inning of a game. Tonight, was a big thing for me, too."

"That's hard for me to believe," Charles says. "As good a hitter as you are…"

"I'm not saying I haven't gotten some big hits," Stephen says. "It's just when the game's on the line and it's all up to me … I've got a history of thinking way too much and screwing up."

"Before I agree with you," Ed says, "let me say that you've been our MVP every year you've played for us. But I've noticed that you've struggled in situations where you had a clear choice between being a hero or a goat. I assumed that for whatever reason, you didn't feel comfortable in the role of hero. It wasn't your story, if you will. Tonight though, you stroked a difficult pitch, right where you needed to hit it. So maybe you had a breakthrough."

"I think I did," Stephen says.

"Right on schedule," Ed says, beaming at Stephen. "It will serve you elsewhere, I promise."

Stephen tries to understand some of the possible implications of Ed's statement while conversations split off into subgroups.

Ed puts his arm around his future wife's shoulder and smiles at his daughter. "This is my dream come true," he whispers to Kelly.

She smiles back at her father. "I'm glad I could be a part of it."

"You here celebrating my engagement and winning the game. That's everything," he says.

After everyone remains quiet out of respect for that moment, Matthew glances at his watch and says, "It's getting late. I've got to go."

"Why are you leaving so early?" Ed asks. "You can't leave before we've finished our Champagne."

"I've got the curriculum committee meeting tomorrow at eight a.m.," Matthew says.

"Oh, that's right," Ed says, before turning away from Matthew.

"And you won't be coming, right…because you've quit that committee," Matthew says.

Everyone looks toward Ed.

"You quit the curriculum committee?" his daughter asks.

"I can only give so much to department politics," Ed says.

"You always hated department politics," Kelly says. "But you always said the most important committee was the curriculum committee. You said, 'whoever determines the curriculum defines the type of psychologists who lead the future.'"

"Your daughter knows you well," Matthew says.

"Well, I don't know," Ed says, shaking his head and seeming to hope the matter would be dropped.

"Why did you quit the committee?" Kelly asks.

"I don't know. I just got tired of being voted down. Matthew doesn't seem to mind, but I resent being treated like a dinosaur. I've just gradually quit going to the meetings and nothing has changed because of it."

"I'm not sure I like being characterized as someone who doesn't resent being treated like a dinosaur. I think I've framed the experience differently than you have," Matthew says.

"I know you have," Ed replies. "I just have no interest in fighting a battle that can't be won."

"I can't believe that, Daddy," Kelly says. "I thought that's what you were all about. Don't you get that that's what tonight's victory is about?"

"I don't want to ruin tonight by bringing my failings as a psychologist into this," Ed says.

"Your failings? Dad, this department is your department," she says. "Yours and Matthew's. It always has been."

"It has been, but it isn't. The committee voted three years ago to cut my History and Systems course from two semesters to one. Now I've got one week of two hour-and-a-half classes to discuss the ideas of William James, even though his volumes of work have more ideas for young psychologists than anything else in American psychology. I'm supposed to spend about that much time on Jungian psychology. There's no time for anyone to read Jung or Freud's original writings. Instead, the assigned readings are summaries and outlines that rob their theories of their complexities, making them seem as shallow and trite as the cognitive-behavioral psychologists think they are.

"I sit in the curriculum meetings and listen to a bunch of PhD psychologists engage in the delusion of modernity, the chauvinism of recent developments, a particular type of cognitive error that my course is supposed to prevent. The great irony for me is that I helped create the thing that is strangling me: Cognitive behaviorism, optimism and optimal behavior. Matthew and I hired the guys silencing us. We did it because we wanted scientific psychology, cognitive behavioral psychology, to have a strong voice in the clinical program. Of course, we didn't realize they'd want to silence the other voices."

Ed's voice trails off. Movement in the circle is minimal: Charles sits up a little straighter; Stephen shakes his cup from side to side, bringing bubbles to the surface; Richard takes a quick breath as he starts to say something but remains silent.

Stephen sits up. "If they're trying to take the department from you," Stephen hears himself say, "I hope you won't avoid facing up to them."

Ed sits up a little straighter. His heavy eyes look into Stephen's. "I don't feel like I need to deal with that at this point in my life," he says. "And I'm a little embarrassed that this seems up for discussion."

"Ed, I mean you got all of us believing we could win this game and we won. We beat the fucking Big Jocks. I'm not sure how you can think that we can beat them and not think that you can fight against the guys changing the department. And you yourself said earlier that it's all about being in the game and giving it everything."

Ed smiles at Stephen, and then looks at his daughter. He pulls Mia closer as he slowly scans his audience smiling at each of them. "Okay, all of you are right, of course. I guess I need a little bit of that resilient optimism I used to love so much."

Ed stands, as he says, "I guess I need to get home if I'm going to make that meeting."

Everyone stands up. Ed holds his cup out. "To the Psychos," he says, and they all take a last sip together.

Chapter 34

AWAKE

RANDY CLOSES THE DOOR of his truck. The sound causes Stephen to stir.

It's six-thirty in the morning. The alarm will be going off in half an hour. Stephen peeks at Ally who sleeps next to him, looking soft, innocent, free. "Does she possess these qualities, or does he give them to her in this moment?" he wonders.

"Both," he whispers.

He walks to his window and looks out at the garden that Randy and his father planted. Randy has referred to it as "Stephen's father's garden" so often that he now thinks of it that way, too. He walks to Nicholas's door, opens it wide enough to make sure that he's sleeping, then closes it.

He walks slowly toward his front door. He opens it and walks across the slate stones toward the main house. He goes into the kitchen, gets some coffee that Randy has made for the family, and walks back out toward the garden.

Though it's mid-July, the morning air is cool and light. He walks into the garden and wonders why he's there, awake for these extra minutes of morning.

He sits on the bench and listens to the bird song. He closes his eyes for a few seconds, then opens them and spots a cardinal who rests on a low-hanging branch of the oak tree twenty or thirty feet from him. He focuses on the bird's mix of colors and textures and then his eyes close again, peaceful.

For a long moment there is no movement in the garden.

He follows his slow-moving thoughts like an egret patiently searching for edible treasures in the marsh. He feels lucky that his father died slowly; it took them that long to do what they had to do. He hopes that he and Nicholas can do that much, even more. He has an image of saying good-bye to Nicholas, forever. It's a soothing image, even though it's of his own death, and includes Ally and some others whom he cannot see clearly.

He sits comfortably with the image.

A breeze moves some leaves on the oak tree nearest him. Thoughts drift in with the breeze. He didn't save his father's life; he helped him die. There really is no saving anyone. There is only being with them, touching them with your heart, letting them touch yours, allowing them to leave when they're ready, and saying good-bye, naturally.

He breathes in deeply, feels calm, awake.

He squints across the field of perennials that his father and Randy planted that will return each year. He focuses on some flower petals spread across the soil from yesterday's rain. He reaches over to clean up the petals but stops. He notices the richness of the blend of the petals with the English ivy and the soil. His eyes focus and then defocus and then focus again on the colors before him- verdant green, lavender, blush, gold, white, black.

He sits, separates the colors, follows an ant that moves onto one of the crimson petals, then onto the soil, and then disappears in the ivy.

Again, there is no movement in the garden.

As we leave him, our young poet is exactly where he belongs.

The End.

DISCUSSION QUESTIONS

1. Who was your favorite character and why?

2. How did Stephen (and eventually Nicolas) moving into the carriage house change the dynamics in Dan and Randy's relationship?

3. How did you initially feel about Ed's attraction to younger women? Did your feelings change when you heard the longer version of his story? How did Ed eventually resolve his fear of loss in his romantic relationships?

4. Discuss the money and power dynamics in Dan and Randy's relationship. How did their family of origin stories impact their beliefs about money and power? How have your childhood experiences impacted your perceptions regarding money and power in intimate relationships?

5. Discuss the symbolism of birds throughout the novel. When do they appear? How does the Kurt Vonnegut poem included in Stephen's grad school application apply to his life?

6. How did Stephen's and his father's separate narratives about Stephen's parents' divorce create such a deep divide between them? Discuss a time when you learned new facts that radically shifted your perspective and feelings about an event from your life.

7. How did you make sense of Stephen's possessiveness and jealousy regarding Ally posing nude for Randy? What helped him shift his narrative so they could heal the breach in their relationship?

8. How did Stephen's instincts regarding Darnell help him connect with the prisoner? What did Stephen do later that caused Darnell to de-compensate? Discuss the "prison" metaphor throughout the story.

9. Why do you think Stephen's memories of being tutored by his sister influenced his self-perception so profoundly? Why was the psychodrama effective even though Stephen knew that the "ideal parents" were just actors? Can you recall messages you received from your family about yourself that were less than ideal? What did you need to hear instead? How might your life be different if you'd internalized ideal messages? How can you work on this today?

10. How might the book have ended differently if Ed had been called out at the plate in the softball game?

11. When people say, "Leopards don't change their spots," they mean we do not change our essential character. What is your opinion of this? Over the course of the novel, Stephen evolves from essentially sleep-walking through life to being fully awake. What experiences have helped you feel more aware, awake and alive?

ABOUT THE AUTHOR

GERALD STEVEN DROSE was born and raised in Charleston, South Carolina. After graduating from the University of South Carolina with his PhD in Clinical Psychology, he moved to Atlanta, Georgia with his wife, Dina Zeckhausen. They co-founded Powers Ferry Psychological Services, a psychotherapy practice that now has thirty therapists in four locations. For two years Gerald produced the "Sex, Love and Marriage" column for the online health information site ShareWIK. com (Share What I Know), writing about how couples therapy transforms relationship dramas.

For over 30 years, Gerald has worked as a psychotherapist helping his clients re-write their personal narratives, recognizing that the stories we tell ourselves limit our ability to love and thrive. He enjoys supervising younger therapists, filling in the gaps left after graduate school training.

Made in the USA
Columbia, SC
24 April 2021